Shooting Scripts

Shooting Scripts

From Pulp Western to Film

Bob Herzberg

McFarland & Company, Inc., Publishers
Jefferson, North Carolina, and London

LIBRARY OF CONGRESS CATALOGUING-IN-PUBLICATION DATA

Herzberg, Bob, 1956–
 Shooting scripts : from pulp Western to film / Bob Herzberg.
   p.   cm.
 Includes bibliographical references and index.

 ISBN 0-7864-2173-8 (softcover : 50# alkaline paper) ∞

 1. Western films — United States — History and criticism.
 2. Western stories — Film and video adaptations. I. Title.
 PN1995.9.W4H45   2005
 791.43'6 — dc22   2005002559

British Library cataloguing data are available

©2005 Bob Herzberg. All rights reserved

No part of this book may be reproduced or transmitted in any form or by any means, electronic or mechanical, including photocopying or recording, or by any information storage and retrieval system, without permission in writing from the publisher.

Cover photograph: Richard Widmark, Patricia Owens and Robert Taylor in Marv Albert's *The Law and Jake Wade*

Manufactured in the United States of America

McFarland & Company, Inc., Publishers
 Box 611, Jefferson, North Carolina 28640
 www.mcfarlandpub.com

To Colleen,
my love,
my companion,
my best friend,
this is for you

Table of Contents

Introduction	1
1. Ernest Haycox and the Grandeur of the West	9
2. Luke Short and Romance in the West	32
3. Frank Gruber and the Distortions of the West	58
4. Norman A. Fox and the Clichés of the West	84
5. Louis L'Amour: Nietzsche Goes West!	101
6. Marvin H. Albert and Violence in the West	133
7. Clair Huffaker and Hellraising in the West	153
8. Saddle Up: Other Unsung Heroes of the Written Page	188
Bibliography	190
Index	195

Introduction

In the twenty-first century, with little western literature coming off the presses, and other fiction (basically the mystery, the science fiction and the thriller) dominating readers' imaginations, it's hard to fathom that at one time the pulp western was king. Usually selling for under 50 cents, sometimes printed in impossibly small typeface, these books sold briskly, but were hardly taken seriously by the intelligentsia.

The popularity of the pulp western, an evolution of the "penny dreadfuls" of the late nineteenth and early twentieth centuries, kept up right through the post–World War II years and into the 1950s; by then it had evolved yet again into the paperback. The original "pulps," those novels of the 1880s and '90s that purported to tell Easterners the "truth" about the west, were atrocious works, usually written by hacks who had no idea of, indeed, had never been anywhere *near*, the west.

Books about Billy the Kid, Jesse James and other outlaws were published and they sold well, perhaps too well, which said a little something about their readers. Eschewing the truth for the sake of colorful exposition and even more colorful dialogue, these books provided mind-numbing action, unrealistic heroism and historical falsehoods all for the price of a few pennies.

According to the early pulps, Billy the Kid killed 21 men (he really killed only four), Jesse James was a hero (as a Confederate guerrilla, he'd participated in scores of murders, with and without brother Frank), and every other villain was called "Black" something or other (Black Pete, Black Bart, Black Percy, etc.). Heroines called villains "varlots" before facing "the fate worse than death," heroes referred to villains as "fiends" and the hero generally kissed his horse more than he kissed the heroine, implying something far sicker than the authors had in mind.

The villains usually coveted the heroine's ranch (as well as the heroine) and everyone else's herds of cattle, horses and, on some rare occasions, sheep. Villains had long black moustaches, dressed in black and even rode black horses, as if the color alone implied a warped mind. Their henchmen were invariably ugly: one-eyed, hook-nosed, either with shaggy hair (black, of course) or bald, tall and fat (for purposes of bullying) and definitely bearded, as if the lack of a razor implied bottomless evil.

Both heroes and henchmen wore two guns, one on each hip. The reason all for this artillery was never explained. In reality, Westerners might wear one pistol, but two? Pistols were, of course, ivory-handled and had long gleaming silver barrels, with little variation.

Heroines were always frail and helpless. They would faint so often, in fact, that an indication of a serious illness probably wouldn't be too far off the mark. Being helpless, they needed the strong, manly hero to save them from the aforementioned "fate worse than death." Heroines were virginal, and to them a "roll in the hay" was something only horses did.

And horses could do anything: untie the hero's ropes, dive into a roaring stream and save a child, play matchmaker for the hero and the rancher's daughter by pushing them together, and even bury a friend. Perhaps the only thing these amazing equines couldn't do was sell insurance.

The supreme irony in many of these clichés, originating as they have in the nineteenth century, is that not only have they become standard plot devices for western literature of the twentieth century, but they have been transferred, with little change, to the western film.

As far as the western novel was concerned, the twentieth century got off with a bang when former Wall Street stockbroker Owen Wister wrote *The Virginian* in 1902. Ironically coinciding with the book's growing popularity was the release of *The Great Train Robbery* in 1903. Lasting a mere 12 minutes, compared to *The Virginian*'s 400 pages, the film shows us a train robbery in progress and the killing of several robbers, complete with scenes of incredibly smoky gunfire. The film caused a sensation. At last, a film with a plot! Before this, the mere act of a person brushing his teeth seemed good enough for a patron to part with his or her hard-earned nickel.

The Virginian was a bestseller, eventually ending up as a classic of the west and of literature, and effectively ensured the success of *The Great Train Robbery*. Between these two works, the Industrial Age would give birth to a renaissance of the old west in both literature and film.

Yet why was this happening? Nostalgia? Those still alive in the pre–World War I period might have lived in the west and might have felt a bit sentimental reading stories about their home turf (even if those stories had nothing to do with the real west—something these survivors instantly recognized).

Was it an escape to a simpler, less hurried past? After all, at the time *The Great Train Robbery* was released and *The Virginian* was published, man learned how to fly, cars rolled off Detroit assembly lines, folks were talking to each other long-distance through little boxes and people paid five cents and went into little rooms to watch pictures move. The days when a person climbed up on his horse to ride for miles just to see a friend were going fast. Communication became easier (though certainly not cheaper) and rural America was rapidly becoming urban America. In short order, outlaws and bandits would become gangsters, and politicians who lied to the people at open-air rallies could now lie to them on the radio.

Crime would change radically; as the new century advanced, modern outlawry would eclipse the heroic symbols of a simpler time. A good example of this was when a crooked official in the employ of gangsters murdered Marshal Bill Tilghman in 1924. Tilghman was one of the west's greatest lawmen. A brave man used to dealing with gunmen face to face, he was caught off-guard when a corrupt Prohibition enforcement officer shot him in the back. Indeed, the concept of one-man law in a small community was rapidly giving way to the machinations of big city politics, complete with corrupt law enforcement and rapidly expanding criminal organizations.

With the violent background of World War I, the rise of gangsterism, and with the Depression just over the horizon, America's fascination with the Old West only flourished. As mobsters robbed, kidnapped and murdered and the law became more bureaucratic and less hands-on, the public relished the spectacle of a tall, two-fisted white man in a large white hat and carrying two abnormally large guns bring justice to the prairie. Riding high atop a handsome white steed named Silver, Tony, White Flash or simply Ted, these broad-shouldered men of action did the right thing for poor homesteaders, victims of outlawry, and nubile ranchers' daughters. The novels of the early twentieth century were just touchstones for what was to come.

To a rapidly growing civilization learning not only to communicate and build better, but also to destroy people on a scale hitherto unknown, the hero of the Old West presented a cleaner, simpler alternative. As tanks and machine-guns made their ugly appearances on the world landscape, and war and ethnic strife took its toll in human lives, the adventures of individuals on a long-gone frontier entranced readers across the globe.

According to the simple values of the western as dictated by the pulps, the American west was built on the pursuit of justice and the defeat of outlawry. In the eyes of the reader outside America, a nation was founded and built on honesty and initiative, not racial, religious or territorial strife.

With backgrounds of Communist revolution in Russia, genocide in Turkey, colonialism in the Middle East and Africa, rising totalitarianism in Asia and an overall policy of ethnic cleansing in all of these places and beyond, a person outside America could still look with envy on a democratic United States, where freedom and equality were the order of the day.

Historians of the day wrote books on what the country had gone through since its inception, though their prose was flowery and their facts were sometimes colored by their own prejudices. The newspapers had these same problems; details were there, but real facts were missing, along with a little thing called insight. These were not necessarily newspapers, but in their own way fictions for a thrill-hungry public (My, how times have changed!). Therefore, to those outside America, the western novel seemed to be the easiest way to grasp the frontier myth that many believed embodied American principles. The cowboy hero made the myth salable to a world hungry for justice, a justice many of them were not getting in nations ruled by despots and landscapes marked by killing fields.

If the western novel gave us myth, the Hollywood western would take that same source material and make it even simpler and more unreal. A good example of Hollywood's almost cartoonish excesses concerning the west was the idea of the singing cowboy. Though singing cowboy movies were never based on novels (excluding perhaps Gene Autry's emasculation of Les Savage, Jr.'s, *Coffin Gap* as *The Hills of Utah*), what a ludicrous conception it was compared to the realities of the west. In these low-budget works, we have a man in fancy shirts with buckskin frills playing a spiffy new guitar and backed by a group of amazingly on-key cowboys crooning nonsensical songs in a background of joy and good will, totally ignoring the sweat and hardship and generally making a mockery of the real-life working cowboy. Forget getting the beef to market, let's all sing a ditty about the beauty of cattle driving! (Don't get me wrong. I love Roy Rogers, Tex Ritter and all the rest. But in what history book is a pioneer singing "Ragtime Cowboy Joe" with backup by the Cass County Boys mentioned?)

The Hollywood western would take a cue from the pulps, and their myths persisted far beyond the post–World War II period to culminate, ironically, in a series of revisionist westerns of the 1990s and early twenty-first century. Suddenly a west that had previously featured only white Christian characters became so populated with persons of color and various ethnicities that one wonders if white Christians had *ever* been in the west. The American Indian, previously seen as attacker and bully, went through a miraculous transformation. In the revisionist westerns, they suddenly became lovable teddy bears who harmed no one, and their possession of tomahawks and bows and arrows were really fashion statements misunderstood by racist whites. Heroines who needed "big strong men" to save them suddenly became prototypes for MENSA, and did everything big Tex or Wild Bill could do, but use the men's privy.

These westerns rebelled against the status quo perpetuated by the western novel and film. Unfortunately, they also started some new clichés of their own, which at present don't seem to be disappearing. The irony of all this is that it actually makes one a bit homesick for the old formula. And I still hold out some hope that in the midst of a revisionist western containing plot elements of racism, abortion, rape, incest and apocalyptic war, some time will be allotted for one lone cowboy who can halfway carry a tune to warble "Home on the Range"…

The Coming of the Dudes

The three biggest western authors, all of whom seem to have been inspired by *The Virginian*, would effectively blaze a trail for every western writer from then on. They were Zane Grey, Maxwell Brand and Clarence Mulford. Their prolific output overwhelmed both readers and critics with sheer volume. In subsequent decades, the postwar western writers, Louis L'Amour in particular, would hark back to the works of these men, finding in them stories of a simpler, bucolic existence, where heroes were made and the west held promise and glory. Those who had actually carved out an existence in the west might strenuously disagree as to both the promise *and* the glory, but such pessimism didn't sell books.

The fact that these three fathers of twentieth century western literature were emphatically *not* from the west means nothing. (Brand was from California, but *hated* the west.) They could write, and they gave the public what they wanted. Though all three men were adventurers of a sort, indeed outdoorsmen, each man approached his chosen profession of western storyteller in different ways.

The works of Zane Grey have been called melodramatic, antiquated and just plain old-fashioned. Indeed, his books contain practically every cliché known to Man, and more; however, no one ever doubted Grey's sincerity. If Grey's way of telling a story seemed corny, at least he treated his characters seriously. A well-traveled man who was constantly seeking story ideas, Grey had apparently spoken to old settlers of the west, including former Army personnel, and gathered so much information for material that a prolific output was assured.

Of course, Grey had his faults. His books were *long*. Brevity was not the man's strong suit. His writing style was elaborate, at times unnecessarily so. Why just describe a mountain? We have to be told *exactly* what each pebble looks like. If a character has certain motivations, we must be told ad nauseam *exactly* what he or she is thinking, as well as that character's ambitions, dreams, likes, dislikes, habits and fears. God forbid the reader should figure things out for themselves!

Maxwell Brand has produced some 30 million words in fiction, or the equivalent of 530 books. He was the creator of two-fisted gunslingers like Destry and Silvertip, and two-fisted surgeons like Dr. Kildare. Though he thought of himself as a poet, this incredibly energetic man banged out 20 to 40 pages of manuscript every day on his Underwood (Remember *them*?).

If one tired of the long, *long* novels of Zane Grey, there was always Brand. His books were usually shorter and his descriptions more concise, but as one would expect in those days, the occasional flowery, moralistic speech might creep in. In other words, Brand's work was made for Hollywood.

The third author of the early twentieth century whose work helped define the Hollywood western was Clarence Mulford. Though everyone seems to think that the creator of Hopalong Cassidy was a marriage broker from Brooklyn, that was simply not the case. Mulford was not "from Brooklyn," even though he later lived and worked there. He was from Skeator, Illinois, and later became a civil servant. He developed an interest in both physical fitness and the west, and he wrote many stories and novels about the characters on the mythical Bar-20 ranch. Though Cassidy is his one creation that we remember today, the writer also gave us Buck Peters, Mesquite Jenkins and literally dozens of other figures all related to each other in one way or another in various series of novels.

Cassidy was an ornery, red-headed codger with a pronounced limp. He cussed and swore and was nothing like the white knight dressed all in black as portrayed by William Boyd. Though Mulford was never crazy about what Paramount did with his Cassidy stories, he apparently liked Boyd personally and tolerated the studio's blasphemy. Indeed, the Cassidy we think of today is more a creation of the actor playing him than Mulford's conception. This would ultimately result in the author himself rewriting several of his Cassidy tales to conform to Boyd's excellent characterization.

In the coming years, dozens of others would try to take the place of these men. Some ended up carving out their own place in the western firmament (Ernest Haycox, Luke Short, etc.). Others were graduates of the blam-blam school of horse opera—hacks merely marking time by grinding out stories and novels which could be enjoyed by only the most gullible readers.

Introduction

This book will concentrate on seven men — Ernest Haycox, Luke Short, Frank Gruber, Norman A. Fox, Louis L'Amour, Marvin H. Albert, and Clair Huffaker — who came after Grey, Brand and Mulford. It is a critical examination of the films made from the works of these western authors, and how Hollywood interpreted (or frequently misinterpreted) the original stories. I'll go into the various changes that took place once the novel was committed to celluloid, and comment on the actors and directors that brought life to these writers' visions.

Since I'm giving my honest evaluation of these authors and the craftsmen who made their works into films, my take on certain individuals might not be pretty. And while some might be screaming for my painfully slow death, I hope others will be enlightened. For I believe that the seven men who gave us these tough cowboy protagonists would want nothing less than total honesty.

The seven authors I examine encompass the years of the Depression through the 1970s. They are not authors who have had only one of their works filmed, nor were they fly-by-nights by any stretch of the imagination. These were authors that Hollywood consistently returned to in their search for film material, especially in the time period mentioned above, a time when both the western novel and the western film flourished.

Many of the plots taken from these novels give us much of our modern conception of the western, years after the black-hearted villain–noble hero–virginal heroine school of writing from the late nineteenth and early twentieth century. Though the old sagebrush stereotypes vanished by the 1930s, one is still amazed that the clichés themselves remained even into the 1970s.

How many westerns have there been where the villain is a cattleman, banker or rancher who wishes to take over everyone's property and become Boss of the Valley? How many westerns have we seen where heroes were quick-draw experts, *always* winning the gunfight, and fighting according to the principles of fair play? How many heroines have we seen who had to be rescued (or at least protected) by a strong, manly cowboy? Some western authors continued to use these clichés into the post–Vietnam era; others had set upon a course of originality even during the Depression. Regardless, Hollywood would almost always use the cliché over the original concept. This might explain why the works of Louis L'Amour make it to the screen ahead of a groundbreaking author like Les Savage, Jr., who had only a few film adaptations of his work, and never above the level of a "B" film.

In the old western novels, there were many ways to describe a gunfight, but one of them has always stuck out in my mind: The firing of a pistol would be described with the now-laughable phrase "guns talked" or "guns spoke." I always wondered why the author didn't continue with this frame of reference and then write "from across the street, a Winchester replied" and finally, "Meanwhile, a sawed-off shotgun peered from a window, laughing its head off!"

In the following pages, you'll become acquainted (or reacquainted) with seven authors whose work Hollywood deigned good enough to transfer to celluloid. For close to a century, the film capital was a place where "guns spoke" on screen and where a western author's work was judged less by writing skill than his pull at the box office.

Welcome to a world where there's "No Sunday west of St. Louis and no God west of Fort Smith," a place which sounds a bit like Hollywood…

1

Ernest Haycox and the Grandeur of the West

Ernest Haycox was born in Portland, Oregon, around the time of the Spanish-American War and died relatively young, at the time of the beginning of the Korean War. There are those writers who see their labors as a creative art, and wait for inspiration to strike them. Then there are those who treat writing as a business, setting regular working hours and even dressing a certain way before sitting down at the typewriter (in those pre–Microsoft days).

Haycox was a writer who dressed in a business suit every day, went to a rented office and sat at his machine from nine to five, hard at work at his job of Author. From the 1920s up to the time of his death at 50, Haycox produced dozens of stories and over 40 novels, usually of the old west. Many of his stories brought to life characters he had been acquainted with in his home state of Oregon. From his pulp western novels of the 1920s and '30s to his far more ambitious work of the '40s, we clearly see an author whose talents were growing with each new work. Haycox had writing in his blood, and his work attained a maturity as the 1940s progressed — ironically, even as his health was failing.

What events shaped this talented man, one of the finest authors, not only of the western genre, but of literature itself? Haycox was born in the Pacific Northwest just before the turn of the century, a time when some might have found it hard to adjust to the industrial age — like Haycox's father. Apparently not satisfied at his occupations of railroad worker and lumberman, the elder Haycox also tried farming and sheep herding. Ernest's parents divorced before he turned 11. After first living with an uncle in the farming community of Mist, the teenaged Ernest was more or less on his own. He went through the usual series of odd jobs in Portland, then later ventured to San Francisco. Eventually he enrolled in high school and improved his education, demonstrating a natural talent in English and history.

Lying about his age, at 16 he joined the Oregon National Guard, then enlisted in the Army during World War I. Stationed in Washington State where he guarded power stations vital to the war effort, he seems to have crossed swords with the Communist-backed International Workers of the World (the "Wobblies") trying to sabotage the stations. It might have been Haycox's first encounter with the Soldiers of Bolshevism; whether this experience helped turn the future author towards the GOP is anyone's guess, though it is quite possible. Later, Sgt. Haycox served in France as a weapons instructor — a prophetic occupation for someone who would write stories about men packing six-guns.

Honorably discharged, the young man returned home and became a commercial fisherman in Alaska, then enrolled in college with the intention of becoming an author. He went to New York, then the hub of publishing, and met his future wife Jill on the journey by train. While living hand-to-mouth in the Big Apple, he was told by magazine editors that they were interested in western stories.

After returning to Oregon, it wasn't long before he rented that office in downtown Portland. Soon he was able to make a good living selling his stories, both "pulps" (for the more action-oriented magazines) and "slicks" (for the more sophisticated *Saturday Evening Post* and others). Serialized in magazines, many of these "slicks" would later become novels.

Though the reading public became acquainted with Haycox through these stories in the 1920s and '30s, Hollywood barely knew the man existed. Infatuated with Zane Grey and singing cowboys, filmmakers were not impressed with good writing, but with phenomenal sales (this assessment, unfortunately, includes Grey). Haycox's material was not from the "rip-snortin', two-fisted" (and totally mindless) school of bang-bang western fiction Hollywood was ordinarily interested in. It would take the eye of a visionary, or more likely an Irishman, to discover what Hollywood had been missing.

John Ford had discovered Haycox's short story "Stage to Lordsburg" in the April 10, 1937, issue of *Collier's* magazine. Years later, the director, never the most reliable source of information, claimed to have bought the story for $2500, while budget records reveal that Haycox was paid $7500. However, according to *The Movies That Changed Us* by former American Movie Classics host Nick Clooney, Haycox was paid $4000. Whatever the dollar figure, had Haycox been paid $1.25, the movie sale would have still been worth it, considering what a hit the film would be and how it enhanced the previously unknown writer's status in Hollywood.

Reportedly a reworking of a short story by Guy de Maupassant, the piece became the touchpoint for one of the most influential westerns of its time. Ford used Haycox's characters as a basis, adding other characters and plot points from Bret Harte's *Outcasts of Poker Flats* which Ford himself had filmed for Universal in 1918. In collaboration with liberal screenwriter Dudley Nichols, Ford created a film in which the "respectable" capitalist characters show cowardice under fire, while society's outcasts, John Wayne's gunfighter Ringo and Claire Trevor's harlot, demonstrate courage.

Originally called Malpais Bill, the character of the Ringo Kid made a star out of John Wayne. It was a powerful performance by any standards, certainly one to be admired considering the hardships the young Duke was put through by Ford's constant bullying. According to Claire Trevor, the usually enraged director would grab Wayne, shake him and scream at him about his acting. Already self-conscious about his reputation starring in Poverty Row westerns and all too aware of the top-notch cast supporting him, the Duke amazingly held his temper and took the abuse. Ironically, Ford's constant harassment forced the rest of the cast to rally around the young actor. Though Ford might have had this in mind all along, there were far too many incidents of the man's bullying of actors to merely accept this as playing head games for a good cause. A nasty man, even on his good days, Ford had bullied John Agar on *Fort Apache*, Harry Carey, Jr., on *3 Godfathers* and also attempted to push around Ben Johnson until the ex-cowboy told him off (and would not appear in a Ford film for many years after that).

Was *Stagecoach* really true Haycox Country? The answer is yes and no. Ford's film owed a great deal to the original story, and the skill with which Haycox wrote it unfortunately did not transfer to the film. Ford was interested in presenting contrasting personalities, more likely class stereotypes, in a tense situation. Haycox's story was a well-written account of a group of diverse westerners, not class stereotypes, on a fateful journey. In Haycox's work, there is almost never a wasted moment; the dialogue, the occasional violence, the emphasis on characterizations over gratuitous action content, only point up the differences between Haycox the writer and Ford the director. In the auteur's films, the time can easily be taken up with mindless fistfights and drunken carousing, subtlety not always being the helmsman's strong suit.

The film has one of the first appearances of the now-clichéd character of "the hooker with a heart of gold," a stock figure still popular enough to propel the previously unknown Julia Roberts to superstardom in *Pretty Woman*. Certainly a more realistic comment on this pathetic cliché is offered by the madam character in Loren D. Estleman's excellent *Mister St. John*: "If I had a heart of gold, they'd cut it out and sell it for whiskey…"

The characters from "Stage to Lordsburg" are more diverse than in the film. There is a smug cattleman, a whiskey drummer from St. Louis with a heart condition, a "proper" woman on her way to marry an infantry officer, an Englishman with a hunting rifle, Henriette the hooker (with a heart of gold) and Malpais Bill — one big happy family. Malpais Bill is out to "collect a debt" in Lordsburg from two scoundrels named Plummer and Shanley (who become the Plummer brothers). In the film, Henriette becomes Dallas (the talented Claire Trevor); the cattleman becomes a crooked banker (played by Berton Churchill in a career where it seems he played nothing *but* crooked bankers); the whiskey drummer with a heart condition is played by Donald Meek, and the gentlemanly gambler is John Carradine (both actors were under contract to Fox around the same time).

Irishman Ford was not about to have a sympathetic Englishman in one of his movies, and so the character is replaced by drunken old Doc Boone (Thomas Mitchell). Mitchell was a veteran stage and screen actor rarely known for subtlety, and whose major quirk as a performer was his tendency to use broad gestures and bellow his lines as if he were still on stage. Apparently Mitchell was perfect to play roaring drunks. As Doc Boone, Ford has him drink whiskey in front of the town's "proper" ladies and defiantly sneer at them. (Behind this bit of business is the director's contempt for those who look down on him for his own alcoholism. Some may call the bit improvising on the set, but it sounds an awful lot like denial.) Ironically, Mitchell's performance as a charming medical lush would inexplicably win him an Oscar. Go figure.

However, *Stagecoach* was a John Ford film and he wasn't about to let you forget it. During the big chase scene out on the flats, with the stagecoach being attacked by Indians, Ford had reached his zenith as a director. Cutting between the action inside the coach and the hard-riding Apaches outside, and punctuated by excellent stuntwork, this heart-pounding sequence would be copied in countless westerns. One man, however, didn't care for it. An obviously jealous William S. Hart stated that, realistically, there wouldn't be a chase scene since the Indians could have easily shot the horses. Fancying himself an expert, the has-been actor probably never considered the fact that the Indians probably wanted to steal the horses, so why shoot them? Ford would only say that the horses weren't killed because the Indians were traditionally bad shots.

Two years later, Haycox seemed to be making a subtle comment on Ford's film in the first few pages of *Bugles in the Afternoon*, written in 1941. Haycox has the hero, Kern Shafter, take a stagecoach to a transfer point

1. Ernest Haycox and the Grandeur of the West

Always standing tall. John Wayne and Claire Trevor in *Stagecoach*, the film version of Haycox's "Stage to Lordsburg" that propelled the Duke to stardom. Ford's film also sparked a comeback for the big-budget western. (Jerry Ohlinger's Movie Material Store, New York City.)

on the way to Bismarck in Dakota territory. Inside the coach, he is seated with the heroine and a young man with a chip on his shoulder. Seeing the disparate personalities on board, we are quickly reminded of the Ford film. However, instead of the cinematic thrills that accompany Ford's Indian chase scene, young Indians ride up to the coach and only *mime* shooting arrows at it. The young man is ready for trouble, but Shafter diffuses the tension by saying that these Indians are purposely trying to frighten them. And if that isn't enough of a reason to calm down, Shafter also states that they wouldn't dare attack because it's winter and they'll need provisions from the fort. This seems to be a far more realistic take on the same situation. Also, Ford never quite explained how a team of horses pulling a heavy coach with people inside is somehow supposed to be faster than a bunch of Indian ponies.

For the Duke, it was the culmination of eight years slaving away in the "B" western graveyard. Producer Walter Wanger had wanted Gary Cooper for the Ringo Kid and Marlene Dietrich as Dallas. Though this actually *does* sound like an interesting casting choice, Ford rejected these and stuck to his choice of Trevor and the Duke. Cooper was already established as a cowboy star, and Dietrich would star in a western that year that would signal a "comeback" for her: *Destry Rides Again*. In 1948, Cooper would reject the script for Borden Chase's *Red River*, forcing director Howard Hawks to cast Wayne. The Duke would give one of the genre's best performances in the starring role. (After seeing this film, Ford reportedly said to Hawks, "I didn't know the son of a bitch could act.")

With the phenomenal popularity of the Ford film, Hollywood suddenly sat up and noticed the talented writer from Oregon. Seeing box office ahead, they swooped in (or rather, circled the sky a few times first) and started buying the rights to Haycox's works, the first filmmaker being no less a Hollywood icon than Cecil B. DeMille. In an almost perverse reply to the liberalism of Ford's film, the conservative DeMille bought one of Haycox's novels that contained elements of the noble pursuit of Manifest Destiny, *Troubleshooter*.

In 1936, when Haycox serialized *Troubleshooter*, an adventure set around the building of the Union Pacific railroad, the project was a controversial undertaking. Up to that point, pulp westerns had emphasized action and romance, sometimes with mind-numbing regularity. Haycox was probably the first to infuse historical accuracy into his western output. It was a far cry from what *Saturday Review* critic Bernard DeVoto called Zane Grey's "preposterous *U.P. Trail*," the novelist's cliché-ridden take on the same subject. Though the story's "romance and action" is made up, the rest of the book was based on careful research (dirty words to a hack like Grey). Haycox read books on the subject, including pamphlets from Union Pacific and biographies on the railroad's founder General Granville Dodge (with a certain town named after him that would figure prominently in Hollywood's mythologizing of the west), and even traveled the route of the original track-laying. (Haycox's dedication to detail was nothing if not painstaking. There are picture-perfect descriptions of terrain in Indian War–themed novels like *Bugles in the Afternoon* and *The Border Trumpet*, as well as gold camp novels like *Canyon Passage*, revealing that the author had actually visited these sites before writing about them.)

On the heels of a revival of the big budget western started by *Stagecoach*, Paramount released *Union Pacific* in 1939, a year that also gave us *Destry Rides Again* and *Jesse James*. With the title changed to glorify one of the largest railroad corporations in the west, and its theme of almost fanatical devotion to getting the job completed no matter what, Cecil B. DeMille gave us a conservative's idea of the prairie that rejected the nobility of the outsider as depicted by Ford and Nichols.

1. Ernest Haycox and the Grandeur of the West 15

Dallas' cowboy. The Ringo Kid (John Wayne) and the hooker with a heart of gold, Dallas (Claire Trevor), exchange meaningful looks in *Stagecoach*. Trevor and the rest of the cast rallied behind Wayne when the burgeoning star was bullied by director John Ford. (Book Castle-Movie World, Burbank, California.)

In *Trouble Shooter*, corporate hatchet man Frank Pease is faced with trouble from Indians, outlaws and greedy big-money interests out to stop the building of the railroad. In DeMille's film, Haycox's romanticism is gone and replaced by bombastic spectacle, with graphic demonstrations of incidents that happen in the novel (Indian attacks, derailments, personal conflicts) — in other words, DeMille's penchant for over-the-top thrills and bad soap opera.

The real Union Pacific corporation reportedly lent the studio its own track workers to use in the track-laying scenes. The crowd scenes are large, the explosions and train wrecks impressive and the pro-corporate propaganda repulsive. The dialogue in DeMille's films had grown more and more laughable as the years went on; there are very few films that hold a candle to the corny, twisted dialogue of *The Greatest Show on Earth*. For once, however, DeMille had based his epic on the work of a fine author and sometimes the two elements didn't gel.

There are the usual name changes. Hero Frank Pease becomes Cap-

The parties can't come to an agreement. Brian Donlevy (left) and Joel McCrea (right) are about to have their talk interrupted by Akim Tamiroff's whip in DeMille's *Union Pacific*. Manifest destiny was never like this. (Jerry Ohlinger's Move Material Store, New York City.)

tain Jeff Butler in a ridiculously implied reference to Rhett Butler. The role is played by Joel McCrea with the usual rock-hard stubbornness we've come to associate with his characters. McCrea himself had said to Preston Sturges, "Nobody writes for me. They usually write for Gary Cooper and if he turns it down, they offer it to me." There might be some truth in this, since DeMille loved working with Cooper and probably offered him the lead role.

Heroine Nan Normandy becomes Mollie Monahan. Though McCrea's performance as Pease aka Butler is adequate, someone should have coached Barbara Stanwyck on her brogue. She was usually a good actress and worked steadily in the western genre, but an Irish accent was clearly beyond her.

Besides Haycox's new dedication to historical accuracy, *Trouble Shooter* was also written at a time when the author was making his novels longer and there was more variety in the plots and greater depth to the characters. Since this is the case, his heroes and heroines usually had far more complicated relationships than a Hollywood film had the time (or inclination) to explore. Besides DeMille's own legendary dedication to painstaking detail, the screenplay reportedly had no less than eight writers working on it, including Haycox, before the director was satisfied enough to shoot it.

Replacing the human complexities beloved by the author, we have the subplot about the "other man," ne'er-do-well Dick Allen. He is played with pre–Harold Hill unctuousness by Paramount contract player Robert Preston. Usually playing oily but charming heels in the studio's films, the talented Preston all but steals the movie from the usually wooden McCrea and the overdone blarney of the miscast Stanwyck. Unfortunately, Preston's character has less to do with Haycox than it does the actor's standard screen persona at the time as seen by Paramount. Usually cast as the hero's pal who goes bad but ultimately reforms himself at the end, Preston's crooked gambler does just that, giving his life to save the hero, and by extension the railroad.

Also cast in his first appearance in Haycox Country was Brian Donlevy as crooked gambler Sid Campeau. Elevated to stardom by his over-the-top portrayal of a psychopathic sergeant in William Wellman's *Beau Geste*, Donlevy gives us a dry run of the crooked gambler he would portray in Haycox's *Canyon Passage* seven years later. Also seeking to gum up the works and stop the spread of the railroad is crooked banker Asa Barrows (Was there ever an *honest* banker in these films?), played with typically disreputable tendencies by Henry Kolker. (This makes two crooked bankers the same year in two Haycox film adaptations.) The film is also packed with future stars Anthony Quinn (soon to be the director's son-in-law), Ward Bond, Evelyn Keyes and Lon Chaney, Jr., as well as familiar western players like Lane Chandler and Iron Eyes Cody, the latter listed in the cast as "Indian"; what a surprise.

With dictatorship growing in Europe, the script ensures that McCrea will give a patriotic speech that speaks more to a nation about to enter a World War than the folks of the 19th century. Though film historians have pointed out DeMille's insertion of a patriotic ending as a preparatory call to arms in a war against fascism, I believe that the reactionary DeMille, and perhaps the conservative Haycox, were thinking of a fight against *all* dictatorships; not only fascism, but also our future allies in war, the Communist Russians, as well.

After Preston's death, McCrea informs us that he will be waiting for them "at the end of the tracks," in retrospect, a rather spooky prediction. Then we see a modern Union Pacific train heading towards the camera, huge and monolithic; the imagery unwittingly implying something to fear rather than celebrate, and even worse, giving us an image of totalitarian-like regimentation.

Twentieth Century–Fox released a film version of the author's *Sundown Jim* in 1942. And so started the decline of spectacle in the film versions of Haycox's works. When the works of Luke Short were filmed, high budgets were not necessary since Short's novels dealt with personalities more than epic events. Though Haycox's books from the late 1930s to the early '50s would be based on historical events, after *Union Pacific* the films would never again be given directors with the stature of a Ford or DeMille. Perhaps one of the lowest budgets given to a film version of Haycox was *Sundown Jim*, clearly filmed by Fox's "B" unit. Directed by the little-known Jim Tinling, *Sundown Jim* was a mere hour and three minutes.

Sundown Jim is played by Jim Kimbrough, Fox's resident singing cowboy. Perhaps Kimbrough's most memorable vehicle was *Rawhide*, filmed in 1937. This film's main distinction is not the cowboy crooner's performance or even the direction, but the fact that it was the only film to feature Yankee legend Lou Gehrig in an acting role. Needless to say, the slugger's dramatic skills were equal to Laurence Olivier playing first base in the Bronx.

Casting a singing cowboy as a character created by Ernest Haycox was tantamount to putting Jerry Lewis in *Farewell to Arms*. It was not as if a Haycox film didn't have songs; the later *Canyon Passage* would be infused with numbers by Hoagy Carmichael. However, casting a singing cowboy in a tale of feuding families bitterly knocking each other off does lighten up the range war elements considerably. Despite a good supporting cast, including Joe Sawyer, Paul Hurst and Lane Chandler, the "B" is badly directed. The film is forgotten today, which is just as well.

Next was another "B" version of Haycox, this time from mighty MGM, "where there are more stars than the heavens." However, looking at the cast here, the heavens didn't miss any stars as they cast this opus.

Clearly made as a "B" film not worthy of the talents of a Gable, Tracy or Taylor, *Apache Trail* headlines Lloyd Nolan as Trigger Bill, one of the wild west's many good-badmen. Cast in a role that is more suited to Wallace Beery, Nolan is a good enough actor to make you root for his charming outlaw, despite his glaring urban accent. Usually cast as gangsters or FBI agents (and a standout as detective Michael Shayne), Nolan is very likable in the film, though his dialogue delivery is more midtown Manhattan than west of the Pecos. Clearly, a performer's accent meant nothing in those days when any actor with a foreign accent was automatically accepted as *any* foreign character. Compounding this miscasting is William Lundigan, who plays his brother Tom.

The film's plot has similarities to *Stagecoach*, with a group of stage passengers stuck at a forded-up way station as word of Apache trouble spreads. Tom is at the center of a romantic triangle, with the beautiful Constance (Anne Ayers) as one side of it. In what seems like another triumph of (mis)casting, the lovely, and very Anglo-Saxon, Donna Reed is cast as Latina beauty Rosalia Martinez, the third point of this triangle.

With the stage passengers under siege and conflict between the two brothers boiling under the surface of MGM's usually innocuous dialogue, there seems to be nothing left but for the Apaches to come along and launch their usual failed attacks. Of course, Trigger Bill gives up his life to save the lives of the coach passengers.

Director Richard Thorpe does a good job considering the less-than-adequate screenplay and the incessant miscasting. The usually excellent Thorpe did a lot better filming Short than Haycox (*Vengeance Valley*). And this may be the paradox. Luke Short was always easier to put on film than Haycox, not because Short was a better writer, but because Short's works had strong plots that constantly *moved*.

Haycox spent time, sometimes a lot of it, establishing a milieu, particularly one where his characters seem to be prisoners of their fate. Marshal Dan Mitchell goes about his sometimes depressing daily routines while attempting to tame a frontier town in *Trail Town*; Frank Pease is the ultimate company man fighting all odds that the Union Pacific would get the railroad built in *Troubleshooter*; after spending eight years in the east, Hugh Kingmead *must* return to his family's abandoned ranch to settle the score with the bad guys in *Return of a Fighter*; the troopers of Fort Grant in *The Border Trumpet* live their lives in a hot, stifling Arizona desert and many give their lives to stop the Apaches.

With the success of *Stagecoach*, Hollywood saw Ernest Haycox as an author whose material might spell more box office. However, few producers (or, for that matter, screenwriters and directors) had the patience (in a land where time was money) to film the author's work as it should have been. In truth, a TV miniseries might have been more appropriate; with no time constraints, a miniseries might have given us the fullness of Haycox's characters, as well as a sharply detailed portrait of the west that he wrote of. The film versions of *Sundown Jim* and *Apache Trail* were clearly double-bill fodder.

In 1945, United Artists, film producers that had literally no studio facilities or stable of stars, only offices, hired independent producer Herbert Biberman to film Haycox's novel *Trail Town* under the title *Abilene Town*. Written in 1941, the novel is another of Haycox's "sprawling" works, chronicling in painstaking detail the story of Marshal Dan Mitchell and his duties as a "day marshal" of the similarly sprawling cow town of River Bend. The name of the town is ironic, for Dan Mitchell never bends. In the novel, the lawman goes through his job with set routines (breakfast, a cigar, barber shop, lunch, a patrol down embattled Race Street, etc.). He is the impartial regulator caught in the middle between the law-abiding but pushy merchants, and the rowdy cattle drover element backed by the saloonkeepers. He is the only one charged with controlling them.

Supposedly based on the exploits of Abilene town marshal Tom Smith (who was murdered by a outlaw with an ax), Haycox gives us a compelling portrait of an embattled officer of the law caught between two factions who run the town. On the one side, the merchants give him absolutely no support, and on the other side, the saloonkeepers want him dead. Doggedly enforcing the law on his noon to midnight shift (before an older man comes on duty and works the quieter midnight to noon shift), Mitchell is a striking portrait in stubborn courage, and perhaps more than a little absurdity. Besieged by all to quit before he gets killed, the fatalistic Mitchell plods on, risking his neck almost hourly in a thankless, low-paying job for usually ignorant, ungrateful townsfolk.

With Herbert Biberman backing the play, the film version set about retaining the fatalism of Haycox's tenacious lawman, but added a storyline with a leftist twist. In later years, Biberman would be indicted by the HUAC as one of the Hollywood Ten. But when the film was made, Russia was still our ally, though not for long. During this brief period of alliance with the Soviets and before the onslaught of the HUAC, Biberman took the time to give us one of Hollywood's few socialist westerns.

Somehow, the thought of turning the conservative Haycox's work into a socialist tract may sound like blasphemy, but Biberman had screenwriter Harold Shumate (who adapted Frank Gruber's *Peace Marshal* for the 1943 film *The Kansan*) cunningly inject some interesting pro-capitalist, pro-religious elements.

Randolph Scott, an actor who usually did right by the western pulps, was cast as Dan Mitchell. The casting was perfect; no other actor could project the same moral rectitude, the strictly by-the-book style of law enforcement that the character of Dan Mitchell demanded. Added to this was the Scott character's huge stubborn streak. Two years before Scott's screen persona would evolve into the Obsessive Pursuer of Justice (or rather Revenge) in Luke Short's *Coroner Creek*, the actor gives us a small taste of things that would come in the 1950s as he worked with Budd Boetticher. Even when working for the talented Joseph H. Lewis, Scott was still able to project an almost fanatical adherence to duty as he fought the outlaw elements in *A Lawless Town*, a 1955 Columbia film that suspiciously

Forever tall in the saddle. Randolph Scott, who had brought to life many pulp western characters, rides tall in *Abilene Town*. Produced by Herbert Biberman, it became the screen's first socialist western. (Jerry Ohlinger's Movie Material Store, New York City.)

copies the plot of *Abilene Town*. In the latter film, the town is seen as "an untamed beast" ready to be turned loose if not for the persistant law enforcement of Scott's beleaguered marshal. When Scott is sidelined, the town is "wide open," the exact same term used in Biberman's film when the outlaw element takes over.

Mitchell also has to contend with his spoiled princess girlfriend,

Sherry (a young and very brunette Rhonda Fleming). In the novel, the romantic interludes between Dan and Sherry are subtle, yet powerful; every meeting, no matter how innocuous, has an undercurrent of smoldering passion waiting to be released. In the book, Sherry is tough and compassionate, another good example of the respect for women Haycox bestowed on his female creations that was just as sincere as Luke Short's.

In Biberman's film, she's a spoiled brat, her mannerisms containing much pouting and childish stomping of feet. Using an element of Luke Short, screenwriter Shumate elevates the lonely saloon gal Rita to a tough but compassionate woman to end up with Scott's hero. A friend of Mitchell's in the novel, a man who loves Rita, is removed for the film. Also gone from the movie is the affair between a merchant's lonely wife and a sophisticated gambler. In a way, this particular omission is a pity, since this doomed relationship is quite touching; however, Biberman's dogma had no time for such capitalist sentiment.

Using the novel's subplot of the merchants' hostility to new homesteaders and elevating it to center stage, Biberman and Shumate bodily threw in a leftist's version of economics into the mix. Towards the end of the film, one merchant adds up what a homesteader would spend in his store compared to a cattleman's and realizes that the sheer volume of poor homesteaders would make more lucrative customers than rowdy, unreliable cowboys. Moving in a radical direction (radical for a Communist, that is), Biberman shows us a scene where Mitchell is listening to the poor but devout homesteaders singing hymns, and giving his silent approval. That Biberman intended the homesteaders of the film to be seen as America's poor, disenfranchised minorities would not be far from the truth. They are protecting their new land from the wild, bullying cattle drovers, who are seen as some kind of fascist entity with lariats and spurs.

Needless to say, when the homesteaders, as personified by handsome (off-screen liberal) Lloyd Bridges, back the marshal in their fight against the drovers, it spells doom for the economic monopoly held by the evil (and so very capitalist) cattle interests. When Scott intones to the drovers that the meek are taking back the town and that they're tougher than we think, it is Biberman's comment on the economic power of minorities, typically ignored by the capitalists of 1945.

In 1946, a bigger budget was set aside for the next film version of Haycox, *Canyon Passage*, based on the novel serialized in the *The Saturday Evening Post*. Produced by Universal, the film starred Dana Andrews as Logan Stuart, a new freighter in a rip-roaring gold camp town in Oregon in 1849. Appropriately set in Haycox Country and shot on location in beautiful Bend, Oregon, the film takes the book's finely detailed characters and gets as close as possible to Haycox's original conception. There is another romantic triangle, with the usually limited Brian Donlevy as George Camrose, a banker who's been embezzling his depositors' accounts so that he can enjoy his true passion, non-stop gambling.

However, Camrose still reserves *some* passion for the third side to this triangle, the lovely Lucy Overmire, played by the lovely Susan Hayward. Unfortunately, Hayward is totally miscast as a sweet young thing from the Oregon gold fields. Consistently mannered, even in her best performances, Hayward was clearly out of place in the western. Fully aware that she was once a poor girl from Flatbush, the star spent most of her years on-screen trying to make us forget it (despite her frequent "Anyone here from Brooklyn?" line she gave at war bond rallies). Her performances in Henry Hathaway's *Rawhide* and the Gary Cooper vehicle *Garden of Evil* are abominably bad; her attempts at an upper crust dialogue delivery out in the old west laughable.

Also in the cast is Ward Bond as the brutal, Indian-hating (and unusually named) Honey Bragg. Lloyd Bridges returns to Haycox Country as Johnny Steele, young hothead extraordinare. For Bridges, it is another of his portrayals of hot-tempered young working stiffs with socialist leanings at which the actor excelled in the shadow of the Blacklist Years.

As directed by horror maestro Jacques Tourneur, *Canyon Passage* seemed to perfectly capture the poetry, and especially the brutality, that is never far from the surface of Haycox Country. In an interview, Tourneur said that he found directing outdoor sequences much easier than directing indoor scenes with three of four people in a room. If that was the case, then he must have been delighted with the set pieces of *Canyon Passage*. These scenes include the burning of Logan's store, an Indian attack and a knockdown dragout saloon fight between the hulking Ward Bond and the taciturn Dana Andrews. The fight is filled with plenty of face-smashing and as much shedding of blood as the Production Code would allow.

Universal's budget was certainly higher than for their usual bread-and-butter pictures during the war years. In coming years, the studio would produce the Oscar-winning Best Picture of 1948, *Hamlet*, and the film that would give Ronald Colman his long-deserved Oscar, *A Double Life* (1947). These efforts would indicate that the studio used Haycox's source novel as the perfect opportunity to produce an "A" western and thus be able to compete with the larger studios. This was certainly the reasoning when Universal merged with International Pictures that same year. With this acquisition, Universal had hopes of abandoning their previous "B" product and emerging as a major player in Hollywood, capable of making "important" films every bit as good as that studio with all the stars in the heavens, yadda yadda.

Suddenly Universal ceased production of their horror movies with Lon Chaney, Jr., their Sherlock Holmes series and their "B" westerns with Tex Ritter, Rod Cameron and Kirby Grant. *Canyon Passage* had major stars, beautiful Technicolor and a 92–minute running time, elements that gave credence to the film's tagline, "Now — Great Motion Picture Entertainment." (We're to assume that films made before this one, like *Gone with the Wind*, weren't.)

The film was even nominated for an Oscar for Best Song, "Ole Buttermilk Sky." Perfectly crooned by Hoagy Carmichael, it unfortunately lost to the audacious and highly overrated "On the Atkinson, Topeka and the Santa Fe" from MGM's even bigger-budgeted *The Harvey Girls*. (Apparently the studio had more songwriters than were in the heavens as well.)

Nevertheless, Oregon's governor, Earl Snell, flew to the film capital and lobbied Universal to hold the film's premiere in Portland. Oregon Senator Wayne Morse praised the film in the halls of Congress and his praise became part of the Congressional Record. As for the author himself, Haycox was honored at the film's premiere, as well as given an honorary degree from Lewis and Clark College.

Haycox wasn't usually called upon to do screenwriting chores, unlike Frank Gruber, whose own western novels seem to come suspiciously close to some of Haycox's own works (in plots, that is, not execution). Though he did work on screen treatments for Samuel Goldwyn, Haycox, the writer and the man, rarely left his home in Oregon for the wilds of Hollywood, where even the author's toughest cowpokes might be helpless.

However, the author *did* do an adaptation for a film called *Montana Mike* in which Haycox is credited with extra dialogue. This would explain why the lines are better than the camera angles, since the film is only adequately directed by journeyman Albert Rogell. The fantasy plot has Bob Cummings as an angel. That's right, Bob Cummings of *Love That Bob* and what seem like half a dozen other TV series, including some show about a female robot which co-starred Julie Newmar.

In the postwar years, Warner Brothers suddenly became enamored of western literature and the talented men who produced them. They had Alan LeMay under contract in the late '40s, would expand Louis L'Amour's short story "The Gift of Cochise" into *Hondo* in 1953, and with the new decade bought the rights to Haycox's *Bugles in the Afternoon* and the Haycox story that became *Montana*.

Montana was directed by an old western hand, Ray Enright, who had previously filmed Luke Short's *Coroner Creek*. It starred Errol Flynn as Morgan Lane, sheep herder extraordinaire, moving his woolly, hay fever–inducing flock onto cattle range. As one can expect from such an explosive crowding of these two contrary species, the prairie was doomed to suffocate in a constant wave of gunsmoke.

With a running time of a mere hour and 16 minutes, it is considered one of Flynn's minor westerns. This is unfair, since Enright's direction is superb and the performances are excellent, despite its "B" running time. Western character man Douglas Kennedy is a standout as the hot-tempered villain and romantic rival for the hand and the rest of the body of Alexis Smith. Nevertheless, this film version of Haycox would be one of Flynn's last good Warner films before the studio decided not to renew the fading actor's contract.

The next film based on Haycox, however, would bring another of the author's novels to the screen with the kind of reverance not seen since *Canyon Passage*. With Randolph Scott again co-producing and starring for Columbia, the studio filmed Haycox's 1937 novel *Man in the Saddle*. Though produced on a lower budget than the Universal film, Scott had Andre DeToth directing. DeToth was a director of European films who came to America before the war and started to direct low-budget works that contained dark material which would fit in perfectly in the postwar years. With films like *None Shall Escape* (about the hunt for Nazi war criminals) and the later *Ramrod* (based on Short's novel), DeToth gained a reputation as a stylist. His westerns emphasized suspense and the darkest aspects of human behavior (that is, sanctioned by the Breen office).

DeToth's genre works with Randolph Scott, whether filmed at Columbia or Warners, were filled with well-chosen camera angles, scenes of sustained tension (particularly when gunmen are stalking each other through deserted streets) and an emphasis on driven, haunted personalities. Scott was shrewd enough to surround himself with competent craftsmen, especially directors who could give the clichés that something extra. Unfortunately, DeToth gave interviews in which it was obvious he didn't respect his star's talent, and hardly acknowledged Scott's considerable input into his westerns. This is a pity since the two had worked so well together. As far as *Man in the Saddle* was concerned, merging DeToth with Haycox might not have been a perfect union, but it was a respectable attempt at filming Haycox Country.

At the beginning of the film, rancher Owen Merritt (Scott) is trying to get over the fact that his sweetie, Laurie Bidwell (for some reason, changed from the novel's Sally), is marrying Will Isham (Alexander Knox). Since Laurie is played by the beautiful Joan Leslie, we can perfectly understand why Owen is upset. Isham, a powerful rancher, is of course trying to squeeze everyone out of the area so that he and he alone can be the undisputed Boss of the Valley. Thrown into this mix is Nan Melotte (Ellen Drew), the local schoolmarm who has always had a crush on Owen.

Also mixed in with all this mishegos is John Russell as Nan's psychotic stalker, Hugh Clagg, Scott's frequent co-star Guinn "Big Boy" Williams as Haycox's wonderfully named Bourke Prine, and Richard Rober as Isham's murderous foreman Fay Dutcher — this has all the makings for a head-on collision into mayhem!

Man in the Saddle is not as multi-textured a novel as *Bugles in the Afternoon* or *Troubleshooter*, it being a combination ranch romance–shoot 'em up. Yet it is also an interesting character study of a group of driven individuals saved or destroyed by their own obsessions.

In the book, Sally Bidwell is a poor but beautiful girl who holds her father's poverty in contempt. Though she loves the tough but honest Owen, she ultimately sets her cap for the wealthy Isham. Will Isham is a proud if power-hungry man, gobbling up the other ranches without a pang of guilt, yet also enraged that his new wife might still carry a torch for Owen. Nan is the lonely schoolmarm, always watching the handsome, now-available Owen from afar, and eventually risks her life for him when he is wounded in a gunfight. Hugh Clagg, essentially a 19th century version of a stalker, is a nasty individual whose own obsession with Nan causes tragedy.

The novel, especially in the opening chapters, perfectly draws a finely detailed portrait of a world filled with the toughest hombres smoking the bitterest tobacco and ready to draw their weapons at the slightest personal insult. In a predictable foreshadowing of trouble, Bourke Prine keeps prodding Owen to have it out with Isham and get Sally back. The other characters, filled with tension, are also waiting for a chance to gun down their enemies at the drop of a hat.

Welcome to Haycox Country!

In the film, Will Isham rather bluntly explains his goal to possess anything and everything he can get his rich, powerful hands on. Though the role is well-acted by Knox, his English accent is clearly out of place. Perhaps Scott and co-producer Harry Joe Brown cast him as a reminder of George Macready, who had played roles like this opposite the star before. As played by Scott, Merritt is tight-lipped and reserved, the actor showing us bitterness that his girl is now married to a creep. He also rolls his own smokes and wears a brown cowhide jacket that the actor apparently liked to wear in his other Columbia films.

In her previous roles, Joan Leslie was usually cast as the heroine who got the guy. Already a star at Warners, where she appeared opposite Bogart, Cagney and Cooper, the actress was still in her early twenties when she decided not to renew her Warners contract. Jack Warner being Jack Warner, he vindictively blacklisted her from working at other studios. Herbert Yates ignored Warner's blacklist. Signed with Republic in 1950, the underrated Leslie would appear in several of the studio's westerns, including a standout performance in the feminist western *The Woman They Almost Lynched*. (This film includes a good knockdown drag-out catfight between Joan and Audrey Totter, the latter playing, of all people, Kate Quantrill!)

Speaking of fights. Scott's Owen gets into a terrific brawl with John Russell's Hugh Clagg midway through the film. In the book, Owen is wounded in a shootout with Isham's men and Nan Melotte finds him and hides him in a cave, where she loyally stays with him and tends to his wounds. By accident, they are found by Clagg and he and Owen have a terrific brawl. However, Haycox gives us a realistic, claustrophobic fight within the small confines of a cave, with the two men grappling within narrow spaces, even crowding Nan aside as she tries to help Owen. In the film, DeToth gives a literal interpretation of "opening up" the source novel, by having the two brawling men knock down the poles holding up the weak roof of Nan's small shack, with piles of accumulated snow falling into the now uncovered room as the two combatants go at it.

The film does not, however, go into the frustrated, stalled passions the novel's protagonists have. As the novel progresses, Isham and Sally, now realizing that they made a mistake, decide that their marriage will be in name only, shunning any physical contact. After Nan spirits the wounded Owen away to the cave, the sweaty passions they have for each other are hard to ignore.

Towards the end of the book, Owen kills Isham out in the woods. The film goes one better for a change, by having Laurie offering to stay with Isham if he divests himself of his wealth and leaves Owen and the ranchers in peace. Ultimately Isham is shot by Fay Dutcher. As he dies, he makes Laurie promise to keep his wealth, already moved by the fact that Laurie does love him enough to stay with him even if he were poor.

In the novel, there is some basis for this. After Isham's death, Sally Bidwell becomes mistress of the spread, forcing the rowdy, sexist ranch hands to bend to her will by sheer force of personality.

Richard Rober, after having played a gunman opposite Audie Murphy in Universal's *Sierra*, is far too cleancut as Isham's hired thug, Fay Dutcher. In the novel, he has a big black beard and is a hulking, usually enraged monster. In the film, Rober is as intimidating as a used car salesman. All in all, *Man in the Saddle* may not have been a perfect visualization of the novel into a film, but it did give us a taste of Haycox's west, however diluted.

Warner Brothers returned to Haycox Country with the filming of *Bugles in the Afternoon*, the author's epic novel of a love triangle played out against the background of Custer's defeat at the Little Big Horn. Kern Shafter (the laughably miscast Ray Milland) is a soldier who enlists with Custer's Seventh Cavalry in Dakota Territory. Formerly a captain during the Civil War, Shafter is now a private, hoping to lose himself in Army life after losing his love to his erstwhile best friend, Edward Garnett (Hugh Marlowe).

The book goes into intricate detail on Shafter's torment and his fierce hatred of Garnett. After enlisting, who should he find as a company captain? You guessed it. Garnett is now a captain over Shafter's embittered private. To top it off, both men are again fighting over a woman, the beautiful Josephine Russell (played by the beautiful Helena Carter). Carter is perhaps a little too English for this material, but then again, so is her leading man. Marlowe is a good, if limited, actor; a little too stiff to convincingly reenact Haycox's versatile Captain Garnett. (In the book, Garnett is a charmer with the ladies, a competent officer, and a dastardly schemer, as he looks for ways to destroy Shafter. Cut from the book is Garnett's romantic affair with a general's wife.)

Starting from the bottom of the cavalry food chain, Kern is promoted to sergeant instantly by his old comrade-in-arms, Captain Myles Moylan. (Another example of strange casting: the usually villainous Barton MacLane as a good guy.) Now that he's become a sergeant literally days after his arrival, Shafter incurs the jealousy of ex–Sergeant Donavan. As played by Forrest Tucker, the actor perfectly captures the Irish trooper's love of a good drink, a good cigar and a damn good fistfight. His battle with Kern, as in the book, is quick, professional and without malice. After Kern wins the fight, the two men are now buddies. Though Tucker does lay it on thick with the brogue, at least he's better at it than Barbara Stanwyck. The previous year, Tucker had played an Irish sergeant in Paramount's *Warpath*, the film version of Frank Gruber's novel, with a plot that's suspiciously close to Haycox's *Bugle in the Afternoon*.

There are certain episodes from the book which transfer well to the film, such as Garnett ordering Kern, and only Kern, to arrest two Sioux warriors who murdered some settlers. What the film doesn't explore is Haycox's lively portrait of General Custer. As seen by the author, Custer is clearly a vital life force; unable to simply put away his horse after arriving at the fort, the general has to ride up and down the parade grounds to expend more of his endless flow of restless energy. In the novel, we see Mrs. Custer being physically carried up to her bedroom by her husband, Haycox giving us a small demonstration of the very real love that the Custers had for each other. (Custer's letters to his wife were reportedly filled with X-rated suggestions amidst the declarations of undying love.)

Haycox gives us some well-detailed scenes of Shafter, now assigned to deliver the fort's mail throughout the territory, riding into blizzards and ice storms. The film also drops the subplot of Garnett's affair with an officer's wife. The book's intricate details of cavalry life are gone, including Shafter, Donavan and their company challenging a rival troop company to a fistfight. The film is merely set on a Warner lot masquerading as a fort used in countless films. Apparently Haycox Country didn't always fit in well with Burbank.

Within the casting, the story needed an actor capable of giving his character a bitter edge; Milland is simply not bitter enough. More appropriately, Warners should have cast Randolph Scott, a larger-than-life actor then under contract to the studio; he had already proven himself (Twice!) in Haycox Country.

At the end, as in the book, Custer leads his men to Little Big Horn. In the novel, Shafter is not in Custer's company at the time and, though wounded, he is able to still give a fatally wounded Garnett, his bitter enemy, a last drink of water. Recuperating in the hospital, Kern is again made a captain, and patiently waits for Josephine's kiss as she leans over his bed. In the Warner's film, Custer's defeat seems to take place over an area about ten feet square, complete with the studio's replicated trees and rubber bolders. Garnett is conveniently shot dead by an accommodating Sioux warrior, Kern is wounded but survives, and he and Josephine clinch; end of film.

As a postscript, the film also has the underrated James Millican as Sergeant Hines— quite a comedown since the actor played Custer in Paramount's *Warpath*. Sheb Wooley played the part this time around.

Next was *Apache War Smoke*, MGM's "B" movie remake of *Apache Trail*, a "B" to begin with. The casting was improved considerably by having Gilbert Roland play Peso, a reprise of Trigger Bill. Not only was Roland one of the genre's more talented performers, but his Latino accent fit in much better than Lloyd Nolan's rather urban cadence.

Unfortunately, we have the same problem here with the protagonists' relationship as in the original. Having Nolan and William Lundigan as brothers was not believable; *Apache War Smoke* casts Gilbert Roland as Robert Horton's outlaw *father*. What an improvement!

Horton is clearly miscast as Herrera, the stationmaster. The Apaches are on the typical warpath, this time because a thief and murderer named Pike (the talented "B" veteran Myron Healey) has killed some braves and stolen their jewelry. Pike is chased on horseback to the way station. Also arriving at the way station is the famous bandit Peso.

This is after we are introduced to the charming scoundrel at the hacienda of a beautiful senorita and her children. We do not know whether this is his wife or lover or even private secretary, and we aren't quite sure whether these are his kids, but the bit does establish him as a ladies' man. It is only afterwards that we learn he's also a master thief and gunman, but this is all right since he's so full of charm.

Also along for the siege is Fanny Webson, a "proper woman." It turns out that she is actually an outlaw who knows the kissing bandit from way back. The folks you run into at these places!

However, this lively con woman is played by Glenda Farrell. After making a career of playing lovable, empowered women in Warner Brothers films of the '30s, her career declined somewhat in the strongest years of the Production Code, when depictions of strong women were considered verboten. Playing a supporting role in an MGM "B" western a mere hour and seven minutes long was not considered a comeback.

By the end of the film, after Peso switches clothes with Pike (Pike had spread the word that Peso killed those Apaches), the charming outlaw forces the murderer out into the open where Apache warriors promptly kill him. Now that they have their man, the warriors ride away and, unbelievably, leave the passengers alone.

With a general decline of "B" westerns due to television, Hollywood held off filming any more of Haycox's works until 1965, when they remade *Stagecoach*. This, however, was more a tribute to John Wayne and John Ford than Haycox, an author who had been dead for 15 years and for all intents and purposes forgotten by Hollywood.

Alex Cord had given good performances in both domestic and foreign westerns, but there was no mistaking the fact that he was not John Wayne. Nor was Gordon Douglas a substitute for John Ford in the director's chair. Bing Crosby, a dozen years after playing a drunk in Paramount's *The Country Girl*, is cast in Thomas Mitchell's Oscar-winning role as the alcoholic Doc Boone, and doesn't exactly make it. In fact, the whole film had a "TV" look about it. Casting such popular television performers as Stefanie Powers, Mike Connors, Robert Cummings, Red Buttons and Ann-Margret as well as Crosby, who was doing TV specials consistently year after year, reminded audiences that the first film was indeed groundbreaking. The remake was like a TV movie of the week, its only saving grace being Van Heflin's tough marshal. Heflin was a talented performer whose underplayed acting style neatly stole the film from the rest of the cast's over-the-top antics.

Another departure from the original was a violent and gratuitous knife-fight over Dallas (Ann-Margret) by two cavalry privates. The scene is clearly unnecessary and, I suspect, a blatant repudiation of John Ford's lionizing of the cavalry. Compare this bloody battle with all those wild brawls Ford's troopers get into where no one is really hurt and the attempt to inflict physical pain is considered fun.

The 1985 TV movie remake of the bloated 1966 remake was even worse, and hardly worth mentioning, except in the casting of the always dislikable Kris Kristofferson, blasphemously cast in the original Duke Wayne role.

With this film, Hollywood put a close to its filming of the works of Ernest Haycox. The author would not enjoy the revival of his works on cable television that a lesser talented writer, Louis L'Amour, would enjoy. This is a shame because Haycox was one the finest writers of western fiction, a man whose skill alone would cause his admirers to refer to his work as belonging in Haycox Country. It's not every author whose works inspire a territory of their own.

Ernest Haycox developed from a writer of pulp magazine stories and novels to outstanding chronicler of historical epics. However, even in his early works of the 1920s like *Guns Up, A Rider in the High Mesa* and *Return of a Fighter*, Haycox's style was far ahead of his contemporaries, even if these early Haycox novels had their rural characters spouting flowery dialogue. (In a letter written to his college English professor in the 1920s, Haycox referred to the dialogue in his first novel, *Free Grass* as "reverse English.") In *Return of the Fighter,* when the hero shows up after being gone a long time, one cowpoke remarks, "We thought you dropped off the calendar." As time went on, the language of his characters would become grittier, their anguish and torments more sharply defined.

The pulp covers of his novels may have shown us the same corny image of a cowboy firing blazing six-guns in the air, but what was between the covers was far ahead of its time — respecting the reader's intelligence, their basic storylines rejecting standard "shoot 'em up" clichés.

In the beginning, Hollywood had discovered Ernest Haycox through the genius of John Ford. Between the talents of Ford and John Wayne, *Stagecoach* became such a success that it revived the big-budget western that Hollywood had ignored since the end of the 1920s. The film triggered Hollywood's interest in Haycox Country and resulted in the epic *Union Pacific* based on the author's *Troubleshooter*. Somewhere along the way, however, the studios' interest continued, but with a meager price tag, and further film versions of Haycox's work were of grade "B" quality. By the time of the *Stagecoach* remake, Haycox's story would become a vehicle for the mostly limited talents of TV performers, and audiences would forget the talented author whose source material was responsible for so much in the genre.

Definitely, Hollywood should return to Haycox Country and give the author his due on film.

2

Luke Short and Romance in the West

There are those western authors who write of the beautiful vistas, the panoramic valleys, the majestic, breathtaking mountains and reams and reams of copy on the quality of ancient volcanic rock on a stretch of land where a chase sequence is taking place. Then are those who just give us the basics on physical beauty of the land, but concentrate more on the problems (frequently romantic) of their protagonists.

If vengeance and inner turmoil motivate a large number of Zane Grey's characters, jealousy, not always petty, motivates the actions of Luke Short's people. Thwarted love, romantic rivalries, dysfunctional entanglements and paranoid jealousies move the stories along as much as the usual clichés of villains trying to get the ranch. In a Short novel, misconceptions over a loved one's romantic allegiance can ultimately topple a ranching empire, destroy a silver mine or get someone killed.

Romantic rivalries play major roles in his novels *Marauders' Moon*, *Brand of Empire*, *Ride the Man Down*, *High Vermillion* and *Vengeance Valley*, to name just a few. He brought up the issue of sexual roles in society decades ahead of the Equal Rights Amendment. His characters, particularly his women, were thinking human beings, not cardboard cutouts.

His career started with his novels being serialized in pulp magazines; in later years he would grow as a writer, but still be stuck in the formula western genre, his fame eclipsed by the even more prolific, but distinctly less talented, Louis L'Amour. His death from cancer in 1975 occurred around the same time Elmore Leonard would write his last gritty unconventional westerns before then turning successfully to the crime genre. The decade of the '70s also gave us the first western novels of a man who would, in my opinion, successfully bring the cynicism of the post–Vietnam era to the genre: Loren D. Estleman. Opposite these men, Short's formula prairie romances must have seemed old-fashioned indeed. Also fighting encroaching blindness and the memories of his son's accidental death in the 1960s, Short's career would end on a bittersweet note; the title of his last novel, *Trouble Country* might have been commenting on the twilight career of an author whose days in the sun had long passed.

Luke Short's real name was Frederick Dilley Glidden and he was born in Kewaunee, Illinois, on November 19, 1908. When his father died, Glidden was barely 13; he was raised by his mother, a high school English teacher. Later, the sophisticated Mrs. Glidden became dean of women at Knox College in Galesburg, Illinois. Though this information might seem unimportant, it has a great deal to do with Luke Short, the Writer.

Unlike most western writers, particularly those writing prior to the 1980s, Glidden treated his female characters with real compassion and sympathy. He brought up the issue of sexism in the old west when his rivals celebrated manliness. In Short's books, intelligent women were frequently having a hard time being independent in a male-dominated west, while in other pulp westerns manly heroes were symbolically waving their Winchesters.

It seems to be a prerequisite for success in the genre that western authors be real-life adventurers as well. Therefore, if Zane Grey was an expert fisherman, Louis L'Amour was an explorer and Alan LeMay was a soldier and a cowboy, it comes as no surprise that Luke Short was a trapper in Canada and, in his later years, an expert skier.

Short would always claim that his pen name came about by accident, not realizing that Luke Short was also a famous gambler, gunfighter and close friend of the Earps and Doc Holliday. Somehow this is hard to swallow; stop and think of how one could possibly come up the combination of names "Luke" and "Short." If this is an accident and he was unaware of Short's reputation, as Glidden has claimed, one wonders why he didn't call himself Jesse James. The ignorance of Luke Short's existence also might call into question Glidden's knowledge of western history. Unlike the works of Haycox, Alan LeMay or Will Henry, Glidden's formula oaters would almost never be based on historical events.

At first his fiction was serialized in magazines, where a writer was sometimes paid by the word. This would probably explain the verbosity of such early works as *King Colt, Hard Money* and *Bounty Guns.* This almost Zane Grey–like lack of conciseness has a lot to do with why Hollywood basically ignored these serialized works once they were published as novels. Also, the length of your average western film was basically an hour (if it was a "B" like those starring a Roy Rogers or Wild Bill Elliott), or 90 minutes (if starring a Randolph Scott or Joel McCrea). Intricately plotted novels like *King Colt* or *Bold Rider* were not what Hollywood had in mind, despite the novels' basically non-threatening, non-controversial formula of squeaky clean romance and adventure.

Still, in a formula opus like *Bounty Guns* in which a young hellion of an outlaw becomes a hero, it also juxtaposes the story of a spoiled, rich girl and her painful growing-up. When her snotty ways finally cause her wealthy father to kick her out of the house, she is forced to fend for herself, and finds the painful reality of what it's like to be a single woman facing discrimination in the old west. Unless she had a husband or worked the dance halls, a woman had literally nowhere to go. Short makes us see this through the hurt and confusion of his heroine, now forced to serve food at the counter of a local café. Though it is tough at first, she soon drops her selfish behavior and learns to respect herself through the independence that a job brings her. Outside of the saloon hall, few western writers mentioned the existence of Working Women, and certainly not with the insight and sympathy that Short brings to the subject.

If anything, Hollywood was not interested in making feminist westerns, but they *were* interested in making good, clean shoot-'em-ups. Ironically, Hollywood would ignore Short's 1930s magazine fiction and instead purchase his 1940s output. Outside of filming *Hurry Charlie Hurry*, based on a story by Short and starring ex–burlesque comedian Leon Errol, Hollywood would start filming Short's novels in earnest in the immediate postwar era.

One might ask why the film capital ignored Short's verbose but basically non-controversial western output of the 1930s and instead film his grittier 1940s works? The answer could probably be found within Frederick Glidden himself.

Unable to join the Army in World War II due to poor eyesight, Glidden worked for the Office of Strategic Services in 1943. Whether this acquaintance with the war and doing his patriotic duty had changed Short is only a guess. Nevertheless, his novels during and after the war years definitely became darker, his heroes became more driven; or so it seems in works like *Coroner Creek, Ride the Man Down* and *Gunman's Chance.* Whether pursued by ghosts of the past, embittered by events of the present or fatalistic about their future, Short's heroes did not have the same agenda as those wild hellions who populated his magazine fiction of the 1930s. Consequently, Hollywood made sure that his dark heroes found a place on the silver screen in the age of film noir.

Ramrod (1947) would be the first Luke Short novel to hit the screen. Being the first, the film is fortunate in having good talent at the helm. The producer was Harry "Pop" Sherman, the man who brought Hopalong Cassidy to the screen. It starred Joel McCrea, an actor who, along with Randolph Scott, would dominate the postwar western; the director was Andre DeToth, an imaginative filmmaker who would give us westerns of high quality, but would ironically always be known as the man who directed Vincent Price's return to the horror field in *House of Wax*, admittedly not one of DeToth's best.

The traditional Short elements are there: Romantic rivalries, jealousy, hidden passions, the usual attempt to take over the ranch, and a strong taciturn man to save the day. McCrea stars as Dave Nash, formerly tough ramrod, now trying to find himself inside the nearest bottle. He blames himself for the death of his wife and kids. Offering him a shot at redemption is Connie Dickason (Veronica Lake), a ruthless woman who has inherited a ranch due to the timely death of her fiancée. She needs a strong man who can go against Frank Ivey (Preston Foster), the self-proclaimed Boss of the Valley. Also thrown bodily into the mix is Bill Schell, a wild roughneck who is the hero's pal. Unfortunately this role is played by Don DeFore, usually cast in late 1940s and '50s comedies as the guy who loses the girl. Usually attired in a suit or a white dinner jacket, his screen character practically screamed pomposity. DeFore is about at home in the role of a wild cowhand as Mickey Rooney would be starring in "The Life of Richard Kiel."

At the end of her Paramount contract, Lake was signed clearly because she was DeToth's wife. McCrea did not like working with her. Always a limited actress, she would enter the 1960s employed as a waitress, and eventually end up doing some low-budget atrocity about saving Hitler's brain. She died of hepatitis at 51.

In *Ramrod*, there are noir elements, as well as a few plot devices Short had used in other novels. Donald Crisp portrays the guilty, do-nothing sheriff in the pay of Ivey, just as J. Carrol Naish would play the do-nothing marshal in the film version of *Ride the Man Down* and Edgar Buchanan would play the do-nothing sheriff in *Coroner Creek*. Veronica Lake's bad girl has to vie with Arleen Whelan's good girl for the hero's affections. The good girl-bad girl plot device would appear in countless Luke Short books. Also, the 1940s Luke Short hero would be a scarred man. McCrea's Dave Nash could be the twin of Larkin Moffitt of the book and screen versions of *Silver City* (*High Vermilion* is the novel). Both Nash and Moffitt were good at their fields; both would retreat to drink and live in squalor due to some horrible accident in their pasts. Both are hired by bosses who need their previously notable skills to defeat an opponent or get the job done. Les Savage, Jr., would also use this plot device in his novel of the California Gold Rush, *Hangtown*.

Predictably, Bill Schell sacrifices his life to hold off Ivey's thugs, making it possible for the wounded Dave to escape. Soon Nash, his gun arm in a sling, faces off against the evil Boss of the Valley with a Winchester, which can beat Ivey's .45 any day, and does. Preston Foster, the man who portrayed this land-grabbing sidewinder, was not only an actor, but also a talented singer and composer; in films he had played gruff heroes and gruff villains and obviously fit into the latter parts much better.

Lake's evil vixen is not an interesting character merely because she is played by Lake; had an actress with more than one expression done the part, Short's Connie Dicason might have been a fascinating film character. The director is plainly responsible for this failure in the casting. Also ringing a false note is the casting of Donald Crisp as the waffling sheriff. Never fully comfortable in the western genre, he would redeem himself considerably in Anthony Mann's *The Man from Laramie*, where his Scottish accent and cultured demeanor fit in perfectly with the auteur's western version of *Hamlet*.

McCrea is excellent straight down the line, being able to do this material in his sleep, and occasionally the wooden McCrea *does* look like he's doing certain roles in his sleep. Unfortunately, this would be his first and last foray into Luke Short territory.

Pine-Thomas Productions was a maker of "B" western-thrillers and adventures in the 1940s and early '50s. The heads of the firm, William Pine and William Thomas, produced their films on such a low budget that the two men were known in the industry as "the Two Dollar Bills." This is actually unfair since Pine and Thomas were also showmen who almost invariably delivered the goods. Their films usually had a modicum of dialogue and a maximum of low-budget adventure; set in exotic locales that were actually filmed on the Paramount lot, the stories moved and they featured action stars like John Payne, Larry "Buster" Crabbe and a certain ex–Warner Brothers contract player who became our fortieth President.

Paramount released Pine-Thomas' *Albuquerque* on February 20, 1948. Based on Short's novel *Dead Freight for Piutte*, it appeared nine months after the release of *Ramrod*. The McCrea film wasn't a big hit (McCrea himself dismissed the film as "lousy"), but *Albuquerque* showed Hollywood that Luke Short could be filmed, and filmed well (and under budget). All they needed was to pick up the story's pace a little. Unlike the slow-moving DeToth film, *Albuquerque* had no such problems, and this is because of two important production factors: the film's star, and its director. Ray Enright was a veteran director of sagebrush sagas, particularly those starring a tall, handsome actor from Virginia.

Randolph Scott was unarguably a giant of the western genre; had there never been a Randolph Scott, many a film version of a western novel (or filmic reenactment of western history) might have starred a dude-like actor like, Heaven help us, Don DeFore. Born in Orange County, Virginia, Scott was a leading man for Paramount in the 1930s, starring in their dramas and romantic comedies. But it was when Scott put on a holster and Stetson and fought the good fight against outlaws that the actor came into his own.

At Paramount in the 1930s, Scott became the Total Westerner in the film versions of Zane Grey's books (reportedly he was chosen by Grey himself to play his heroes). The association with the works of Grey and the energetic direction by genre veterans like Henry Hathaway taught Scott well.

Later, as a hands-on producer, usually in partnership with Harry Joe Brown, Scott was smart enough to see the potential of filming the pulp westerns of the '40s and '50s. He would appear in films based on the novels of Ernest Haycox, Max Brand and, of course, Luke Short. The actor wisely employed scenarists like Kenneth Gamet and Alan LeMay. By giving himself good material and surrounding himself with the genre's best supporting players (Edgar Buchanan, "Gabby" Hayes, Guinn "Big Boy" Williams, etc.), Scott made westerns of lasting quality. The actor said that if the story wasn't set 90 percent outdoors, it wouldn't work. (This is also Scott the Producer talking, since the great outdoors need no sets to be built.) In his own way, the actor would become almost as much an auteur as Anthony Mann and Budd Boetticher.

In Short's novel and the Paramount film, Cole Armin (Scott) arrives in a New Mexico town to work for his Uncle John (George Cleveland, usually cast as lovable old codgers called "Gramps"). However, Uncle John is the scheming owner of a freight line that hauls gold ore into town. In true anti-capitalist, pro-monopoly fashion, Uncle John wipes out his freight-hauling competition through devious means and now seeks to destroy the small hauling operation of young (and of course handsome) Ted Wallace (played by young and handsome Russell Hayden) and his sister Celia (Catherine Craig). (The author must have had a special affinity for the name; more than one Luke Short heroine is named Celia.) Hayden, having played the hot-tempered Lucky of the Hopalong Cassidy films, was ideally cast as the hot-tempered Ted Wallace.

Our hero resolves to help Ted, as does his sidekick Juke ("Gabby" Hayes), a character who is very un–Gabby-like in Short's novel. Bernard Nedell plays Sheriff Linton, a waffling lawman. Letty Tyler is a bad girl secretly working for Uncle John until she changes sides and becomes a Wallace partisan (as well as Wallace's girlfriend). She is portrayed by Barbara Britton, Scott's leading lady in *The Gunfighters*.

Perhaps the best casting of all is that of Lon Chaney, Jr., as Uncle John's psychotic henchman, Merkil. Backed up by his horror film reputation, Chaney had the talent to make one truly frightened of his villains, and he doesn't fail here, though he is also allowed some unusual comedic moments. Unfortunately, Scott would not work with him again, which is a pity, especially since both actors would end up at Warners at about the same time in the early '50s.

The film is fast-moving, without even a modicum of noir-like camera angles or atmosphere of dread that DeToth would put into his westerns. Ray Enright was not the stylist DeToth was, but he *did* know his way around a western. A frequent collaborator of Randolph Scott, Enright directed the star in eight films. Their next teaming, however, would signal a turning point in the star's career. Again turning to Luke Short for source material, Scott would cement his image as the ultimate Lone Cowboy in one of his best films.

Columbia Pictures was a company that made some truly fine westerns, and it was the studio where an acknowledged giant of the genre like Scott would do his best work. He teamed with producer Harry Joe Brown, and the two convinced the studio to buy the rights to *Coroner Creek* (written in 1945). In the late 1940s, when film noir was at its height of popularity, its bleak style would soon influence other genres. Outside of two Robert Mitchum films, *Pursued* and *Blood on the Moon*, and the later Randolph Scott vehicle *The Doolins of Oklahoma*, the film version of *Coroner Creek* became the perfect realization of film noir transferred to the west.

Instead of rain-soaked city streets, we were given prairies filmed on cloudy days. Reflecting the violence of the crime thriller, fistfights became far more brutal; heads were banged into the ground, eyes were gouged and trigger fingers were stepped on. The evil women who popularized noir films now became the double-crossing daughters of powerful ranchers, as if conveying the dark side of the typical rancher's daughter heroine. Our heroes were in pursuit of something, or someone, or were themselves pursued. In Short's novel, hero Chris Deming is haunted by the memory of his late fiancée having been kidnapped by Indians and then raped by the white villain. She eventually commits suicide with the man's knife.

In the film, Deming is a typically laconic Scott character — a man of integrity, speaking only when needed, but tough and defiant enough to fight any insult to his dignity. Gradually, from the 1930s on, Scott was moving towards this character; in this film version of Short's novel, Scott fully makes the character his own for the first time. As time went on, he would add shadings and some grim humor (mostly when directed by Boetticher), but in the meantime, this tough customer would get his fullest opportunities for mayhem in *Coroner Creek*.

As in past Short novels, this film version has two women fighting over our hero. Kenneth Gamet's screenplay gives considerable screen time to hotel owner Kate Hardison. Blonde in the novel, she is portrayed by the beautiful brunette actress Marguerite Chapman. As in the novel, Kate becomes the hero's conscience, trying in vain to dissuade Chris from his path of vengeance. Two years later, in Ray Enright's *Kansas Raiders*, Chapman tries to dissuade Audie Murphy from the path of outlawry. Since the talented war hero-turned-actor is playing Jesse James, we can only assume that Marguerite was not successful.

Deming tracks the man responsible for his fiancée's death to the town of, you guessed it, Coroner Creek. (Who picks the names for these towns?) This, after a good establishing scene (which starts the same way in the novel) of Forrest Taylor's good hombre setting up a meeting with Apache Charlie Stevens to get information on "the blonde man with the scar." This unredeemable louse turns out to be Younger Miles, who has apparently used his ill-gotten gains in the stagecoach raid to open a freight outfit and become Boss of the Valley. As portrayed by Columbia contract player George Macready, Miles is a cold (and cold-blooded), emotionless creep. This brilliant but warmth-challenged individual has married the sheriff's daughter and driven her to drink with his coldness. By the way, did I also mention he was cold?

Abbie Miles (Barbara Reed) is the daughter of Sheriff O'Hara (Edgar Buchanan), another of Short's long line of morally weak lawmen. However, as portrayed by the talented Buchanan, O'Hara (as in the book) is played for tragedy as well as comedy. When he admits to himself that Abbie has stayed with Miles only to keep her proud father in the sheriff's job, it is a very moving moment.

Another Luke Short trait transferred to this film is the respect for its female characters and their rejection of the stereotyped roles they were forced to play in a male-dominated west. Kate Hardison runs a hotel. Her rival for Deming's affections, Della Harms (Sally Eilers), runs a ranch and holds sway over obnoxious, lazy male ranch hands.

Abbie's ambitions and needs are suppressed by the dominating Younger Miles, causing her to drown her lost dreams in booze. Unlike the more empowered Kate and Della, Abbie has allowed a bullying, abusive male to dictate her life and she suffers for it. Her concern for her father's fragile ego also distracts her from her own needs. When Scott's tenacious Chris Deming comes to town, the cowpoke indirectly sets into motion a series of events that not only free the town from Miles' ruthless domination, but also frees Abbie from her failed marriage to the freight-hauling heel. This plot device of Scott's cowpoke riding into a strange town and, through his own personal vendetta, freeing the town from its crooked boss, would be repeated even more powerfully in *Decision at Sundown*.

In *Coroner Creek*, it is only when Abbie puts some Miles between herself and her husband (sorry about that) and gets a job in the local café, as does many a Short female protagonist, that she feels better about herself. In the novel, Abbie is helped on this road to self-discovery by the brother of Chris Deming's fiancée, a fellow named McDonald, who also happens to work for Younger Miles. The character is absent from the film's screenplay without any discernable loss.

After taking a room in Kate's hotel, Chris is asked to take a drunken Abbie back home by buggy. Unfortunately, he runs into Ernie and the Rainbow Crew, Younger Miles' wild boys. As Ernie, Forrest Tucker easily plays his most vicious character. When Ernie orders Chris to get out of the buggy and reaches over to pull him off, Chris jumps him. Typically, the Randolph Scott character is not one to be *ordered* what to do. After the Rainbow crew separates them, all is forgiven and Abbie is taken home to her loving husband, who will verbally abuse the downtrodden woman for embarrassing him.

Soon, Chris takes a job as Della Harms' foreman, angering Miles and especially the jealous Kate. Almost immediately after taking the job, Deming is grabbed by the vicious Stew (Douglas Fowley) and taken back to the Rainbow bunkhouse. As in the book, Ernie has Chris held by the others as he beats him unconscious and then steps on his trigger finger, a particularly violent act for movies at the height of the Production Code.

Though Andy (Wallace Ford) is ordered to ride away, Deming has filled him with defiance. The ranch hand finds his gun and returns to Rainbow, holding the gun on the others as Deming angrily fights Ernie with one hand. The fight is violent and well-choreographed, as were most of the fights in Scott's films. This has Chris compensating for his broken right hand by biting Ernie and then giving his opponent a head-butt, one of the first times the move is seen on screen outside of slapstick comedy. After knocking Ernie out, Chris barely pauses before he crushes the bully's fingers under his boot. By this time, even the Rainbow Crew (and perhaps the audience) are sickened by this wanton violence.

Gradually, little by little, Deming foils Miles' plans, the cowpoke's presence indirectly causing Abbie to break from Miles (her father does so as well). "It's good to get off your knees," says O'Hara, after arresting Stew for killing Andy (off screen). However, this move towards honest law enforcement leaves Miles unimpressed, as the freight magnate kills O'Hara and releases Ernie and Stew from jail.

Pursued by Deming, the two felons hide out in the loft of a livery stable. Even Kate helps out. At one point, she accidentally shoots Stew out of his hiding place, the film giving us the cliché of a woman being clumsy with a gun (she only succeeds in disarming the villain by accident), an unwitting rejection of Short's undercurrent of feminism.

Rather cruelly holding Stew in front of him as a shield, Deming pushes the vicious gunnie right in the path of Ernie's bullets. This is *after* Stew admits to Chris his pathological fear of getting shot ("It's like a hunk of iron in you," Stew whimpers.) After the pathetic Stew is riddled by Ernie's bullets, Deming guns down his former finger-busting opponent.

Finally cornering the unarmed Miles in an old shed, Deming forces the disgruntled freight man to defend himself with his late fiancée's knife. Frightened, Miles climbs up an old ladder and, of course, happens to grab a rung which breaks off. Plummeting to his well-deserved death, Miles lands on the knife in true poetic justice fashion. Deming then checks his gun and finds it empty; he couldn't have killed Miles if he wanted to. Over the soundtrack we hear Kate intoning the Bible, "Vengeance is mine, I will repay..." (A statement she did *not* make previously).

RKO bought the rights to Short's *Station West*; shot in 1948, the resultant film underlines the connection with film noir by casting in the lead Dick Powell, the star of *Murder My Sweet*, one of the first American movies to start the trend. Almost in homage to his Philip Marlowe in the previous film, Powell's cowpoke, Haven, is an ornery, defiant cuss who lives to pick fights with all the film's characters. When Steve Brodie's Lt. Stellman sits next to him at a bar, Haven insults the officer and rejects his company. The barkeep is played by movie villain John Doucette; after hearing the obnoxious Haven's insults, even *he* is outraged by his harsh treatment of the lieutenant. (A couple years after the end of WWII, this ridicule of an American soldier, even from the nineteenth century, was tantamount to treason in the movies.)

When Haven plays up to the saloon's gorgeous owner, Charlie (played by the gorgeous Jane Greer), he is accosted by Charlie's chief hatchet man, Mick Marion (Guinn "Big Boy" Williams). In Charlie we again see Short's casting a woman in a non-traditional role; Charlie is still beautiful and sexy—and she runs a saloon, Short once again rejecting the usual cookie-cutter role that was expected of women.

When Mick starts getting under Haven's already thin skin, the cowpoke splashes whiskey in the big man's face. The two then clash out on the street, cheered on by what seems to be half the town. The assorted sharpies

Up the down staircase. Jane Greer as an empowered saloon boss-bandit queen opposite intrepid (and testy) military intelligence agent Dick Powell in *Station West*. Transferring the two stars of film noir to the western resulted in a respectable but imperfect film version of Short. (Book Castle-Movie World, Burbank, California.)

place bets on the fight, including future TV star Raymond Burr as crooked lawyer Mark Bristow. (In the western novel and film, was there ever an *honest* lawyer?) The subsequent fight imitates the brutality of the battle between Chris and Ernie in *Coroner Creek*, *sans* the busted trigger fingers.

Also featured in his first film role is Burl Ives as a hotel clerk who happens to also (Surprise!) play a guitar and sing. The role is definitely *not* connected to Luke Short, but it is still interesting to see the jovial Ives, probably playing the happiest hotel clerk in the west, and doing more ballad-singing than checking in guests. Ives would practically repeat this amiable character in Universal's *Sierra*, Audie Murphy's second starring western for the studio, playing a singing, guitar-playing mountain man. However, the balladeer's film image would change radically within a few years when he played Big Daddy in *Cat on a Hot Tin Roof*, and won the Oscar for a powerful performance as the vicious Rufus Hennessey in *The Big Country*.

As the plot progresses, we realize that Charlie is in charge of a gang of ruthless men (Is there any other kind of gang?) who rob gold shipments, and that the roustabout Haven is actually an officer in Military Intelligence trying to find out who murdered two soldiers guarding said shipment. For Powell, this is typical casting by this time. Having shed his crooner image by playing a tough private eye, Powell was now getting typecast as tough detectives and military intelligence officers (even in the west). As Haven, Powell plays the strident Army agent with jaw clamped tight and piercing stare aimed at everyone in the cast; besides these off-putting mannerisms, however, we're also trying to forget his *urban* accent. Perhaps Powell himself realized the miscasting; after *Station West*, the actor would make no more westerns.

Hollywood next released the fourth film based on a Luke Short novel that banner year of 1948, *Blood on the Moon*, based on *Gunman's Chance*. The casting is as perfect as the studios would give us in any film version of Luke Short. Still emulating film noir, RKO cast the star of Warners' noir western *Pursued*, namely Robert Mitchum.

Already under contract to RKO and years away from serving jail time for a marijuana conviction that would only increase his popularity, the sleepy-eyed Mitchum portrays Jim Garry, cowpoke with a past. Having been a no-good crook most of his life, Garry rides up from Texas, summoned by his erstwhile fellow crook, Ted Riling. This charismatic roustabout is played by Robert Preston in another of his long line of performances playing charming heels, years before *The Music Man*.

The film is very close to the book; this is certainly no surprise since the author himself did the adaptation. Still, even if Short hadn't gotten involved, the studios rarely changed the author's work on screen. It was as if Short's books, with their fascinating plots and constant action, were made for movies. The film version of *Gunman's Chance* is a good example of this.

When Jim Garry has his camp run down by cattle, he is taken to the camp of old man Lufton, a cattleman in a range war with the homesteaders of the aptly named Massacre Valley. Since both sides desire the graze that cattle needs, the war is being stirred up by Riling in an elaborate scheme which involves cheating both Lufton and the federal Indian agencies out of huge sums of money.

Also figuring in the plot is Amy Lufton (Barbara Bel Geddes), playing another one of Short's feisty, take-no-guff women. Her sister, a variation of Short's bad girls, has been leaking information about her father's movements to Riling. After Riling hires two gunmen to help terrorize Lufton's outfit and two innocent men are killed during a cattle stampede started by these murderous imps, Garry realizes his mistake.

Through with Riling's murderous activities and his own self-loathing, the cowpoke breaks with the charming crook as the two meet in an out-of-the-way tavern in a one-horse stop called Commissary. However, the break becomes the fracturing of limbs when the two men fight to the death in a set-to that is not only extremely bloody for the late '40s, but one of the best fight scenes in a western. When the lights are knocked out, Robert Wise, one of the best directors of film noir, uses the darkness to his advantage as the two men try to kill each other. Illuminated by brief splashes of light from outside, we see the fury of the struggle and are totally convinced of Garry's attempts to reform, as well as seeing Riling dropping his veneer of charm and becoming the snarling brute he really is.

In the book, this sequence is a turning point, showing Riling as a hot-tempered monster whose previous self-control has been permanently shattered by the fight with Garry. An example of this is when he suddenly murders of one of his homesteader pawns with a hatchet!

In the book, Garry kills Riling in town, with the now psychotic crook dying in the dust of Sun Dust, with no witty bon mots or last words. However, since Riling is portrayed by the charismatic Preston, the dying outlaw looks at Garry with a little regret and gives a last charming smile before croaking.

Blood on the Moon is undoubtedly the best film version of Luke Short. Robert Wise gave us one of the darkest westerns to hit the screen. Wise had worked for Orson Welles as an editor on *Citizen Kane* and for Val Lewton's unit at RKO, first as an editor, then as a director, before finally coming into his own with *The Body Snatcher*, Boris Karloff's best film. Having directed a horror film with class and restraint, the director would graduate to major works like the outstanding *The Set-Up* with Robert Ryan, again using darkness and grainy film stock to his advantage. Using razor-sharp editing, lighting that emphasized shadows and some of the most violent sequences in a western prior to the advent of Anthony Mann, the director brought Short's tormented people to life as few filmmakers had.

Filming on location outside Sedona, Arizona, of course, had its challenges. The area was prone to snowstorms and heavy cloud cover, forcing the shooting schedule back considerably. (This, as well as good friends Mitchum and Preston playing sadistic pranks on leading ladies Barbara Bel Geddes and Phyllis Thaxter.) Bel Geddes, already saddle-sore from a lack of riding experience, was still able to give a heartfelt performance as the gutsy and passionate Amy, fully justifying Wise's casting her despite a lack of western film experience. Wise was able to bring the film in on time and schedule, justifying Dore Schary's faith in *him* (the studio was going to replace Wise with Jacques Tourneur).

Never sell 'em short. The lobby card for the best film version of Luke Short, *Blood on the Moon*. Even in a lobby card, there is an emphasis on the empowerment of women. (Jerry Ohlinger's Movie Material Store, New York City.)

Next in the constant parade of Short novels to hit the screen came *Ambush*, based on Luke Short's novel ... *Ambush*. This time the producing studio was MGM. This meant that a Short novel was going to get first-class treatment. Not that the previous films based on his works were lacking (with the exception of *Hurry, Charlie, Hurry*), but this time the film was made with MGM's full production gloss.

Renowned as the studio with "more stars than the heavens," MGM gave the author his due in a medium-budgeted film that starred one of the biggest leading men of the time, Robert Taylor. The actor was MGM's longest-lasting star, working at the studio for close to 25 years. Around the time of *Ambush*, Taylor gave his notorious testimony at HUAC, being a friendly witness for the committee's prosecution of alleged Communists. His director was Sam Wood, a man who was one of Hollywood's most vindictive anti–Communists (and, if one believes in rumors, a vicious racist, anti–Semite and union-buster).

In *Ambush*, Taylor portrays a man trying to stop a Red Menace of a different kind. The actor portrays Ward Kinsman, one of those crack Indian scouts that western novelists are always writing about — the *only* ones who can stop the Indian attacks. In *Ambush*, this scout is no different. Kinsman is such a famous scout that even Charlie Stevens' Apache chieftain knows him personally and, of course, hates his guts.

A young white woman has been kidnapped by the Apaches and her sister Ann Deverall (Arlene Dahl) arrives at the fort to get the cavalry to rescue her. Kinsman turns down the job, knowing that the competent Major Breverly (which rhymes with revelry) and played by MGM contract player Leon Ames, can get the job done.

Then the subplots start coming in at blinding speed. Lt. Linus Delaney (Don Taylor) is romancing, albeit quietly and tastefully, Martha Carnovan (Jean Hagen), the battered wife of Tom Carnovan (Bruce Cowling). For Short, once again there is a sympathetic portrait of a woman, bringing up the issue of wife-battering that was rarely mentioned on screen at the time, much less in a western. As played by Jean Hagen, years before her screeching bubble-brained silent screen star in *Singin' in the Rain*, the role has much sympathy, yet also much dignity, in line with Short's treatment of women. The Carnovans are Irish, but Short's treatment of them is not stereotyped, despite Tom's fondness for liquor; the dignified Lt. Delaney is also Irish, his love for Martha is genuine and he doesn't drink. In the novel, after Martha fights off one of Tom's attacks with a skillet, we are allowed to feel her revulsion, and what an insult it is to her dignity to find herself standing on the camp grounds holding a skillet as everyone stares at her.

After going on a drunk that causes him to be punched out by Kinsman, the hopeless rummy is thrown in the guard house. Soon, however, Carnovan breaks out and runs into Major Breverly; unfortunately, it's with a bayonet. Now with their commanding officer sidelined, the troop is under the command of Capt. Ben Lorrison (John Hodiak), an efficient, by-the-book officer who lacks the street-smart instincts of a real Indian fighter. Totally underestimating the cunning of Charlie Stevens' Diabolito, he leads his men, like Custer, into an Indian trap. Though the character of Lorrison is treated with a certain amount of respect in the book, including his actually winning the fistfight with the hero, the film has him die with absolutely no dignity, as he's riddled with bullets by Diabolito himself.

Kinsman, however, gets a chance to blow away Diabolito as the evil chieftain pretends to be a corpse lying among his victims. Having rescued Ann's sister, Kinsman is now able to return to Ann, with whom he has fallen in love. The former hostage is, of course, alive and well and we are to assume that nothing happened to her during her captivity. (Yeah, right.)

In another clichéd plot device, Tom Carnovan escapes jail yet again (not bad for a drunk) and is bumped off by the Apaches. In the book, Linus is allowed to end up with Martha. In the film, reflecting Louis B. Mayer's puritanical dictates, the alleged affair-that-never-was causes the two to separate at the end, despite the fact that Tom Carnovan is dead and nothing is standing in their way. In Short's book, the battered woman is allowed happiness at the end; to MGM, the two lovers must live unhappily.

The film is loyal to the book, even if there is a neurotic compulsion to change all the characters' names; Brierly becomes Breverly; Loring becomes Lorrison; Ann Dunnifun becomes Ann Deverall and Riordan becomes Carnovan. One wonders why MGM didn't change the Apaches to the Sioux just for variety.

For Sam Wood, it would be his last film. He died of a massive heart attack some time after its release, the old reactionary not living to see the box office response to his film or, for that matter, the Rosenbergs caught for selling the A-bomb to the Russians.

MGM's next foray into Short-land came in 1950 when they filmed *Vengeance Valley*, a novel containing more than the usual elements of false allegiances and dysfunctional personalities; it also speaks of the need for folks to take personal responsibility for their actions. With cast and crew assembling outside Canyon City, Colorado, in July under the direction of Richard Thorpe, the production was ready to begin filming; all they had to do was wait for their star to show up. With a mere ten days' rest after finishing Fox's *Mister 880*, the up-and-coming Burt Lancaster began his first western in the role of Owen Daybright, the goodie-goodie foreman of a ranch run by the dysfunctional Strobie clan.

Signed with producer Hal Wallis at Paramount, Lancaster had been typed in bread-and-butter action pictures since the mid–1940s, with the exception of two outstanding film noirs directed by Robert Siodmak (produced by Universal, not by Wallis). Lancaster himself said he wanted to "clean up these contracts," meaning Wallis' cheesy pictures, so he could make his own films. When Lancaster turned down the lead in *Dark City* (which was given to Charlton Heston for his Hollywood film debut), Wallis loaned Lancaster out to Fox for *Mister 880* and then MGM for *Vengeance Valley*. Wallis' assistant, producer Paul Nathan, would refer to Lancaster's role of Owen Daybright as "a typical John Wayne part" and "very heroic." Nathan was wrong on the former, though not the latter. Owen Daybright was not in any way, shape or form the Duke — and certainly not the John Wayne character we would come to know and love by 1950, much less the take-no-prisoners Duke of the Cold War years.

Indeed, the role is hardly even suited to Burt Lancaster; certainly not the devil-may-care action hero of the early '50s, nor the dynamo of the Elmer Gantry years. Lancaster had always projected a quick intellect on screen; he is nobody's fool. So as the film progresses, the audience is wondering when Lancaster's Owen is going to wise up. However, to be fair, Owen Daybright does have to deal with some tough situations.

In many a western there is the powerful ranching family; screwed-up, selfish, drowning in jealousies and petty power struggles. Practically every single western writer has chronicled the misadventures of these wealthy oddballs and how the hero crosses paths with them. In *Vengeance Valley*, Owen Daybright has been "adopted" and raised by rancher Arch Strobie (Ray Collins) to be a kind of surrogate brother to Arch's son Lee (Robert Walker). Two things destroy whatever tranquility is involved in this arrangement. One is that there are enemies around them looking to destroy the Strobies; the other is that Lee is played by Robert Walker.

Whether playing a gay psychopath in *Strangers on a Train* or a pseudo-intellectual Commie heel in *My Son John*, Walker projected the closest thing to a twisted persona we'd see in films of the early '50s. Exuding the sneaky as well as the deranged, Walker excelled at portraying the Dark Side as the shadow of the Blacklist Years approached. He was a chronic alcoholic and brawler in real life; his death just a few months after finishing *Vengeance Valley* only underlines the all-too-real aberrations within the character of Lee Strobie.

Already serialized in *The Saturday Evening Post*, *Vengeance Valley* is certainly a good example of how Luke Short had grown as a writer. The

Frederick Dilley of the 1930s magazine serials wouldn't have come up with this plot or its clever execution.

The novel begins on what would normally be the middle of the story. Ne'er-do-well Lee Strobie reveals to Owen Daybright, his mature, restraining big brother figure, that he has knocked up the town's cute waitress, Lily Faskin (Sally Forrest). At the time, Forrest seemed to have a monopoly on playing unwed moms.

Impregnating this beguiling gal is one thing, but Lee is already married to Jen (Joanne Dru). Complicating this mess is that Lee is being trailed by Hub and Dick Faskin (John Ireland and Hugh O'Brian), Lily's two hulking, macho brothers. When they find out their sister is pregnant out of wedlock, the two outlaws plan to reward the prospective father with bullets instead of cigars.

Lee, being a ne'er-do-well, allows people to believe that *Owen* is the father. Being too much of a gentleman, Owen refuses to set the record straight. Meanwhile, Arch Strobie is blind to all of this; Lee is his favorite, the son he spoils endlessly, though it's obvious he *respects* Owen and treats him like a man. Lee, craving that same respect and jealous of Owen, also gets back at his hated big brother by trying to cut cattle deals behind his back.

Still, Owen refuses to squeal on Lee. This is seen by Short as a distinct character flaw, since Owen is cleaning up Lee's messes all through the book and the movie. Predictably, Jen starts to fall in love with Owen, but he will not be worthy of her love until he breaks with Lee and starts to fight for himself. In Short's world, women must be respected and misguided men like Owen must earn that respect.

At the end, when the Faskins attempt to kill Owen (having been indirectly put up to it by Lee, of course), Owen is able to kill both of them. When he sees Lee riding away from him instead of helping him, it finally dawns on Owen that Lee is not his pal any more. After giving chase, Owen is forced to kill his "kid brother," and then finally reveal all to Arch. He and Jen are now free to marry.

Vengeance Valley reminds one of *Paper Sheriff*, one of Short's mid–1960s novels. In that, the sheriff hero is married to the "bad girl," Callie. His decision to marry her was based on the fact that he had gotten her pregnant. Unfortunately, she loses the child and our noble hero is stuck with this whining, arrogant tart — a member of the ruthless Ordley clan, Short's hillbilly version of the Borgias. And, of course, there is a "good girl," again named Jen, who is the town's prosecuting attorney, another of Short's non-traditional occupations for his female characters.

This twist of having the hero marry into the villains' family, in essence linking him by marriage with murderers (whom his own wife is covering up for), was perhaps *too* offbeat for Hollywood. This is a pity, since *Paper Sheriff* would have been good film material. Unfortunately, by the 1960s Short was considered old-fashioned, not worthy of filming. Considering the familiar themes of Short's novels (confused, dysfunctional family relationships and women in positions of power fighting over the hero), Short seems to have discovered the nighttime TV soap opera formula years before *Dallas*, *Dynasty* and *Knots Landing*.

In 1951, Paramount shot *Silver City*, the film version of Short's 1949 novel *High Vermillion*. In the early '50s, Paramount was making a series of westerns usually starring the horribly miscast Edmond O'Brien, an actor more suited to urban thrillers. These Paramount westerns were usually, but not always, produced by Nat Holt (who had worked on Randolph Scott movies). The dominating characteristics of these films have been wide screens, Technicolor and a not-so-subtle political subtext reflecting the hysteria of the Cold War.

As in most big studio products of the time, Indians weren't just a bunch of screaming guys with war paint who were trying to kill whites and steal their horses; the screenwriters injected an unhealthy undercurrent of Fear. The Indian wasn't merely out to steal your horse and scalp you, he was out to *change your social system*! This portrait of American Indian tribes being seen as Bolsheviks on painted ponies was usually played up big in the Paramount westerns, a small sample of Hollywood's terror of the Red Scare.

Silver City doesn't have Indians, but it does have a "get back to work" ethic that must have delighted reactionaries in the Cold War years. In the book, Larkin Moffitt is an assayer, evaluating the value of gold and silver claims by weighing and analyzing the samples that folks bring to his tiny office. However, it turns out that Larkin had previously been a geologist and engineer, one of the finest in the west. He's been lowering himself with this sometimes thankless job due to the fact that he's committed the Great Mistake in his past that all heroes have made, causing them to lose themselves in a) rotgut whisky, b) jobs not worthy of their talents, and c) phonics. (All right, the last one I made up.)

In the film, Larkin Moffitt and his stuffy pal Charlie Storrs (Richard Arlen) are in a mining shack guarding the mine's payroll when two bandanna-wearing hombres enter with drawn guns. Since the taller one of the two is screenwriter and character villain Frank Fenton, we know that these men are up to no good. Storrs is knocked out, but then revives enough to hear what he believes to be Larkin's collusion with the bandits.

In many of his westerns, O'Brien has never been able to hide his New

York accent, and is usually forced into bellowing his lines to show himself to be a tough man of the prairie. His "hardbitten" persona has instead become that of a strident moron, and it seriously causes one to wonder what any western gal would see in him (Helen Wescott in *Cow Country* and Polly Bergen in *Warpath*, as a couple of examples).

After the bad guys escape, Larkin grabs a gun and fires at the fleeing suspects, then gives chase. After beating up Fenton as they struggle on top of a moving train, he grabs the payroll off the stunned outlaw and makes a spectacular dive into a lake hundreds of feet below as the train passes over a trestle bridge. No one has recorded what Short has said about this opening scene, that is, if the author ever saw it, but I bet it wouldn't have been kind. No such derring-do takes place in the book; it is a total invention of western pulp writer Frank Gruber, now credited as screenwriter for this film. Considering Gruber's own copious output of pulp westerns and mysteries, one is not surprised. If the word "contrived" is in the dictionary, Frank Gruber's picture will probably be next to it.

In Short's novel, Moffitt *had* committed a payroll robbery to keep his pompous girlfriend, Josephine, in diamonds and furs. Unfortunately, he was caught and subsequently ostracized by all, particularly his pal, now ex-pal Charlie Skoors. The next scene is the way it begins in the book; we meet Larkin examining ore samples brought in by Dutch Surrency (Edgar Buchanan, doing his second Luke Short character in three years). The old man has also brought his daughter Candace; a pretty blonde in the novel, she seems to have darkened her hair for the film, since she is now played by Universal siren, Yvonne DeCarlo. Recognizing Moffitt's talent, Dutch wants to hire the former mining maven to help dig his claim. In the book, Larkin is tough, but does have moments of self-pity; the film drops the self-pity (not good to see all that emotion in the McCarthy Era) and points up O'Brien's hardbitten persona from his film noir movies, a dubious proposition at best. Reluctantly, Larkin joins up with Dutch, not realizing that he's going to be taking a trip into his past.

Who should come to the Vermilion mining camp but Josephine, now with her new husband in tow — Charlie Skoors. In a long Hollywood career, Richard Arlen has appeared in practically every genre, usually for Paramount. The studio apparently liked the actor enough to hire him back again and again during his 40-year film career, from *Wings* in 1927 to *Apache Uprising* in 1965. Arlen had done westerns (including being pathetically miscast as Buffalo Bill), and approached them about the same as he did his other work. A shrewd underplayer, the actor wisely let the other cast members of his films froth at the mouth as he smoothly delivered his lines in a sober, restrained fashion. Perhaps you may not like Charlie

Skoors, but you'll like Arlen's subtle performance, making his character's motivations understandable, if not admirable.

Now with Larkin on their side, the Surrencys have nothing to worry about; that is, until the appearance of rival mine owner R.B. Jarboe. In the film, Jarboe is supposed to be ruthless, but since he is played by the likable Barry Fitzgerald, he is charming and funny, his ruthlessness couched in wry humor. Opposite the overplaying O'Brien, it is hard to hate Fitzgerald's Boss of the Valley, and one feels a little sorry when he is killed by his black-suited henchman Taff, in a typical double-cross. Fitzgerald was not usually cast in westerns, but his musical Irish brogue sounded better suited to the west than the New York or Southern California accents of most western players. Historically, many Irish came west as pioneers and soldiers. In Paramount's *California*, Fitzgerald's Irish politician fits into the western milieu much better than Ray Milland's British-accented cowboy.

Midway through the film, Taff attempts to beat up Larkin as his thugs hold a gun on him, just as Ernie did with Deming in *Coroner Creek*. However, before anyone thinks of stepping on trigger fingers, Candace arrives and saves him (in the book, he's saved by Dutch). Holding a gun on Taff's men just as Andy held a gun on Ernie's boys, Candace tells Moffitt to "take him." In the book, this fight scene is much bigger and far more brutal, including the two combatants taking their fight into the mud-covered street *a la The Spoilers*. In the film, the "fight" never leaves the confines of the small room. One does get the impression that, having shown a fight atop a moving train at the beginning, Paramount cut the budget of this battle to save a little money.

Jarboe tries everything to foil Dutch and Larkin, even going to the lengths of getting Dutch's well-paid men drunk. In true pro-capitalist style, Larkin initiates a brawl which wrecks the saloon that is getting the men drunk and keeping them from their labors. This scene probably would have shocked pro-labor filmmakers of the Depression era, but probably brought smiles to supporters of HUAC. If anything, screenwriter Gruber had no problem parroting the reactionary line in his films; his next project, *Warpath*, was even more inflammatory.

Josephine thinks she still has her hooks on Larkin, much to the anger of Candace. As in most of Short's novels, good girl and bad girl have a confrontation scene, though amazingly none of these confrontations result in any catfights. As Candace tells off Josephine, however, the audience is still mystified as to why either of them would bother fighting over O'Brien's embittered sourpuss.

As in the book, Charlie Skoors imagines Larkin and Josephine are having an affair and goes gunning for the engineer. Here's where actor

John Dierkes becomes significant to the plot. As in the book, a no-account thug named Arnie is hired to kill Dutch. In the film, this charming guttersnipe is played by veteran western villain Dierkes, reportedly one of the nicest actors off-screen.

When the revenge-crazed outlaw tries to shoot Larkin, he misses and our hero gives chase — boy, does he give chase — right through a lumber mill (including a dangerous and unnecessary ride on a log flume by both hero and bad guy) and then into a railroad yard. Suddenly things happen too fast, and perhaps too neatly. Larkin kills Arnie, Taff kills Charlie and Larkin kills Taff; *King Lear* it isn't, but it sure comes close.

After this horribly contrived denouement, Larkin comes together with Candace; kiss, fadeout, end. The best film version of Luke Short is *Blood on the Moon*; *Silver City* is probably the worst. As one can tell from the title change, it is more a work of the poison pen of Frank Gruber than the subtle and far more literate Frederick Dilley Glidden.

The next film based on Short, however, was much better. Shot in 1952 at Republic, *Ride the Man Down* showed Frank Gruber and Paramount where they had gone wrong. The screenplay is by western writer Mary C. McCall, Jr. For the first time, a woman is in charge of a Luke Short screenplay. Shot in glorious black and white by Republic's ace director Joseph Kane, the film stars Rod Cameron as Short's driven ranch foreman Will Ballard. His employer, old man Everts, has died before either the book or the film starts. Everts had been a power in the valley, not exactly a Boss of the Valley, but not chopped liver either. Everts was a larger-than-life figure who had fought off both Indians and others trying to get his land, including the evil Bide Mariner (Brian Donlevy ludicrously given top billing over Cameron). Now with Everts dead, the vultures are coming out, hoping to grab all that free range with its endless bounty of grass and water, a veritable gold mine for a cattle outfit. Standing in their way is Everts' feisty daughter Celia (Ella Raines) and her tough foreman.

Besides this typical old west battle for grazing land, there are the usual Short elements. There are two women battling over the hero, though at first this will not be apparent, since both Will and Celia are engaged to others. Will is engaged to Lottie Priest, the wimpy schoolmarm. As played by Barbara Britton, she is pretty, but of course she is also a pouting, whining pain in the butt. She wants Will to quit, leave Celia, take her somewhere glamorous, like back East, etc., etc. As we all suspect, this prim brat is not fit for a manly man like Will Ballard.

If anything, Celia is luckier, if only slightly. She is engaged to Sam Danfelser (Forrest Tucker). Because this character is played by Tucker, a master of underplaying, his Sam Danfelser sides with Celia, but he also harbors resentment. Will has usurped him of his role of manly man around the ranch of his own fiancée, and as the film goes on, he also desires Celia's property since his own ranch borders on hers. Tucker's western characters have always been ambiguous; the actor excelled at playing bad men turned good, or heroes who had done bad things or cavalrymen who could do wild, un-cavalry-like things. In short, audiences were usually not aware of just where a Forrest Tucker character stood until towards the end. As Sam Danfelser, after siding with the good guys, Tucker join forces with Bide Mariner and betrays his main squeeze for all those grass and water rights.

Prominent in the film is another of Luke Short's vacillating lawmen, Sheriff Joe Kneen (J. Carrol Naish). Also in the cast, besides Chill Wills in one of his rare performances where he's not overacting, are Republic regulars Jim Davis, Roy Barcroft and Douglas Kennedy.

Since this is a Republic film, Kane injected some good action, especially a fight scene between Cameron and Tucker that wrecks the inside of another man's shack. For the two tall actors, it is only one of their many film brawls in a Republic western. Their next film would be *San Antone*, a solid, well-written "B" that has a post–Civil War background and two women (for once, literally) fighting over the hero in a plot that could have easily been written by Luke Short.

By the end of *Ride the Man Down*, Sheriff Kneen develops a backbone and he and Bide Mariner riddle each other with bullets at a railroad station, Sam Danfelser is gunned down by our hero, and Celia and her foreman discover that they love each other. We can now assume he'll probably get a big raise.

Two years later, Republic shot *Hell's Outpost*, based on Short's modern western *Silver Rock*. Rod Cameron returned for his second film based on Short's work. Made with the typical Republic expertise, the film was set in the present-day 1950s. Cameron portrays ex–Korean War vet Tully Gibbs, a good man scarred by his war experiences who tries to attain wealth and power in his grab for a silver mine. The beautiful Joan Leslie plays Sarah, a woman who will temper his greedy ways by the end of the film. Though thought of as a limited actor only capable of grade "B" westerns, Cameron excels as the obsessive Gibbs, learning the hard way that riches won't compensate for his psychological pain. Cameron had already played the same type of character in *Stampede*, as a rancher reacting with bitterness to his brother's murder. (The film was written by future director Blake Edwards.)

After this film, it was a full five years before a Luke Short work would make it to the screen. In 1959, Paramount was given a second chance to do right by the Master and filmed his short story, "The Hangman." Robert Taylor, a star at MGM who excelled at playing uncomplicated handsome leading men in the '30s, became a better actor with his portrayal of bitter, grim-faced protagonists in the postwar era. The hardbitten soul he would bring to countless film noirs and crime films eventually transferred to the western. This is certainly apparent in the film version of Short's *Ambush*, the stark black-and-white photography and lack of music emphasizing this new darkness in his sagebrush heroes. He was the grim older brother to John Cassavetes' wild young cowpoke in Rod Serling's *Saddle the Wind*; the driven buffalo hunter in Richard Brooks' *The Last Hunt*, and the hardbitten marshal held captive by Richard Widmark's charismatic psycho in the film version of Marvin H. Albert's *The Law and Jake Wade*.

Now Taylor portrayed Marshal Kinzie Boyvard (instead of the story's Will Minifree), nicknamed "the Hangman" for an attitude towards outlaws that dispenses with anything close to Miranda rights. (The old west obviously had no Miranda law, but film producers of the 1950s like to think that old west lawmen had the same regard for the rights of criminals that 1950s lawmen were supposed to have.) Boyvard tracks down an alleged robber, Johnny Bishop (Jack Lord), a man whose only crime is actually holding fresh horses for the real robbers. Boyvard is tough as nails, but obviously burned out. To this merciless man, "there is always one more rat to catch." As the film progresses and he realizes that the town is trying to protect the suspect because apparently he *is* a good man, the marshal's cherished beliefs start to crumble.

Also bombarding him with speeches on the Quality of Mercy is an alleged witness to the robbery who apparently isn't too reliable. Named Celia, after many a Luke Short heroine, this beautiful woman is played by Tina Louise years before her "three-hour tour" on *Gilligan's Island*. At the end, after finally arresting Bishop, "the Hangman" does the decent thing and lets him go. Inevitably Boyvard rides off with Celia. For Taylor, it is the umpteenth time in the 1950s where he ends up with a leading lady half his age; a symptom of Hollywood May–Decemberism that still hasn't let up. (Look under the Films of Harrison Ford and Sean Connery)

Expertly shot in black and white by cinematographer Loyal Griggs, the film is also directed by one of the screen's underrated geniuses, Michael Curtiz. At this time, the auteur was coming to the end of his Paramount contract, having recently directed Elvis Presley in the profitable *King Creole*. Despite the box office failure of *The Hangman*, Curtiz would continue to work in Hollywood until his death two years later.

As the '50s progressed, so did the need for better film plots. After 1954, the "B" western made by the big studios was dead. Afterwards, only the low-budget films put out by tiny independents like Lippert, Howco and Astor would take up the slack. By 1959, Republic, the studio that had produced literally hundreds of "B"s, started to close its doors. Eventually so would Allied Artists, their name change from Monogram having absolutely no effect on disguising the cheapness of their product.

They were replaced by the western shows produced for television; it was as if a world had come to an end. Cowboy heroes like Wild Bill Elliott, Roy Rogers, Rex Allen, Gene Autry and Allan "Rocky" Lane were basically through as far as films were concerned. With the studios now producing "A" westerns in full color and wide-screen and with stars like Kirk Douglas, Gregory Peck and, of course, the Duke, the material they did would have to be better.

It was not as if western plots didn't have the age-old clichés of villains trying to get the ranch or cattlemen and sheep herders trying to push each other off the range, but these "A" westerns tended to be less formulaic. Reflecting the film versions of Broadway hits and best-selling novels, western characters became more complicated and the dilemmas posed became morally ambiguous. Right wasn't totally right any more, and what we would have considered evil in the pre-war days might not have been *truly* evil in the 1950s.

Case in point is the wonderful *Decision at Sundown*, where Randolph Scott decides to avenge his wife's ruination and subsequent suicide by going after the man responsible for her downfall, crooked town boss John Carroll. It is almost the same type of vengeance quest Scott's Chris Deming had performed in *Coroner Creek*, except for the savage twist director Budd Boetticher and his writers give us at the end. At this point, we gradually find out that Scott's wife was not an innocent woman being taken advantage of, but a "loose woman" who gladly cheated on him. It is the kind of formula-defying twist Luke Short would never have come up with.

It might have been this lack of cynicism in his work, this steadfast dedication to "old" plots in which romantic triangles moved events far more than economic or social conditions, that kept Hollywood from filming more of his work. With the rise of auteurs like Anthony Mann, who frequently emphasized sadism, and western plots which used the Indian Wars as a euphemism for racial conflict, Short's "ranch romances" must have seemed old hat indeed.

Short tried television, providing scripts for the Warner Brothers shows *Sugarfoot* and *Cheyenne*. He also worked on television pilots that didn't sell. After the new decade dawned, he suffered the tragedy of his son's death; then the death of his longtime literary manager.

Short had never broken out of the western mold, despite "new" elements in his work, like characters suffering through unwanted pregnancies (*Paper Sheriff*) and his usually strong female protagonists fighting off rapists (*The Man from Two Rivers*). Novels like *Donovan's Gun* and *The Deserters* were well-written, but offered nothing new in the age of Grassy Knoll and the Tet Offensive. Ironically subplanted by a less talented writer, Louis L'Amour, whose simpler, often asinine novels would amazingly become best-sellers around the world, Short continued pumping out his westerns and skiing in Aspen as the 1970s progressed.

Finally on August 18, 1975, the author, now almost totally blind, lost his battle with cancer. He died at the time of an almost universal revulsion with the direction America was going. With a less-than-graceful exit from the quagmire in Vietnam, and a cynicism about our government in the wake of Watergate, the type of novel that Luke Short produced had rapidly disappeared. He wouldn't live to see a renewal of belief in America accompanying the feel-good Reagan years, a time that would have welcomed Short's "ranch romances."

Unlike Louis L'Amour, whose work would experience somewhat of a Hollywood revival through cable TV, Short would continue to be ignored by Hollywood. His west wasn't the glamorization of the Desert Man popularized by L'Amour or a re-enactment of the building of the west made famous by Zane Grey. His west was powered by personalities; at times they were ornery and wild, at times driven and dysfunctional, but in the end they were eternally romantic. Certainly few western writers of the time carried with them a persistent feminism that empowered their female protagonists as Short did. Years before the Equal Rights Amendment, Luke Short's females owned saloons, managed hotels, bossed ranch hands and argued their cases in court as full-fledged attorneys.

And this element of his work is just a small part of how good he was. In Short, Frederick Dilley Glidden was one of the best.

3

Frank Gruber and the Distortions of the West

Authors Short and Haycox lent a respect to the pulp western. These men labored to provide interesting plots; they created fascinating, even likable characters; they demonstrated a thorough knowledge of the west and, especially in Haycox's case, they had an original point of view concerning historical events. Both men worked hard to entertain the reader, with nary a word or sentence wasted; their expositions were descriptive without boring the reader, the dialogue lively without sacrificing realism.

Then there are the western writers at the bottom end of the scale — like for instance, Frank Gruber.

Gruber was a blessing to the pulp western; unfortunately, the pulp would never quite be squeezed out. Gruber's works always sold well, and to an undiscriminating readership he delivered the goods, namely fast action and lively plots. Making the reader think was never one of his priorities. Indeed, opposite Gruber, Haycox and Short must have been considered highbrow. For if Louis L'Amour's plots were at times simple, even cartoonish, Gruber's westerns were pure delirium.

And as far as Delirium is concerned, thy name is Hollywood.

Born in Elmer, Minnesota, on February 2, 1904, Gruber started writing for trade journals and for various small newspaper organizations, eventually making it to editor. The ambitious young man started to sell detective stories to pulp magazines in the early '30s, including the yardstick of pulp mystery magazines, *Black Mask*. He created those lovable conmen detectives, Johnny Fletcher and Sam Bragg, then he branched out into a Simon Lash detective series. Realizing that westerns sold well (Gruber was anything but a man who didn't respect a buck), the up-and-coming author sold western stories that were serialized in several magazines. Perhaps this might explain their episodic nature once these stories were expanded into books. Haycox and Short had the grace to edit their works once they expanded them into novels so that the transition to a longer format wouldn't be noticeable. If Frank Gruber ever edited his work, it was probably with a bone-saw.

In Gruber's westerns, what might start out as an interesting, even fascinating plot suddenly goes off in an entirely different direction, all signs of originality disappear and the action grinds to a screeching halt (*Fort Starvation* and *Town Tamer* are good examples of this). Entertaining the reader ceases to be a concern and, unfortunately, like many a quick-buck hack, Gruber pads the narrative. In a good many of his western novels, the plots are so badly constructed that any problems the hero encounters could easily have been solved in the first few pages.

In his highly uninformative book on fiction writing, *The Pulp Jungle,* Gruber boasted that he had written 65 motion picture screenplays and had no fewer than 25 of his novels sold to the movies. However, when Gruber wrote these words in 1967, the author had no idea that decades later this "information" could easily be checked on a computer. A quick look at the Internet Movie DataBase reveals that Gruber worked on 19 screenplays, not including adaptations and "additional dialogue." Instead of the 25 books sold to Hollywood that he claimed, the film industry bought eight of his novels and eight stories, these "stories" not including screen stories written especially for the studios. To be fair, perhaps the pulp author included his many western teleplays for shows like *Tales of Wells Fargo* and *Shotgun Slade*, but somehow this seems doubtful, since he also claimed to have written over one hundred TV scripts!

Hollywood, which knew how to make a quick buck and always respected those who followed suit, had already filmed a Gruber story as *Death of a Champion*. However, the first Gruber novel Hollywood would film would be a western. In 1943, United Artists filmed Gruber's 1941 novel *Peace Marshal* as *The Kansan*. It starred aging Richard Dix as rootin' tootin' town tamer John Bonniwell. Much younger (and presumably much thinner) in the book, Bonniwell is practically the most famous marshal in the west, that is, next to those ubiquitous Earp boys.

When he was in Hollywood in 1941, Gruber had submitted a copy of *Peace Marshal* to the Ned Brown Agency. Some time afterwards, Brown himself submitted it to producer Harry "Pop" Sherman, who was producing the Hopalong Cassidy series for Paramount. But there was trouble in Hopalong paradise; by early 1942, the series' box office was falling. Looking at William Boyd's later surrender to the image of Hopalong Cassidy, it's shocking to believe that at that time Boyd didn't want to be typecast as the black-clad Bar–20 foreman. Besides having to deal with a dissatisfied star (Boyd was talented, but not easy to control under the best of circumstances), "Pop" Sherman also had to deal with his ace director Lesley Selander working for other studios and not concentrating all his energies on the Cassidys. With a backlog of unproduced pictures, Paramount wanted to cut loose the declining series.

By the early '40s, United Artists was in desperate straits; their usual quota of independent pictures was drying up. With their exhibitors screaming for product, UA urgently needed projects to distribute.

In 1942, UA struck a deal with Paramount Pictures to purchase 21 of their projects slated to be produced during the 1942–43 "season." These included not only the Hopalong Cassidy series, but Sherman's "A" products—sagebrush melodramas like *Buckskin Frontier* and *The Woman of the Town* starring Richard Dix, Jane Wyatt, Albert Dekker, Victor Jory and Lee J. Cobb. (Cobb and Jory would appear as villains on the Cassidy series.) Former Warners directors Lloyd Bacon and William McGann, as well as journeyman George Archainbaud, helmed this group of "A" "specials." However, despite the fact that the budgets exceeded $350,000, these men were not good western directors; their lack of expertise indirectly shortchanged Sherman's sincere efforts at making good westerns. The first Frank Gruber novel to make it to the screen might be a good example.

Sherman reportedly paid Gruber $1000 for the rights to the author's meandering tale of a town tamer and, unfortunately, the many, *many* distractions the lawman has to deal with before the predictable Big Showdown. In *The Kansan*, future Gene Autry director George Archainbaud does as good a job for Gruber as he does for the old singing cowboy, which is mediocre.

In the film, the New York opening is dropped from the book and fortunately so are many, *many* of Gruber's long, talkative scenes on the train as the brothers journey west. This includes interminable scenes of cardplaying to pad out the time. Screenwriter Harold Shumate (bless him) removed many of these.

In the film, John Bonniwell is a man wanting to hang up his guns. However, he is recruited to be the new marshal of the little village of Broken Lance (a name the unimaginative Gruber would use several times). The crooked city council is run by banker slash Boss of the Valley Steve Barret (changed from Ferd, and played by the underrated Albert Dekker) and his much smoother brother, Jeff (Victor Jory).

Somehow it is hard to believe Dix as a town-taming marshal; old, fat and moving without any of the grace that a gun hawk would naturally have, the aging actor delivers his lines in a haze, with a voice getting more and more husky as the years went on. Randolph Scott would have been a far better choice. (His town-taming marshal in *Abilene Town*, also with a screenplay by Harold Shumate, is all the proof you might need.)

Wounded in a gunfight, our geezer lawman is hospitalized. United Artists did not make cheapness the cinematic art that the other studios had, and so their "hospital" consists of the one bed Dix is in, and we just see one small corner of the room. Bonniwell is nursed back to health by Eleanor Sager, a combination of *two* young lasses in the novel, Eleanor Simmons and Lou Sager. She is played by Jane Wyatt with all the matronly wholesomeness she would project 15 years later as the mom in *Father Knows Best*. Obviously Eleanor is the marshal's love interest, despite the fact that the actor playing opposite her is old enough to be her father.

Another actor in the cast giving us an idea of things to come is the man playing one of the Barrets' underlings, Kelso: future western star Rod Cameron. The part is small; he's an outlaw who challenges our aging hero and is wounded for it. Formerly a stunt man before he became a contract player for Paramount, Cameron's star was on the rise, especially in the "B" western field. In fact, had Cameron been cast as Bonniwell, the actor would have easily brought out the danger inherent in the character.

As Steve Barret works to consolidate his control of the town by buying up lots to build property on (something Gruber's power-mad Joe Jagger does in *Buffalo Grass*), his smoother, more subtle brother Jeff works in a different way. Victor Jory's performance as a gambler with some scruples neatly steals the film away from the overrated Dix. He joins Steve in his schemes to bilk the town, but bucks him several times to help Bonniwell.

Also cast in this opus is the tragic Willie Best. Cast in the stereotypical role of Bones (based on Gruber's racist stereotype named Mose), the underrated Best bows and scrapes and predictably gets scared at the least bit of trouble. His eyes light up and he smiles when Bonniwell keeps shaking a fistful of coins at him, bidding the victimized African-American to do some moronic task. One is truly sorry Bones doesn't fling the coins back in the overrated town tamer's face.

In the meantime, Bonniwell arrests Steve for his crooked activities. The angry banker-speculator tells Bonniwell he won't get away with it and threatens some kind of reprisal. Then we never see or hear from Steve again. The mysterious disappearance of the would-be Boss of the Valley seems to imply that the Broken Lance Jail is in reality a dark pit of human misery on the same level as Stalin's Lubyanka Prison, and that Steve has vanished off the face of the earth like some Prairie refusnik. Or more realistically, perhaps Decker was just needed on the *Woman of the Town* set. The film has practically the same cast and is made by the same company around the same time.

When outlaw Ben Nash (the ubiquitous Douglas Fowley) and his gang move out to attack the town, for some strange reason they start from way out in the hills; this is so Bonniwell will have plenty of time to stop them. In fact, when the Nash gang has to cross a certain bridge to make it to town, Bonniwell and his posse decide to blow up the bridge! Since there are very few territories in the west that are divided by something on a scale of the Grand Canyon, one wonders why blowing up one small bridge will actually stop the gang from somehow getting to the town. It seems that screenwriter Shumate cut most of Gruber's boring dialogue scenes, but kept the author's cartoonish logic.

Bonniwell does blow up the bridge, killing Nash and most of his gang—and unfortunately Jeff Barret as well. (Jeff had the misfortune of loving Eleanor. Since the under-aged woman is slated to end up with the creaky town tamer, film convention dictates that Jeff must die.) Bonniwell is wounded in the skirmish that follows, and the aging marshal is back in the "hospital" once again being tended to by Eleanor. The town is tamed; May–December clinch, end of story.

Shumate cut sequences from the book that positively reeked of padding; Gruber gets so far off the plot that he includes a shooting contest with a "Mr. Woodson" (Jesse James). This does not come as a surprise since Gruber had always been fond of including famous historical figures in his westerns. *The Bushwackers* features Confederate guerrillas Quantrill, Anderson and Todd, and *Bugles West* has Generals Custer and Shelby, the James boys and even Sitting Bull! Throughout these fictionalized reenactments of history, Gruber treats these people as name-dropping cartoon stick figures, devoid of any sense of reality or historical insight.

This is certainly borne out in *The Pulp Jungle,* where the author dictates his rules on depicting outlaws. Addressing would-be writers, Gruber explains that one can write about Jesse or Frank every three or four years, and if that doesn't do, you can fill in Sam Bass, Butch Cassidy or any fictitious outlaw. In other words, Gruber is telling the would-be western writer that one outlaw is just as good as another. He also informs us that the outlaw *must* be treated sympathetically, the felon always having been forced into outlawry by circumstances like the (Civil) War. Not only does this statement show a total ignorance of history, but it neglects to explain the criminality of outlaws like Butch Cassidy and the Hole in the Wall Gang, whose exploits occurred decades after the end of the Civil War.

Another Gruber trait, demonstrated literally dozens of times in *Peace Marshal* and many of his other works, is the idea that if two characters are having a conversation, keep having more characters enter the scene to make it more interesting. The interminable poker games that fill his westerns are nothing more than excuses for lots of boring dialogue. When his heroes are entering or leaving hotels, they usually run into a half-dozen or so people who couldn't move the plot forward with a hi-lo. Fortunately, Gruber's next work would be far better; perhaps this is because Gruber wasn't the only writer on the project.

Signed with Warner Brothers in 1943, Gruber found himself at the same studio as another famous western writer, though this author was far above him talent-wise: Frederick Faust, whose most famous pen name was Max Brand. Faust was making $2000 a week and working on the screenplay for the Errol Flynn starrer *Uncertain Glory*. In fact, Gruber was in very exalted company at the Burbank studio. He would recall having lunch at the Warners commissary and listening to right-wing author Ayn Rand arguing politics with Dalton Trumbo and John Howard Lawson, two of the Hollywood Ten. Gruber would also recall Faust keeping a thermos of whiskey in his office, as well as forsaking the fascinating personalities at the Warner commissary to get drunk at Musso & Frank's in Hollywood.

Gruber wrote the screenplay for *Northern Pursuit*, a wartime adventure directed by Raoul Walsh and starring Errol Flynn, Julie Bishop and Helmut Dantine. Though it was not a western, Gruber adapted his usual contrived plotting to this wild tale of Nazi intrigue. Just as many a Gruber hero would pretend to infiltrate the outlaw gang to get the goods on them, Errol Flynn's Canadian Mountie pretends to turn traitor to infiltrate a gang of Nazi saboteurs run by Helmut Dantine. (In real life, the heroic Dantine was an anti–Nazi activist and early survivor of Dachau.) The dialogue is good; a future member of the Hollywood Ten, Alvah Bessie, gives us some good anti–Nazi propaganda, and even more lines were contributed by, of all people, $250-a-week contract writer William Faulkner. Gruber was indeed fortunate in working opposite such famous company for his first screenplay.

His next screenplay for Warners, *The Mask of Dimitrios* (based on Eric Ambler's *A Coffin for Dimitrious*), starred Zachary Scott in his film debut, beginning his career as the studio's resident cinematic heel. Also in the cast were Sydney Greenstreet and Peter Lorre. (Coincidentally, Lorre plays a writer.) Though he didn't originate the material, Gruber used all his best instincts as a mystery writer to come up with a memorable work. With his (or more likely, Ambler's) lines delivered by such experts of intrigue as Lorre, Greenstreet and Scott, Gruber came up with what was undoubtedly his best screenplay.

Unfortunately, this also meant that things were going to go downhill afterwards. One of his stories was filmed toward the end of the war by Republic as *Oregon Trail*. A "B" starring the dramatically limited Sunset

Carson in three roles, the film gave us a chance to see Carson give a bad performance in all of them. Afterwards, Carson started on his short-lived career as Republic's most handsome, yet most boring cowboy hero.

More of Gruber's mysteries were made into films at this time, including Eagle-Lion Studios bringing his Johnny Fletcher and Sam Bragg characters to life in *The French Key*. Continuing at the same studio, he also wrote two films using the Bulldog Drummond character created by H.C. McNeile. For Universal, he adapted two Sherlock Holmes stories as *Terror by Night* and *Dressed to Kill*, two of the worst Holmes films made by the studio.

For Republic, he did the adaptation for *In Old Sacramento* in 1946; it was the first attempt by "B" cowboy great Wild Bill Elliott to move into higher budgeted "A" films. Elliott himself reportedly told off director Joseph Kane, angry that he was leaving the world of "B" oaters and losing his loyal base of child fans. Cast as the black-cloaked highwayman, Spanish Jack, Elliott has to pay for his sins by being shot and killed at the end. As he predicted, this death scene outraged many of his young fans.

At the end of the decade, Gruber wrote the screenplays for *Fighting Man of the Plains* and *The Cariboo Trail*, two cheap oaters produced back-

Fool's gold. Gabby Hayes, Randolph Scott and unidentified player (left to right) looking quite silly in a publicity shot for Frank Gruber's *Cariboo Trail*. Randy, Gabby and producer Nat Holt had done much better work elsewhere. (Jerry Ohlinger's Movie Material World, New York City.)

to-back by Nat Holt for Twentieth Century–Fox release. The casts were essentially the same: Both starred Randolph Scott as the hero, both have character men Bill Williams and Douglas Kennedy in support, both have Victor Jory as the villain, and both have up-and-coming western star Dale Robertson (in *Cariboo Trail* he's the second lead; in *Fighting Man* he's Jesse James, another example of Gruber's name-dropping).

In *Fighting Man*, Scott is an ex-bandit who becomes one of Gruber's many town tamers. In *Cariboo Trail*, Scott is a cattleman hoping to start a ranch until he is opposed by Victor Jory's Frank Walsh, another in a long line of would-be Bosses of the Valley. Both films are minor Scott, though usually minor Randy is much better than the efforts of many others. The writing, however, is appropriate for Gruber; both films are mediocre. (When Randy and "Gabby" Hayes have to use a wild, back-kicking jackass to help them escape from an Indian camp, it's time to leave the theater.)

Again at Fox, Gruber did the screen story for *Dakota Lil* (1950) starring the usually wooden George Montgomery as, of all people, Tom Horn (presumably long before his being sentenced to hang for murdering a child) and Rod Cameron as cigar-smoking saloon boss Harve Logan. The wonderful Marie Windsor is saloon songstress Dakota Lil, who ultimately helps Horn get the goods on Logan. With little effort, Cameron and Windsor steal the film from the limited Montgomery. Though the film does show off Windsor's many charms and gives Cameron one of his few villain roles, the film could have been better, though it is hard to improve upon Lesley Selander's direction.

However, the next Gruber work to become a film would be an outstanding "B," a good example of what one could do with a low budget when the talent was there behind the camera. *The Texas Rangers* was released by Columbia with a screen story by Gruber. Again starring George Montgomery, the Wooden One gives one of his better performances in a well-written film with direction by the excellent Phil Karlson, a man who could put real spark into even the cheapest production. Karlson and his screenwriters recycled Gruber's clichés about the ex-outlaw now spying on his old gang for the good guys and turned it into an almost noirish exercise in vengeance, bloody shootings and a bangup climax on a runaway train.

Montgomery is Johnny Carver, member of a gang of bank robbers that includes Sam Bass, John Wesley Hardin and the evil Dave Rudabaugh (the ubiquitous Douglas Kennedy), a teaming of famous outlaws that historically makes no sense, but is another example of Gruber's obsessive name-dropping. It's amazing that Sam Houston, Abe Lincoln and Cochise don't show up in the film as well.

Karlson keeps the action moving, not giving the audience time to think about the plot's many inconsistencies. Wounded and captured after a bank robbery, Carver is sent to prison. Here, Karlson shows us a pair of brutal guards torturing Carver, a touch of historical reality totally at odds with Gruber's usual contrivances. Brought before the Texas Rangers, Carver is offered a pardon by the governor if he helps bring in his old gang.

Of course, he gets into the gang with no problem. However, his younger brother, now a Ranger who changed his name, is forced to bring in Johnny. Before he can do so, however, the kid is killed by Rudabaugh. Suddenly imbued with a Sense of Justice, Johnny becomes a Ranger for real, and goes through with the plan to trap his old gang. Joining Carver is Buff Smith (perennial postwar western sidekick Noah Beery, Jr.), who gets killed by Rudabaugh as well, giving Johnny even more reason to even the score.

By the end, Johnny blows away Rudabaugh. In this sequence, Karlson has Johnny turn Rudabaugh's own gun on himself during a struggle; the shot is fired below camera range, implying a painful below-the-belly gutshot. At the end, Johnny is reunited with pretty newspaper editor Helen Fenton (the lovely Gale Storm).

The film was a successful enough for Paramount to take notice. In 1950, the studio of Bob Hope and Martin and Lewis signed Gruber to a contract to write screenplays for their "A" westerns, and to doctor the scenarios for their non-western film output.

Perhaps aware of Gruber's penchant for bodily throwing historical characters into his works, Paramount assigned him the task of doing the screenplay for *The Great Missouri Raid*, a semi-fictional recreation of the James' boys exploits in Missouri.

It was an audacious film to start the new decade with, but hardly an original one. With some minor changes, and the glaring omission of ham actor supreme Henry Hull, the film is essentially a remake of the far better *Jesse James*, made by Fox in 1939 (and which Fox would remake in 1958). All the details are there, almost down to the Jesse James-as-social-victim fantasy. The original had elements of a leftist point of view, and this film would be the closest the conservative Gruber would come to making a social comment in his westerns. There is further irony in the casting: Ward Bond, a major reactionary figure in the Blacklist Years, played the James boys' less-than-honest pursuer, Major Trowbridge; while Anne Revere would play Jesse and Frank's mom, just before her own blacklisting. Having both blacklister and blacklistee on the same set must have been the basis for some lively discussions, but unfortunately the same passion doesn't make it into the film.

3. Frank Gruber and the Distortions of the West 67

The rest of the casting is according to Paramount stock company standards. Macdonald Carey is Jesse; Wendell Corey is Frank; Ellen Drew is Bee (Jesse's wife was nicknamed "Zee"; was Paramount afraid of a lawsuit?); Bruce Bennett, late of Warner Brothers, is Cole Younger; Edgar Buchanan is the James boys' adopted father Dr. Samuels (reuniting Buchanan with Ellen Drew, his co-star in *The Man From Colorado*); Anne Revere, trying to show the same outrage that she did in *Body and Soul*, is Mrs. Samuels; James Millican is Sgt. Trowbridge; and his big brother is Ward Bond as Major Trowbridge.

To Gruber's credit, he does use certain aspects of history not mentioned in the previous Fox version. Sgt. Trowbridge and his blue bellies are at the Samuels farm and they're going to hang Dr. Samuels unless he tells them the whereabouts of Frank James, reputedly a Quantrill raider. In the whitewashed Tyrone Power version, no one attempts to hang Dr. Samuels and no mention is ever made that Frank (and, in reality, Jesse) belonged to a gang of murderers headed by Quantrill. When Frank does arrive and a shootout starts, Sgt. Trowbridge is killed and his big brother, the Major, vows eternal vengeance on the Jameses.

When Frank goes to see Trowbridge to find out if the governor's offer of amnesty is real, the Major says it is and tells Frank to have his boys ride in unarmed and there will be no shooting. Of course, the duplicitous officer sets up an ambush and some of the gang are slaughtered, but Frank and Jesse escape. Now the James-Younger gang are social as well as literal outlaws, and they decide to do all the things they'll be world-famous for, namely, rob banks, trains and stagecoaches (which we all know just naturally leads to hero worship by the populace).

Macdonald Carey and Wendell Corey are clean-shaven and have hairstyles from the 1940s rather than the 1860s, as does Bruce Bennett as Cole Younger. Carey and Corey, in fact, always had underplayed acting styles (as well as off-screen reputations as alcoholics), and their performances, though adequate, lack the personal charisma one might find in the real-life Jameses. Bennett, repeating his performance as Cole Younger from Warners' *The Younger Brothers* of the previous year, is good as Cole, but he is given little to do since this is not *his* picture, but the Jameses'.

Of course, Gruber's scenario is episodic, just like his novels. Though the author does put some interesting twists into the proceedings (Frank ends up with a wife, for instance, as he did in real life), the film is still hurtling to its predictable conclusion. The direction is handled competently by the usually pedestrian Gordon Douglas in one of his few Paramount films. (He would sign with Warners in the '50s and eventually direct the sci-fi classic *Them!*).

Another asset to the film, despite the fact that he doesn't enter until the last few minutes, is the excellent performance of Whit Bissell. A talented Broadway actor, Bissell is a standout as the cold-as-ice little back-shooter, Bob Ford. The actor brings to the role a portrait in real evil as a scary little man who sees himself as the new head of the gang. When Ford asks Jesse to remove his guns, we know what will happen next, but Bissell's cold-blooded way of making the request is what we remember. Ultimately, his Ford is far more frightening than Carradine's hammy, cowardly version in Fox's *Jesse James* 11 years before.

Also revealed to us by Ford is that a crazed pickpocket killed Major Trowbridge. Delivered matter-of-factly by Bissell, the revelation of this important piece of information is a shock; not because the major dies, but because Gruber and Douglas kill off the film's main villain (depending on your point of view) without showing us. We can only assume that Bond had to leave the set to appear in a John Ford film. For whatever reason Trowbridge is not shown getting his comeuppance, it's seriously clumsy filmmaking.

Again working for Paramount, Gruber did the screenplay for *Warpath*, based on his novel *Broken Lance* (that name again!). *Warpath* is a controversial film, not only for its inflammatory content, a symbol of reactionary attitudes at the height of the blacklist years, but for where the author might have gotten the idea for his material.

In his *Western Films: A Complete Guide*, Brian Garfield writes of *Warpath* that "the plot is a bald imitation of Haycox's *Bugles in the Afternoon*" (Haycox's novel was written years before *Broken Lance*) and that "Gruber was a numbed veteran of the hack clichés and a mainstay of lower-case pulp magazines." With this last statement, Garfield was absolutely right. However, to be fair to Gruber, one might quibble with the charge that Gruber stole *Bugles in the Afternoon*, though certainly not much. It is true that comparing Gruber to Haycox is like comparing a hot dog to a filet mignon, but the viewer can judge if Gruber stole *Bugles in the Afternoon*.

Both Kern Shafter of *Bugles* and John Vickers of *Broken Lance* are former officers in the cavalry rejoining the Army years later and starting over again at the rank of private. They both meet commanding officers who happen to be former comrades and who, out of sympathy, promote them to sergeants. The basic difference between the two men is their reasons for rejoining the cavalry. Kern Shafter was an officer who caught his former best friend, a fellow officer, having a tryst with his fiancée. After Shafter challenged his rival to a duel, he wounded him with a sword and was then dishonorably discharged. Wandering the west in the intermit-

3. Frank Gruber and the Distortions of the West 69

tent years, he finally decided to lose himself back in the Army and joined the Seventh Cavalry just before Custer led his men to their deaths.

In *Broken Lance*, John Vickers is a former Army officer rejoining the Army (coincidentally, the Seventh Cavalry) to find the men responsible for murdering his fiancée, having discovered that the killers changed their identities and joined the Seventh.

Gruber liked the plot so much, it seems he not only stole it from Haycox, but himself as well. *Broken Lance* is copied shamelessly in Gruber's 1954 novel *Bugles West*.

Since Broken Lance sounded too much like the film *Broken Arrow* for comfort, Paramount felt the title *Warpath* was more appropriate. But whereas the earlier film promoted brotherhood with Native-Americans through interracial marriage, *Warpath*, as written by Gruber, heightened animosities. Certainly the tenor of the times encouraged this point of view.

On February 7, 1944, the Motion Picture Alliance for the Preservation of American Ideals, a right-wing organization consisting of performers and craftsmen, was organized at the Beverly-Wilshire Hotel. The violently anti–Communist director Sam Wood was elected president, and its membership included reactionary ideologues like Cecil B. DeMille, Adolphe Menjou, Ward Bond and Walt Disney, as well as crooked pro-studio union leader Roy Brewer. Also upholding the organization's dictum on censoring alleged left-wing propaganda were screenwriters Borden Chase, James Edward Grant, Richard Macauley (author of several Warner Brothers proletarian screenplays)— and Frank Gruber. As the years went by and the Cold War got chillier, the organization's power grew, eventually providing many a friendly witness to the HUAC.

Reflecting the bigotry inherent in genre films during the McCarthy era, the Sioux are seen as the Other, a savage people who live for nothing but the extinction of Our Way of Life. Seeing the Indians as another kind of Red Menace would be a regrettable trait in many major studio westerns of the early '50s, particularly the Paramount westerns as written by their ace sagebrush scenarist, Frank Gruber.

At the beginning of this opus, a nasty outlaw is called out in the middle of a dusty cowtown street by John Vickers (Edmond O'Brien, an actor of decidedly urban bent constantly miscast in westerns). The outlaw is quickly gunned down by Vickers. As it turns out, the felon is one of three, count 'em, three evil men responsible for the murder of his girl. When Vickers has reliable information that the other two might have enlisted in the Seventh Cavalry, the former cavalry captain rejoins the military, apparently super-confident that he can nab the two felons and leave the Seventh whenever he pleases. In reality, there were dozens of desertions in Dakota Territory, particularly from Custer's Seventh.

Unfortunately, Vickers has a run-in with two drunken soldiers harassing Molly Quade (Polly Bergen) at the railroad depot. Knocking them aside easily, Vickers then arrives at the fort to join up and is promptly assigned to the platoon under the very same sergeant he had knocked around at the depot. This tough noncom is the redoubtable Sgt. O'Hara (Forrest Tucker, again giving us the Dark Side of the Cavalry).

At first, O'Hara gives Vickers all the crappy tasks—literally. He is assigned to clean out the stables. After superior officers check out Vickers' record, he is promoted to Master Sergeant, and now it is O'Hara's turn to clean up after the horses. During Vickers' stay there, he also meets sutler Saul McQuade (Dean Jagger), a man who likes Vickers, but might be harboring a secret.

Gen. Custer (James Millican) leads his men to their deaths, though we don't see this (it might cost too much). Instead, we concentrate on the wagon train party Vickers and his men are escorting through Sioux territory. When a little Indian boy foolishly fires an arrow at a wagon, the paranoid wagon boss fires a rifle at the child, killing him. The Sioux capture everyone, including Vickers, Molly, Private "Irish" Potts (Wallace Ford) and Private Fiore (Paul Fix), the film's two Irish stereotypes. Gruber would refine this bigotry in his screenplay for *Denver and Rio Grande*, with Paul Fix repeating his role as a brogue-accented clown.

Now held captive at the Sioux camp, the tribe promptly brings out a new prisoner—O'Hara! Now that Vickers realizes that O'Hara is one of the men he's hunting, and with the enthusiastic tribe prompting them, the two men fight. Ultimately, they both knock each other out as the braves register disappointment. (Were they taking bets?)

Apparently O'Hara had sneaked a derringer pistol into camp. Knowing that death and torture await, the sergeant sacrifices his life, firing a fatal shot off-camera, thus distracting the Sioux guards and allowing Vickers and Molly to escape. We later find out that McQuade, the second of the murderers, died (conveniently off-camera) trying to warn Custer. Now free of his quest for vengeance, Vickers can now settle down with Molly with his full rank restored.

Despite the good production mounting, the film has great flaws, particularly in its choice of leading man. Edmond O'Brien is far too citified for westerns. The burly actor, on his way to winning a 1955 Oscar for *The Barefoot Contessa*, tries to compensate for his lack of a western persona by projecting pigheadedness instead. Constantly scowling and barking his lines with all the charm of a neutered pit bull, O'Brien's vengeance-seeking hero is totally devoid of sympathy. One cannot root for his mission since it's extremely hard for an audience to like him. O'Brien's performance in Lesley Selander's *Cow Country* is hardbitten, but far more subtle than in the actor's Paramount westerns, where Cold War hysteria seems to have transferred itself into a quest for (personal) subversive enemies. It was not until O'Brien's performance as the old codger in Peckinpah's *The Wild Bunch* that the actor would give his best performance in the genre. (It's also hard to believe that O'Brien played this toothless old man just 18 years after playing the male lead in *Warpath*.)

Next up was *Silver City*, the film version of Luke Short's *High Vermilion*. I have also commented on this in the chapter on Luke Short. Suffice it to say that Gruber's screenplay turns Short's novel of mining camps and romantic rivalries into a convoluted series of contrived incidents and hazy character motivation, effectively removing all traces of Short's real-life knowledge of mining operations. Edmond O'Brien, by the way, plays his part so hardbitten that it's obvious he's in serious need of anger management.

Gruber would next doctor the screenplay for Paramount's *Flaming Feather*, another heart-tugging tale showing the Indians as warped savages; this time they are stupid enough to follow a depraved white man named "the Sidewinder." Starring Sterling Hayden, a genre veteran far more charming than O'Brien (and an ex–Communist party member who gave names to the HUAC), *Flaming Feather* is another twisted tale of vengeance.

Avenging the murder of his Mexican ranch hand and the burning of his ranch, Tex McCloud (Hayden) goes after the Sidewinder. Unfortunately, also hunting the evil, snake-named villain is the Army, as represented by Forrest Tucker as heroic, but interfering, Lt. Tom Blaine. Though his lieutenant is a good guy, he is also a strictly-by-the-book greenhorn. Fortunately, he's aided by Edgar Buchanan as Sgt. O'Rourke (a name Tucker would make famous on his later hit TV show *F Troop*). It is to Tucker's credit as an actor that, although he is typecast as a cavalryman, the actor still comes up with so many variations on the part, having played both officer and noncom, drunken wild man and naïve bureaucrat. (Ironically, Tucker was also in the cavalry during World War II.)

It turns out that Lucky Lee (Victor Jory), the friendly storekeeper, entrepreneur and fiancé of the cute Nora Logan (the cute Barbara Rush), is actually the Sidewinder! As a cavalry patrol under the command of Blaine heads out to Lucky's hidden claim, Lucky has ordered "his" Indians to kidnap Nora and wipe out the patrol. But the cavalry fight back, finally chasing the Sidewinder to some fortifications within the cliff's face that strangely resemble the homes of Pueblo Indians. (Apparently Gruber and Paramount had no qualms about slandering the Pueblos.)

During the attack, Lucky grabs Nora, throwing her over his shoulder like a sack of laundry and carrying her away. (A VCR slowdown will show that Barbara Rush has her hand out so Jory can take it and expeditiously throw her over his shoulder in a convenient Fireman's Carry.)

Ultimately, Hayden and Tucker defeat the Pueblos (??) and the Sidewinder is killed. Hayden and Babs are together and Sgt. O'Rourke tells Tucker that he's finally cavalry(!).

Late in the year, Gruber finished the screenplay for Paramount's seafaring picture *Hurricane Smith*, starring two men who are *not* the personification of nineteenth century privateers, John Ireland (taking a hiatus from film noir) and Forrest Tucker (looking strange out of uniform). Gruber's screenplay emphasized every cliché the sub-genre was known for, except perhaps a dictatorial captain which would have made the film more interesting.

In 1952, Paramount shot *Denver & Rio Grande*, with an original screenplay by Gruber. Though the film has Gruber's typical manufactured situations, it does show some realism in a variation on the theme of the range war. Instead of showing us cattle outfits at each other's throats, this film depicts railroad crews battling each other for possession of territory where they can lay tracks. The film's highlight is a wonderful head-on collision between two trains, done with actual nineteenth century rolling stock, not the usual badly matched miniatures that the studios' special effects experts relied on.

However, before great scenes like this, we must have schlock.

Edmond O'Brien, wearing his hat at an arrogantly jaunty angle, and still showing a bitter scowl, plays Jim Vesser, bullheaded surveyor for the railroad. He confronts his ex-pal Bob Nelson (Paramount contract player Don Haggerty) and his boss, the gun-toting McCabe (Sterling Hayden as an effectively smarmy bad-guy). Both sides are trying to put down stakes for the laying of track. Soon an argument ensues, resulting in a fistfight. Realistically, we do wonder what they're fighting about, since it's hard to lay track on what is obviously an indoor set.

During this melee, McCabe accidentally kills Nelson. Johnny Bluff (one of the screen's best bad-guys, the great Lyle Bettger) arrives in time to frame Jim for the killing.

Traumatized by the supposed killing of his friend, Jim retreats from all responsibilities (as O'Brien's mining engineer became a common assayer in Gruber's screenplay of *Silver City*). However, this is the early '50s, and with HUAC at the height of its power, we have to have a benign capitalist give our tormented hero a chance. And so Gen. Palmer (Dean Jagger, returning to Gruber country) hires Vesser as a surveyor for the Denver & Rio Grande (take *that*, Union Pacific!).

In the meantime, Paul Fix returns as engineer Moynihan, another one of Gruber's Irish stereotypes, this time doing comedy bits opposite 1930s comedienne Zasu Pitts.

Many gun battles ensue during this railroad war, with McCabe and his evildoers fighting Vesser and his noble Denver & Rio Granders. Finally, betrayed by Johnny Buff (Did anyone expect Lyle Bettger *not* to betray someone?), McCabe is shot by his supposedly loyal henchman while atop a dynamite-laden car heading down the tracks. Vesser shoots Johnny dead and McCabe dies in a spectacular explosion. The Denver & Rio Grande flourishes and, by extension, so will our nation. Certainly in the Blacklist Years, any interference with capitalism was literally considered treason.

In 1953, Paramount shot *Pony Express*, based on Gruber's screen story, with a screenplay by western novelist and future director of TV's *Gunsmoke*, Charles Marquis Warren. The film is sheer nonsense. We are to assume that Buffalo Bill (a miscast Charlton Heston) and Wild Bill Hickok (an even more miscast Forrest Tucker, again looking strange out of uniform) have teamed up to see that villains do not stand in the way of the Pony Express (an organization that lasted only a couple of years). Only in Gene Autry's *Last of the Pony Riders* do we have so passionate a defense of the Pony Express' legitimization of its low-paying wages and gung-ho attitude for its riders in the face of exhaustion, permanent injury and death. The film repeatedly drums into our heads (as it does in corporate head Gene Autry's far-from-subtle film) that the Pony Express never fails—and damn any pinko rider who whines about job safety! For Gruber, it is another fanatical pro-company message for the Blacklist Era, with Buffalo Bill and Wild Bill Hickok doing all they can to thwart the film's (leftist?) villains.

Perhaps most insulting of all is the way our two heroes treat the tomboyish Denny (a miscast Jan Sterling). The two big men repeatedly laugh at her, despite her adoration and loyalty, and essentially treat her like trash. Ultimately the little tomboy sacrifices her life for these two macho morons. Rhonda Fleming is the beautiful heroine; it is inferred that since she wears dresses and generally appears more "feminine," she is allowed to live. Sterling's character wears pants and is a tomboy, so of course she gets killed.

However, even after Denny's death, Buffalo Bill, though saddened, forgets his grief and goes off to deliver the mail. In the early '50s, the Company must always come first.

Pony Express was the last film on Gruber's Paramount contract. The next time the author would return to the studio was a dozen years later for the film version of his novel *Town Tamer*. After leaving Paramount, Gruber next contributed the screen story for *Rage at Dawn*, one of Randolph Scott's cheapest vehicles, done in 1955 for the dying RKO studios. Scott owed RKO a picture on a contract signed in the 1940s, which would be the only reason he would appear in this boring chronicle of the exploits of the little-known outlaw Reno brothers. The actor had otherwise worked for just two studios in the 1950s, Warners and Columbia.

Next Universal shot *Backlash* (1956). Based on Gruber's novel *Fort Starvation* which was serialized in *Rance Romances* in 1952–53, the film has a production team that's given us some of the finest westerns: The director was John Sturges; the screenplay was by Borden Chase, the scenarist for Anthony Mann's greatest westerns; and producer Aaron Rosenberg was behind some of Universal's major films during the 1950s.

Richard Widmark portrays John Slater, dutiful son out for revenge. Gruber's story deals with a small stockade built by six prospectors in the middle of Piute country. When the tiny "fort" is attacked by warriors, five of the prospectors are massacred, and though their remains are mutilated, it is clear that there was cannibalism involved. Hence, the stockade was renamed Fort Starvation. The sixth man betrayed his comrades to the Indians and absconded with $60,000 in gold. Among the five dead soldiers was John Slater's father.

Once again, Gruber had come up with a fascinating plot — and then promptly dropped the ball. The book soon becomes a series of Gruber's prized meetings between several shallow characters. Later, our intrepid hero joins the outlaw gang of ex–Quantrill man Jim Bonniwell, who coincidentally has the same last name as the title character in *Peace Marshal*.

Prominent in Bonniwell's slovenly group of hardcases is a young hot-shot gunsel named, believe it or not, Johnny Cool, a title no gunfighter in his right mind would realistically give himself. (Gruber's character is no relation to Henry Silva's wonderful portrayal of a hit man with the same name in *Johnny Cool*, produced by Frank Sinatra in 1963.) Unfortunately, despite his fascinating name, the character is one of literally dozens of Gruber's short-tempered, fast-draw young gunmen who are forever sneering at the hero and challenging him to a gunfight (see the character of Marshal Hunsinger in *Town Tamer* as an example). Here, the character is played by William Campbell, who had already portrayed other felons of both the nineteenth and twentieth centuries, including Caryl Chessman.

Typically, since the source material was a Frank Gruber novel, things were changed. Fort Starvation is now Gila Valley. Instead of having gone to Yale back east, our hero is now a Texan. (Who could believe an Eastern college boy as a rootin' tootin' Man of the West?) The Piutes responsible for the massacre are changed to Apaches (in Hollywood's view, one tribe was as good as the other). Susan Orpington, the daughter of a retired colonel who had investigated the massacre, is now a widow of one of the survivors and her name is changed to Karyl Orton. The roughneck Bonniwell, who is paired with Slater in much of the novel, becomes a crooked (and older) rancher who happens to have $60,000 with which to buy up land so that he can be Boss of the Valley. He is played with appropriate oiliness by the always excellent John McIntire, a character actor used by everyone from Mann and Hitchcock to Aldrich and Richard Fleischer.

Sturges and Chase give us a gritty western, reminiscent of Anthony Mann's films with James Stewart, though without the themes of the duality of Man's nature (this is, after all, still Frank Gruber).

That same year, RKO made *Tension at Table Rock*, the film version of *Bitter Sage*. In the novel, a Jesse James–like outlaw named Sam Older is justifiably shot down by his erstwhile friend Wes Tancread. The people of the west sing Older's praises literally; a song about the ex-robber and murderer is sung portraying Older as a Robin Hood who gave to the poor, and presumably loved children, animals and small birdies. Older's killer, Tancread, is seen by all as a Bob Ford backshooter, a Judas who supposedly took reward money to betray his friend, the god-like Sam Older. As the years pass and the legend grows Older, Tancread, alias John Bailey, becomes the printer and typesetter for a newspaper crusading against the rowdy cowboy element in the little Kansas cowtown of Sage City. (One wonders how this translates into the title of *Bitter Sage*, but Gruber never let little things like plausibility get in his way.)

As usual, none of Gruber's plots actually make it to celluloid intact. Wes Trancread (the incredibly dimpled Richard Egan) is now a famous gunfighter who is sick of killing and adopts an alias. He comes to the aid of Sheriff Fred Miller (Cameron Mitchell), a character who is nowhere in the book, and helps him fight the cowboy element drifting into town. Laura, the sweet young heroine in the novel, is missing. She is replaced by Dorothy Malone as Miller's wife, Lorna. DeForest Kelley as Jim Breck, a hired gunman, and John Dehner, as council member Hampton, almost steal the picture from the taciturn leads.

As directed by Charles Marquis Warren, the film is another cheap screen treatment of a Gruber "town tamer" novel — kind of a *Peace Marshal* for the atomic age. Warren was probably Paramount's second most controversial western scenarist after Gruber (though this wouldn't be apparent during the early '50s), having written the inflammatory *Arrow-*

Upstairs/downstairs. Edmond O'Brien (top) as a pathetic drunk being defended by a stalwart Alan Ladd in *The Big Land*. O'Brien's performance is quite moving, but the direction and screenplay failed the film. (Book Castle-Movie World, Burbank, California.)

head and the sexist *Pony Express*. Though Warren and screenwriter Winston Miller (who has the same last name as the heroic sheriff) attempt to change the material for the better, the film is basically indistinguishable from dozens of other westerns.

Now it was Warner Brothers' turn to film a Gruber novel, giving the project a wide screen and full Technicolor treatment. Originally serialized under the title *Buffalo Grass*, Gruber changed the novel's title to *The Big Land* to coincide with the Warner film. As usual, Gruber starts off with a good idea, and for once actually lets it play itself out instead of going off in half a dozen contrived directions.

The novel begins at the tail end of the Civil War. Two Union soldiers, Chad Morgan and Joe Jagger, find a Confederate soldier dying on the battlefield. Next to the dying Reb they also find a chest filled to the top with gold, which happens to be Gen. Jo Shelby's war chest. Though Morgan feels guilty about taking the gold, the ambitious Jagger has no qualms about it, even shooting the dying Reb to make sure no one will tell.

The two men decide to start a town in Kansas not far from the trail

3. Frank Gruber and the Distortions of the West

Who says the land ain't big enough? Virginia Mayo and Alan Ladd strike manly poses in *The Big Land*, one of Frank Gruber's better works. Like many of Ladd's productions of the late 1950s, it failed at the box office.

herds. The town grows, but the partnership goes downhill, with Jagger growing more surly, resenting Morgan's more honest, but less profitable way of doing business. At the end, the two have a time-honored showdown in the dusty main street of the town they started.

Still under contract to Warners, and working through his own production company, Jaguar Productions, Alan Ladd was cast as Chad Morgan, with Edmond O'Brien returning to Gruber Country in the supporting role of Joe Jagger. However, there are the usual radical alterations. Though Ladd's Morgan is still a war veteran, the subplot of finding stolen gold has disappeared along with the book's tomboyish teenage heroine. The film has our heroes attempt to forge an alliance of farmers and wheat growers against crooked cattlemen.

In the film, Edmond O'Brien's Joe Jagger loses whatever evil streak there was in him and becomes a pathetic alcoholic instead. His sister in the novel, Helen Jagger, remains a classy woman in the capable hands of Warner contract star Virginia Mayo; but like her brother, the character loses any duplicity she had in the book. Mayo and her husband Michael O'Shea were friends of the Ladds, and the actress had starred opposite

Ladd in his first film under his Warner contract, *The Iron Mistress*. The chemistry between the two is definitely there; however, the writing isn't.

The film seems to go from one clumsy event to another. Wheat is grown, cattle are moved, and Ladd and Ginnie spar briefly. O'Brien's performance as Joe Jagger is very good, even touching at times. He's obviously not the man Ladd's Chad Morgan is, and the poor fellow takes a drink when faced with the least little problem. So you know when evil cattleman Brog (!) and his shadow Joe Cole arrive and beat him up, he's going to reach for that Bacardi.

As played by Ladd buddy and frequent film villain Anthony Caruso, Brog (which rhymes with grog) cuts an appropriately evil figure. Standing tall in his black Stetson, drawing back his long coat so his hand can reach for his .45, and smiling the wickedest of smiles, Caruso was in his two-dimensional villain element.

When Morgan is away with the cattle, Brog and Cole arrive and try to bully the settlers. Jagger tries to draw on them, but his arm is caught halfway in the air when the two bullies gun him down. At the end, Brog and Cole stampede the cattle throughout the homestead. Apparently, the murder of Jagger, the heroine's brother, was not sufficient grounds for Morgan to go after the two gunslingers, but when harmless cows are made to run when they don't feel like it, now our hero is pissed!

Morgan faces down Brog and Cole and amazingly blows away both of them. He and Helen clinch, and we assume the settlers will start from scratch.

Unfortunately, critics and the public were not enthused. When it premiered at New York's Paramount Theater (the showcase for many Ladd films), *New York Times* critic Bosley Crowther savaged the film. "Synthetic too is the story..." said Crowther in an obvious dig at Gruber, and opined that the star gives "a pasteboard cutout of the performance he gave in *Shane*." It was another in a long line of box office disappointments for Ladd that would soon cause Jack L. Warner to cancel his lucrative contract.

There would be no further film versions of Frank Gruber's works for a full eight years. Though he was already considered old hat for the movies, apparently he was appropriate for TV. Gruber would profit enormously from the young medium, submitting half-hour teleplays to the western shows *Lawman* and *Sugarfoot*, and creating the series *Shotgun Slade* and *Tales of Wells Fargo*, the latter starring former *Cariboo Trail* cast member Dale Robertson.

In the made-for-television *Gunfight in Black Horse Canyon* (expanded from the *Tales of Wells Fargo* series), Rod Cameron, who had a small role in *The Kansan*, steals the film as a good-badman opposing Robertson's Wells Fargo detective.

Then suddenly in 1965, two, count 'em, two films based on Gruber were released. The first was perhaps the better film, though that's not saying much. Released by Columbia, *Arizona Raiders* was a remake of *The Texas Rangers* which was filmed for the studio by Phil Karlson in 1951. Audie Murphy is a distinct improvement on the original's George Montgomery; unfortunately, it was made at the time Murphy's career was on the wane. Though the talented hero-turned-actor turns in a good performance, the film is a mass of clichés that is not helped by Mary and Willard Willingham's screenplay.

As with most of Audie's later films that were written by the Willinghams, there is a little voiceover narration used to give us a (simplistic) historical background and introduce a villain (as they did in the Murphy vehicle Gunpoint).

In *Arizona Raiders*, a fellow appears before the camera dressed as a nineteenth century newspaper typesetter. With quiet dignity, he addresses the camera, telling us some things about Confederate guerrilla chief William Clarke Quantrill. First of all, besides the bizarre sight of a nineteenth century character breaking the fourth wall and talking to a twentieth century invention, we have terrible shots of former Republic stunt man Fred Graham as a kind of Quantrill mannequin. We see him trying to remain frozen and look deadly as the typesetter mentions his name. (For a wax figure, Graham moves a lot.) Indeed, this opening alone perfectly captures the persistent sense of delirium and illogic that is so much a part of the works of Frank Gruber.

It is the end of the Civil War and Quantrill and his bushwackers are raiding Lawrence, Kansas. There are scenes of some men shot in the back while running away which director William Witney obviously took from the Columbia stock library. Prominent among this bunch of Confederate Bad Boys is Clint Cooper (Murphy), whose character's name is a clumsy merging of western film stars Clint Eastwood and Gary Cooper. Joining Audie is his good friend and genre veteran Ben Cooper as sidekick Willie Martin.

When disgruntled bushwackers attempt to kill Quantrill, our ethically challenged hero saves him! Almost immediately after this, Federals raid Quantrill's hideout and Clint and Willie are sent to prison. Soon, however, the two men are released by Cpt. Tom Parker (Buster Crabbe) to be recruited into the Arizona Rangers (subbing for the Texas branch in the original).

It was the Willinghams' amazingly lame-brained perception of history that somehow put the days of Quantrill and the end of the Civil War (1865) just before the formation of the Arizona Rangers (around the turn of the century). There are yet more discrepancies. Besides the time lapse of 35 years, Crabbe's character is called Tom Parker, not the name of the real-life Arizona Ranger captain, Tom Rynning. And since when did the Rangers recruit ex-bushwackers straight out of Union penitentiaries?

Even for the implausible Frank Gruber, the Willinghams one-upped the old pulp writer in bizarre plots that bordered on science fiction.

The reformed-badman-who-infiltrates-his-former-gang plot was old hat when *The Texas Rangers* was filmed in 1950, but at least that film had Phil Karlson as its director. William Witney, a good action director who had made his bread and butter for Republic directing serials and westerns, was clearly no Phil Karlson. Audie was a far better actor than Montgomery and certainly a more appealing hero. Ben Cooper is a better sidekick than Noah Beery, Jr., in the original, and Buster Crabbe, a former cowboy hero himself during the '40s, shows dignity and class as the Ranger captain. Unfortunately, the plot is too fantastic to take seriously.

A.C. Lyles produced a series of westerns for Paramount, populated by casts of aging performers. These actors usually included Rory Calhoun, Richard Arlen, Lon Chaney, Jr., Dana Andrews, John Russell and former starlets like Jane Russell, Virginia Mayo, Linda Darnell and Joan Caulfield. By the mid–60s, Gruber was still earning a living from TV residuals, but with both film and television gradually attaining more realistic content in their material, the works of Frank Gruber were slowly but surely disappearing from the list of projects to be filmed. With Lyles' production of *Town Tamer*, based on the author's 1957 novel, Gruber was to have his last hurrah on the American screen.

The novel deals with Marshal Tom Rosser, a tough, fast-draw lawman of the type that was already becoming a cliché by the 1960s. Rosser is opposed by Riley Condor, a clichéd saloon boss villain we've seen literally hundreds of times. As the novel begins, Condor has hired Lee Ring to kill Rosser, because those are the kind of things a saloon boss does.

While seeing his girl, Carol, Tom ducks out of the way just as Ring opens fire. Unfortunately the shot kills Carol and Ring escapes, as does Riley Condor.

Rosser soon becomes a drunk. He is wallowing in his whiskey when a railroad exec named James Fenimore Fell offers him a chance to be a "town tamer" for a new village out west where tracks are to be laid. At first, the hiccupping lawman refuses the offer, but when he realizes that his archenemy, the vulturistic Condor, could be taking up residence in this very same town, Rosser accepts the railroad man's offer.

Now come the subplots. Sweet young Susan Tavenner is the abused wife of gambler–drunkard–rat's behind Guy Tavenner. This handsome sharpie has charmed the innocent gal into leaving her folks and marrying him. After this whirlwind fairytale, reality hits her. Tavenner steals her money and gambles it away, beats her frequently and, later in the book, rapes her. It is in the character of Susan that Gruber is probably the most effective. One actually feels sorry for her when she's abandoned and then uses her last money, including pawning a family brooch, to buy her way to the town where Tavenner is. After she finds Tavenner, the abuse continues, finally leading to rape. One almost cheers when Tom Rosser punches his face in midway through the novel.

Ah, yes, the novel. If readers thought the old pulp maven would grow with the years, they were sadly mistaken. The book is still the typical series of talkative card games and the hero meeting half a dozen people outside his hotel and holding repetitive conversations, usually ending with hysterical exclamation points.

Suddenly realizing, after 170 pages, that the only way to stop the madness is to throw down on Condor personally, Rosser kills the saloon boss and his merry men in a time-honored gun duel in the streets. Soon it is discovered that Guy Tavenner had married and abandoned another woman and is not legally married to Susan, which now makes the 20-something gal free to end up with the fiftyish Rosser.

In the film, the aging Dana Andrews is cast as Rosser, giving his usual non-existent 1960s performance. (In Lyles' *Johnny Reno*, Andrews practically repeats this sleepwalking demonstration of non-acting skill as a federal marshal in a town dominated by lynch law.)

Cast as the young and innocent Susan Tavenner is the ex-girlfriend of Howard Hughes, 40-something Terry Moore. However, what is amazing about her is the fact that, unlike Andrews or any of the other cast members clearly too old for their roles, Moore is still beautiful, giving us an example of agelessness that would shock Oscar Wilde.

Pat O'Brien is crooked Judge Murcott; Lon Chaney, Jr., just returning from filming *Witchcraft* in England, is Mayor Charlie Leach; Bruce Cabot is Riley Condor, exuding so much oiliness that a dermatological soap should be used immediately; Barton MacLane is railroad boss James Fenimore Fell; Richard Jaeckel, another youthful-looking actor who must have had his portrait hidden in a closet somewhere, is cast as young, hot-tempered Johnny Honsinger; Coleen Gray, a long way off from *Red River* for Howard Hawks, is Carol Rosser, now elevated to being the marshal's wife; Jeanne Cagney is café owner Mary Donley (Lyles and James Cagney were good friends off-screen); and, in the film's best performance, DeForest Kelley (yep, Dr. McCoy) is the slimy Guy Tavenner. Very close on the future ship surgeon's heels, giving the film's second best performance, is the wonderful Lyle Bettger as Lee Ring.

Undoubtedly giving the film's worst performance is the actor playing the desk clerk in the hotel where Tom Rosser is staying while he's "taming" the town. Lacking dramatic skills is one thing, but you'd think the character's creator would know him better than anyone. That's right, Frank Gruber himself plays the hotel clerk, giving a performance that would cause any potential guest to immediately check in someplace else.

Limply directed by Lesley Selander, the film is still fun, with its risible dialogue and ridiculous situations. In the Lyles westerns, characters get into knockdown drag-out fistfights at the drop of a hat, the long shots not hiding the fact that the aging leads are replaced by 20-something stunt men (even if one of them was former Republic stunt man Dale Van Sickel, then pushing fifty).

Selander, a western helmsman who could put real class into his films, had directed the best of the Hopalong Cassidy films, directed Buck Jones, helmed RKO's Tim Holt series and gave us the finest Rod Cameron westerns for Allied Artists. However, once he signed on with Lyles and Paramount, his reputation as a western director who could squeeze production values out of the most meager budget took a hit. He would direct several films for Lyles, the director's declining skills unable to save the films from horrible scripting. Forced to keep to a budget in the age of Cinerama, Selander had to shoot his Indian-fighting scenes in what was clearly a soundstage with a horribly painted backdrop pretending to be an Arizona skyline. Considered too old-hat to direct films like *Soldier Blue* and *The Stalking Moon*, Selander quietly retired in 1969.

By the late 1960s, for all intents and purposes, the film industry was through with Frank Gruber. The last gasp, as ever, would come from Europe. The Spanish production of a Gruber story would become *Comanche Blanco* (*White Comanche*). Featuring the blatant overacting of another *Star Trek* actor, William Shatner, as half-breed Johnny Moon (and Notah) and the sadly exploited Joseph Cotten as Sheriff Logan, the film was triple-bill fodder in this country.

A changing Hollywood was now holding the plots and contrivances of genre films in contempt. It was apparent that what worked in films and TV in the past was not going to work any more ever, certainly not in a newer and hipper film industry.

In the western, perfect heroes and innocent heroines were out. So were contrived plots that bodily dragged in the likes of Gen. Custer, Sitting Bull, Quantrill, Billy the Kid and Butch Cassidy in one film. Fighting for the almighty corporate structure, be it a mining operation, a growing town, or a railroad just wasn't relevant any longer. Neither was the idea of a hero fighting for the downtrodden. A western hero was considered more genuine simply fighting for himself — like the characters played by Clint Eastwood. Also, scenes of the hero running into a half-dozen individuals and padding out the time with mindless babble were also passé when directors like Peckinpah killed off ten men in less than two minutes, blood-squibs literally exploding off the screen.

The plots of Frank Gruber were dead. Soon the author would go the way of his plots, dying quietly in 1969 in Santa Monica. In truth, it is hard to imagine if Gruber would have survived either the New Hollywood or the new publishing industry. His material was from a far simpler time. A time when heroes were good, villains were bad, and no one had any problem imagining a meeting between Sam Houston and the Dalton Brothers.

4

Norman A. Fox and the Clichés of the West

At first glance, there seems to be nothing special about the works of Norman A. Fox. He had written western stories for all the usual magazines since the 1940s. His output was prolific, but the writing style was not much different than dozens of other sagebrush scribes. As an author of wild west tales, Fox delivered the goods, and sometimes that is more important than those who see their works as Great Art (like all too many filmmakers). His work seems undistinguished, especially opposite those writers who were promoted zealously by their publishers, like L'Amour and Gruber. Yet as far as Hollywood was concerned, in the mid–1950s Norman A. Fox's novels were regularly filmed, making the author a brief star of sorts to the film community.

The films made from his works starred western giants Randolph Scott, Audie Murphy and James Stewart, as well as an urban actor uncomfortably transferred to the west, Tony Curtis. His works contained the usual clichés, though it seems that Fox respected his readership enough to keep the action moving and give us likable characters, a talent L'Amour and Gruber didn't always possess.

In 1953, Universal filmed Fox's serialized novel *Roughshod*, written in 1950–51, as *Gunsmoke*. The film is fairly loyal to the novel, except in the minimizing of the characters of saloon gal Cora Dufrayne and transforming the widowed Dr. Farrell from a young second lead hero to the old, fat comic relief figure played by Chubby Johnson in the film.

The screenplay was written by D.D. Beauchamp, known as "Bud" to some of his colleagues. Beauchamp had written screenplays for Abbott & Costello vehicles like *Abbott & Costello in the Foreign Legion* and *Abbott & Costello Go to Mars*. In the *Abbott & Costello Book* (Apple Book film series), writer Jim Mulholland considers the latter the team's worst film.

The prolific Beauchamp had worked for Universal and Republic, and written screenplays for western stars Audie Murphy, Rod Cameron and Kirk Douglas; he wrote Budd Boetticher's excellent *The Man from the Alamo*, but also did the screenplays for the execrable *Son of Belle Starr* and *Jesse James' Women*. In other words, Bud Beauchamp's material usually alternated between passable quality and low-rent schlock, with the latter dominating his résumé.

In his screenplay for *Gunsmoke*, the results were basically a mixed bag of stampeding cattle, double-crossing bad guys, ambivalent gunmen and a west where everyone is an expert at wisecracks.

The novel begins as Reb Kittredge rides a stagecoach towards the ludicrously named town of Sleeping Cat. The gunslinger has been summoned by Telford, Sleeping Cat's resident Boss of the Valley, to work as one of his bully boys and aid him in destroying the homesteaders. When the evil Jimson brothers attempt to rob the stage, Reb thwarts them. Unfortunately, this incident also tips us off on whose side the ambivalent gunman will fight; the author destroying anything close to suspense in the narrative.

The film begins with cavalry troops chasing gunmen Reb Kittredge (Audie Murphy, in a piece of flawless casting) and Johnny Lake (Charles Drake; ditto) over the Montana countryside. After escaping the blue bellies, the two comment on just finishing up their work in "Johnson County." While Norman Fox implies Kittredge's participation as a hired gun in the infamous Johnson County War, the film makes this detail plainer, though without mentioning the pernicious character of the gunmen of Johnson County. The two men then go their separate ways, with Reb riding towards Billings.

When a gunman opens fire on Reb, the bullet kills Reb's horse and the ex–Johnson County gunsel is forced to carry his saddle to the stage route. After hailing a stage, Reb jumps into the coach and finds himself sitting on the lap of the beautiful Rita Saxon (Susan Cabot). Though Reb announces playfully that he likes sitting there, Ms. Saxon does not share the feeling.

After arriving in Billings (the actual city being a distinct improvement over a town called Sleeping Cat), Kittredge is challenged to a gunfight by Dan Saxon, Rita's father (the always excellent Paul Kelly). Saxon is under the impression that Reb had been hired by Telford to kill him, and decides to beat them to the punch. Forced to defend himself, Reb wounds the old man. Though Rita despises Kittredge for winging her old man, Dan sees something else in the reluctant gunfighter, namely himself as a wild young man desperately in need of direction. "He's a roughshod," Dan says to Doc Farrell (Chubby Johnson) while he's being patched up.

In a card game where the stakes are Saxon's ranch, the old man ends up losing his property to Kittredge on the turn of a card. Telford must now seize a ranch owned by *Kittredge*, a far tougher customer than old man Saxon, and putting the gunman in direct opposition with his erstwhile employer. As usual in these films, the old man owes notes on the ranch; in order to pay these off, the cattle must be brought to market and sold. Murphy would practically repeat this storyline in the film version of Wayne Overholster's *Cast a Long Shadow* in 1959.

From the beginning, Kittredge shows a natural talent as a rancher, bringing the ornery ranch hands in line. All of them, that is, except for Curly (Jack Kelly), the obnoxious foreman who has his own ideas about Rita. Two years later, Kelly would again perform opposite Murphy in a radically different role: portraying Audie's real-life war buddy Sgt. Kerrigan in the film version of the hero's memoirs, *To Hell and Back*.

Fox's plot, the ambivalent gunman fighting for a spread of his own and, subsequently, a chance to rejoin honest society is kept by Beauchamp, but the scenarist adds some touches of wry humor that were not in the novel.

Curly tells Reb that he wouldn't be so big if he weren't "wearing that gun"; according to the universe of western clichés, at that point Reb is supposed to take off his holster and the two men would "have it out" and the result would be a well-deserved beating for Curly. However, Beauchamp has Kittredge say that he has no intention of taking off his gun and then walks away, leaving Curly fit to be tied.

Meanwhile Telford is not through with Kittredge and his newly won cattle. Hiring Reb's old pal Johnny Lake as his trigger man, the evil Boss of the Valley orders cattle stampedes, sets fire to the prairie, denies credit to Reb's men at the general store and even hires Curly to help shoot up their camp. The only thing he hasn't done is tie Susan Cabot to the railroad tracks.

As portrayed in the film, Reb is one tough hombre who likes to push the envelope. With a stubborn streak a mile long, Kittredge defies the all-powerful Telford, tweaks Curly's fragile sense of self-esteem and flirts nonstop with the reluctant Rita. With Audie Murphy playing Kittredge, the Texan gives the gunfighter just the right amount of playfulness to offset the character's ornery streak. Whether beaten up by Telford's thugs or getting his face slapped by Rita, Audie retains the twinkle in his eye, proving his ability to bring light comedy to his usually grim western roles.

In the film, Murphy and Beauchamp bring a less-than-grim approach to the material; in the book, Reb Kittredge is far more stubborn, and perhaps more than a bit foolhardy. In one scene, he is surrounded by the psychotic

Jimson brothers (the same group of gentlemen whose stage robbery Reb thwarted at the beginning of the novel), and he still defies Telford. Confronted with an almost certain beating, a sensible man would have backed off, but not Norman A. Fox's Reb! The Jimsons respond to his pluck by kicking in his rib cage. In the film, he is merely roughed up by Johnny Lake's men, without a fraction of the Jimson brothers' brutality.

Indeed, there are several changes from Fox's novel. In the book, Rita is half–Mexican. Perhaps not wanting to bring a racial issue into the proceedings, the film opts for the casting of Susan Cabot, a dark-haired Jewish actress playing a dark-haired white Christian, with the appropriately last name of Saxon. Cabot's performance is excellent, bringing independence to the usually clichéd role of heroine in a 1950s western.

Beauchamp's screenplay also kills off the subplot of a young, widowed doctor who ends up with Cora Dufrayne, the saloon gal, a much more complex woman in the novel than Mary Castle's quickie portrayal in the film. However, Castle *does* get a chance to sing "See What the Boys in the Back Room Will Have" from *Destry Rides Again*. (Universal's westerns were full of song retreads the studio owned the rights to. Whenever there was a scene where a saloon singer had to belt out a number, the songs were almost invariably "Take Me to Town," "True Love" or "Little Joe.")

At one point during the film, chuckwagon cook Jesse White is told to turn his wagon around and the real driver's hands are clearly seen in the film behind White. The director was Nathan Juran, which was probably the reason there were no retakes. Juran is also responsible for the gaffe in the climactic fight scene in *Tumbleweed*, made the same year. When hero Audie Murphy takes a swing at villain Russell Johnson during their edge-of-the-cliff fistfight, Audie's punch misses by several inches, yet Johnson still falls backwards. In *20 Million Miles to Earth*, a mustachioed Italian farmer stabs the film's Venusian monster in the back with a pitchfork. In the next shot, we see this same farmer standing behind a cadre of police, this time holding a shotgun, presumably watching himself stab the monster. Somehow, one can expect this level of efficiency in a film directed by the man who helmed *Attack of the 50 Foot Woman* and *The Boy Who Cried Werewolf*.

Perhaps the most significant change from book to film is in the role of Johnny Lake, a character who doesn't exist in the novel. As played by Universal contract player Charles Drake, Johnny is an older version of Reb, tough yet principled. Drake would be Audie Murphy's most frequent co-star and be paired with the actor in his most successful films, including *To Hell and Back* and *No Name on the Bullet*, his character usually acting as a maturing influence on the stubborn Texan. As Johnny, Drake brings a toughness to the role that easily *could* have been written in by Norman Fox.

Because Audie Murphy played the starring role, the film was deservedly popular, and its success drew Hollywood's attention to the profitability of filming more of the works of Norman A. Fox.

In 1955, Warner Brothers found their next Randolph Scott vehicle in the film version of Fox's 1951 novel *Tall Man Riding*. A ranch-and-town story which had all the heavy drama that Beauchamp's screenplay of *Gunsmoke* lacked, *Tall Man Riding* would be Scott's last film before beginning his collaboration with Budd Boetticher. In an extension of his screen persona as a grim-visaged hunter looking to even the score, the actor appears more tightlipped than usual as Larry Madden, Man with a Mission.

The novel begins in the middle of the night in some forest in the west in a Land Far, Far Away. Larry has been awakened from his slumber by the far-off sounds of gunfire. Packing up his bedroll and saddling up, he rides right into the middle of a murder attempt. Seeing a group of shooters attacking one man, our fair-minded hero buys in and his skill with a gun drives the marauders away. Larry is then taken aback by the identity of the man he rescued, Rex Willard (William Ching), the husband of the girl he left behind and the son-in-law of Tuck Ordway!

Okay, just who is Tuck Ordway? Ordway is the biggest man in the valley, not exactly its Boss, but big enough. Fanatically stubborn and obnoxious to a fault, Ordway is the man who, many years earlier, drove Larry Madden through the town of Little River with a whip and ran him off. It seems that both Madden and Ordway were (are) the most stubborn men in the universe, both men refusing to compromise when Ordway tried to make Madden obey orders before his marriage to his daughter Corinna. This role is played by Dorothy Malone with alternating moments of breathlessness (Was she forced to run around the studio?) and bitterness displayed towards Madden. For Malone, who was also Scott's leading lady in Columbia's *The Nevadan*, it was just another poorly written role of sagebrush heroine before her ship came in two years later. At the 1956 Academy Awards, Malone would win the Oscar as Best Supporting Actress for Douglas Sirk's *Written on the Wind*.

Directed by western auteur Lesley Selander, *Tall Man Riding*'s ambush scene is done in the middle of a bright sunny day, with Randolph Scott having no trouble driving off three gunmen. (At one point, one outlaw recoils after being hit with a bullet, the sound of Randy's gunshot dubbed in a full second *after* the man recoils.)

After politely escorting Willard to the gates of Warbonnet, Norman Fox's version of the Hearst Mansion, Madden warns Ordway that he'll be back. Madden has employed the services of lawyer Ames Ludington (John Dehner) to help declare Tuck Ordway's claims to his own land invalid.

Dehner was one of the genre's most talented actors. Though born in Staten Island, New York, the actor was constantly hired to play crooked western lawyers, bankers and sometimes seedy gunmen, all with a slight southern accent. His rich voice was used in hundreds of radio programs and he excelled as radio's Matt Dillon in the 1950s. In 1953, the busy actor was signed to portray Telford in *Gunsmoke*, but then Donald Randolph played the role instead. Here, Dehner finally gets a chance to appear in a film based on a Norman A. Fox novel, though it could hardly be called one of the actor's career highlights.

After entering Little River, Larry hits Perlo's Pleasure Palace and promptly insults everyone in sight, including Sebo Perlo (John Baragrey). Saloon singer Reva (the tragic Peggie Castle) hears Madden's taunts and starts to admire him for his pluck. Castle was a talented actress and her abilities were never fully utilized in the film capital. Selander would use her in a few B westerns, appreciating her talent to play tough, independent women years before Women's Lib. Though her role is clearly a supporting one, we do get to hear Peggie giving a rare singing performance, her voice so good that the actress was not dubbed in by a real singer.

However, despite all this laughter and song, there are other more dangerous individuals who stand in Madden's way. Besides Tuck Ordway (Selander regular Robert Barrat), there is Sebo Perlo's hired gunsel, the Peso Kid, as played by Warner contract player Paul Richards. Richards had dark, greasy hair, so Selander cast him in the role of a nasty pistolero. Far too old to play a "Kid," the actor also struggles with a Spanish accent (though it isn't as bad as his Southern twang while playing a Confederate bushwacker in *The Black Whip*).

Though Madden is the stalwart hero, the character was part of a downhill spiral for the Randolph Scott persona. For the Warner films of the 1950s especially, the character became more and more inflexible: too righteous, too uncompromising, a little too damn dedicated to duty. In Warners' 1952 *The Man Behind the Gun*, the Scott character himself admits his own hard-nosed attitude, repeating a litany of "duty" that he must adhere to which caused him to kill his best friend for being a traitor. Fortunately, *Tall Man Riding* would be the last film Scott would star in before Budd Boetticher's films loosened up the Scott persona considerably, or at least called attention to the character's darker aspects.

Riding a stagecoach outside town, Willard is attacked by crooked deputy Jeff Barclay (Mickey Simpson) and the Peso Kid. During the skirmish, Peso kills Willard and the news gets back to Madden.

Angrily, Madden accosts Deputy Barclay in his office, and before you can say "Why, you dirty—!," a huge fight erupts, one of the best Selander ever directed. The fisticuffs start in the tiny marshal's office with the smashing of chairs, the destruction of a pot-bellied stove and breaking the barred window. The two men quickly take the fight outside and are soon rolling under horses and buckboard and doing some unmanly hair-pulling and face scratching before Madden delivers some final knockout punches to the disgruntled deputy's face. Madden tenaciously forces the beaten man to admit that it was the Peso Kid who killed Willard.

This knockdown drag-out is in the Fox novel, with the author describing it rather archly as "two men trying to kill each other." However, in the novel, the fight is between Madden and a character named Mace Stroud, the crooked land locator working for Sebo Perlo. Perhaps realizing that there were *too* many bad guys, screenwriter Joseph Hoffman deleted the character from the script. Hoffman had worked on the screenplays for *Duel at Silver Creek* with Audie Murphy and *Rails into Laramie* with John Payne and Dan Duryea, so he knew how to avoid the pitfalls of padding the narrative. (However, Hoffman would end up writing for TV series like *My Three Sons* and *Nanny and the Professor*, a far cry from the two-fisted oaters he wrote for Universal and Warners.)

After the fight, Larry visits his erstwhile enemy at Warbonnet and the two challenge each other to a gun duel that will finally settle years of mutual hate. Aided by Hap Sutton (western veteran Lane Chandler, whose career went back to the silents), Ordway arrives at the location of the purported duel, an abandoned saloon cloaked in darkness. When Madden gets there, he remarks that the building is "darker than the inside of a boot," but agrees to go on with the duel. After the two men enter the building from two different entrances, they are to open fire. This shootout in a pitch-black empty building is in the novel, but Lesley Selander turns the scene into a stylistic tour de force, with a blackened film screen illuminated by jabs of flame from fired guns. After Ordway is wounded, a rear door opens; sunlight reveals Ordway blindly searching for the pistol on the floor right in front of him. To Larry's horror, he realizes that Tuck Ordway is blind! After Corinna accuses him of wounding a blind man, Madden is now more alienated from the family than ever.

In the meantime, Ames Luddington reveals that Tuck Ordway never filed on his land. Warbonnet is now Public Domain, something that will start a stampede that will make the Oklahoma Land Rush look like a slow waltz. Soon Luddington joins Perlo in his mad schemes to be Boss of the Valley.

Now the big land rush sequence. With everyone hoping to carve up

Warbonnet like a Thanksgiving turkey, everyone, including Tuck, Hap and Corinna, ride out to the property to put up their stakes. Somehow Madden beats everyone to the property — everyone, that is, except Perlo and Luddington. After Ames wounds Madden, the cowboy finally fires his attorney with bullets. Warned by Corinna, Madden kills Sebo Perlo before he can ambush him.

The killing of Perlo is filmed less than gracefully by Selander. John Baragrey, the actor playing Perlo, has to fall from his horse after being shot. Selander gives the actor a pony! This is so Baragrey will fall a mere three feet to the ground. Unfortunately, the pony bit is laughable; instead of cheering the villain's death, we are given the impression that Perlo is about to get his picture taken by his parents.

After Ordway and Corrina arrive at the property, Madden tells them that his stake has been planted in order to save the property for them; he is returning Warbonnet to his former hated enemy. Moved by his generosity, Corinna realizes that there can be a future for the two of them.

There are the usual changes from the book. The character of Sebo Perlo is old, fat and chews cigars; he is not the young, handsome, oily character as played by Baragrey. But perhaps the most significant change from novel to film is that Willard not only lives, he is allowed to end up with Corinna. Now having reunited his former gal with his pompous rival, Madden rides off to conquer the mountain range known as Tumbling Wall, never again returning to River City. (Or is it Little River?)

The performances are basically good, with Peggie Castle practically stealing the film as the sophisticated saloon gal. The actress made Reva a far more appealing character to end up with Madden than the usually broomstick-up her-butt Corinna, a one-note performance by Malone. The worst performance, however, has got to be Paul Richards, who is atrocious as the sleazy little Peso Kid. In the book, Fox maintains the pidgin English stereotype of the character, with long "e"s any time the little gunman says "is" or "senor" or just about any other standard word in the English language.

In his *Western Films* Brian Garfield wrote, "hardly a line or nary a scene is not cliché" and that the film is a "textbook for rance romance formulas." Garfield wasn't kidding. Though the film was escapist fun for the undemanding, it seemed to emphasize Fox's tendency to give us corn in place of realism. In this realm, Fox was probably not much different than other pulp writers, where contrivance and cliché carried the narrative. Western writers like Les Savage, Jr., however, would constantly attempt to destroy the genre's clichés, despite the fact that the author's work would be censored by editors. Because of what Savage had to go through, this does seem to indicate that other authors had to endure this humiliation as well, forcing them to keep to a formula that was safe and non-threatening. (As an example, one particular western novel by Lewis B. Patten contained child molestation. The book wasn't published until after Patten's death.)

In 1956, Norman Fox certainly didn't have time to worry about the clichés of the recent Warner film. Universal had bought the rights to his 1953 novel *The Rawhide Years*, the story of a Bayou youth and his coming of age in the west.

Unlike *Tall Man Riding* and *Roughshod*, Fox here minimizes the clichés and gives us a touching coming-of-age story about a nameless youth, Will Yeoman (named after a damaged ship), who never knew his parents, and goes through the book searching for his identity.

The novel begins with Will as a 16-year-old working for Carrico's gambling house. He aspires to leave the clip joint and promises to send money back to Zoe, Carrico's no-good female accomplice who merely uses the innocent youth. When Will tries to leave, Carrico whips him mercilessly. The attack is interrupted by big Matt Comfort, an ambitious rancher whom Will saved from being cheated at cards. After Comfort saves him, the two sail on the next packet headed west. Comfort also brings with him a large wooden Indian figure which will be the McGuffin of the plot.

Fox wrote the character of Matt Comfort as a father figure for the wondering, nameless youth — a firm yet compassionate man whose addition to the story is to guide Will to a happy existence. Fox has the youth promise himself to one day pay back Comfort for his generosity, leading us to expect some conflicts to erupt or barriers to be thrown in the youth's way that might stop him from repaying Comfort. Then Fox shocks us by having Matt Comfort knifed to death in his cabin, thus killing off what we thought was going to be a major character.

When Will discovers Comfort's body, he chases the felons and discovers the wooden Indian being lowered into a launch. During the struggle, Will falls overboard and is forced to fend for himself in the thriving hamlet of Fort Benton along the Missouri. Now without his Comfort zone, the youth is also pursued by Marshal Littlejohn, a tenacious lawman who will never stop until Will is caught.

Years later (Rawhide Years, by the way), Will has become a cowboy, as Matt had wanted him to. Accompanied by a charming but dangerous saddle pal named Buck, Will returns to Fort Benton, drawn by his desire to help Matt's daughter Libbie and her mom in their battle against rustlers.

Now the clichés return with a vengeance that will shock even the Hatfields and McCoys. Will works at the nearby ranch for a crook named

4. Norman A. Fox and the Clichés of the West 93

Millard and his foreman Blucher. These enterprising pixies are actually responsible for the rustling and also head a gang of river pirates. As if that isn't enough, they also possess the wooden Indian, which is revealed to be full of jewels and other goodies grabbed off ships wrecked by the pirates. Suddenly an engrossing coming of age story becomes *North by Northwest*.

Will realizes that Zoe is a no-good tramp willing to betray him to the Law, kills the two-faced Buck, captures Millard and Blucher, returns the jewelry-filled wooden Indian to the authorities, saves the ranch and clinches with Libbie, all the while learning that it's not what a person's name is, but the strength of his character that counts.

The moral is fine, but the plot is basically Louis L'Amour, down to the part where our manly hero feels the need to protect the helpless heroine. If anything, Libbie Comfort is a feminist, and far more realistic than L'Amour's fleeting concessions to female empowerment by having them as the hero's occasionally competent sidekick. Still, by the end of Fox's novel, Libbie realizes that there are situations which "need a man," the author thereby sabotaging a very interesting character.

In the film, Will Yeoman is dead for all time. Instead of a 16-year-old river youth, he is rechristened Ben and is played by the Bronx-accented Tony Curtis. Donald Randolph, Telford of *Gunsmoke*, is Carrico. The film then follows the plot; Comfort and Ben escape Carrico and sail off on a riverboat; Comfort is murdered; his wooden Indian full of jewels is stolen, and other assorted hijinks.

Added to the film are William Demarest as Comfort's duplicitous brother and Arthur Kennedy as Harper, the script's Buck clone. At the time, Arthur Kennedy was playing charming heels for Anthony Mann in *Bend of the River* and *The Man from Laramie*. Zoe (Colleen Miller) now owns a saloon with a smarmy European character named Boucher (instead of Blucher, and played by Peter Van Eyck). Instead of being pursued by the novel's Marshal Littlejohn, Ben is hounded by Marshal Sommers (William Gargan, continuing a lifetime of playing cops and detectives).

At the end, after much shooting, lynching and mindless chase scenes, a dying Boucher confesses all, allowing Ben to live happily ever after with Zoe. Certainly the relationship Will had with Libbie did have its charm, so cleaning up the novel's duplicitous Zoe and allowing the hero to end up with her removes one of the novel's main assets.

The adaptation was done by that old hand at comedy-western screenplays, D.D. Beauchamp. However, the actual screenplay, full of murders and near-riots, was written by the tragic Earl Felton. A screenwriter since the 1930s, Felton later worked for RKO and wrote several of their film noirs, including the classic *The Narrow Margin*. Afflicted in both legs with polio as a child, the screenwriter barely worked in the 1960s, and ultimately shot himself to death in Hollywood on May 2, 1972.

Curtis is obviously miscast. Never at any time, especially while making his early Universal westerns, has the actor proven that he was made for the sagebrush genre. Riverboat sharpies of the nineteenth century didn't sound like they were from the Tremont section of the Bronx (Universal also shamelessly miscast Curtis in swashbucklers). Though Curtis would later prove himself an actor of versatility in films like *The Defiant Ones* and *Sweet Smell of Success*, putting him in a western was tantamount to not respecting the material. Years later, Curtis was considered to star opposite Burt Lancaster in the filming of Alan LeMay's *The Unforgiven*, until saner heads prevailed and United Artists cast an actor more at home in the genre, Audie Murphy.

The last western film made from a Norman Fox novel was again made a Universal. *Night Passage* (1957) was a tale of two brothers, one good, the other not so good, and their involvement with train robbing outlaws. As one can tell, the story is nothing much, emphasizing Fox's penchant for sagebrush clichés. Far more interesting was the film's somewhat tortured production history.

Universal had bought Fox's 1955 novel with the idea for it to be the next collaboration between Anthony Mann and James Stewart. Universal's Mann-Stewart films (as well as the pair's films for other studios) had been huge box office, and the collaborations are seen to this day as some of the best westerns ever made. These works brought a darkening of Jimmy Stewart's standard good-guy persona, and brought more unrestrained violence and sadism to the genre than there was up to that time. The films dealt with retrieving one's soul, fighting unhealthy obsessions, defeating fear, and man coming to terms with his dark side — themes that advanced the genre and coined the overused label "adult western."

Fox's novel tells the story of Grant McLain, a former troubleshooter for the railroad, now reduced to playing the accordion for workers' camps along the track route. When an opportunity arises for Grant to get his job back on the railroad by delivering a payroll, our two-fisted hero accepts. Unfortunately he runs smack into the Utica Kid and his gang. (The Utica Kid, by the way, is in reality Lee McLain, our hero's brother. That's right, Grant vs. Lee.) The brothers are at loggerheads, the two battling for the soul of Dickensonian railroad waif, Joey.

Though the plot was drowning in clichés, the film *could* be box office gold if directed by a genius like Mann and starring the infallible Jimmy Stewart (whose profit participation deals with Universal made him not only of the richest stars, but one of the most powerful in Hollywood).

With a script put together by Mann's usual scenarist, Borden Chase, filming started in Durango, Colorado, in October, 1956, and after only one day's shooting on the picture, Mann quit. Perhaps this was only a delayed reaction to something eating at Mann's craw; more to the point, the script itself. Chase's script, envisioned by Mann as a dark comment on the duality of man, now had scenes of rampant accordion playing, slapstick fight scenes, wisecracking outlaws and silly songs. Suddenly a work by Anthony Mann became a Gene Autry movie.

Though James Stewart would later say he accepted the role because it gave him a chance to play the accordion on-camera, Universal wisely dubbed in the squeezebox tunes. Unfortunately, they couldn't dub in Stewart's voice during the alleged singing interludes. Though Stewart was one of the finest actors ever seen on a movie screen, the star's singing was as good as his accordion playing, or for that matter, his script doctoring.

By this time, Stewart had tired of being involved in films containing scenes of sadistic beatings, being shot through the palm of his hand and being dragged by ropes through campfires, the usual elements of an Anthony Mann western. After expressing his displeasure with Chase, Stewart saw that the script was appropriately changed. Now with the actor's enthusiastic backing, Mann's journey into darkness soon became as family-friendly as a Dumbo cartoon, except for the shooting.

Caught in the middle of this crossfire between director and star was Audie Murphy, ideally cast as the Utica Kid, though his role is clearly subservient to Stewart's; in fact, the talented war hero–turned–actor doesn't even appear in the film until a half-hour into it. Now helmed by commercial director James Nielson, *Night Passage* might as well have been called *Day Frolic*. The film's sudden removal of its dark tone brought about a split between Mann and Stewart, and the two old friends did not speak for years.

As for the film eventually directed by Nielson, our story begins with accordion player Grant McLain, former railroad troubleshooter, now trudging on to his next gig, picking up nickels at a workers' camp. Before this, however, he has a cheap meal at the café of pretty Charlotte (Charlie) Drew (played by pretty Dianne Foster). In the novel, when they were little boys, Grant and Lee fought over the attentions of flame-haired Charlie (who apparently became a brunette for the film). Charlie continues to carry a torch for Lee and hopes to have him give up his life of looking great while robbing trains, and eventually marry her.

Now that this is established, Grant finally arrives at the workers' camp, where he is to "entertain." The place is populated by stereotypical Irish characters who apparently like to fight at the drop of a hat — and unfortunately do. We can only assume that Mann would not have shown this sequence, especially as it descends to the level of a John Ford slapstick fight scene. Neilson's film is not the only place where the Irish are stereotyped. At one point in Fox's novel, an Irish brakeman is revived after being found unconscious on the tracks. After coming to, the man quickly expresses a desire to have a swig from someone's whiskey bottle, the booze apparently having a magically rejuvenating effect.

After this touching fight scene, Grant is brought before railroad boss Ben Kimball (frequent Mann player Jay C. Flippen), who offers the squeezebox maven a chance to get his old job back and, in so doing, regain his self-respect. Here, Fox goes way out on a limb and gives us a premise that only stuns us with its lack of believability. This big railroad hires an accordion player, albeit a former railroad employee (and an embittered one at that), to deliver a payroll to workers at the end of track, and so avoid the payroll getting stolen by outlaws Whitey Harbin and the Utica Kid. Even for Fox, this was stretching credibility a bit.

While journeying to the railroad, Grant spies a man named Concho (Robert Wilke) chasing down a little boy and trying to beat him with a rope. Grant rescues the boy, Joey (Brandon DeWilde), hits Concho in the head with the rope, then knees him. Anthony Mann would have had the two wrestling around for 15 minutes over the edge of a cliff. Soon both Grant and Joey are riding on the next train out, with the ex-troubleshooter-musician hoping to deliver the payroll to those brawling, useless riffraff the film portrays so movingly (who would probably squander the money as soon as they got it).

Now after a full half-hour, the Utica Kid rides up to the camera for a full closeup. Attired in a waist-high leather jacket and black Stetson, Audie is sharp as a tack. Though the outfit is clearly anachronistic, the actor does look like a candidate for Mr. Blackwell's list of the Ten Best Dressed Outlaws. Off-screen, Murphy had tried to get the studio to give him costumes that were less gaudy and fit the times; judging by this film, he failed. As usual, Murphy exudes charm, making this young outlaw one of the most personable badmen that ever pointed a .45.

During Grant's journey to self-knowledge and fat paychecks, he finds time to croon two little ditties written especially for this film, "Follow the River" and "You Can't Go Far Without a Railroad," the latter a pro-corporate love song to the arrogant, exploitative nineteenth century railroad industry. During these touching musical numbers, we discover that Jimmy Stewart is no singer and one almost wishes for the arrival of Whitey Harbin and his gang to pull their big stickup.

Before you can say "You can't go far without a railroad," the train is stopped by Whitey Harbin and his men. The charismatic outlaw is played by Dan Duryea in a nervous repeat of his laughing outlaw in *Ride Clear of Diablo* (he even has the same first name), though this Whitey has a much thinner skin. Periodically he is mocked by the Utica Kid, who ribs the touchy badman mercilessly. For Duryea, the actor had worked with the film's two stars and its previous director before. In fact, all three actors had done much better work elsewhere.

Back on that wayward train, also on board and glaring daggers at Grant and Joey, is big Concho, the man Grant had beaten up to save Joey. Thinking fast, Grant shoves the payroll into little Joey's shoebox(!).

Predictably, Whitey takes over the train; Concho hits Grant in the head with his pistol, literally knocking him off the train; and the Utica Kid commandeers the railroad boss' car, meeting the man's cute daughter Verna (Elaine Stewart). Meanwhile, Concho and Harbin grab Joey (and his strangely ubiquitous shoebox) and kidnap Verna, and flee back to their (as it will turn out) less-than-secure outlaw lair up in the hills.

At the lair, both Whitey and the Utica Kid try to get close to the pretty Verna, with the leather-jacketed one easily aceing out the high-strung outlaw boss. The gang has returned from this so-called desperate robbery with nothing to show for it but the attractive daughter of a railroad baron, a disabled train and a skinny little blond kid with his stupid shoebox. The gang, unable to summon up even a modicum of the charm possessed by the Utica Kid, basically loaf around waiting for someone to enter the scene and keep it going, as if taking a page from the Frank Gruber style of writing.

Suddenly, this desperate gang's hidden lair gets more people wandering into it than an Internet café. In what seems like a matter of minutes, Grant, Charlie and a two-faced informant named Renner will arrive to try to liven things up — unfortunately the script and direction are so mediocre, they all fail miserably. First there is Grant, who shows up and expresses the desire to join the gang. There is absolutely no response from anyone about this except the Utica Kid, who is against it. Since the Utica Kid is against something, Whitey says he's *for* it, and accepts Grant into the gang. However, his membership in the gang will probably last no more than ten minutes since others are suddenly arriving at the so-called hidden lair.

After Grant shoots Concho dead, he and his little brother Lee decide to go outside and talk things over. Anthony Mann would have made a 15-minute fight scene out of this talk; Neilson just keeps it as it is: Talk. This is what happens when the director of *The Naked Spur* and *Bend of the River* is replaced by the future director of *Gentle Giant* and *Where Angels Go, Trouble Follows*.

Finally the two stars of the film meet. Both actors are excellent in this scene, with the less experienced Murphy more than holding his own opposite Stewart. The men (particularly Grant) discuss saving Joey's soul. Lee hopes to train Joey to be just like him (a charming, well-dressed outlaw, we presume). Both men refuse to give in and after Grant and Lee finish this little Appomattox, Charlie arrives and she and Lee talks things out.

Audie Murphy is particularly good in this scene, as we see the charming mask drop off and the embittered little brother come out. He mentions how much he likes being a thief, and is cheered by the looks of people when he takes things from them. Indeed, Murphy makes the character far more interesting than Stewart's goody-two-shoes (and far more colorful than in the book, where he is just a standard badman). When Charlie hears Lee refuse to let go of either Joey or his life of crime, she breaks off their engagement. Realizing that she's in love with Grant, Lee responds wryly, "...And he calls *me* a thief."

The two brothers soon return to the saloon-lair (Was this meant to be a low-rent version of William Saroyan's *The Time of Their Lives*?). Then, to the audience's horror, Grant plays the accordion again. He belts out "You Can't Go Far Without a Railroad" (badly), and then prompts Lee to join in! Before you imagine the ads for the film screaming "Audie Sings!," I should tell you that Murphy *talk-sings* his stanza, the Medal of Honor winner realizing full well that he was no singer.

Despite the fact that Stewart and Murphy's rendition of this song mean absolutely nothing to us, it is the moment when the Utica Kid becomes Lee, the brother of Grant, a man working for the railroad, and that family is far more important than the (apparently) boring life of a train robber.

But first, the arrival of Renner (Dennis the Menace's TV dad, Herbert Anderson), a double-dealing informant we saw in earlier scenes working at Kimble's elbow. He announces to Harbin that Grant is a fink working for the railroad. Appropriately (and finally), all hell breaks loose. Though he faces nine men with quick-draw reputations, Grant is still able to heave his bulky accordion at the kerosene lamp overhead and kill the lights before anyone can pull a gun.

Trapped behind the bar with Verna, Grant discovers a convenient trap door that is nowhere in the novel and the two escape and meet up with Charlie outside. Before he goes out the trap door, Grant takes a last look at his accordion, which is now in flames. The audience, we presume, applauds mightily.

In the book, Lee realizes that he must save his brother and jumps behind the bar as well; he is shot and mortally wounded during the gun battle. The good guys arrive and arrest the gang as Lee dies.

However, that's too simple for the film. The Utica Kid escapes, grabbing both Joey and the payroll. Grant, Verna and Charlie give chase. Whitey Harbin and his gang of misfits chase *them*. It all ends at an abandoned mining operation complete with convenient ore buckets and shafts to hide behind while being shot at. (It seems that these mines go bust simply for the excuse of using these abandoned facilties as locations for gunplay.)

Grant sends Verna out on the first ore bucket suspended across a canyon, supposedly so she can escape Whitey's gang (one must notice that Grant let Verna take a chance on this unwieldy conveyance first). Charlie remains with Grant during the coming shootout. Meanwhile, the Utica Kid and Joey remain above the scene, up in the hills, as the youth begs the outlaw to help his brother. Finally disgusted with Lee, Joey rides down to the shootout and has his horse shot out from under him.

Now Lee rides to the rescue. Since Audie is doing the shooting, the old war hero efficiently guns down most of the gang before finally taking that bullet while protecting his brother. Murphy's death scene is quite moving (as Lee's wasn't in the book), with Stewart cradling the actor in his arms as he dies.

Whitey and his men are wiped out, the payroll gets returned, Grant gets his old job back, Joey will work for the railroad, and Grant walks off with Charlie (Dianne Foster, who's half Stewart's age). In the novel, the trio becomes a family unit, with Joey now being adopted as Grant and Charlie's son.

Another change from the novel is the deletion of Cranby, a lily-livered character who works for the railroad. An absolutely useless wastrel and sniveling coward, it's been *arranged* for him to marry Verna (who, in a true piece of dysfunctional character motivations, is marrying him in order to stick close to her father). Also missing from the film is Charlie's feistiness. At one point, the red-headed gal picks up a gun dropped by Cranby and empties it at Harbin's men. (Joey exclaims cheerfully, "She's the most fightingest woman I ever saw!" His admiration for Charlie is appropriate since she will end up as his mom by the end of the book.)

Though Fox's novel is definitely not the heartwarming comedy the film is, the author's contrivances border incredibly close to parody. One still wonders why this big railroad would have Grant deliver payroll money. The accordion player's shabby way of dress is no excuse for thinking that his appearance will deter the gang. If that was the case, why didn't the railroad simply just hire one of their own people to dress shabbily and carry the money?? Who had to hire an embittered ex-employee-accordion player who can't even carry a tune?

This film called an end to Norman A. Fox's brief but lively run at being Hollywood's favorite literary source of sagebrush entertainment. Though he would write for TV westerns, no film would be made from Fox's work until he wrote the screenplays for two dramas filmed in Canada between 1979–81.

Fox's works, filled as they sometimes were with the conventions of the day, were still worthwhile. Never really aspiring to be the Great American Novelist, the author still gave us shoot-'em-ups that delivered the goods. His work did not make one think, but they kept us entertained. And in the World of the Western, sometimes that's accomplishment enough.

5

Louis L'Amour: Nietzsche Goes West!

Louis L'Amour had reportedly made the remark that he could sit down with his typewriter in the middle of busy Santa Monica Boulevard and still write. If that were the case, one can only assume that any faults in his writing style were due to his being distracted by traffic.

The legend is that L'Amour rarely proofread his novels or bothered to rewrite, and there does seem to be some truth in this. Not as flowery with his prose as Zane Grey (who seems to have influenced L'Amour's plots rather than his way of delivering them), L'Amour's way of describing characters almost makes a mockery of the painstaking descriptive passages that Haycox and Short labored to present in their works.

In L'Amour's books, evil henchmen are usually referred to as "rough-looking men." His heroes are almost invariably "tall and wide-shouldered," with customary thick black hair and green eyes. The hero's weaponry always seems to be a Russian .44 handgun or a Spencer rifle with a revolving cylinder. The land is usually red with clay, and his deserts always seem to have the same "dust devils," the plant life is usually "catclaw" or "mesquite." The same plots were used over and over again with relentless abandon. The hero was basically the same, with little variation, in novel after novel.

In short, creativity was not Mr. L'Amour's strong suit. Yet an eager readership around the world didn't care; L'Amour's books sold in the millions. However, as author Richard Wheeler once wrote of L'Amour, his work "has turned away better educated readers, particularly women, from reading westerns."

The standard characteristics of L'Amour's novels, predictability, an almost cartoonish lack of logic, strong action content and a persistent vision of the western hero as infallible superman, appealed to a Hollywood of the 1950s, its box office already reeling from competition from television, as well as the blacklist years. To Hollywood, L'Amour's heroes were no whining leftists complaining about social justice; his heroes were the stuff of Nordic legends. "Tall, wide-shouldered" men who had the power to survive the desert, the snowstorm and the wilderness. In short, they were perfect men who abhorred the little human frailties that plague all of us, and had contempt for anyone who couldn't keep up with them. To a nation that had won a war against a people who promoted themselves as superior beings, Louis L'Amour's heroes held a vicarious appeal to western readers that lasted decades after.

And what of the man who created these flawless cowboy automatons?

Born Louis Dearborn LaMoore in 1908 in Jamestown, North Dakota, the boy grew up in a family of avid readers. While still quite young, Louis devoured the works of Shakespeare, Jack London and Zane Grey. The last two particularly would have an influence on the writings of the future author. (It is quite possible the young man also became acquainted with Plutarch, since his material will refer to the great man's work in at least one novel, *To Tame the Land*.)

At the tender age of fifteen, the young man was struck with wanderlust (or "yondering," as he would later call it in his memoirs) and shipped out on a freighter. Besides his experience as a seaman, the adventurous youngster would travel around the world and work in professions as varied as elephant handler to fruit picker and presumably even found time to squeeze in service as a tank officer in World War II, not an easy rank to attain, especially for ex-seamen and ex-elephant handlers. After the war, he returned to the States and took up residence in Los Angeles, where he decided to become a writer. At first he sold detective stories, then decided to switch to westerns, which were then very popular.

He was chosen to continue the series of novels featuring Clarence Mulford's Hopalong Cassidy character when Mulford retired; L'Amour used the now-laughable pen name "Tex Burns." L'Amour's conception of the Cassidy character is interesting in view of his later success. Taking a cue from Mulford's own rewriting of the character to conform with the William Boyd film characterization (the Hopalong Cassidy we know today was created more by the actor playing him than by the original author), L'Amour fashioned a Cassidy that was part Superman, part symbol of eternal justice. As played by the talented Boyd, Hoppy was tough but wise, full of humor and laughter but quick to size up situations, flawed but quite human. These character traits did not suit L'Amour for Hoppy any more than they would his later heroes.

By then, however, actor and creation would become one in real life as well as on screen; William Boyd had bought all rights to the character from his good pal Mulford and in time would reap enormous benefits from a revival of Hoppy-Mania — television, radio, toys and other merchandising enterprises.

Riding the crest of Hoppy-Mania, the books sold, and L'Amour, or rather Tex Burns, would benefit. But works for hire never paid as well as works under one's own name. L'Amour wanted to create his own people. Men that strode the earth like giants — and women who had to keep up with them.

Still, as he was writing and selling his western stories, fate (or more likely Batjac Productions) intervened. John Wayne and his partner Robert Fellows bought the rights to L'Amour's short story "The Gift of Cochise." After longtime Wayne scenarist James Edward Grant wrote the screenplay, L'Amour expanded the story into a novel. In his *Western Films: A Complete Guide*, novelist-historian Brian Garfield comments that the novel was essentially based on the screenplay, and never credited as such.

Grant had been a big-city reporter and columnist for the *Chicago Herald-American*, specializing in crime and sports, which, particularly in Chicago, sometimes overlapped. Segueing into novel writing, Grant wrote *Whipsaw*, which was purchased by MGM and made into a movie with Spencer Tracy as the undercover man infiltrating a gang of jewel thieves. Brought out to Hollywood by Irving Thalberg, Grant would prove himself a talented scenarist, writing such films as MGM's *Johnny Eager* (which won an Oscar for Van Heflin) and Republic–John Wayne classics like *Angel and the Badman* and *Sands of Iwo Jima*. Though talented and highly intelligent, like other Hollywood writers, Grant also had his demons. A chronic alcoholic, Grant would consume four bottles of bourbon a day and predictably develop a nasty temper. Frank Capra detested Grant, claiming that it was the writer's influence with John Wayne that caused him to be fired from the production of *Circus World* in 1963. (Capra never once considered the real reason for his firing, which was that the feel-good helmsman was clearly the wrong director for the job.)

Grant expanded L'Amour's short story into *Hondo* a full three years before the screenwriter joined Alcoholics Anonymous. Yet it was the tormented scenarist's talent which was mostly responsible for bringing the western author some much-needed attention. Like Brian Garfield, film historian Jon Tuska would also take L'Amour to task for never giving Grant the credit for turning, let's face it, a mediocre magazine story into the successful film it became. L'Amour, a writer who supposedly cherished truth and honesty in both his characters and his life, would end up using someone else's creation as a yardstick for his future heroes. Certainly Grant's screenplay and Wayne's performance give far more humanity to L'Amour's protagonist than there is in the original story.

In "The Gift of Cochise," Angie Lowe lives out in the desert with her

Looks like trouble a-comin'. Geraldine Page, John Wayne and Ward Bond as Desert Man's Woman, Desert Man and Old Grizzled Guy in *Hondo*, with Louis L'Amour characters created by James Edward Grant. (Jerry Ohlinger's Movie Material World, New York City.)

children, Jimmy and Jane. Her husband Ed is a wandering scoundrel who likes a good drink and good company and basically forsakes his family for months at a time. Surrounded by Apaches, Angie's fighting spirit inspires in them a strange and totally unrealistic respect for her. (In the real world, they would have captured her two minutes after she took up residence, and the cabin itself would have been burned to the ground.)

When Ed Lowe sides with drifter Ches Lane in a saloon gunfight, the two men gun down their three antagonists, but Ed is mortally wounded. Before he dies, he mentions his wife's name. After getting information on the family's general whereabouts, our big, wide-shouldered hero promises to find them. During his many weeks of searching, Ches battles Apache warriors, starvation and the elements. Finally captured by the Indians, he survives the usual indignities until Cochise, seeing a manly man before him, promptly deposits Lane with Angie. This is the warrior chief's "gift," get it?

In the film, the Duke portrays *Hondo* Lane, who rides in out of the desert, Shane-like, to defend the lonesome Angie (a miscast Geraldine Page) and her son (the daughter apparently moved back east to live with relatives, I guess). In the film version, Ed Lowe is played by Leo Gordon, and since the role is played by Leo Gordon, Ed is now a worse skunk's behind than he was in the story.

Throughout the film, Hondo and Angie survive their various perils and, through it all, an American family is formed in the lonely desert. For Wayne, it was the first film of a Warner Brothers contract that would include *Blood Alley* and *The High and the Mighty*. The actor would initiate the Budd Boetticher-Randolph Scott collaboration by producing *Seven Men from Now*.

Though there are critics who maintain that John Wayne was the perfect visualization of Louis L'Amour heroes, there are major differences between the characters created by the author and those "created" by the Duke; one trait in particular points up these differences, and that is humanity. The Duke, even at his most vindictive, as in *The Searchers*, could command sympathy. Though he made his fame by playing strong, seemingly infallible men, the Duke's characters were quite fallible; he was a man who could enjoy a drink, another man's company, a good laugh and even spar with a woman on an equal level. Despite his toughness, he played a wide variety of flawed men, many of whom buried their pain under an iron exterior (*Sands of Iwo Jima*, *The Searchers*, *Wake of the Red Witch*, etc.). He could even miss a target or fail in whatever plan he tried, his "never apologize" remark in *The Searchers* notwithstanding. He treated women with respect when they did not play games with him.

L'Amour's heroines usually had to follow their men and submit to their will. His heroes had an almost excruciating prejudice against those helpless individuals who couldn't survive in:

A) the desert
B) the frozen wilderness
C) Apache country (or Sioux, Kiowa or Comanche, depending on L'Amour's mood)

Hondo, however, had its share of problems. Wayne and Fellows decided to follow the studio's suggestion that they make it in 3-D, a dubious proposition at best. In order to fight the encroachment of TV, the film industry used this procedure, fully guaranteeing audiences an abundance of thrills, even if they did have to wear silly spectacles.

Three dimension, where the visuals resulted in characters and objects seemingly flying out at the audience, was a gimmick for desert adventures, jungle films, horror opuses, science fiction flicks and, of course, westerns. Suddenly Apache lances thrown at the cowboy hero somehow made their way into the audience; flaming arrows, ditto; during fight scenes, cowboys' fists flew off the screen into patrons' mouths; the long barrels of Winchesters uncomfortably protruded at shocked ticket-buyers; and in Warners' *The Command* (1953), Frank Lovejoy's actual spit from tobacco juice could be seen and enjoyed by multitudes. (In a revival of the film at New York's Film Forum in the 1990s, I was forced to witness this particular magic of cinema wearing my 3-D glasses, and unfortunately on a full stomach.)

Realizing that 3-D cameras could be unreliable, Wayne pressured the studio for an extra camera so as not to hold up production in case of a breakdown. When the 3-D apparatus did break down, Warners still wanted their extra camera back, resulting in angry telegrams between the studio and Wayne, who was on location in Camarga, Mexico. When the film premiered, however, theater owners were threatening to boycott 3-D films. Ultimately, after a week of 3-D lances shooting off the screen, Wayne and Fellows wisely decided to release the film in a "flat" print, letting the film's story and characters win over the audience instead.

Apparently it was a good move. At the height of the Blacklist Years and with TV terrorizing the nation's movie exhibitors, *Hondo* was a hit, earning $4.1 million domestically. The Duke had returned to the west with a vengeance, and would continue with a series of hits that emphasized his growing stature not only as one of the most popular stars ever, but as an American Icon. Though the film version of L'Amour's story gets a certain amount of credit for this lionization, the Duke had certainly started on this road in the 1940s with fine performances in *Red River* and especially *Sands of Iwo Jima*.

With the phenomenal success of *Hondo*, Hollywood started to take a look at the works of Louis L'Amour. Before the emulsion dried on the flat prints of *Hondo*, Universal filmed L'Amour's *Four Guns to the Border*, the author's tale of four outlaws who come to the aid of a father and daughter under attack by Indians. Tough outlaw Cully (Rory Calhoun) and his fellow miscreants Dutch (John McIntire), Bronco (George Nader) and Yaqui (Jay Silverheels, who obviously fit the name better than his co-stars) run into Simon Bhumer (Walter Brennan) and his daughter Lolly (Colleen Miller). In this picture, the aim was to run "the gauntlet through the Devil's Playground of Apache Hate!" (according to the film's tagline).

After Cully provokes a fistfight with the Sheriff (Charles Drake, one of Universal's more talented contract players), the gang robs the bank and then heads out of town fast, as bank robbers tend to do. They run headlong into the Apache as the warriors are attacking Bhumer and Lolly. Just an hour from the border, the Fab Four come to the defense of the beleaguered pair. During the subsequent proceedings, and in typical "B" movie style, Cully's three cohorts are killed by the Apaches.

In the meantime, before one can sing "On the Good Ship Lollipop," Cully and Lolly are having smoldering kissing scenes. Adding to the realism, director Richard Carlson had camera set-ups which accentuated the erotic, including having Brennan spill water on Ms. Miller's blouse to make it cling and raise the film's sexual content.

Eventually, a wounded Cully, Bhumer and Lolly escape. Back at the Bhumar ranch, the impassioned Lolly begs the wounded outlaw to surrender to Drake's persistent lawman, promising to wait for him when he's served his debt to society. Ultimately, Cully surrenders.

The film was praised as "satisfactory fare for the outdoor trade" with some attention going to Ms. Miller for her obvious sex appeal. Not as successful as *Hondo*, the film was the first step in lowering L'Amour's material to the category of the "B" movie. Ultimately, it was one of Universal's rare associations with the works of Louis L'Amour; they wouldn't film another of his books until 1964, the year of *Taggart*.

The film also marked the first association with L'Amour by western star Calhoun who in subsequent years would star in several film versions of L'Amour's work, and co-produce as well. Somehow this seemed fitting. Calhoun's standard screen persona was that of an expert at all things western, a well-traveled man, a man who knew the land, the Apaches, firearms, you name it. He was the perfect actor to portray L'Amour's "desert man" who could lead a group of travelers out of Apache country; he could tell the survivors how to ration their water, and he could win a knife fight with any warrior. The actor also seemed to have the requisite physical description of black hair and green eyes of which the author was fond.

First came *The Treasure of Ruby Hills*, starring the underrated Zachery Scott playing one of his few good guys. The rest of the cast, Carole Mathews, Barton MacLane, Dick Foran and Lola Albright, all actors who were doing "B" films at the time, seemed to underline the fact that film versions of L'Amour had quickly become programmers unworthy of decent budgets.

Next, Allied Artists shot L'Amour's *Stranger on Horseback*, starring Joel McCrea as Rick Thorne, a circuit court judge whose courage is only matched by his skill with a hog-leg. The villain of the piece is one of L'Amour's long line of evil cattle barons who want to become Boss of the Valley, this time played by John McIntire (of *Four Guns to the Border*). The cattle baron's immediate family are a dysfunctional lot; however, since these people are created by Louis L'Amour rather than Luke Short, they are obviously not that interesting, without even the modicum of tragic dimensions Short would have brought to them. The film's only saving grace seems to be the always enjoyable Emile Meyer, who plays the sheriff with the actor's all-too obvious East Coast accent. All in all, the film is based on a work of L'Amour's that is not one of the author's best.

In 1956, Columbia shot *Blackjack Ketchum, Desperado*, the title of the film obviously concocted to boost the box office with the name of a recognizable outlaw. Based on L'Amour's *Kilkenny*, the film is very loyal to the book. Howard Duff, having already played a sympathetic Sam Bass at Universal, stars as Blackjack Ketchum, one of the west's most vicious outlaws, though you'd never know it from the film.

In the book, Kilkenny is another one of L'Amour's Aryan Supermen of the West. He is handsome, tall, wide-shouldered, a tough brawler, a quick draw, a man whose name brings terror to those who hear it; in other words, a perfect human being. And in the book, what does this Terror of the West really want? Just to start a small ranch way out in the desert and be left alone in peace. Unfortunately, those damn untermensch won't leave him alone. There's always some baddie who wants to bully him. (It is never inferred that this arrogant human being perhaps *draws* this kind of trouble to himself. L'Amour has used this premise for countless heroes, along with the exact same conflicts.) Ultimately paired with him is the beautiful Nita Riordan, a "perfect" woman who will ultimately go live in the desert with her man because he wants it that way.

Blackjack Ketchum rejects this Nietzschean nonsense and instead pits Duff's dressed-in-black good gunman against Victor Jory's villainous Jared Tetlow, another of L'Amour's long line of cowmen who want to be Boss of the Valley. Again, there is the attempt by L'Amour at showing a dysfunctional cattle baron's family, and again the author fails. The powerful but morally weak cattle families in Donald Hamilton's *Smoky Valley* and *The Big Country* are much more screwed-up — and much more fascinating.

Ultimately the film is better than the book, not only in the removal of Kilkenny's arrogance, but also in the desperation the superb actors bring to their roles. Jory is ideal as the big, bad rancher whose carefully constructed façade of legality disintegrates as Blackjack fouls up his plans. The killings are now getting beyond Tetlow's firm control. This is graphically demonstrated when his hired killer, Havelik, murders the marshal. Tetlow quickly chastises Havelik, telling his hired gun that the murders were just flimsy indictments on a piece of paper; with the lawman's murder, Havelik has just given the authorities a corpse. As tensions grow, Tetlow himself will pull the trigger on a café owner who just serves him coffee. (Caffeine does make one more tense.)

Another plus is the fine performance of Maggie Mahoney (a.k.a. Margaret Field, and the mother of Sally Field). Her Nita Riordan has a strength and defiance that is clearly not in the book. In the novel, Nita is seen as beautiful and tough, but gunplay, according to L'Amour, is clearly a man's game, letting Kilkenny handle all the action. In the film, when Tetlow tries to bully Nita's father, the feisty gal orders the cattle baron and his thugs off her ranch. When the cattle boss tries to sweet-talk her, Nita pulls a gun and fires at him, her draw every bit as quick as Blackjack's. (She's even dressed all in black.) In a later sequence, after Tetlow has had her father murdered, the angry woman indicts the rancher in public, giving him a stinging slap across the face. L'Amour's heroines weren't usually allowed to go this far.

Though a "B" production, *Blackjack Ketchum, Desperado* was solid and (certainly for its touch of feminism) enjoyable entertainment. Ultimately we know that Duff is not playing the real Ketchum, and indeed, who would want to play an outlaw whose greatest notoriety is the way he died? (The real Blackjack was hanged, whereupon the noose tightened a bit too much and decapitated him.)

The Burning Hills was the next L'Amour outing, produced by Warner Brothers. Casting Warner contract players Tab Hunter and Natalie Wood was an obvious grab for the teen market; Ms. Wood was partially responsible for the box office success of Warners' *Rebel Without a Cause*, co-starring her with James Dean. Indeed, Dean would almost certainly have been cast in Hunter's *Burning Hills* role had he not met his untimely death on the highways. (Dean was also set for Paul Newman's role as Billy the Kid in *The Left Handed Gun*.)

If Hunter's performance as Trace Jordan did not match his later flawless performance as the young hellion in Phil Karlson's *Gunman's Walk*, the reason might be lack of direction. Though Stuart Heisler was a talented helmsman on his own, he did not win the affections of his two stars, both of whom detested him for his lack of communication with actors.

Born in Los Angeles in 1896, Stuart R. Heisler started out in the studios in silent days as an editor, and continued into the talkies, cutting the Eddie Cantor films *The Kid from Spain* and *Kid Millions*. Signed with Paramount in 1936, he cut films there until making his directorial debut with *Straight from the Shoulder*, a comedy with Ralph Bellamy; this led to his directing the second unit for John Ford on *The Hurricane*. After returning to Paramount, Heisler directed the "B" horror outings *The Monster and the Girl* and *Among the Living*, two films distinguished not only by their noir-like elements, but their left-leaning social commentary. Keeping in line with these critiques on American society, Heisler filmed *The Remarkable Andrew*, an anti-capitalist fantasy written by future member of the Hollywood Ten, Dalton Trumbo. (It also featured a fantasy sequence with Rod Cameron as a noble Jesse James, Trumbo's arch screenplay depicting an outlaw as a symbol of Americanism.)

In 1947, Heisler directed Susan Hayward in her first Oscar-nominated performance in *Smash-Up: The Story of a Woman*, casting doubts on Wood and Hunter's assertion that Heisler didn't direct actors. In 1950, he was signed with Warners where he directed Bogie, Cooper and Reagan (the latter giving an outstanding performance in *Storm Warning*, from a script by Richard Brooks which attacked the Ku Klux Klan).

Wood had already worked with Heisler on the Bette Davis vehicle *The Star* and vividly recalled the director's callousness at an American Film Institute tribute to Bette Davis. Heisler decided to add a scene (not in the script) in which Natalie would dive off Sterling Hayden's boat and swim to shore. Frightened of the water, she begged the director to use a double, a suggestion Heisler ignored. Some say Davis threatened to walk off the picture if Wood didn't have a double; some say her mother threatened to pull Natalie from the film. For whatever reason, the scene was not shot; however, the female lead of *The Burning Hills* was not about to forget the director's cruelty.

The film was produced by one-time Warners contract player Richard Whorf (who worked opposite Cagney and Reagan). Whorf was a former actor who never really enjoyed being in front of the camera; later, as a producer of westerns, he was certainly no Harry Joe Brown or Nat Holt. His memos to the Warners hairdressing staff in which he stipulated that Wood's hair was to be "shorter" and "fluffier" and that Tab Hunter was to have no whiskers were rather ridiculous. Whoever heard of a man on the run who had time to shave every day?

Hunter asserted that the director was a hack, but at least he and Wood got along well. They would reteam for another Warners excursion into teen angst, *The Girl He Left Behind*. On *The Burning Hills*, the studio was considering dubbing Natalie's lines with a Latina actress, but Wood was nothing if not a pro. Tutored by a studio dialect coach, the actress painstakingly developed a convincing enough accent to pass muster. In fact, it is the same accent she would use four years later playing another gal named Maria in the Oscar-winning *West Side Story*.

The script would conform to the original story, one of L'Amour's many plots showing his manly heroes going out in the desert with his female "other half" and fighting off those inferior bad guys. Yet screenwriter-novelist Irving Wallace would improve immensely on L'Amour's writing, and the performances of Hunter and Wood, though not their best work, made L'Amour's usually obnoxious characters appealing. Between the talents of Heisler, Wallace, Hunter and Wood, and backed by wonderful color photography by Ted McCord, a work by Louis L'Amour never looked this good.

In the novel, Trace Jordan and his partner have rounded up some wild horses, hoping to start a ranch. When Jordan returns to their corral, he finds his partner shot in the back and the horses gone. The trail leads to a town dominated by the infamous Sutton-Bayliss clan. (The art of tracking is rather pompously addressed by L'Amour in his typically condescending manner; in the screenplay, Wallace actually makes it sound as informative as it's supposed to be.)

Once in town, Jordon is told by the sympathetic bartender (usually-cast-as-a-villain character actor John Doucette) that there is no law and that the town is controlled by the Sutton-Bayliss outfit, run by patriarch Joe Sutton (Ray Teal, one of the orneriest screen bad guys).

On the street, Jordan sees the S-B crew try to manhandle Maria Cristina Colton. The cliché would have our manly hero coming to her defense. Amazingly, Jordan keeps his place and it is Maria who uses her quirt to whip the obnoxious men out of the way, almost running her buckboard over them as she heads out of town.

In the novel, we are told that Maria is proud and defiant, although to the casual reader it actually appears that Maria, like other L'Amour creations, has serious problems relating to other human beings, particularly men. Her personality in the book is alternately obnoxious and borderline psychotic; although justifiably bitter at the murder of her father by the Sutton-Bayliss boys, she treats those around her with contempt, including her supposedly cowardly brother. She clearly has a sado-masochistic relationship with Jordan once the two are alone in the hills, with "romance" interspersed with plenty of punching and scratching. Certainly Wallace's screenplay is to be credited for toning down Trace Jordan's macho attitude and Maria's hatefulness.

Jordan pays a visit to Joe Sutton's stronghold (which our hero easily gets into, overcoming a guard and unloading his gun with one dexterous hand movement). When Joe argues with Trace and the rancher goes for a gun, Jordan shoots him.

In the novel, Trace guns down the rancher in the street. However, when Trace makes his getaway, L'Amour seems to have made a glaring mistake; at least there is one on Page 14 of the Bantam edition. After Jordan mounts his big red horse and rides away, "guns talked, but no bullet hit him." Hours later, he is lying in the hills with a bullet wound in his torso. Who gave him the wound, the Shootout Pixie?

Our hero is later found by Maria, feisty senorita, newly reborn with charm and personality courtesy of the lovely Ms. Wood. There is a telling moment when Maria does show the bitterness against whites that she has in the novel. Finding Jordan lying wounded in a stream, she mutters, "Gringo!" But this bigotry is quickly forgotten once she sees that the gringo is handsome, blonde Tab Hunter. Nursing him back to health (or at least good enough to get into two rough-and-tumble fight scenes), the two young people find a common purpose in their hatred for the Sutton-Bayliss clan.

Heisler emphasizes close-ups of the pair, their physical proximity practically screaming sexual attraction between the two young people. This is particularly obvious when the half-naked Hunter puts up his arm to stop Maria from leaving; Heisler's camera frames Wood's lovely face over his bare shoulder, as her look inquires what he wants. Later on, when the couple is alone in the cave, Jordan tries to kiss Maria. Instead of slapping and scratching Jordan, as she does in the novel, the shy girl just looks down. Understanding her shyness and not wanting to force himself on her, Jordan doesn't go through with the kiss.

Wallace's approach to their relationship is far more mature than L'Amour's having Jordan stake his claim on the Mexican girl by calling her "his woman" constantly and then trying to paw her; or for that matter, Maria's violent responses, complete with personal insults. In the novel, we're supposed to admire these people despite their dysfunctional relationship. However, thanks to Wallace's screenplay and the performances of appealing actors like Hunter and Wood, the Warner film does for its characters something the author himself couldn't do: Make the audience root for them.

The S-B crew arrive at the Cristina-Colton sheep ranch. Prominent among them is the psychotic Jack Sutton (Skip Homeier, playing young psychos ever since causing a sensation as the Hitler Youth member in the Broadway and film version of *Tomorrow the World*). When Jack wants to beat the truth out of Maria, he is stopped by ranch foreman Ben Hindemann. The short, blocky-faced foreman in the book becomes tall and handsome Claude Akins for the film. Unfortunately, when his back is turned, Hindemann gets two bullets in it from Jack's gun; Wallace shocks not only the movie audience, but those who have read the novel as well (Hindemann lives all the way to the end of the book).

Once in the house, the gang take over, beating Maria's brother and the Latina herself getting roughed up by Mort Bayliss (Earl Holliman, usually cast in westerns as either dumb young men or *evil* dumb young men). Just as the gang tries to figure out how to solve this problem called Maria, the Latina gal takes matters into her own hands, drugging everyone's coffee with jimson weed (named, we assume, after the psychotic Jimson brothers in Norman A. Fox's *Roughshod*). The resourceful gal escapes to join Trace in the hills.

Looking to lessen the odds, Jordan spies a group of Apaches camped in a clearing and fires his rifle at them. Now alerted to danger, the warriors lie in ambush and attack the Sutton-Bayliss lads. After the warriors and the S-B crew massacre each other, Jack escapes with Jacob Lantz (Eduard Franz), the wise and noncommittal half-breed tracker.

When Jack catches up with them in some picturesque hills overlooking a roaring stream, he jumps Trace and a huge fistfight ensues, literally all over the hills, as Maria looks on worriedly. After tumbling into a stream, the fight continues until Sutton is unceremoniously drowned. After the friendly Lantz tells them where they can find the nearest fort, the young couple embrace happily and start life anew.

Wallace elevates L'Amour's simplistic plot by making Joe Sutton a crooked rancher trying to keep homesteaders from filing claims and, of course, seeking to become Boss of the Valley. Thus, Jordan's trek is not merely to escape Sutton's thugs, but to enlist "federal help" to help save the homesteaders. Though Joe Sutton is merely wounded by Trace early in the film, it is implied that Sutton will now be put out of business once the couple arrives at the fort and implicates the rancher. An interesting irony to the scene of Joe Sutton's shooting is the fact that Tab Hunter will again shoot and wound Ray Teal two years later in *Gunman's Walk*.

Gunfight under the O.K. Corral. Rory Calhoun about to fire a burst of his hoglegs in ***Utah Blaine***. Calhoun seemed to be the perfect embodiment of L'Amour's fabled Desert Man, despite the fact that the actor was far more likable than the author's creation. (Jerry Ohlinger's Movie Material World, New York City.)

In 1957, Columbia starred Rory Calhoun as *Utah Blaine*, another one of L'Amour's all-purpose superior beings who just happens to be a well-known gunman. Utah Blaine is "the fastest gun in the west," something that might be news to Kilkenny. When Utah (hard to disrespect a hero named after a State) rescues a rancher from a lynching, the grateful man bequeaths half his property to his rescuer. Utah, who like many a L'Amour gunman just wants his own spread somewhere far away from evil (and inferior) civilization, gladly accepts. However, the rancher is battling Russ Nevers (Ray Teal at his slimiest) over the property. In short order, the rancher is murdered, thus leaving the whole shebang to Utah.

Also residing in the same valley is Angie Kenyon (Susan Cummings), another of L'Amour's physically beautiful but basically subordinate heroines. Like many of his women, she is ogled by many men, but is, of course good enough only for a man as physically beautiful and just as superior as she is. (In the novel, towards the end, no less than *three* men want to rape her, including the staid banker.)

Utah is aided by the hulking Gus Ortmann (Max Baer, Sr.). In both book and film, Utah must beat him in a fistfight to gain the giant's respect. In many of L'Amour's novels, his heroes must all go through this rather useless and especially painful routine, the author obviously seeing these battles as some kind of noble ritual for his superior heroes, and not the mindless exercises in brutality that they really are.

Though wounded and beaten, hunted and despised, Utah rises above his inferior enemies with a triumph of the will and the withering blast of his hog-legs. Certainly Rory Calhoun, a talented genre veteran, brings more likability to the character than originally written. Also to the film's advantage is the direction of Fred F. Sears, former "B" western performer (he was a regular in Charles Starrett's Durango Kid series), who became the studio's ace budget director, reportedly directing over 50 films in nine years! Tragically, Sears would die in 1957 while still in his forties, with overwork a possible contributing factor.

Next up was Allied Artists' *The Tall Stranger*, again starring Joel McCrea. This time McCrea is Ned Bannon, former Union officer, now just a drifter left for dead on the trail. Picked up by a wagon train, the cowpoke resolves to fight villains within the train and others who hope to become bosses of the valley. The heroine is Virginia Mayo, now too old to play L'Amour's original cute young thing. Her appearance is also a painful reminder of her co-starring with McCrea in Raoul Walsh's excellent *Colorado Territory* of eight years before.

Columbia then released *Apache Territory*, based on L'Amour's *Last Stand at Papago Wells*. Co-produced by and starring Rory Calhoun, the film is directed by an old hand at Columbia westerns, Ray Nazarro. Though Sears could bring true style to his low-budget efforts, Nazarro was no slouch either, as he kept the action going from beginning to end.

A lone rider arrives at an Apache water hole (Papago Wells, though not called that here). That rider is Logan Cates (Rory), desert man par excellence! Also arriving coincidentally is Jennifer Fair (the subtlety of the name baffles me as to the girl's character), and gambler–underhanded sharpie Grant Kimbrough (the always fascinating John Dehner).

Kimbrough wants to run off with Jennie, and defies Logan's warnings about the Apaches. Also stumbling into this Grand Hotel–like conclave is a small cavalry detachment consisting of Leo Gordon as L'Amour's arrogant troublemaker Zimmerman; genre veteran Myron Healey as Webb, a beleaguered trooper, and several other blue-bellies.

Also showing up in this melange of humanity is Tom Pittman as young Lonnie Foreman and Carolyn Craig, a year before screaming her lungs out in *House on Haunted Hill*, as young Junie Hatchek. In both novel and film, the shy, hesitant love developing between the two young people is easily the story's most charming aspect. Another character in the book is a rather large woman who goes insane and walks hysterically into a sandstorm, a sequence far more chilling than the many Apache murders.

All in all, the book seems like what it is, a blatant steal of *Stagecoach*. And if these people aren't enough, they also have a friendly Pima Indian (the future chief of the Heckowas on *F Troop*, Frank DeKova). For once, Calhoun is surrounded by excellent players; with their obvious enthusiasm, as well as the film's tense conflicts, *Apache Territory* is one of the best-ever film versions of L'Amour.

In 1954, a year after leaving his long-time employer Paramount, Alan Ladd had organized Jaguar Productions. Warner Brothers was committed to financing and distributing two Jaguar films a year, as well as paying the star a whopping $150,000 per film and a percentage of the gross. Jack L. Warner would never be crazy about the deal; however, buoyed by the enthusiastic response to *Shane*, he accepted the arrangement. Later on, seeing the public's indifferent response to Jaguar's films, the studio boss would look for any little excuse to kick Jaguar and Ladd off the lot.

Producer-screenwriter Martin Rackin would leave Jaguar by the time of the box office failure of Frank Gruber's *The Big Land* and be replaced as production head with the up-and-coming Aaron Spelling. According to director Edward Dmytryk, Rackin was "a first-class raconteur, but a second-class screenwriter," though he would say he was a good "production executive." Perhaps because of Rackin's departure, the film version of Louis L'Amour's *Guns of the Timberlands* was postponed half a year to January 1959.

Warner Brothers proceeded to reluctantly film the project, hiring Robert D. Webb to direct. Webb had guided the King's film debut, *Love Me Tender*, proving that Elvis could act as well as sing. The gimmick of using a popular singer in a western would be repeated here, with Frankie Avalon essentially doing an Elvis. After this film, Avalon would sign with AIP for their moronic beach party series.

With a screenplay by Aaron Spelling, the film turns L'Amour's story (an evil eastern businessman hoping to gut the forest and become another Boss of the Valley) into something totally different. First of all, the hero of the book, young Clay Bell, is now played by the middle-aged Lyle Bettger. And since Bell is played by Lyle Bettger, he is obviously no longer the hero.

Alan Ladd, a star for decades, but underrated by Hollywood as an actor, portrays Jim Hadley, a character who is nowhere in the novel. Jeanne Crain plays Laura Riley (changed from the more attractive-sounding Colleen). The always excellent Gilbert Roland is cast as Hadley's partner Monty, who, of course, goes bad.

At one point, hoping to open up a logging road closed by the townsfolk, Monty uses dynamite. The explosion ultimately kills Bert Harvey (Avalon), but not before the young man belts out a few contemporary numbers that wow the forest folk. Louis L'Amour was never like this!

The film deletes the various battles between the businessman's forces and Clay Bell's men, including the climactic knockdown, dragout fistfight between the hero and villain. Filming outside of Reno, Nevada, Ladd was subjected to all sorts of mishaps, including snakebites, a fall from a horse and the flu. To top off these physical calamities, he was also coming off a string of flops, the last of which turned out to be *Guns of the Timberland*. With little hesitation, Jack Warner spitefully canceled Ladd's lucrative contract. But Louis L'Amour didn't have anything to worry about. The next studio project would be considered by the author to be the best film version of his work—even if it hardly resembles his work.

In 1960, Paramount, a studio filming L'Amour for the first time, gave us *Heller in Pink Tights*, basically a cannibalism of L'Amour's *Heller with a Gun* (a baffling title since there is no one in the book named Heller). Paramount had supposedly bought the L'Amour novel as a starring vehicle for Alan Ladd when the actor was still under contract to the studio. However, Ladd's last film under his Paramount contract was *Botany Bay*, released by the studio on October 29, 1953. L'Amour's novel came out in 1955, a full two years after Ladd's contract ended, calling into question whether *Heller with a Gun* was actually set to be a Ladd vehicle.

The film does at times seem like a battle between director George Cukor (the most prestigious director ever for a L'Amour adaptation) and producer Carlo Ponti, who cast his gorgeous but semi-talented wife Sophia Loren in the lead role. The screenplay was by Dudley Nichols, who also did the screenplay for Ernest Haycox's *Stagecoach*. At the time, Nichols was dying of cancer, and the screenplay would be rewritten by blacklisted writer Walter Bernstein.

Produced by a man who was using the project as a showcase for his wife, and directed by a filmmaker who was known as a "woman's director." This film version of a L'Amour novel would be changed radically. Predictably, the film's focus switches from Steve Forrest's gunman, Clint Mabry (in place of the novel's King Mabry), to Angela Rossini (Sophia Loren), an Italian-sounding character named for the sexy Neapolitan star that is clearly not in the book (the heroine is named Janice Ryan). One wonders why Paramount, who had Ms. Loren under contract, decided to cast her in a western. Another example of shocking miscasting is the usually talented Anthony Quinn playing the book's red-headed Irish actor Tom Healey. The youthful Margaret O'Brien plays the youthful Della Southby (named Dodie in the book), but the film is stolen out from under all these better known players by the stage actress Eileen Heckart as Della's mom, Lorna.

George Hoyningen-Huene, whom Cukor had used on the 1954 *A Star Is Born*, was hired by the director as the film's "visual and color consultant." It appears that for this reason and this reason alone, Loren is wearing a blonde wig. Had the film not been produced by Ponti or directed by Cukor, the role could easily have been filled by blonde western actress Peggie Castle, without the wig, but with more genuine emoting.

Also changed is L'Amour's frozen wilderness that the acting troupe travels through. Their journey could have been through Griffith Park in Los Angeles. L'Amour always said that *Hondo* and *Heller in Pink Tights* were two of his favorite filmizations of his works. If this was the case, then apparently these were his favorites because they were major films with big stars, not because they followed his original stories. *Heller*, in particular, essentially throws away L'Amour's rather pedestrian story and the film becomes a charming, sophisticated comedy set in the west (humor was never L'Amour's strong suit).

A traveling troupe of actors headed by Tom Healy (Quinn) comes to a wild town to perform. Prominent among the performers is Angela Rossini (Loren), a gorgeous, beguiling flirt whose charms have helped keep the group afloat—in more ways than one. Usually poor and always outrunning creditors, this merry band of thespians sees a change in its fortunes when it eventually crosses paths with gunman Clint Mabry (Steve Forrest). During a high stakes card game, Mabry "wins" Angela at the turn of a card — and this persistent gunman intends to collect his winnings. When the troupe is chased out of town again, Mabry rides with them to protect them from Apaches.

Certainly director Cukor and screenwriters Bernstein and Nichols give us a far more interesting tale than is found between the covers of L'Amour's novel. In the book, Mabry hooks up to the troupe and protects them from bandits who are trailing them. Why bandits would go out of their way into a frozen wasteland to steal this troupe's meager profits makes little sense, and credit is to be given to Bernstein and Nichols for fleshing out the plot.

Loren looks horrible in a blonde wig. Always a limited actress, she amazingly won a Best Actress Oscar three years later for *Two Women*. Clearly out of place in the old west, Loren's Neapolitan tart is able to charm every male in sight and then abandon them at a moment's notice. Unfortunately, the Italian actress was tense under Cukor's extremely demonstrative direction, which called for the director himself to act out all the parts for his actors, whether they were male or female. This extremely dated style of direction might have worked for Cary Grant and Katharine Hepburn in the 1930s, but opposite a narrow actress like Loren at the beginning of the Swinging '60s, this approach only further undermined the film. Add to this Cukor's ambitious plans for Loren's role. The flamboyant director, always interested in the real-life stories of theater people, envisioned Loren's Angela Rossini as part Lillian Langtry, part Adeh Isaacs Menen. Unfortunately, what he got was an Italian starlet in a silly blonde wig.

As shot by the gay director, the film is almost a dig at male-female relationships. Nowhere is this cynicism more apparent than in the sequence where Mabry "wins" Angela in a poker game. Angela herself twists men around her finger with ease, whether they be Quinn's underplayed Healy or Forrest's wily gunman.

Another Cukor touch is the confusion of genders so dear to the auteur. When Apaches capture the empty wagon the troupe was forced to abandon, the wild braves don the colorful costumes, mostly those of the actresses. Here Cukor gives us a sexually ambivalent scene in which aggressive males dress like women and "camp" it up with loud whoops. Later on, in order to escape the bad guys who are planning to kill him, Mabry is forced to dress in Angela's cloak and ride out of the theater pretending to be a woman. Another example of this sexual ambiguity is seen in the title; instead of the more manly-sounding *Heller with a Gun*, we are given a title where *With a Gun* is replaced by *In Pink Tights*, seemingly implying the presence of transvestites in the old west. It's obvious L'Amour missed this subtext totally, as did most reviewers in those still innocent days of 1960. (In *Education of a Wandering Man*, L'Amour's rambling, chronologically inept memoirs, the writer claimed to have left the *Heller* set with his wife Kathy so they could look at the desert location where *Shalako* was set. *Shalako* was not written until 1962, two years later.)

Unfortunately, the film ended up as another in a series of bombs starring Sophia Loren. Marketing the film for traditional western action fans (most of whom were young males), Paramount failed to see that not one film ever directed by George Cukor ever captured the imagination of those same young males who embraced *Gunfight at the OK Corral* and *The Magnificent Seven*.

Amazingly, the film was praised by the likes of Bosley Crowther. The *New York Times* critic thought the film was "colorful, humorous, sentimental and even exciting," and that Loren was "warm and natural." One wonders, indeed, what they put in the coffee in the *Times* break room.

It would be four years before another L'Amour novel would be committed to film. (Though he was credited with a book called *How the West Was Won*, the book is a "novelization" based on James Webb's screenplay, and emphatically not an original work.) Next Universal released *Taggart* (1964), the long space in time without filming a L'Amour novel an indication that perhaps Hollywood was losing interest in his works. By the '60s, Marvin H. Albert had effectively taken over as Hollywood's resident western author. (And unlike L'Amour, Albert could write screenplays *and* novelizations!)

By this time, L'Amour's Supermen Gunslingers had learned to talk, and what they said wasn't always pretty. Several of them had views which were not only arrogant, but downright inflammatory. Shalako alone would express a vicious sexism that was clearly *not* meant for female readers. Brionne would praise the wonderful experience of suffering, expressing to his female companion the Nietzschean theory of pain and hardship making one stronger. The hero of *The Quick and the Dead* harbors a contempt for soft easterners that borders on the deranged.

In the novel *Taggart*, it is the heroine's turn. In the first few pages, Miriam chatters on and on about what a woman should do for her man, along with the *true* definition of what love is. (It is important to italicize that word since it emphasizes that L'Amour never states that these characters are just expressing their point of view. They are saying what we are *supposed* to feel. In L'Amour's universe, there is clearly no room for any other points of view.)

In the book, Taggart is a gunman chased by a crooked marshal. This superior gunman also happens to find Miriam, an aging maiden who's never been with a man, but seems to know all about love and marriage.

She and her brother are looking for gold in the desert. Joining them reluctantly is the brother's bitchy half–Apache wife, Consuelo. Speaking of the Apaches, they happen to be menacing our merry band of dysfunctional travelers at every turn. The film is not far from this plot, and its saving grace (besides Dan Duryea's usual enthusiastic performance) is the direction of western veteran R.G. Springsteen. It's unfortunate that Murphy (seen in other Springsteen movies) was not cast in the lead role, since it was perfect for him. TV star Tony Young was clearly too lightweight for the role.

Kid Rodelo was written in 1966 and it's obvious that the film's Spanish producers bought the rights before the ink was dry on the galleys. Directed by Richard Carlson in his second crack at filming L'Amour, the film's shoddiness and lack of production mounting, as well as its intention to cater to adolescents, was typical of the low standards typified by the Euro-western. It also indicated that Hollywood's interest in mounting a major film based on L'Amour was clearly a thing of the past. Two years before the making of *Kid Rodelo*, United Artists had filmed Marvin H. Albert's *Apache Rising* as *Duel at Diablo* with James Garner and Sidney Poitier, and Fox filmed Clair Huffaker's *Rio Conchos* with Richard Boone (still playing two years later in double-bill houses). In the 1960s, Albert and Huffaker would now be regarded as Hollywood's premiere sagebrush authors, leaving L'Amour and his supermen heroes far behind.

Kid Rodelo starred American actors plainly on the decline. Don Murray, no longer a star as he had been at Fox, was Kid Rodelo; Broderick Crawford, an alcoholic actor squandering the years since his 1949 Best Actor Oscar, was the villain; Janet Leigh, an actress whose days as a leading lady were clearly behind her, was plainly overage as a L'Amour ingenue. And when there is a shortage of English-speaking actors in a foreign film, the director might just cast himself, which is exactly what happened. Carlson, another alcoholic thespian, is also far away from his glory days in Universal sci-fis of the 1950s.

The film's premise, that of another disparate group of individuals looking for riches and menaced by the Apaches at an Indian waterhole, seems like a poor man's *Last Stand at Papago Wells*, which was clichéd to begin with. Opposite the "spaghetti westerns" starring Clint Eastwood and Lee Van Cleef, this European shoot-'em-up was clearly cheap claptrap, a horrible decline in prestige for L'Amour since the days of the Duke producing and starring in *Hondo*.

Not that the author was doing badly. In his 30 years as a top selling author, L'Amour would see 250 million copies of his novels in print, and translated in 20 languages. Not bad for a man who had once cleaned up after elephants.

Though L'Amour would profit from the use of his character for the *Hondo* TV series, the world of film beckoned again, and unfortunately it was again the world of low budget European co-productions. Once again, foreign investors backed a film version of L'Amour. This time the book was *Shalako*, another L'Amour chronicle of a superman gunslinger coming to the aid of helpless and morally inferior easterners. This time they are Europeans, since the European locale they are filming in is supposed to be the west — get it?

With no fewer than 36 European investors and partnerships backing *Shalako*, director Edward Dmytryk claimed that his film would be "a different western." Compared to *True Grit* and *The Wild Bunch*, his film was different, though not in the way he had envisioned. Due to a strike in Mexico, the film's shooting location was moved to the desert outside Almeria in southern Spain. Almeria was the usual shooting location for spaghetti westerns and in some cases, war films; in fact, *Play Dirty* with Michael Caine was shooting within flaming arrow distance.

Western authors are usually on the conservative side of the political spectrum, so one wonders what L'Amour must have thought of the leftist

...And God created shooting women. Brigitte Bardot uses her Winchester to fire at critics of her performance in *Shalako*. Caught between the polemics of Edward Dmytryk and Louis L'Amour, this British western convulsed audiences all over the world. (Jerry Ohlinger's Movie Material World, New York City.)

sensibilities of *Shalako*. As directed by ex–Communist Dmytryk (one of the Hollywood Ten), the film plainly rips European imperialism and racial superiority. However, Native Americans don't come off any better in this film either, looking like drooling, homicidal psychopaths and crazed butchers, gleefully maiming the Europeans and murdering their helpless women. Indeed, out of all the film versions of L'Amour, this Euro-western was the most violent, and the most inflammatory.

To completely understand the aims (or misfires) of this film, one must go into the Dmytryk oeuvre. As an up-and-coming "B" director in the early forties, Dmytryk's output was mostly negligible. However, as World War II raged on, the director concentrated on films which attacked fascism. These films would be distinguished by their refusal to attack our enemies on terms of race or nationality, but rather by political affiliation. A good example of this would be *Behind the Rising Sun*, a film set in pre-war Japan which showed the rise of Japanese militarism through the eyes of one Japanese family. (Unfortunately, all the Japanese characters are played by Caucasian actors in laughable makeup.) Postwar, Dmytryk used the genre of film noir to attack a supposedly contented America, showing crime and corruption behind respectable pillars of society.

Then, in 1947, the director made *Crossfire*, a film which attacked anti–Semitism. It was universally praised as an important work (that is, until the release of *Gentleman's Agreement*), and Dmytryk was finally noticed as an emerging talent. Then, not long after making *The Sniper*, a film which attacked our society's treatment of serial killers, the HUAC came knocking. After serving a few months in a minimum security prison for being a member of the Communist Party, the director shortened his jail term by naming names to the Committee.

Perhaps as a consequence, the director was now given top-notch film assignments directing stars like Bogart, Tracy, Gable and Elizabeth Taylor. Like Elia Kazan, another ex–Communist whose act of "naming names" brought him renewed offers of work, Dmytryk was now doing major films like *The Caine Mutiny*, *The Young Lions*, and *Raintree County*. Still calling himself a liberal (though his former comrades might have used other names), his films continued to attack the darker aspects of capitalist society, though in varying degrees, depending on the film. In *Raintree County*, the target is the aristocracy in the old South, and to a lesser extent, racism; in *The Young Lions*, it is anti–Semitism again, as well as fascism; in *Broken Lance*, a wealthy cattle baron is seen as a feudal despot, with range wars seen as ruthless capitalist competition; in *The Carpetbaggers*, a millionaire is portrayed as a dysfunctional, unfeeling sociopath, with money seen as the root of his neurosis. In most of his films, no matter where they're set, there is usually a well-dressed representative of the bourgeoisie who has opened the door for totalitarian oppression. Perhaps there is no better example of this than in a scene towards the end of *The Young Lions*. The town's pompous mayor (John Banner, himself a German Jew who fought in the U.S. Army during the war) tells the American colonel (Arthur Franz) whose forces liberated Auschwitz *not* to have the camp's surviving rabbi read a prayer for those still dying because it would upset the Germans who allowed the atrocities to happen.

In the 1960s, however, perhaps as a delayed backlash to his informing on his former friends, Dmytryk's Hollywood film offers were getting less and less important. Though they were still major films with top stars, the actors performing in them were declining, with their best work clearly behind them (Gregory Peck, Bette Davis, Robert Mitchum, Alan Ladd). Given nothing but clichéd war films and bad soap operas, Dmytryk was now forced to turn towards Europe as the decade came to a close. Which brings us back to that schlock classic, *Shalako*.

The film stars Sean Connery ("Bond in buckskin!" the ads raved). Having the Scottish-accented Connery out west was tantamount to starring Charles Nelson Reilly as James Bond. Why Connery accepted this part, complete with toupee, mystified Dmytryk at first; that is, until he found out that the star was getting $1,000,000 of a reported $5,000,000 budget, and a percentage of the profits. Some sources say that the former James Bond got $1,200,000 plus 30 percent of the profits. Whichever figure it was, the money enabled Connery to invest in a little winter villa in Spain.

However, Spanish villa or no, Connery was horribly miscast. A fading American star would certainly have been far more appropriate; for instance, Rod Cameron, his career declining in the U.S., was making westerns in Germany, Spain and Yugoslavia. The part of Shalako, with its implied arrogance (in the novel, it is more than implied!), the character's knowledge of the desert and Apache culture, perfectly fit Cameron's screen persona from the 1940s on. Though Cameron might have been considered too old for leading lady Brigitte Bardot, her pasty makeup certainly erased all traces of the sex kitten of only ten years before who had become a sensation in Roger Vadim's ... *And God Created Woman*. Buried in Euro-pancake, the erratic Bardot appears far older than she was.

For this film, Bardot's salary was reportedly $350,000 and a cut of the profits. After a hefty delay, the aging sex kitten finally appeared on the set in Almeria in a white Rolls-Royce, though by no means did she arrive alone. Bringing along her chauffeur, hairdresser, makeup artist and a small platoon of still photographers, the wrinkled ingenue did not impress Sean Connery. "She's all girl," said the man who was Bond, *James* Bond, "but only on the outside." Ironically, Bardot's Gallic snobbery would fit in perfectly in a story ripping European colonialism.

Early in the film, a mountain lion is surrounded by a group of cowboys and European aristocrats banging tin plates at him and obviously driving the beast crazy. After this outrage, the Countess Irina (Bardot) raises her rifle and kills the lion. These would-be colonialists are having their sport, and little do they realize that by the end of the film *they* will be in that trapped animal's position.

At the beginning of the novel, Shalako Carlin is riding through the desert on a horse with no name listening to nothing more disturbing than the desert wind. As he rides, the author describes to us the sheer magnificence of this man. He begins sentences with "the man named Shalako" several times, as if trying to push us into a state of awe at the sheer perfection of this obviously superior being. The first few pages also contain sentences telling us what "most western men" would do in certain situations out in the desert. The plot is another recycling of a familiar L'Amour theme, basically that of the superior man joining a bunch of non-westerners (Easterners, Europeans, settlers, lost members of a wagon train, etc.) and using his physical strength and skill with a gun to protect these helpless sheep. Despite this L'Amour cliché, however, the book is well-written, giving the reader a vivid picture of a punishing, merciless land. What it also gives us is a full-blooded portrait of a nasty, arrogant man at the center of it all who we're supposed to root for as the hero.

In the book, Shalako is not only forced to stay and fight for these hapless schlemiels, but he must also be on his guard for Tats-ah-das-ay-go, the hulking Apache warrior also known as Quick Killer. Obviously this man is not known for his people skills.

In the film, Quick Killer is himself disposed of in the plot, and Connery is not given a real formidable opponent anywhere in the film nearly as deadly. His fight with Woody Strode's Chata at the end is boring and anticlimactic. The omission of this powerful villain in the narrative also deletes Shalako's bloody hand-to-hand battle with Quick Killer near the edge of a cliff at the book's climax. Especially poignant is Shalako's Apache cry to Quick Killer when the psychopath goes over the edge: "Warrior! Brother!" However, L'Amour quickly avoids the horrible implication: If Quick Killer is a homicidal maniac and our hero Shalako feels a kinship with him, what does that say about L'Amour's Western Man?

Before the credits roll, we are treated to some lines on screen presumably written by Louis L'Amour from Hollywood, telling us about all the Europeans who came to the American west. However, these lines, written as an explanation for why there are so many European characters in the film (and probably why there are so many European *actors* in the film), only shows us that L'Amour's idea of Europeans out west was certainly at odds with that of leftist director Dmytryk. To the former Communist, the Europeans are interfering colonialist clods. To L'Amour, they're clods, but they're still human beings who can change for the better.

As the film begins, Shalako Carlin is huddled in the shadow of a hill, coming out of a presumably restful sleep. Then he awakens his horse (who is lying down next to him), mounts and rides off over the hills as the credits roll up on screen and we hear the laughable title song; it is called (What else?) "Shalako." The singers croon the title song, extolling Shalako's manly virtues, including the attraction that women naturally have for the toupee-wearing scout. After a couple of minutes of this little ditty, it becomes obvious that the lyrics are far more suited to James Bond than Shalako; with Connery playing him, the European backers of the film no doubt hoped audiences would make the connection.

As our desert superman rides the hills, he hears gunshots. He quickly rides to the rescue of the Countess Irina, a European noblewoman whose stringy hair is bleached too blonde and who wears far too much makeup and lipstick to resemble a human being any more. Brigitte Bardot couldn't act, and her stiff line readings, buried in a guttural French accent, only emphasize the fact that Connery is given a leading lady far beneath him. To further emphasize the Bond connection, one wonders why the producers didn't cast Honor Blackman as Irina instead of as the snotty Lady Julia Baggett.

After Shalako kills two Apaches and rescues Irina, Shalako "frees" her guide, a cowboy sent out to ride with her. Unfortunately, the poor man is naked and tied up in such a way that the slightest movement will send the sharp point of a lance through him, which is exactly what happens, Dmytryk lovingly coming in for a closeup of the bloody lance. Again, this action does not endear us to the Indians. As for Dmytryk, this makes one wonder about the self-confessed liberal's sincerity.

After this scene, Shalako and Irina ride back to the camp of Baron von Hallstatt (Peter Van Eyck). Being that these are "cultured" Europeans, the Baron is having his own wine and cheese party where everyone is dressed to the nines in tuxedos, boiled shirts and flowing evening gowns. This aristocratic crew is populated by neurotic, money-hungry imperialists the likes of which are *not* in L'Amour's novel. Even their names are changed — slightly.

Lady Irina Carnevan becomes Bardot's Countess Irina Lazaar; Sir Charles Daggett becomes Charles Baggett (Jack Hawkins); the bitchy Edna Baggett of the novel becomes the bitchy Lady Julia Daggett (Honor Blackman); Julia Paige and Laura Davis, daughter of a U.S. senator, disappear. The French nobleman Count Henri becomes a British-accented American politician, Henry Clarke (Alexander Knox). Also bodily thrown into the film to emphasize the bigotry of the Senator, is the character of Elena, his Latina wife (well played by the underrated and very Anglo-Saxon actress Valerie French).

On the American side is Don "Red" Barry as Shalako's sidekick Buffalo Harris. Long past his heyday as a "B" western star for Republic, Barry does well here, though his having a pronounced red feather sticking out of his Stetson is a tempting target and far too dangerous for a seasoned old Apache fighter to wear. In the next ten years, he continued to appear in shoddy films; in 1980, the former western star, now dying of cancer, shot himself in the head.

Shalako warns the Baron's party that this is not a simple junket in the country and that the Indians mean business. The Baron ignores Shalako, who then decides to ride for help. With great timing, after Shalako leaves, the Apaches attack. Dmytryk was never the classiest director. Even during the years of the Production Code, when the amount of violent content in films was restricted, Dmytryk's scenes of violence were always crude (such as the bayoneting of a Chinese baby in the director's wartime *Behind the Rising Sun*).

After 1966, with the death of the Production Code's ban on showing extreme screen violence, Dmytryk's full tastelessness came to the fore. During the big Apache attack, flesh is ripped open with abandon; flaming arrows bury themselves in bared chests; no man gets shot without giving a bloodcurdling scream as well.

Inevitably, the evil Bosko Fulton and his men steal the horses, a stagecoach and other supplies from the Europeans. Ultimately going on the list of stolen property is Julia herself. The selfish, materialistic woman is glad to leave her aging husband and gleefully goes with Fulton.

We already know that Julia is shallow since she can't stand blood. When men are dying and she is forced to be in their proximity, they amazingly reach out in their death throes and try to manhandle her, causing her to shriek as she is pelted with gallons of stage blood. This happens no less than twice in the film; once when someone pulls an arrow out of a man's chest and again when a man is shot in the head and falls on top of her in a runaway stagecoach. However, instead of demonstrating Julia's weak character, these laughable scenes show Dmytryk's traditional crudeness as a filmmaker, as well as an undercurrent of sexism.

Shalako returns and helps the Continentals as they fend for themselves in the desert. Later, when Bosko Fulton scouts the perimeter, Apaches attack the stagecoach containing Julia. Bosko's cutthroats are slaughtered in appropriately bloody fashion, and Julia is humiliated before meeting her horrible death.

L'Amour's villainous Rio Hackett has disappeared for the film, but we still have the evil Bosko Fulton. Certainly Stephen Boyd makes the character far more attractive than the antagonistic psychopath L'Amour created. (Offscreen, Boyd would get into bitter arguments with his ex-fiancée Bardot, sometimes holding up an already unhappy production.) However, in the book, when Fulton threatens the Baron and subsequently Shalako threatens Fulton, the violence of L'Amour's hero is clearly on the same level as the bad guy's and one can hardly tell the difference between the two. When the same scene is played out in the film, the screenwriters water down the violence of Shalako's threats, and instead the scout accepts Fulton's help, knowing that the surrounded party will need the extra gun. The Shalako of the film shows a wisdom that is more due to Ian Fleming's Bond rather than the quick-tempered Neanderthals written by L'Amour. (Connery, usually a good judge of scripts and what would work for him, might have helped "clean up" the character before shooting.)

The Europeans are a truly dysfunctional lot. Sir Daggett would be thrown in debtors' prison if he returned to England, and it is evident that Julia married the older man for his money. Julia also hungers for the handsome but evil Bosko Fulton as L'Amour never would have allowed in the book. Senator Clarke has lost an election, it is inferred, because of his marriage to a Latin-American (thereby demonstrating American racism, you see). The Apaches are routinely referred to as savages with much more vehemence in the film than in the novel. The Baron's marriage to Irina is arranged; neither one loves the other, and it is obvious a marriage of fortunes is the real goal.

With the possible exception of the arranged marriage (and even this isn't dwelled upon), it's obvious that the film's characters owe more to Dmytryk's leftist leanings than L'Amour's Nietzchean survivalism. However, even as Dmytryk hits American racism and European colonialism, his portrait of American Indians is far worse than in any "reactionary" film. Woody Strode's Chata is articulate, but his words are threats and bitter hatred directed towards Shalako; it is never explained why the warrior hates him so much. The Apaches are portrayed as bloodthirsty savages, more than justifying the Europeans' racist assessment of them. When they grab Julia and manhandle her, the audience is justifiably outraged. However, in Dmytryk's leftist view, Julia is a materialistic bitch who fully deserves her horrible death. (A hulking Apache stuffs her jewelry down her throat — in Dmytryk's view, literally forcing her to choke on her materialism.) This scene caused one critic at the press screening to quip, "Breakfast at Tiffany's?"

After the various bloody killings, the stage is set for Shalako's *mano-a-mano* with Chato. Any one of Connery's screen fights as 007 make this set-to look like the boring cliché it was; certainly the film needed Quick Killer badly. Besides the casting of the actress who played Pussy Galore opposite the actor who played Bond, there is another in-joke: As the party is besieged on the mountain ridges by the Apaches, someone offers wine, with the grizzled Shalako expressing his hope that the wine is chilled. (At least, the director didn't have him say "shaken, not stirred.")

At the end, after much killing, Shalako bests Chatta in hand-to-hand battle, with the warrior's father begging the scout to spare his son. Amazingly, instead of wiping the Europeans out, the warriors allow the group to leave in peace and even bring them some horses! Even L'Amour would find this unbelievable. In the book, Shalako mentions how Indians would always murder a smaller, weaker group of opponents, and take their property without the slightest hint of guilt. Having the movie Indians aspiring to a European's (alleged) idea of fair play makes no sense, and totally repudiates L'Amour's vision of them as no-nonsense fighters.

If the director and his international backers wanted to make a statement against fascism in the west, they could have easily concentrated on the most fascist-like character in the book, namely Shalako. His views are, of course, Nietzschean. He's also European-educated, as are most of L'Amour's heroes. Though this kind of background is unusual for a real-life Indian scout, it makes sense when one realizes that *L'Amour* had traveled to Europe as a young man, and cherished the things he learned there.

Shalako, however, has contempt for all non-westerners who have never lived the hard life he has. Though articulate, he is a violent man, and holds violent views. Besides his (and Buffalo Harris') sexism, he expresses the "fact" that Indian women would love to have thieves and warriors (or, it is inferred, murderers) as husbands, and that the entire culture lives for stealing and fighting (killing). "In The World According to Shalako," Indians torture helpless human beings to test their endurance and for fun, and he expresses the view that a man should have more than one woman in his home; this last comment makes a mockery of Luke Short's respect for women in his own novels.

In L'Amour's books, it seems that sex is not as arousing to a man as his sheer love of his own abilities to survive. This philosophy is blatantly brought home to us on the cover of Bantam Books' 1980 printing of *The Strong Shall Live*. Not only is the title alone a chilling reminder of Nazi racial doctrine, but the cover of this volume of short stories shows a buckskin-clad man astride his mount, the barrel of a rifle unusually thrust upwards between his legs.

With Connery (no slouch at expressing sexist sentiments himself) playing the hero, Dmytryk removes the scout's hang-ups with the opposite sex that the character has in the novel. (Coincidentally, sexism was also a major character trait of James Bond.) Still, casting Connery as the hero gave Shalako an implied arrogance without the character's vanity-laced speeches from the book.

After the film's 1969 release, audiences the world over, including yours truly as a gangling youth of 13, laughed uproariously at Edward Dmytryk's "different western." Critics, most of whom were doubled over with the same tears of laughter, were equally contemptuous. *The London Times* wondered whether the filmmakers knew "just how funny it all was," while the *International Herald Tribune* dubbed the film "embarrassingly bad." In his autobiography, Dmytryk speaks of his decision to make the film as being hoisted on his own petard; however, the director drew the line at quoting the critical responses, some of the worst he'd ever received in an already declining career.

Next on the list was MGM's medium-budgeted film version of L'Amour's 1963 novel *Catlow* shot in 1971. The studio basically ignored the description of the title character in the novel and cast Yul Brynner as L'Amour's lovable Irish outlaw. Brynner is dressed all in black, exactly like he was in *The Magnificent Seven*, the first film that showed that Brynner could appear in westerns despite his incongruous accent. (Was there ever a western with Yul Brynner when he *wasn't* dressed in black?)

The talented Richard Crenna is the marshal hot on his trail. Certainly the film gives both characters a humorous bent that was clearly beyond L'Amour's abilities, and their tit-for-tat one-upsmanship adds to the film's atmosphere of (sometimes) harmless fun. Ultimately Crenna is allowed to get the girl, and the wily but charming Catlow is allowed to get away (as he does in the book), but the woman Catlow ends up with in the novel is removed from the film. Also gone from the film is the marshal's grim seriousness and his various showdowns with the real bad guys, particularly a well-written stalk-and-shootout in the woods.

The film was successful, its freewheeling humor and bawdiness a refreshing tonic to L'Amour's dead-serious tomes about western supermen. Unfortunately, at the film's climax, this humorous tone is abruptly jolted when one of Catlow's men gets an arrow in the throat, reminding one rather uncomfortably of *Shalako*.

Certainly *Catlow*, the novel, has another fault which is typical of L'Amour, and that is the inconsistency of some of his characters. At certain points, decent men become bad and bad men suddenly become good without any rhyme or reason. This sudden shift in a character's standing is less due to L'Amour's attempt to show ambiguity than a lazy author's forgetting what he had written about a certain character a mere few pages before. The author had always claimed that he rarely corrected his work, and it seems evident that he didn't bother going back on certain pages to check where his own characters stood. It is just one of the reasons why film versions of his books are better than the books themselves, with a studio editor making the appropriate corrections that the author didn't.

In 1973, it was back to Europe again for another film version of L'Amour, *Un Hombre Llamado Noon*, based on *A Man Called Noon*. In this Euro-production, directed by Peter Collinson, two actors made their second foray into L'Amour country: Richard Crenna and Stephen Boyd.

Crenna portrays Rubal Noon, a gunman with amnesia. The film begins like the book; someone has tried to kill Noon as he escapes from his hotel room and the confused man hops a freight out of town under cover of darkness. In the film, Collinson gives us stylish camera angles and swish-pans, the director obviously relishing an arty, fancy-pants European approach. In the beginning, as Noon straps on his hardware before his hotel room mirror, an assassin aims a rifle from across the rooftops. The director pans back and forth between Noon, the assassin and a hungry dog scavenging by a garbage can. Of course, just as the gunman is pulling the trigger, the dog overturns a can and causes the seasoned hit man to jump, spoiling his aim. Creased in the head by the bullet, Noon crashes through his window and unrealistically survives the fall.

After hopping a freight, he meets Rimes (Stephen Boyd), a tough hombre who could be either Noon's ally or his enemy. Later, he meets Fan Davidge (Euro star Rosanna Schiaffino), a rancher who is a virtual prisoner of the bad guys. As in the book, Noon takes a protective interest in the supposedly helpless damsel.

In both book and film, Rubal Noon slowly regains his memory. It turns out that the master gunfighter was once a famous hunter. When his wife and children are murdered by outlaws, the embittered survivalist devotes himself to hunting another species of animal. Now renowned as a famous gunman, Noon has set up a refuge in the hills, complete with escape elevator and books (with a library consisting of, we presume, L'Amour's favorite writers).

Chased by the villainous Judge Niland (Farley Granger in a sad decline from his days with Goldwyn), the villainess Peg Cullane (Patty Shepard, frequent co-star of Spanish horror auteur Paul Naschy) and their easily disposable henchmen, our three heroes, Noon, Rimes and Fan, hold up in Noon's ubermensch Fortress of Solitude.

Gradually the villains are killed off by our intrepid trio, including Noon himself sending a huge, obviously rubber boulder down on a screaming Judge Niland (Granger looking quite ridiculous). With Noon occupied, a wounded Rimes is forced to face off with the villainess. However, the sidekick will not shoot at a woman, even one as badly dressed in black as Peg.

"You won't shoot at a woman!" the evil tart cheerfully crows.

However, Fan declares that *she* has no reservations about shooting a woman, and in record time blows away the screaming villainess. In the book, Fan doesn't kill her, though she does shoot off a couple of Peg's fingers.

Now with his memory returned, our heroic hunter fakes Noon's death with a phony gravesite and walks off with his new sweetie Fan, and followed by the ubiquitous Rimes.

This film was the last (to date) theatrical film version of L'Amour's work. From the late 1970s on, L'Amour's books would become movies-for-television, then ultimately become highly rated cable movies. The films made specifically for the Turner cable stations by the talented Tom Selleck would be a factor in renewing the popularity of L'Amour's work in Hollywood. Obviously an admirer of the author, Selleck made films that captured the best of L'Amour and wisely removed the more obnoxious elements of the author's work. As played by Selleck, L'Amour's heroes completely lost their arrogance and superiority; they were strong, but now also understanding, even compassionate.

These heroes were tough and proud, but not too proud that they wouldn't accept a woman's help in a pinch. Aware of the changing times and the need for a more balanced view of a woman's role in society, L'Amour tried to show spunky women in his books by the 1970s. Unfortunately, these efforts seemed insincere. Though the heroine of *The Quick and the Dead* is allowed to brandish a shotgun at the villains and the heroine in *Shadow Riders* stabs a would-be rapist with a pointed stick, these samples of empowerment pale in comparison to the heroics of the male protagonists, the ones who are primarily responsible for ending the villains' outlawry.

L'Amour's books are still in print and still sell, though certainly not with the fervor of his sales from the 1950s to the '70s. With westerns themselves rarely being filmed (and there are times publishers seem to take their cues from Hollywood rather than the reading public), coupled with the trend towards political correctness, L'Amour's Aryan Supermen have become as dead as the concept of a woman's place in the home and Separate But Equal.

Though he never credited it as an inspiration, it's possible that the author may have been in awe of at least one famous western character created by Jack Schaeffer in 1949, *Shane*. This character might have been a model for some of L'Amour's heroes. Yet for all of L'Amour's Flints, Conaghers, Fallons, Kilrones, Kilrennys, Kilroes, Radigans, Sitkas, Shalakos, Chanceys, Brionnes, Tuckers, Landos and other one-word titled tributes to strong, perfect, superior men, in western literature there would only be one Shane.

Schaeffer's perfect, almost mythic gunman captured the reader's imagination. He won every fight, drew and shot his gun accurately, rode a magnificent horse, moved with grace, was handsome, attracted the farmer's wife, was worshipped by the little boy narrating the tale and was basically a perfect man, obviously endowed with Olympian gifts by the gods. Yet Schaeffer's perfect hero had one glaring difference from L'Amour's protagonists, and that is the fact that Shane never tried to dominate anyone, or arrogantly bend someone to his will.

Shane also didn't give long-winded speeches on the way people *should* be. In an early L'Amour novel, the badly written and episodic *To Tame the West*, if we were not told by the youthful hero what a peace-loving gunslinger he was (the young man tells his story in first-person), we would easily assume he was merely a bully.

There were times L'Amour could be boring and repetitive (*The Rider of Lost Creek, The Last Fast Draw, The Sacketts*), his plots used over and over again, his characters inconsistent and even cartoonish, but at his best he could weave a compelling narrative. Being a well-traveled man, he conjured up environments whose climates he described vividly (the frozen wasteland in *Heller with a Gun*, the scorching desert of *Kid Rodelo*, to name one of the many scorching deserts he'd set his characters in). His supermen protagonists were sometimes a bitter pill; when his heroes were just ordinary men who never picked up a gun (who, unfortunately, became expert killers by the end of the books), the author gave us far more likable heroes (*North to the Rails, The Man from Skiberdeen*).

Ultimately, Louis L'Amour gave us heroes, regardless of their lack of charm, who went through adventures that pleased the world.

Considering that the author had over 250 million books in print and had his work printed and read in over 20 languages, L'Amour became the King of the Western novel. Even one of his superior heroes might actually be impressed.

6

Marvin H. Albert and Violence in the West

If there was ever a western novelist who matched Frank Gruber's prolific output, not only in westerns, but in all genres, it is Marvin H. Albert. The major difference between the two writers is that Albert was truly talented, a rarity in an author who, as the phrase went, just "cranked 'em out."

Louis L'Amour wrote stories that were set in burning deserts and icy wastelands. However, if his west was cruel, Marvin Albert's west was nightmarish. In my opinion, there's never been a western author whose works were so relentlessly violent, and whose characters felt so much pain, from without and within.

Albert's depictions of the west as an endless landscape of pain and terror are something far removed from Haycox's granduer and Short's romanticism. Whether Fawcett (Albert's main publisher) was far more open to depictions of violence and gore is unknown; what is certain is that Albert had far too many books in him to be known by just one name. He was also Al Conroy, a writer whose works were a bit less violent than his doppelganger, the prolific Mr. Albert. He was also known as Mike Barone, Ian MacAlister, J.D. Christilain, Nick Quarry and Anthony Rome.

As one can surmise by the last two names, they belong to private eyes created by the prolific Mr. Albert. Tony Rome would be the most famous of all of Albert's creations. Portrayed by none other than Frank Sinatra in two major films for Twentieth Century–Fox, the houseboat-dwelling, tough private dick seemed to cap a successful decade for the author. Indeed, it was hard to be in America in the 1960s and not come in contact with some book or film that was authored by Marv Albert.

He authored thrillers and westerns, did screenplays and novelizations; brought the private detective out the film noir, war-ravaged world of the 1940s and put him, sometimes uncomfortably, in the more violent, TV-saturated, Vietnam era; gave us pulp westerns whose racial conflicts between white man and red seem to mirror the social conflicts of urban America; he would continue giving us genre works in his adopted nation of France almost up to his death in 1996.

Despite the violence of his novels and films, the versatile writer occasionally departed from his usual path and gave us works whose innocuousness stands unequaled in American literature. How else can one explain a work like *That Jane from Maine*?

In the western world of Marvin Albert, the author gleefully rejected the old cliché of the capitalist seeking to become, by violence and treachery, the Boss of the Valley. Though these were mostly paperback westerns, Albert threw in topics of racial violence and society's hypocrisy. He brought us tales of misguided heroes and charismatic villains who mirrored the hero's buried darker side. Eschewing the old plot of the evil cattleman seeking to gobble up everyone's ranch, Albert's tales spoke of pursuits, sometimes useless ones, in which his heroes had to conquer not only the villains, but the violence within themselves.

Albert was already a seasoned writer of stories and magazine articles when he gave us his first western to be filmed: *The Law and Jake Wade*, written in 1956. Two years later, it was brought to the screen by no less a studio than MGM, "which had more stars than there were in…" yada yada yada.

In the novel, Jake Wade is a lawman in the thriving community of Coldstream — a well-respected marshal who is friendly with all the townspeople and is even engaged to the storekeeper's daughter, the beautiful Lorna Short. Lorna fairly detests all outlaws and criminals and is happy to be engaged to her upstanding, tin star–wearing fiancé. But as in most good stories with dysfunctional characters, the Truth Will Out.

The first thing outed is that fact that this upstanding lawman had once worked the other side of the street. At the beginning of the novel, 40-something outlaw Ben Swift is being held in the Bannertown jail, about to be hanged for murder. The night before the hanging, a masked man breaks into the marshal's office and forces the lawman to release Swift. After escaping into the hills and eluding the usual tenacious posse, Jake removes his mask and it is revealed that he and this hardened killer once knew each other. Jake gives Swift the use of his spare horse to make a getaway and then proposes that they go their separate ways. Swift refuses because only Jake knows the whereabouts of the bank money stolen a year ago by the two men and their former gang.

In the novel, Ben Swift is a charismatic outlaw, an expert tracker, a

6. Marvin H. Albert and Violence in the West

Fit to be tied. Richard Widmark, Patricia Owens and Robert Taylor (left to right) in a tense production still from Marvin H. Albert's *The Law and Jake Wade*. The MGM film toned down Albert's traditional violence and replaced it with an enjoyably witty performance by Widmark. (Jerry Ohlinger's Movie Material World, New York City.)

good shot, a particularly dirty fighter and a very vindictive man. Not only won't Ben forget about that hidden bank money, but he still harbors bitterness towards Jake, his former pupil in outlawry, and his "betrayal" of the gang. Apparently Jake had broken Ben out of jail because he and the gang had saved Wade from being lynched after the bank robbery. However, it never once occurs to this lawman that he is now letting a murderer loose on society. Only his commitment to a twisted kind of morality seem to matter. The lawman believes rather naively that if he saves Ben's life, the outlaw will take up non-violence and forget all about that beautiful bank money.

Swift effortlessly tracks Jake back to Coldstream and kidnaps both Jake and Lorna, forcing the ex-felon to lead them to the bank money. During this wacky journey through hell, Lorna discovers her fiancé's criminal past and looks on him with disgust. Jake himself is put through the ringer as he is tied up and beaten, all the while going through anguish that these merry psychopaths, particularly Ben, were once his friends.

As ever, the self-loathing Jake eventually gains the upper hand. Unfortunately, instead of blowing away this bastard for all time, Jake gives Ben yet *another* chance, escaping with Lorna to the nearest town and waiting for Ben to catch up with him so they can have it out. He even leaves Ben's horse where he can find it!

MGM's film doesn't improve on the book, except in its casting of Ben Swift. Though Robert Taylor is the nominal star as an overaged Jake Wade (in the book, Jake is in his late twenties), the film is neatly stolen by Richard Widmark as charismatic badman Clint Hollister (inexplicably changed from Ben Swift). In a 1958 edition of the novel that ties in with the movie, both stars are quoted as praising the MGM film.

As in the book, Wade breaks Swift (Hollister) out of jail. Hollister trails Jake to Coldstream. He and Lorna (now called Peggy) are taken prisoner and forced to embark on a journey to get that hidden money. Peggy is played by the lovely Patricia Owens, the actress already making a rather dubious name for herself as the leading lady in the cult horror hit of the same year, *The Fly*. Though her role was bigger in *The Fly* opposite her sugar-devouring co-star, Owens acquits herself well as the beleaguered heroine.

The outlaw gang is certainly a sight to behold. Robert Middleton was already making a name for himself in westerns of the 1950s, usually cast as villains. Here, the tall, balding actor plays the novel's Latino badman Otero (here called Ortero) with a mixture of toughness and principle, the character still feeling a grudging friendship for the imprisoned marshal.

Eddie Firestone plays Burke and DeForest Kelley, an actor also familiar to fans of westerns (he's outstanding as Richard Widmark's pal in *Warlock*) is Wexler. Henry Groves, the young punk from the book becomes the dangerous (and far less naïve) Rennie, is played by Henry Silva, an actor capable of oozing almost as much charisma as Widmark.

Throughout the film, the gang takes the imprisoned pair through mountains and valleys until finally the Apaches appear. In the novel, the journey takes so long one is almost under the impression Wade buried the bank money in the Urals. Unlike the lonely clearing that the Indians storm in the book, the film places the Apache ambush in a ghost town. Predictably, the outlaws and the Apaches pick each other off until just Jake, Peggy, Ortero and Hollister are left.

When they finally get to the Bank Money Burial Ground, Jake pulls a hidden gun, cold in the ground for a full year, out of the saddlebag and points it at Hollister. Giving the killer yet another chance, Jake and Hollister stalk each other around the ghost town until the moment of the Big Gundown.

Richard Widmark gives an excellent performance as the wily Hollister. In the novel, Ben Swift is the perfect outlaw — highly intelligent in the ways of surviving the wild, as well as in dominating an enemy. Swift is an accurate marksman, a cruel opponent in a fight and a man whose psychopathic tendencies don't lessen his personal charisma. In other words, a charming but evil bastard, an outlaw whose natural talent and leadership skills are good enough to beguile a young Jake Wade into following him on any path. As in many an Albert western, the hero must break with this evil half and reassert his better nature — or go down with him when the Law comes calling.

In the book, if the reader actually thought there might be some hope for Ben Swift, that hope is dashed after Swift's enraged beating of Lorna, an act that will cause a break with the sympathetic Otero. The beating is not included in the film, nor is Swift's knockdown, drag-out fight with Jake, a set-to complete with much choking, ribs-kicking and eye-gouging. Eventually Albert would transfer this same violence to his private eye melodramas.

The film was successful, and one wonders why it took six years before the next Marvin Albert western was filmed. Perhaps this is because the author was too busy to find the time to sell the film rights to any more of his books. Though this is an exaggeration, the fact that Albert *was* busy isn't too far off the mark. In the late 1950s, Albert wrote *Apache Rising, Renegade Posse, The Reformed Gun, Bounty Killer, Party Girl, That Jane from Maine, Pillow Talk* and even found the time to squeeze in a novelization of the hit TV series *The Untouchables*.

A recurring theme in many of Albert's westerns is the story of the upstanding lawman character forced to deal with an outlaw who used to be his friend, this conflict forcing the goodie-goodie hero to confront his darker half buried within him. This theme, utilized to its fullest potential in the Anthony Mann films *Bend of the River* and *Man of the West*, was well-handled by Albert. In novels like *The Law and Jake Wade, Renegade Posse* and *The Bounty Killer,* the figure of law and order is usually a tough, no-nonsense officer with more than a little pretentiousness. Usually these heroes have absolutely no charm and very little personality except for their stubborn devotion to seeing the villain behind bars. In other words, Albert's heroes were squares.

In Albert's westerns, the villains are usually charming and charismatic. They smile a lot, especially when compared with the usually grim, humorless hero. They charm the women, most of them anyway, and it is inferred that had things worked out differently, the heroine would have ended up with the villain. (*The Bounty Killer* is a good example.).

Years later, in the fall of 1963, Universal cameras were filming in the mountains outside St. George, Utah. The sometimes grueling on-location shoot was for Audie Murphy's latest western, *Bullet for a Badman*, based on Albert's 1958 novel *Renegade Posse*.

Once again, Albert gives us an interesting doppelganger story, a hero and villain who were the best of friends; one has gone over to the side of the law, the other is a good man who became a dangerous outlaw. Throughout Albert's narrative, it's apparent that the two men share many qualities; both are decent men who possess a talent for violence; both love the same woman; the outlaw had a son by this woman and he's later adopted by the lawman; and of course it is inferred that either protagonist could easily have switched places with the other with no discernable difference.

Sam Ward is a notorious outlaw who has escaped prison and quickly organized his equally notorious gang. Though his ambitions supposedly go no farther than robbing the town bank, there seems to be an ulterior motive to Ward's visit to this alien territory.

Logan Kelliher is a former ranger, now a farmer. Years before, Logan and Sam had been rangers. When Logan was wounded in a shootout, he was cared for at Sam's house by his wife Susan. Then, inevitably, Sam turned bad, and was sent up the river for murder. Meanwhile, with a baby on the way, Susan fell in love with the man she was nursing, Logan. Albert is careful to point out that she and Sam have been divorced, though one gets the impression that in those free-wheeling days of the old west, folks didn't always make their splits official on a piece of paper. Now Logan is seen as a father to Ward's little boy (also named Sam).

In the novel and film, Ward sends henchman Ira Snow to scope out the town and find his wife and son. When Snow drifts in and reports to Sam that he's located them, Sam vows to kill Logan for "stealing his wife and son," and then decides to steal them himself—that is, after the bank job.

Logan has gone everywhere for a loan to pay off Owens, the book's arrogant Boss of the Valley. Finally, before you can say Debt Consolidation, storekeeper George Tucker, just to spite Owens, lends Logan the money.

In the Universal film, retitled *Bullet for a Badman* (at least in this country), the plot is about the same, with the exception of cutting down the character of Owens. Director R. G. Springsteen was a former Republic "B" western director. By the 1960s, he was directing Audie Murphy films at Universal and then A.C. Lyles' westerns at Paramount. No one was ever going to nominate Springsteen for an Oscar and he knew it. Universal's budget was pathetic, but R.G. did what he could, giving us a cliché-ridden but interesting moral tale. Like Jake Wade, Logan Kelleher is forced to confront his past, and finally bring closure to those little details that have haunted him throughout the years. Gordon Kay, Springsteen's producer at Republic, was reunited with his favorite helmsman at Universal.

As the film begins, Logan Kelleher (Audie Murphy) is married to Susan (Beverly Owen, just before joining the cast of *The Munsters* at Universal). They also have a little boy named Sammy. After borrowing the money from George Tucker (Edward C. Platt, just before being cast as the Chief on *Get Smart*) and then paying off the note, Logan runs into Jimson Diggs at Owens' saloon. In the book, Diggs is a "short, scrawny, hard-bitten ex-buffalo hunter" who is now a barfly; in the film, he is a tall, beefy, ex-buffalo hunter who seems to be surrounded by flies. He is played by former Warner Brothers contract player George Tobias, later Mr. Cravets on *Bewitched*.

Logan is about to leave the saloon, but he is braced by Bayard Owens' arrogant son Jeff (Berkeley Harris) and his shadow, dandified gunfighter Pink Gladden (Skip Homeier, Audie's nemesis in *Showdown* from the same year). The relationship between Jeff and Gladden seem to be that of two men with the same interests: being bullies. However, their buddy-buddy relationship, with Jeff mimicking the older gunfighter and Gladden backing Jeff on every play, seems to imply something more between them than just being saddle pals. After all, it couldn't have been easy being a gunfighter named Pink.

Also introduced in this Grand Hotel-like saloon is Aaron Leach (Alan Hale, Jr.). As one can tell from his last name, he is not a person with sterling values. Most people forgot that Hale portrayed big, hulking brutes beating the daylights out of Robert Taylor in the actor's MGM films of the fifties. However, pre–*Gilligan*, Hale also seemed to excel at playing the big, lovable, not-too-bright sidekick, as he did so well in Warners' *The Man Behind the Gun* and the Audie Murphy version of *Destry*. In *Bullet for a*

Murphy's Law. Hero Audie Murphy in a relaxed mood between shots of *Bullet for a Badman*. Universal cut back on both Albert's violence and the budget for this film version of *Renegade Posse*. (Jerry Ohlinger's Movie Material World, New York City.)

Badman, Hale is back to being a brute; that is, until he went on that "three-hour tour" almost immediately after his scenes were out of the way. While shooting was still in progress, he supposedly flew from Utah to Hollywood for the *Gilligan's Island* audition. This might explain why Aaron Leach doesn't appear as often as he should in the film.

6. Marvin H. Albert and Violence in the West   141

Meanwhile, somewhere out on the trail, Sam Ward (Darren McGavin) has received word of the location of his wife and son by Ira Snow (Murphy friend and a frequent player in Audie's westerns, Mort Mills). Then Sam does something in the film he doesn't do in the book: shoot a kidnapped bank teller in the back. We presume this is to show Ward's violent behavior, though Albert's narrative didn't need this gratuitous killing to show us Ward's viciousness.

Once again, the screenplay is written by the Willinghams, Mary and William. In this film, their clichés not only make themselves at home but, like some annoying party guest, refuse to leave. Unfortunately, it is the Willinghams' atrocious screenplays which were mostly responsible for Murphy's swift career decline in the '60s.

Ward, Snow and company head for Fort Griffin's bank. Of course, once they are inside the bank their cover is blown and the usual shootout commences, including Logan getting off a shot that wounds Sam. In the book, the shootout is exciting; in the film, we yawn. Springsteen is obviously forced to cut his costs, and during this so-called desperate battle, we hardly see the surrounding town. It seems that all the bandits' horses make their getaway around one lonely corner, when in reality the robbers would have scattered in all directions. Predictably, the outlaws are shot down one by one, including Ira Snow. As Snow melts away, he is able to pass the saddlebags of money over to Sam before the latter rides away with Logan's bullet in his side.

Once on the trail, Logan meets (ta-da!) the Renegade Posse. With the exception of George Tucker, the posse clearly consists of the Fort Griffin's worst citizens; Jimson Diggs, Aaron Leach and Jeff Owens and his "other half," Pink Gladden. Not revealing that he knew Ward personally, Kelliher reluctantly joins this band of doomed misfits to track down his former friend.

The wounded Sam comes upon the cabin of Ira Snow's wife Lottie (the lovely Ruta Lee). Basically an unsentimental tart, the widow Snow has no time to cry snowflakes over her dead hubby, and soon she proposes to go off with Ward to Mexico with the money. This charming idyll is rudely interrupted by Logan, who enters the cabin and captures Ward at gunpoint. It is the first time the two have seen each other in years and the accusations are hot and heavy.

Seeing *exactly* who the posse members are, Sam decides to set them all against Logan. (In *The Bounty Killer*, Albert's charming outlaw Burt Farradin tries to do the same thing against law-sanctioned bounty hunter Luke Chilson.) When everyone (except Logan and Tucker) vote to knock off Sam and take the money, this interlude is rudely interrupted by the Apaches. The Indians then chase the happy group to a box canyon.

Soon both Indians and whites are being picked off, including George Tucker. In the book, Albert looks like he is setting up a premise where a reformed Lottie will help Logan down the line and then, BANG, an Apache puts a rifle slug in her skull. Perhaps more than any western novelist, Marvin Albert had Murphy's Law working 24/7.

Soon, the Apaches are chased off. Now the moment you've been waiting for: The two old friends reunite to fight the posse, both men still showing teamwork. In record time, Jeff, Leach and Diggs are killed off and Gladden escapes.

Missing from the movie is the book's sequence where Logan is able to return Sam to Fort Griffin, and the subsequent showdown between Logan and Owens' men. Predictably, the Universal film goes the cheap route. The wounded Sam is instead brought back to the Logan farm (removing the need for the Fort Griffin set). He meets his son there and, as in the book, both Logan and Susan are worried that Ward will spill the beans about the boy's lineage.*

When Pink Gladden, who's been trailing the pair, shows up at Logan's spread and attempts to kill him, a wounded Sam throws himself in the bullet's path. Logan then guns down Gladden. Afterwards, Sam dies in his old friend's arms, and Springsteen's camera pulls back to show Kelliher reunited with his family.

Murphy is good in the role, though a better director could have given him more to do than just, in Murphy's own words, "Shoot straight and look somber." But Springsteen was, after all, a competent craftsman, not a auteur like Mann, Boetticher or Selander. Released in September 1964, the film did well, but was clearly double-bill fodder. Though still profitable in places like Europe and Japan, in America the "B" western field dominated by Murphy was starting to dry up. In Murphy's heyday of the early 1950s, the budgets of his westerns were around half a million dollars; this would be the same budget that producer Gordon Kay would give the actor's films of the early '60s. Though this might sound frugal, in the eyes of Hollywood, it meant that an Audie Murphy film was no longer a product saleable enough to spend a decent budget on.

Throughout the years, Darren McGavin has received a great deal of praise for his role in this film; opposite Audie's colorless good-guy, there

---

*Ironically, this same situation was enacted in the screen version of Les Savage, Jr.'s Return to Warbow. In Savage's novel, the hero is fighting bad guys who have framed his father for murder; in the screenplay, the author changed the storyline to the point where the father-and-son plot was totally twisted around. In the film, a charismatic outlaw (played by Phil Carey) is the father of a little boy whose mom is now married to the hero. Columbia released Return to Warbow on January 27, 1958; later that year Renegade Posse was published. Interesting coincidence, isn't it?

is a perception that McGavin has "stolen the film." Not so. Audie still beats Darren in the western accent department; McGavin is clearly too contemporary and too Hollywood to convincingly play a western character. (See his performance as a cavalryman in *The Great Sioux Massacre*.) He is also one of the few clean-shaven outlaws in the west; for that matter, his gang has spent some time in the barber shop as well.

As written by Albert, the character of Sam Ward is a piece of work. Like Ben Swift, Ward can do anything. He is highly intelligent, yet also highly dangerous. Ward is handy with both gun and knife, can ride a horse like a master, and is clever enough to work head games on everyone around him. Even when he's tied up, posse members are warned to stay away from him, as if he had the bite of a rattlesnake. In *The Law and Jake Wade*, the situation is reversed; it is the lawman who is tied up, with Swift warning Henry not to go near him if he knows what's good for him.

Meanwhile, Walter Mirisch produced for United Artists the film version of Albert's 1957 novel *Apache Rising*. Directed by Ralph Nelson as *Duel at Diablo* (1966), the sprawling film is the best-produced film version of a Marvin Albert western. James Garner, having shot to overnight fame in Warners' hit TV series *Maverick* in the late 1950s, would turn down all western scripts for the next seven years until this one came along. Speaking to a reporter from the *Hollywood Citizen-News*, Garner explained, "Truth is, I've been looking for a good western for a long time. This is a good one and when it came along, I decided it was time." This is a compliment to both Albert and director Nelson, whom Garner also praised.

The result, predictably loyal to the novel since Albert did the first draft of the screenplay catches some of the book's gory violence, as well as Albert's well-trod terrain of misery and suffering in the old west. The rights to the novel were originally owned by producers Stuart W, Cramer and Michel Grilikhes, who eventually sold the rights to Nelson-Engel Productions and Cherokee Productions (James Garner's company) for $75,000. Albert's screenplay was "rewritten" by Grilikhes; I put rewritten in quotation marks since the screenplay is basically the novel in script form, with the possible exception of building up Sidney Poitier's part. Raymond Strait, author of the book *James Garner* seems to believe that Albert was not "a polished screenwriter." If that was the case (and Albert certainly developed into a Hollywood screenwriter pretty fast), Grilikhes must have merely added suggested camera set-ups (also doubtful since Ralph Nelson hardly needed a screenwriter's help with camera angles). The upshot of all this seems to be that, since Albert did most of the work, ex-producer Grilikhes just decided to give himself a co-screenwriting credit.

All not so quiet on the western front. Sidney Poitier, James Garner and troopers (in background) await an Apache attack in *Duel at Diablo*. Predictably, Albert's screenplay retained the novel's angst. (Larry Edmunds Bookshop, Inc., Hollywood, California.)

The novel and film begin the same way. Army scout Jeff Remsberg (James Garner) is riding the barren, burning deserts of Apache territory when he spots lovely, red-headed Ellen Graff. (Her name is changed to Grange and she's apparently turned blonde for the film.) She's also played by Swedish actress Bibi Andersson, giving us just enough Stockholm in her accent to thoroughly convince us she's from the west.

Also spotting the thirsty Swede are a pair of Apache warriors. Jeff blows them away and rescues Ellen, who, in her delirium, speaks to him in Apache. It seems that Ellen had been kidnapped not long ago and forced to have a child with Nachee, the son of Chata, the Apache chief. The little boy is still in the warrior's camp and she's been trying to return to him.

Remsberg takes the poor woman back to her less than grateful husband, Willard Grange (who was once Millard Graff in the book), who runs a freight line. Though Willard is a hypocrite and a racist, at times we can't help but like him because he is played by Dennis Weaver, an actor far better suited to playing nice guys rather than villains. Knowing of her intimacy with Nachee, Willard would have preferred his wife either die or never come back. In Willard's eyes, being married to an ex-squaw would be bad for business.

In Albert's book, racism rears its ugly head with impunity, as the author points out the hypocrisy in a white-run west where morality is based on hatred. Of course, the Apaches are also racist in their treatment of the captured white woman. When she returns to the tribe, the squaws treat her like dirt, and the warriors give her contempt, mixed with leers. Though written in the mid–1950s, the story was more suited to the 1960s, when issues of race made their way to the headlines. To the moviegoing audience, *Duel at Diablo* became very topical.

Two mavericks. Sidney Poitier and James Garner confer in Albert's *Duel at Diablo*. Released in 1966, the film struck a chord with audiences who saw the Apache wars depicted onscreen as a euphemism for the racial turmoil of the 1960s.

A further reason for the film's concern with racial issues would be brought up in its casting. Given second billing after Garner was America's first black superstar, Sidney Poitier. In the novel, Remsberg almost has a gunfight with Tolliver, a principled gambler. Tolliver is basically a supporting role; he will help the cavalry fight off the Apaches later in the book, but dies anyway.

As Tolliver, Poitier is as an unusually dandified horse-breaker who is dressed in a fancy suit and wears a cool Stetson. He is also allowed to yell at the white lieutenant, Scotty McAllister (more unusual casting, the British-accented Bill Travers). White characters didn't usually get yelled at by black ones in films of the 1960s, unless of course they were played by Sidney Poitier. When asked about his role, Poitier said, "In the film, I'm a guy, not a Negro." (Perhaps this is a comment on the unbelievably noble roles he was called upon to play, portraying victims of racism who persevered rather than fought back. Case in point, his turn-the-other-cheek doctor in *No Way Out*.) Nevertheless, with Poitier bringing dignity to the role of Tolliver, we almost forget the bad performance of Bibi Andersson as Ellen.

Early in the film, Scotty hands Jeff a little pouch which contains the scalp of his dead Indian wife. Told that the town's trigger-happy marshal won it in a card game, Jeff resolves to visit the marshal and find out who killed her — and even the score.

After this, Remsberg arrives at the stable just in time to rescue Ellen from three drunken louts. Their fight is far more violent in the book, but Albert still manages to lovingly transfer a good bit of eye-gouging into his screenplay.

The troops are ready to move out to stop Chata and his merry band from killing everyone in the southwest and Jeff is enlisted to join them, temporarily postponing his plans for bloody retribution. Joining them for a free escort with his freight wagon is Willard, who, as an afterthought, mentions to Remsberg that his wife has gone back to the Apaches.

Hearing this, Jeff splits from the detail and tracks Ellen to Chata's camp. With little trouble, the ex–Maverick swoops in and grabs both Ellen and her baby, throwing them both on a second horse. With Apache squaws cursing in the background, the three escape.

They arrive just as Scotty's command is decimated down to a handful of troopers, and outsiders like Tolliver and Willard. The freight man is less than pleased to see his wife-in-name-only, this time accompanied by a little one. With everyone short of water, supplies and temper, the situation is desperate. Under covering fire by troopers, Jeff sneaks out of the canyon to get help.

Much of Albert's genre work deals with suffering — real physical suffering — before things get better. Never has the author been more effective in describing the physical torture of a man out on a burning desert than in *Apache Rising*. The reader actually feels the pain in Jeff's parched throat and his not being able to swallow. We also share his feelings of helplessness as he sees his thirsty horse stagger to his death.

In record time, Jeff blows away three warriors who had been trailing him and grabs their water and a horse and rides for the fort.

After informing the colonel of the siege, Jeff accosts Clay Dean (veteran bad guy John Crawford), the town's trigger-happy, crooked marshal. When Dean refuses to say where he got the scalp, Jeff stomps his trigger finger, forcing Dean to admit that it was *Willard* he got the scalp from.

Finally the cavalry arrives and quickly arrests Chata and his chattel, but not before the Apaches torture Willard to the point of shooting himself. Jeff and Ellen, who have fallen in love, can now live a new life with their little baby.

Garner is excellent, surprising those who thought he could only do comedy-westerns. He wisely underplays, his performance more powerful because of it. The entire film, like the novel, is grim; an aura of pain and torment hovering over the endless desert the characters travel through. Much of this is reflected in Garner's acting; unlike Bret Maverick, there are no smarmy wisecracks from this poor soul.

Poitier is his usual unflappable self, giving the 1960s a rare portrait of a black man always in control of the situation. Weaver's is the third good performance, giving us not so much an obvious villain, as a portrait of callousness. There is one scene, however, where even he can be tender to Ellen's baby, Weaver giving his character more depth than is usually the case with "B" western rapist-racist-murderers.

The sour note is Andersson, giving a performance that only emphasizes the glacial expressions and cardboard acting of the Ingmar Bergman style of filmmaking. Even during the attempted rape scene, her screams of terror seem unconvincing, as if she fully expected Garner to come and rescue her. It's not as if Hollywood didn't have starlets with western film experience that could have done this role much better. What was wrong with Diane Baker, Judi Meredith, Ruta Lee or Linda Lawson?

The film was a critical and box office success. Even *The New York Times*, never a connoisseur of sagebrush sagas, recommended it. Robert Alden (apparently Bosley Crowther couldn't lower himself to see a western) praised Garner's performance. While acknowledging that the film is "raw and ugly" and that Jeff Remsburg "suffers agonies," the critic also writes a passage about Garner's character that could be a coda for all the western heroes created by Marvin H. Albert. Alden emphasizes the character's "tiredness with the pointless struggle [that] is evident in every line of his weather-beaten face." When considering Albert's works, it comes as no surprise that phrases like "agony" and "pointless struggle" appear. It seemed only natural that France, a nation that gave us Albert Camus and Jean-Paul Sartre, would embrace Albert as a great artist, the kind of praise sorely lacking from Albert's own countrymen.

Then in 1966, your typical Spanish-Italian co-production spaghetti western outfit came along and bought the rights to Albert's *The Bounty Killer*. The novel deals with bounty hunter Luke Chilson and his pursuit of psychopath Burt Farradin and his equally psychotic gang.

In the film, Albert's usual plot of a charismatic psychopath being pursued by a humorless lawman is taken for a ride. Instead of two similar personalities battling each other within the roles society has given them, we have an indictment of the society that gave them those roles.

Luke Chilson becomes Luke Chiltern and Burt Farradin suddenly turns Latino and is called Jose Sanchez. Now instead of the mirror-images of lawman and killer, the likable psychopath himself is a split personality. The townsfolk love Jose Sanchez, even as he kills them.

A further reason for Sanchez's acts of violence is a typical motive of European leftist filmmakers: American racism and the chasm between America's rich and poor. Nevertheless, putting a social-political spin on the villain's motives sounds more than a little spiteful. Leftist spaghetti western filmmakers freely used the genre to attack America (where these films are set), despite the fact that they were cynically aiming their films at the American marketplace. Anybody for a Lenin T-shirt?

The film is known as *A Price for a Man*, *The Bounty Killer* (the filmmakers' cynical attempt to have audiences confuse their film with the more popular "B" with Dan Duryea and Rod Cameron) and finally *The Ugly Ones*(!). Under any title, the film is trash.

In 1967, Universal returned to Marvin Country and filmed *The Man in Black* as *Rough Night in Jericho*. Written under Albert's alias Al Conroy, the novel features one of the author's patented series of trouble-shooting men of action. But unlike Tony Rome or Nick Quarry, the character of Clayburn was situated in the old west.

A former town tamer for the Remsberg Detective Agency (an in-joke), Clayburn was a gambler who played the odds and percentages. Fond of a buck and a good woman, though not necessarily in that order, Clayburn was also a tough fighter. His fistic encounters with hulking henchmen were usually the most violent, gory part of the novels. The gambler-troubleshooter also kept a sharpened knife up his sleeve and was able to throw it with deadly accuracy. Despite his cynical edge, he is still the hero and will, of course, end up doing the right thing.

The novel was published in 1965 and in less than two years, Universal commenced shooting the film. Perhaps the studio noticed the profits from *Duel at Diablo* and thought they could duplicate its success. Wisely, they hired Arnold Laven as the director. Laven was a co-producer–director–writer on many a "B" western of the 1960s, and on TV co-created *The Rifleman* (which Sam Peckinpah tried to steal credit for).

The novel begins with a stagecoach driven by ex-detectives Greco and Clayburn innocently rumbling across the prairie. Suddenly, a sharpshooter and killer named Alex Flood fires his rifle at the coach, riddling it. Back in the ironically named town of Glory Hole, the shot-up coach is returned to Mrs. Velma Lang, a lovely widow who's just started a new stage line.

It seems that Glory Hole is under the huge, pudgy thumb of Wheelock, a Boss of the Valley, second grade. We are introduced to this prairie fascist when he lynches a scared storekeeper for the accidental killing of one of his men. During the attempted lynching, Wheelock stares down the weak young deputy marshal, Jace Harcourt, before breaking into the cell. Harcourt, wracked with guilt, tries to drink himself to death.

Wheelock and his merry men (including Alex Flood) are the police — and the criminals too. Their efficient operation consists of taking money from every merchant in town — or else. It's a western version of the protection racket.

Chief among the gang's opponents is the pretty Mrs. Lang. To protect his investment, Clayburn is forced to side with the beguiling widow, despite his obvious reluctance.

At the end of the novel, Clayburn tracks Flood to another mountain range where, as in the beginning of the novel, the two gunslingers stalk each other for seemingly countless pages.

This cyclical course of the plot is also shown in the death of Wheelock. Out of fear, Jace backs down when he is about to kill the town boss with a double-barreled shotgun. Towards the end, the now-courageous lawman blows Wheelock away with the exact same type of gun, as he should have done at the beginning.

In the film, Clayburn becomes Dolan and is played by Universal's handsome leading man George Peppard. In a radical casting decision, the studio cast Dean Martin, then a box office winner with his Matt Helm spy comedies and the star of his own free-wheeling comedy-variety series, as the villain. Perhaps this was Martin's attempt to expand his acting range. He would play another bad guy the next year in Fox's *Bandolero*, though a sympathetic one. Here, the comedian-singer is cast as Alex Flood, who has now been promoted to town boss, yet still retaining his position as assassin.

Flood shoots up the stage at the beginning and wounds the Greco character, now rechistened Bill Hickman (John McIntire). After returning the stagecoach, they meet Mrs. (now called Molly) Lang, and played with glaring British accent by Jean Simmons.

Since Marvin Albert is co-writing the screenplay, the theme of hero and villain sharing character traits is brought to the fore. Martin and Peppard are allowed to bond and recognize each other as kindred spirits as Clayburn and Flood never do in the book, despite sharing similar stalking techniques.

In the film, Flood owns the town, especially the saloon with the ubiquitous name of Pleasure Palace (Aren't they *all* called Pleasure Palace?).

There are scenes in the saloon with the two men drinking and gambling together which Albert didn't have in the novel. It's evident that these antagonists both like and respect one another. At one point, Dolan yells out a warning to Flood when a cowboy pulls a gun on him. The response is another bloody Albert fistfight, with Flood gratuitously slamming the poor man's head into the wooden bar several times.

When Flood threatens Dolan with hanging, the lines are delivered by Martin in an almost *friendly* way. Flood is a violent man, but he has no heart for killing Dolan. Coincidentally, Dolan wants to destroy Flood's empire, but not the man. Both men are also ex-lawmen, further establishing the two as mirror images of each other.

This connection doesn't prevent the unwelcome visit of henchman Yarbrough (an unusually nasty Slim Pickens) to Lang's coach yard. This time, though, the violence factor is ratcheted up several notches by Albert and Laven. After Dolan is whipped several times by Yarbrough, the two men grapple and we see the usual hair-pulling and eye-gouging before the battle's more violent conclusion: Yarbrough is brained with a singletree. Clayburn doesn't kill Yarbrough that early on in the book, and certainly not in such a gruesome fashion. Perhaps Pickens was needed on another set.

Soon Dolan, Hickman and Jace grab several of Flood's men off the street and lock them in jail, "cutting down the opposition." It also cuts out the excellent back alley shootout in the book. Nevertheless, the result is the same. Without his boys in town terrorizing the populace, Flood and his remaining men ride right into a trap. A full two years before *The Wild Bunch*, this climactic battle is unusually gory (though not for Marv Albert). In the late '60s, most American westerns were still being filmed as expanded TV programs, with violence that would be acceptable to an audience watching NBC's *Saturday Night at the Movies*. However, as far as this picture is concerned, the title, *Rough Night in Jericho* (which sounds better than *Rough Night in Glory Hole*) was clearly an understatement.

At the end, after Flood guns down Bill Hickman, Dolan gives chase. Stalking each other in the hills, Flood wounds the gambler, but Dolan returns the favor by throwing his knife into Flood's chest. Unlike the Flood of the novel, since the role is played by Dino, the personable crooner is allowed to deliver a final witty bon mot to his old pal Dolan and then give a charming smile before croaking.

The two leads would continue working for Universal Studios in the immediate future, with radically different results. Martin would go on to star in the box office smash *Airport*, with the singer's percentage deal with the studio netting him millions in profit. Peppard would star with Mary

Everybody doesn't love somebody sometime. Jean Simmons getting belted by an uncharacteristically brutal Dean Martin in *Rough Night in Jericho*, the film version of one of Albert's Clayburn novels. (Jerry Ohlinger's Movie Material World, New York City.)

Tyler Moore in *What's So Bad About Feeling Good?*, about a toucan which makes people feel happy.

Twentieth Century–Fox would feature Albert's Tony Rome character in two films. Therefore, the author went from working with Dino to working with another member of the Rat Pack, Frank Sinatra. After several TV projects (including bringing Nick Quarry to the small screen) and writing the sceenplay for his mobster novel *The Don Is Dead*, the author moved to France in the early 1980s.

There he created more crack private eyes for the French pulp market. Forgotten by his fellow countrymen, but beloved by the French intelligentsia, Albert died in Menton at the age of 72 in March 1996.

His private eye novels were filled with the two elements prized highly by admirers of pulps: passion and violence. His westerns still had passion, though most of us basically remember the violence. Albert's heroes usually were decent men smoldering with rage. The fact that they share an unusual bond with brutal villains doesn't make them any less sympathetic. And perhaps it is this refreshing duality in his pulp characters that will be his lasting legacy.

7

Clair Huffaker and Hellraising in the West

There is one other western author in the postwar years who paralleled Marvin Albert's ideas about the west and how the taming of it was affected more by personalities than incidents. Albert gave us honest lawmen with secrets buried within them; occasionally these men would be mirrored by an extroverted outlaw who shared the lawman's violent past, but accepted his antisocial personality without guilt. The dynamic of honest yet colorless lawmen opposite colorful, fun-loving psychopaths would be repeated in the works of Huffaker, but with a difference. Whereas the tone of Albert's westerns were marked by misery and angst, the works of Clair Huffaker were filled with uplifting adventure. Whereas violence was frequently brutal in Albert's books, in Huffaker's novels it was vicarious and thrilling.

In Albert's work, the characters, particularly the lawman hero, try to suppress their tension; in Huffaker's books, the characters are fun-loving extroverts who start fistfights for the hell of it. Of course, there was extreme violence in Huffaker's books, including many deaths. Yet the author did not dwell on bloody details, as did Albert; nor was suspense or an increase in tension a major factor in his books. Instead, one gets the impression that Huffaker wanted the reader to have as much vicarious fun as his characters seemed to be having.

This is not to say that Huffaker didn't get serious. Apaches massacre most of a family early in *The Guns of Rio Conchos*; a colorful gunfighter learns to love and respect decent folks in *Badge for a Gunfighter*; a marshal's best friend is murdered and there is a rape in *Posse from Hell*; after several gruesome murders, there is racial antagonism in *Flaming Lance*; and there is nothing amusing about the greedy protagonists of *Guns of Thunder Mountain*. In Huffaker's books, the hero is allowed to be wild and carefree, unlike Albert's where he is hounded by hidden demons.

Clair Huffaker was born in Magna, Utah, on September 24, 1926. He joined the Navy and served in the South Pacific during World War II. After returning to the States, the young veteran went to college, becoming an honor student at Princeton and then enrolling at New York's Columbia University. After traveling to Europe for more years of study, the young man returned to the States and became a writer for Time, Inc. where his articles would appear in both *Time* and *Life* magazines. As a freelance writer and editor, Huffaker produced over 200 stories and feature articles. Using his background as a native of Utah, he would expand a few of his stories into short western novels.

He was not as prolific as Marvin Albert, but the two men shared a busy writing period where both produced their definitive pulps: In the late 1950s, Huffaker copyrighted seven novels, most of which would be made into films. This, as well as writing for the sagebrush shows *Rawhide, Lawman* and *Bonanza*, made the ex–Navy man one of the busiest scriptwriters in Hollywood. Thanks to three men, the 1960s would be even better.

Those three men were superstars and icons of their time — and continue to be icons today: John Wayne, Elvis Presley and Audie Murphy. They would star in film versions of Clair Huffaker's works, each actor projecting manliness and integrity, each one in his own way having a huge impact on the times. It is interesting to see how each actor's screen persona affected the film versions of the author's works.

Elvis was a cultural icon, affecting art and life as well as music; his starring in a film version of a Huffaker novel, helped Hollywood accept the novelist. Audie was a real-life hero whose screen persona as a western version of the citizen-soldier perfectly fit Huffaker's homage to the fighting men of the west. The Duke was a larger-than-life figure who was already making his impact as an American cultural icon; his influence on the macho aspects of Huffaker's work was considerable, but it stopped short of sexual domination, and instead gave it a welcome dose of humor.

Between Huffaker's two Audie Murphy screenplays was an assignment from Twentieth Century–Fox. In 1960, the studio filmed Huffaker's novel *Flaming Lance* as *Flaming Star* (perhaps due to too many westerns featuring marauding Indians with *Lance* in the title).

As in many of Huffaker's westerns (like Albert's for that matter), a character's name is significant. In *Seven Ways from Sundown,* the villain is an unrestrained hellraiser and killer named Jim Flood; that is, Flood as in a torrent. (Marvin Albert's sharp-shooting killer in *The Man In Black* is named Alex Flood.) In *Posse from Hell*, the hero is named Banner, as in flag, or badge of pride. In *Guns of Rio Conchos*, the hellraising hero is named Riot. The corrupt hero of *Badge for a Gunfighter*, who accepts

7. Clair Huffaker and Hellraising in the West   155

money from the villain before his reformation, is called Cash. And so it is that Elvis' character in *Flaming Star* is named Pacer, clearly meant to symbolize one who measures distance, perhaps across racial lines.

At the beginning of the novel, Clint Burton and his Kiowa half-brother Pacer are working the Burton homestead when they spot the new Kiowa chief, Buffalo Horn, watching them from afar (Rudolfo Acosta, in another of his many appearances in a Clair Huffaker film).

In the film, Pacer (Elvis) and Clint (Steve Forrest) are about to enter their home, which is suspiciously dark and quiet. Suddenly we hear "Surprise!" and a birthday celebration begins. Needless to say, someone prompts Pacer to grab a guitar and sing a real hoedown number the likes of which would have shocked any homesteader.

At this shindig, we meet Sam Burton (John McIntire) and his Kiowa wife Neddy (Dolores Del Rio). Also there is Clint's blonde girlfriend Roslyn (the same first name as the heroine of *Guns of Rio Conchos*), played by Fox contract starlet and future genie Barbara Eden. One of the party guests is Tom Howard (genre veteran L.Q. Jones), oldest son of the Howard family. Since he is played by L.Q. Jones, he's an obnoxious moron who makes racist remarks to Neddy, raising the ire of Pacer in a foreshadowing of tragedy to come.

After this celebration, the Howard family returns to their home, where Kiowas spring from hiding and kill most of the family. Director Don Siegel shocks us by having a warrior suddenly come out of the dark and slam a tomahawk into Tom Howard's skull. Everyone else is the recipient of either flaming arrows in the chest or worse. (Pretty Dorothy Howard is seen screaming briefly before a sweaty brave envelopes her with his body, Siegel letting our imagination fill in the picture.) However, Will Howard (Douglas Dick) escapes through a secret trap door on the property.

When Clint and Pacer approach the Crossing, a little two-building hamlet not far from the Burton home, the reception is not pleasant. After entering the general store for supplies, they are met by an angry Angus Pierce (the eternally young Richard Jaeckel). He tells them of the attack and, while he's at it, calls Pacer dirty Indian names and brandishes a rifle at him. Led by Dred Pierce (Karl Swenson), the entire Crossing is up in arms. After the Kiowa massacre, the first target of their hatred is the tanned, guitar-slinging rockabilly cowpoke before them. Though regretting the massacre, Pacer is also growing militant. He starts to see a growing bigotry coming out into the open after years of phony tolerance by the people of the Crossing.

Back home, the Burtons' dinner is rather rudely interrupted by a visit from Dred Pierce and his ignorant fellow townsfolk. The meeting results in Neddy being insulted and Pacer wounding the miscreant. Later, the Burtons discover, to their horror, that their former friends have slaughtered their cattle out of sheer spite. "This is worse than Indians," declares Clint, apparently forgetting that the Kiowas don't kill cows, but *do* kill helpless people.

Meanwhile, the new Kiowa chief, Buffalo Horn (thus named for his laughable headgear), has been bending Pacer's ear with dreams of Kiowa retribution, and practically begging the rock 'n' roll icon to join him.

Pacer's attitude is changing. First there is the visit by two hardcase cowboys riding by to water their horses. However, when Neddy appears, they figure to refresh more than their horses, with one of them even planting a kiss on the middle-aged Del Rio. (Apparently there seems to be something white cowboys of 1950s westerns find incredibly attractive about Latina actresses playing Native Americans. For more information, look at the career of Katy Jurado.)

When Buffalo Horn appears, Neddy suggests that she and Clint visit the tribe's camp to see if they can Stop the Madness. Clint says he'll think about Buffalo Horn's offer (the charismatic chief promises no harm will come to Pacer or his family), and he and his mom travel back home in their buckboard. Okay, remember Will Howard, the wounded member of the Howard family who escaped by that trap door? *Now* he shows up!

Lying in wait with a gun, Howard kills the buckboard's Kiowa escort and then shoots Neddy. Though Pacer rides over and pistol-whips the man to death, it is too late; Neddy is seriously wounded and needs medical help. But is too late. Neddy has wandered out into the wilderness, looking for the Flaming Star of Death (there had to be a reason for that title).

It is a moving scene, and the person more touched by it than anyone was the star. Presley loved his own mother dearly; refusing to see even his screen mom die, Elvis urged Siegel to delay shooting the scene. In the next scene, angry that townspeople have delayed the doctor's arrival, Pacer pulls a knife on the physician. Watching Elvis in this scene, one senses a very real anger coming from him, as if his own mother had died needlessly.

After Pacer draws a gun on his own brother, Clint bitterly orders him out of the house. Pacer now rides to join up with Buffalo Horn.

Meanwhile, Sam Burton is out hunting up strays when he is attacked by a party of young warriors who apparently didn't get Buffalo Horn's memo about not attacking Pacer's family. Though the old man is riddled with arrows, the feisty veteran riddles all of the braves in return with bullets.

After Clint buries his father, the young man is attacked by Buffalo Horn and his band. When Buffalo Horn rides towards him, Clint blows him away (in the novel, he is shotgunned in the face). However, during the skirmish, Clint is wounded in the leg with a Kiowa lance, though it is not flaming.

Found by Pacer, he is hidden by him and his wound is treated. Now in order to protect his brother, Pacer strips down to his shirt and fights the murderous Kiowa band, turning their own Indian fighting tactics against them. Inevitably, one by one he knocks them off, proving that no one messes with the King.

Pacer ties his wounded brother to a horse and sends it to the Crossing. Later, when Pacer rides in mortally wounded, he tells Clint to live for the future, and that he is going off to find the Flaming Star of Death and die in the hills. When Clint limps after him, he falls and a horse is brought to him by Roslyn as *The End* comes up on the screen over the young couple.

It is a moving finale, though the better ending would have been what Clint and Roslyn do in the novel. Now that his family is dead, Clint fires the house so no one else can use it. Then he and Roslyn ride off, presumably to another town, the young woman never returning to her family and the two of them cutting themselves off from the racists at the Crossing.

Incredibly, this film was originally to star Marlon Brando. However, before the Fat Ham could say yes, Elvis agreed to star. The teaming of the King and crime movie specialist Don Siegel surprised most of Hollywood, with cynics thinking the King would fall flat on his guitar attempting to act. They seemed to have forgotten that Presley gave a good dramatic performance in *Love Me Tender* and an even better one in Michael Curtiz's *King Creole*.

Before shooting could commence on the Fox ranch in Thousand Oaks, California, the King would have to be anointed—in red dye. Elvis would be made darker than his "white" co-star, Steve Forrest, and the King would be given a pair of specially made brown contact lenses costing $500. Eventually, the lenses were not used, but this didn't stop studio interference. Fox wanted Elvis to sing several numbers in the picture, including one from horseback; the suggestion infuriated the singer-actor. In retaliation, Elvis purposely blew his lines, almost leading to the first real blowup between director and star, a relationship that had otherwise been amicable. And amicable was not a word many in Hollywood would have used to describe the usually tempestuous Don Siegel.

According to the director, after the studio decided they wanted Elvis to sing *ten* songs in the film, he held an emergency meeting with Clair Huffaker. Nunnally Johnson wanted nothing more to do with the project, and Huffaker (who Siegel describes as always wearing cowboy attire) agreed to do the rewrite, dropping every song except the title and the surprise party number. In *A Don Siegel Film*, the director's memoirs, Siegel paints himself as the Genius whose decisions have saved many a film, and implies that Huffaker agreed with *him*, although it's extremely doubtful that the author would have stood for ten songs (some sources say eight) in a tragedy about race war. (In his book, Siegel also tells off an incredible number of film executives and top professionals, *always* getting the last word in, and never once getting punched in the nose.)

In a clear case of he-says/she-says, Siegel describes the unfortunate casting of future horror starlet Barbara Steele in the role of Roslyn, eventually played by Barbara Eden. Describing Steele as too tall for Elvis, as well as a person who couldn't act, Siegel insisted that producer David Weisbart replace the British-accented actress. When Steele was finally replaced, Siegel describes his meeting with her as amicable, with Steele herself thanking the director for "being so kind."

In a later interview, Barbara Steele claimed that in a scene immediately after the massacre of her family, the studio wardrobe people had her riding away in crisp new clothes. In an attempt to instill some realism, Steele wiped her outfit in mud and consequently "they went bananas." The actress used terms like "out of control," "furious" and "berserk" to describe the reaction to her attempts to add some realism to the scene. All through the interview, the actress refers to her tormentors at the studio as "they," though it's hard to imagine Don Siegel not being part of that select group. Sharply different from Siegel's version, Steele says she walked off the film and ultimately left Hollywood, even when "they" threatened to blacklist her. As for her thanking Siegel for "being kind," it's evident that the actress herself sees nothing to thank the studio or Don Siegel for.

All concerned did a good job of acting and writing. Huffaker's screenplay, co-written by the very liberal Nunnally Johnson (he did Fox's *The Grapes of Wrath* 20 years before), euphemistically pointed up the horrors of race war years before the riots of Selma and Birmingham. Thanks to Presley's involvement in the project, the picture was a huge hit. Critics and the public loved this new Elvis, and to this day it is considered the film that showed that Presley could act. Unfortunately, in subsequent years, Colonel Tom Parker would systematically dismantle the promising film career of the King by putting him in a string of atrocities that wasted his talents.

Another consideration is the fact that Huffaker's novel has more than a passing resemblance to Alan LeMay's 1954 saga of Kiowa savagery, *The Unforgiven*. Starring Burt Lancaster and Audie Murphy, the film version of that novel was released in April of 1960. *Flaming Star* was released in

The king and his ... genie? Elvis Presley protects Barbara Eden in a posed studio shot for *Flaming Star*. The film is still fondly remembered for giving the King a chance to act. (Larry Edmunds Bookshop, Inc., Hollywood, California.)

December. Therefore, both Huffaker's novel and its film version came later than LeMay's classic.

I won't make any snap conclusions, but the two stories *do* have similarities. Both are set in Texas. Both have families living in the midst of war-mongering Kiowas (the Zacherys in *The Unforgiven*, the Burtons in *Flaming Star*). In *The Unforgiven*, there is a major plot point dealing with someone of Kiowa blood, the daughter, living with a white family. In *Flaming Star*, the one with Kiowa blood is the mother, but the focus is on the half-breed son. In *The Unforgiven*, the revelation of the daughter's Kiowa ancestry is a scandal that draws racist antagonism from other white settlers. In *Flaming Lance*, a Kiowa massacre of a white family draws out the settlers' racism, which they direct at the Burtons' Kiowa son, as well as his mother. In *The Unforgiven*, the family's matriarch is killed and the children must defend themselves against the Kiowas in an apocalyptic battle in which the daughter kills her Indian brother, proving loyalty to her white family. In *Flaming Star*, the Burtons' sons are left alive to battle the Kiowas, during which the Kiowa brother kills the Indians (his tribal brothers) who go after Clint, proving his loyalty to his "adopted" family.

Between the release of these two films, however, was something that might make the public forget these glaring plot and character similarities. In September 1960, Universal released *Seven Ways from Sundown* starring their ace western star, Audie Murphy.

Shot in the spring of 1960 at Universal Studios and in the desert outside Las Vegas, *Seven Ways from Sundown* was a fine character study of a naïve young lawman and a charismatic outlaw. The words "character study" had almost never been used to describe a film starring Audie Murphy, this prejudice coming from critics belittling the actor's talent. Yet there is no doubt that Murphy more than holds his own opposite stage and screen veteran Barry Sullivan, who gives an excellent performance as the colorful badman.

In Huffaker's novel, a young man named Seven Smith rides into the Devil River camp of the local Texas Rangers. There he meets crusty Sgt. Hennessey and the martinet Lt. Herly. When a young woman named Joy, the daughter of the supply store's proprietor, shows a liking for the young number-monikered ranger, it arouses Herly's jealousy. Hoping not to give Seven a chance to experience Joy, Herly sends the green ranger out on a mission to apprehend outlaw Jim Flood, bringing along Hennessey.

The man they are sent to pursue, Jim Flood, is a yardstick for hell-raising outlaws. A highly intelligent and strangely principled felon, Flood is a murderer and robber, a charismatic fellow who charms the folks he comes in contact with and spreads merriment to the populace with his unrestrained hedonism — that is, when he's not killing them. The pursuit lasts for weeks, and then months as the pair track Flood across mountains and valleys, from Texas, through Mexico, and then into Arizona and New Mexico. After Hennessey is killed and Seven captures Flood, months pass, and lawman and outlaw bond, each man developing a respect for the other.

Through their long trek back (at the end of which Flood will be hanged for murder), the two men team up to keep Flood from the hands of ornery badmen, bounty hunters and marauding Apaches.

Seven finally returns with Flood after being away for the better part of a year. After days of incarceration, however, Flood breaks loose. Shooting up the area around the camp, Flood fires into the darkness and hits Joy, wounding her in the arm.

Later that night, Flood returns to see Seven, but the young man waits for him with a double-barreled shotgun. After telling the outlaw that he thinks "considerable" of him, a tearful Seven opens up on Flood with both barrels.

When the film opens, there is gunfire coming from a saloon. We are introduced to Jim Flood (Barry Sullivan) as he flees the saloon firing his six-shooters. After this, he tosses lanterns into the building, setting it on fire. More gunfire follows. It is an audacious entrance, Flood pointedly being introduced at night, making the arson he perpetrates seem far more destructive.

When daylight comes, the small hamlet is a row of charred buildings. Riding into the village is the green new ranger, Seven Jones (Audie Murphy). Not only has Smith now become Jones, but the angry townsfolk are ready to tar and feather the ranger until he pulls his rifle from his saddleboot. These scenes establish that both men are not to be taken lightly. By the time they meet, the line between good and evil will be blurred even further.

At the ranger camp, Seven meets Hennessey (John McIntire, years after co-starring with Murphy in *World in My Corner*), and the coldblooded Lt. Herly (Kenneth Tobey, who would play the villain opposite Murphy in *40 Guns to Apache Pass*).

An interesting subplot is the death of Seven's older brother, Two Jones. Hired as a ranger, Two is killed in the line of duty by Jim Flood, though the killing wouldn't have taken place had Two not been abandoned by a ranger who didn't give him backup where it counted. Nowhere in the book is it mentioned that Seven has a brother who's a ranger. This is ironic since Seven will unknowingly be escorting his brother's killer to be hanged. (Of course, Flood doesn't tell him.)

At the camp, Seven meets the storekeeper's daughter, Joy Karrington (instead of Harrington, played by Venetia Stevenson). Instantly taking a liking to the handsome young ranger (Murphy was nearing the age of 36 when he played the novice lawman, but still retained a youthful demeanor), Joy visits him when the rest of the rangers are at a dance. The hesitant love between the two is even better in the film, where both Audie and Stevenson bring a charm to their awkward characters. During one scene, when

Joy's back is partially turned, Seven reaches out to her, his hand frozen for a moment until he thinks better of it and forgets the idea.

Out on the trail, Hennessey incessantly trains Seven in using a hog-leg, tossing out rocks and twigs for targets when the ranger least expects it. The two lawmen trail their quarry through the west and they get a good idea just how popular Flood is with folks he takes a liking to. He gave one youngster his folding knife (possibly creating a future sociopath), and left a trail of jilted saloon girls that would enrage Gloria Steinem.

When the lawmen track Flood into snow-capped mountain terrain, Hennessey is shot dead from across the slopes. The sudden death of a major character is as shocking in the film as it is in the book. We thought Hennessey would live throughout the film, teaching the young man what it's like to be a ranger.

But in Clair Huffaker's universe, there's nothing like life itself to teach one about life. At one point in the book, Flood himself derides "book learnin'" as something for "second raters," saying that a first-class man lives

Murphy's Law, part II: Lawman Audie Murphy (left, with gun) captures charismatic outlaw Barry Sullivan in *Seven Ways from Sundown*. Murphy was renowned as one of Texas' most famous sons, but this is the only film in which he protrays a Texas Ranger. (Larry Edmunds Bookshop, Inc., Hollywood, California.)

"hard and fast." (Of course, Huffaker expresses these pearls of wisdom in a book.)

Ironically, after Seven captures Flood, it is the outlaw who opens up a new world of life experiences for the young man. Also thanks to Flood, Seven meets a young saloon gal and loses his virginity, prompting Flood to say "a man without some stallion in him ain't worth a damn…"

After Hennessey's death, Seven continues the chase until he shoots Flood while the outlaw attempts to scale a snowy mountain slope. At first resentful of the man who murdered his friend, Seven is soon taken under the outlaw's spell.

One does wonder, however, why Flood lets the young man actually transport him all the way back for a hanging. The trek takes months in the novel and, except for that one abortive attempt to escape, Flood allows himself to be incarcerated again in the ranger jail. Though Huffaker certainly implies that Flood will eventually escape, an assumption as predictable as the sun rising, it still doesn't explain the outlaw's acquiescence to being Seven's prisoner.

To Herly's astonishment, Seven rides in with his prisoner. Reunited with Joy, Seven tells her how impressed he was by Flood, who is eternally free to do as he pleases. Joy wisely counters that Flood is like the big buzzard who felt free enough to almost devour her pooch earlier in the film, and Seven finally sees her point.

Back at the jail, Flood recognizes Herly as the ranger who let Two Jones die. After killing Herly and escaping his cell, Flood rides hell-bent for leather, waving goodbye to Seven and firing aimlessly at Joy, who is again hit in the arm.

Later that evening, Flood rides back to the house, hoping to run off with the young ranger for a life of murder and mayhem. Here, the book scene is improved upon by screenwriter Huffaker, with irony in practically every line. Helping with this improvement are the performances of Murphy and Sullivan, both actors giving the scene a touching sadness not common in preludes to western shootouts.

Seven tells the outlaw that people can't live the way Flood does—and that he must stop him. The outlaw desperately pleads with him, offering him a Mephistophelean chance to rule the world ("There are things we can do you've never dreamed of!"). Unwittingly, Seven brings up the subject of Two Jones and the man who murdered him, the young ranger not realizing that he's talking to the very same man. Feeling a twinge of guilt, Flood walks away, pushing back his jacket flap so it clears his holster. At that point, Seven warns the outlaw to turn around, calling him Jim for the first time. Flood draws and fires, but the move is purposely clumsy; Seven's isn't. In the novel, Seven is still a bad shot, and is forced to kill Flood with a scattergun; in the film, the boy has become a man, and since Audie is playing him, you know that any shots he fires will be accurate by film's end.

After Flood dies, Seven picks up his fallen cigars and tucks them back into the gunman's shirt pocket. We assume that where Flood is going, he'll have no problem getting a light.

It's an excellent two-character study, and Murphy and Sullivan are nothing short of superb in their roles. The supporting players also do their jobs well, particularly McIntire and Stevenson. (Reportedly the actress was carrying on an affair with Murphy. Whether this is true or not, the chemistry between the two is definitely there.)

When Universal shot *Posse from Hell*, based on Huffaker's 1958 novel, the decline in the budgets of Audie's films began in earnest. All through the early 1960s, in fact, it seemed that the studio was biding its time until the star's seven-year contract was up in 1965. Needless to say, after the star filmed that year's *Gunpoint*, the studio cut him loose, already considering him a hasbeen. Unfortunately, they never once considered him for *Ride to Hangman's Tree* or *Rough Night in Jericho*.

But that was years away. For now, Audie Murphy was top dog in *Posse from Hell*, giving a moving performance as an embittered cowboy out for vengeance. Caught between the cowardice of the townsfolk and a grueling search for four of the west's deadliest psychopaths, the star is at his tight-lipped best, ironically giving us more than a glimpse into the life of a soldier on a combat mission.

In the novel and film, four very sick individuals ride into the incongruously named town of Paradise (Huffaker's ironic names again). After taking over the incredibly named Rosebud Saloon, these four pixies, Crip (Vic Morrow), Leo (Lee Van Cleef), Chunk (Henry Wills) and Hash (Charles Horvath), bully and terrorize everyone in their sight.

Director Herbert Coleman would only helm two films, both with Audie Murphy, but he had years of experience as a producer and assistant director for Paramount. From the first shot of flames rising, which, as the camera pulls back, we see are flames in a streetlamp, to the final uplifting shot of two hurt people leaving a cemetery hand in hand, Coleman's film holds our attention and never lets up.

After Crip and his men enter town and dismount from their horses, Coleman's camera focuses on the rifles in their hands, with particular close-ups on their trigger-fingers. These are audacious opening shots and hook us right away, Coleman and Huffaker obviously treating this film as much more than a low-budget western.

7. Clair Huffaker and Hellraising in the West   165

The town's lawman, Marshal Webb (Ward Ramsey, a year after starring in the studio's monster epic *Dinosaurus!*), takes a routine patrol of the streets, accompanied by his shaggy dog. The lawman suddenly hears a little voice calling out to him just before a shotgun blast cuts him down.

At the Rosebud, Crip returns through the back door with a smoking shotgun. Worried about her drunken Uncle Billy (Royal Dano), Helen Caldwell (Zohra Lampert) runs into the saloon and is promptly taken captive with the rest. When some of the townsfolk enter the Rosebud hoping for a negotiation with these maniacs, Crip takes his next victim, former Republic cowboy star Allan "Rocky" Lane. (After watching so many films of Lane as the perfect hero who triumphs over all villainy, it is still a shock to see him blown away in an instant.)

Among the negotiators are Seymour Kern (an excellent John Saxon in an offbeat role), as well as two other Republic veterans, Walter Reed and Harry Lauter. During this scene, Crip's evil really comes to the fore. When Crip asks Kern if he's married, the bookish banker shakes his head. After finding out that Lauter is a family man, Crip has *him* go to the saloon doors to issue his demands—then blows him away.

During all this madness, and after (presumably) more murders, the Gang of Four are also able to rob the local bank and kidnap Helen. The next morning, Banner Cole (Murphy) rides into Paradise to visit his old friend Marshal Webb. Soon he finds his brother-figure laid out on a saloon table and dying. Banner is an embittered gunfighter cut off from people and their problems, and it seems that Webb is one of his few friends. As the dying lawman begs Cole to believe in people again and learn to like them, he also admits that he told everyone Banner was to be his deputy. Cole is less than pleased with this arrangement. A lone wolf who fights his own battles and never had to rely on others to save him (very much like the real Audie Murphy), Cole has nothing but contempt for the cowardly townsfolk who let the massacre happen.

Now forced to honor his dead friend's wishes, Banner must play at being lawman, but with a definite take-no-prisoners style. When the town's physician tells Cole that handcuffs are in the top drawer of the marshal's desk, the gunman replies, "I don't need any" while brandishing a Winchester.

While forming a posse, Cole, the seasoned gunfighter, bluntly tells those men that volunteered what they'll be facing. When the volunteers quickly take back their offers, Murphy gives the wryest smile, having anticipated that reaction. Also joining the posse is Johnny Caddo (Rudolfo Acosta returning to Huffaker Country). Despite the racist treatment the townsfolk give the Indian, he still wants to join the posse "because it is what a man must do."

Prodded by the bank's president (Ray Teal), who is worried about the stolen bank money, Kern joins the posse. At first, the bookish easterner is repelled by the gun he's forced to wear, but as the film progresses he will be Cole's most loyal posse member.

Soon, the posse find traces of Helen's presence in the woods ("She was treated badly back there," says Johnny Caddo). When the posse finds Helen, Cole prevents her suicide, telling the despondent woman that a gun isn't the answer to her misery.

After Helen is taken away by Uncle Billy, the posse find the killers holed up in a farmhouse and launches an attack. When the gang tries to escape the farmhouse, Cole turns Hash into hash with several well-fired bullets.

Further out on the desert, the posse, now cut down to Kern, Johnny and Cole, scores another victory when Cole is able to kill Leo. And it is here that we finally see a close-up of Lee Van Cleef in his death scene. Writhing in pain and self-pity, the future spaghetti western star makes the most of this scene. It would be one of Van Cleef's last roles before a car accident sidelined him, causing the studios to basically ignore him in the early 1960s. Considered over-aged in a declining genre in the U.S., Van Cleef's career was saved by appearing in Europe opposite Clint Eastwood in one of the films in Sergio Leone's *Dollar* trilogy. Van Cleef became an international western star, appearing in films where he gave us his own particular breed of anti-hero. His screen character was a sharply defined persona appearing in a subgenre where the cliché of western film heroism was taken for a ride.

Back-tracking, Cole and Kern discover that the two killers are waiting in ambush; they are too late to save Johnny from being killed by Crip. Now, according to Leo's dying prediction, the two killers are riding back to Paradise, to tear the town apart and "kill every mother's son of 'em." Here, Huffaker portrays the killers as an apocalyptic evil capable of wiping out the town and killing everyone in sight. This assertion of destructive power on behalf of just two men gives our heroes' pursuit a further urgency.

Our two heroes find Uncle Billy's shack and Cole runs into Helen. Drowning in self-pity, the abused woman is told by Cole that she will have to learn to live with her pain and that the world will not stop for her. This scene is interrupted by Uncle Billy flying in through the door full of buckshot.

As Cole and Kern search for the killers outside, a wounded Chunk finds Helen alone. In one of the film's best moments, the rape victim blows away one of her rapists, and then takes the buckboard back to town.

After Kern is sidelined, Cole and Crip stalk each other in the woods. Even when Cole gets his side full of buckshot, he keeps on coming, finally emptying his pistol into Crip, thus avenging the murders of Webb and Johnny.

Executing a fireman's carry, the wounded gunfighter transports Kern back to Paradise. The film is a celebration of male bonding and the brotherhood of fighting men. Therefore we have one of the film's best lines when townsfolk reach out to examine Kern. Cole, still carrying him, says, "Touch this man and I'll kill ya."

Cole revives much later and is looked after by Helen. She tells him that even though the attitude of the townspeople towards her is bad, she will learn to live with it. Afterwards, Cole is offered the job of town marshal, but faces an uphill battle because of the town's hypocrisy. The doctor explains that Cole and his men have shown up the town for cowards, and that there is a prejudice against fighting men.

Later, Cole and Helen go to the cemetery and he puts flowers on Johnny's grave. Then, walking hand in hand with her, and to the accompaniment of surging music, the two hurt people walk out of the cemetery, looking forward to embracing life. It is one of the most uplifting endings to an Audie Murphy film, and even more touching when one realizes that its life-affirming message is meant for, symbolically, a combat veteran and, literally, a rape victim. These two lost people are, in their own ways, victims of war-related trauma, and must "learn to live with it" (their pain).

Posse from Hell was a search-and-destroy mission transferred to the west. Forced to deal with a town's cowardice and the pain of a friend's death, Murphy's honest portrayal of a disillusioned gunfighter was the emotional center of the film. A war hero who knew first-hand about losing friends in battle and then exacting punishment on an implacable enemy, Murphy gave one of his best performances, with author Huffaker, also a war vet, perfectly tailoring his story to fit his star. Huffaker had said that the roles Audie played in his screenplays, "put [Audie] in a situation where he has to do something bigger than life. So it really kind of fit him in a way."

For instance, in the novel, Banner Cole *is* Marshal Webb's deputy. The film improves upon this by having Cole as a gunfighter whom Webb wanted to make part of society. Webb wanted to crack Cole's hardened shell and get him to like people again. By pushing Cole apart from society, Huffaker presents a man with few family or friendship ties as the only one who can stop the killers who have wrecked the town. Audie, not a lonely man, but an isolated one due to his war experiences, fit this role to a T.

The novel also gives Banner a snotty girlfriend named Pat. For the film, Huffaker fortuitously elevates Helen Caldwell, still a rape victim in the book, to center stage. Indeed, her ending up with Cole is far more satisfying, the denouement emphasizing the union of two hurt souls against the world, and their joint refusal to buckle under.

One must make note of the scenes between Murphy and Zohra Lampert as an exercise in two different acting styles working together to make a fine scene. During shooting, Zohra, a Method actress who liked to improvise her lines, started to ad-lib, thus throwing Audie off. Murphy took Lampert aside and spoke with her. From what one can see in the film, Murphy, the ex–war hero with no theatrical training, was apparently able to form a compromise with her. Whatever he said, it worked. Their scenes together are restrained and natural, with Murphy telling her to get over her ordeal a key scene.

In retrospect, the two films based on Clair Huffaker's stories and screenplays are two of Audie's best films of the 1960s. These two films came at the beginning of the decade and, unfortunately for their star, things would go downhill from there. It wouldn't be a stretch to say that Huffaker was the actor's best scenarist. The western author was able to capture the essence of Murphy's screen persona in two radically different characterizations, and in both cases give us minor classics of the genre, as well as two representative works in the Murphy canon.

Meanwhile, over at Twentieth Century–Fox, another Huffaker screenplay made its way to the light of day. *The Comancheros* was based on the sprawling novel by former Chicago journalist turned novelist Paul I. Wellman. (I love the term "sprawling novel." As if the book were relaxing on a divan.)

It would star the Duke himself, and the screenplay would be written by Huffaker and Wayne's principal screenwriter, James Edward Grant. The film deals with the efforts of a mismatched pair of fighting men to stop gunrunning south of the border; it would not be the last time that Huffaker would use this plot. Unfortunately, by the time of the low-budget European co-production *The Deserter* 11 years later, the idea had become a pathetic cliché.

At the beginning of the film, a duel is in progress. Ladies' man–gambler–adventurer Paul Regret (Stuart Whitman) wins the duel, but unfortunately the dead man was the son of a local politician, and despite the legality of the duel, Regret is charged with murder and sentenced to be hanged. Regret escapes on a riverboat where he meets the beautiful Pilar Graile (the beautiful Ina Balin).

Distracted by his pursuit of the Holy Graile, Regret is truly sorry when he's handcuffed in bed the next morning by the redoubtable Cpt. Jake Cutter (the Duke). This big Texas Ranger is a crack manhunter, and since he is played by John Wayne, he is a stubborn man who refuses any friendship or leniency for the hedonistic Regret.

When Regret pulls a derringer on the lawman, Big Jake slugs him (he had unloaded the weapon beforehand). As in most Huffaker screenplays (and apparently most Grant screenplays), once a punch is thrown between two protagonists, the male-bonding process has begun.

After riding into Comanche country, Regret does escape, and Jake is forced to return to ranger headquarters empty-handed.

Company Major Henry (good friend and frequent Wayne co-star Bruce Cabot) has another mission for Big Jake: He is to stop the flow of repeating guns to the Comanches by white renegades called Comancheros.

Our larger-than-life-hero soon meets the man who is a contact for the repeaters, the horribly named Crow (Lee Marvin, a year before playing Liberty Valance). With a piece of his scalp missing, Crow is a typically ornery Lee Marvin character. In another example of male bonding, according to the dictates of Clair Huffaker and James Edward Grant, Jake and Crow have a drunken fight in the saloon, with the two staggering men then leaving the place arm in arm.

When Jake and Crow become involved in a midnight card game, one of the card players is Paul Regret. The Frenchman recognizes the Ranger, but does not blow his cover. Cutter is winning all the games. As everyone else takes their loss in stride, Crow accuses the Ranger of cheating. When Cutter's back is turned, Crow draws on him, but rather than eat Crow, Jake guns him down. Now that his mission is put on hold by the death of the Comanchero contact man, Jake puts Regret under arrest.

Traveling through Texas countryside, the two visit another of Jake's friends, prairie widow Melinda Marshal (Joan O'Brien). However, it is the woman's daughter who is the real focus of this scene. Not only does she effortlessly steal the scene, but she gives the film its warmest moments, simply because it is real. This little blonde charmer is played by Aissa Wayne, the Duke's baby girl. When Cutter holds her in his arms, Aissa is playing with her father's neckerchief, apparently not caring that a motion picture camera is on her; her smile is quite genuine. As for the star, holding his adorable little girl in his arms, he is smiling from ear to ear; in fact, we've probably never seen the Duke this cheerful on camera.

Traveling back toward Ranger headquarters, the two get a meal at the Scofield place, where Mrs. Scofield is pregnant (her husband is Wayne's former Republic pal, former cowboy hero Bob Steele). Unfortunately before the baby arrives, the Comanches do. It is apparent that the defenders are

Lookin' for Trouble: John Wayne and Stuart Whitman (left to right) work for the Texas Rangers to stop the gunrunning in the film version of Paul I. Wellman's *The Comancheros*. Screenwriter Huffaker would use this plot several times. (Jerry Ohlinger's Movie Material Store, New York City.)

outnumbered by the attacking Indians. Realizing this, Regret quickly takes a powder, grabbing a horse and riding off to parts unknown. Just when it looks like another pogrom will happen, Regret returns with a platoon of Texas Rangers. During the subsequent battle, the Indians flee, and Regret is considered such a hero that the baby is named after him.

With the Rangers vouching for Regret, Circuit Court Judge Thaddeus Breen (Edgar Buchanan) finds that the Frenchman was actually a Texas Ranger at the time of the duel, and therefore couldn't have committed the murder. Now an honorary Ranger, Regret volunteers to accompany Jake into the Comanchero camp with a wagonload of rifles.

The two men are met by the wonderfully named Horseface (Jack Elam) and his gang. After a brief skirmish, the two are soon hung by their wrists in the hot sun. Only through the intervention of Pilar do they escape massive heat stroke.

The leader of the gunrunners is Pilar's father, simply called Graile (and played by Nehemiah Persoff). Incredibly, this evil villain invites the two Rangers to dinner at his mansion. Apparently Graile runs his "community" like a dictator or, more likely, a commissar, with the felon hanging anyone in his domain who commits even a petty crime. This pseudo–Marxist madman is planning, like Huffaker's Col. Perdee in the later *Rio Conchos*, his own empire in the west.

The rangers soon arrive and meet the Comanches and Comancheros head on. Graile is stabbed to death by a relative of one of his victims as they attempt to escape the Marxist paradise. After the villains are disposed of, Regret and Pilar, who are in love, are wished a farewell by Big Jake Cutter, who officially releases the Frenchman of all his obligations.

The film is supposedly directed by Michael Curtiz. However, Curtiz was dying (he would pass away months after the film's premiere), and the talented helmsman would have trouble remembering certain scenes and have a pathetically feeble grasp on the many details of the mammoth production. To avoid a disaster, the film's producer, genre director George Sherman, asked Wayne to direct the film without credit. Having already cut his teeth as a director on the recently completed *The Alamo*, and possessed of a secure enough ego not to care about the credit, Wayne agreed. Though there are many scenes of horses crashing to the ground that recall the battle scenes in Curtiz's *The Charge of the Light Brigade*, the film's tone is more the Duke than the man who allegedly said, "Bring on the empty horses."

The film was shot in Moab Valley, Utah, a favorite location for John Ford, thus emphasizing Wayne's contribution in the director's chair. The characters are likable, the humor is relatively amusing, the action fast without the usual Michael Curtiz flourishes— all hallmarks of a typical Wayne film. In fact, Huffaker's script fits the style and screen character of John Wayne so well, the star would remember the screenwriter's work and hire him years later for two films at Universal.

On the downside is Stuart Whitman's attempt at playing a Frenchman. The actor's French accent comes and goes, and is not good even when it's there. Truly, the cause of some Regret.

In 1964, Fox filmed a Huffaker novel from the 1950s, *Guns of Rio Conchos* as *Rio Conchos*. Despite the title change, the film version would retain the main plot of gun-smuggling.

In the novel, hellraising cowpoke Riot Holiday and a fellow outlaw are tracked by eight Comanche warriors. After the death of the second man, the marauders chase Riot across the prairie, even shooting an arrow into his chest. Barely escaping with his life (while taking the lives of several of his pursuers), Riot is treated by the decent McAllister family. Unfortunately, Comanches attack their cabin and slaughter the entire family except for their daughter, Roslyn (the same name as the heroine of *Flaming Lance*) and their grown son Thaddeus (or Tad).

Riot escapes as well, though he still has a steel arrowhead imbedded in his chest. Told he has six months to live, Riot decides to cram 30 years of living into 128 pages. He starts a fight in a saloon for no reason at all (one patron, familiar with Holiday, cries out "Riot!"). Though Huffaker implies that the hellraiser's death sentence is the reason for this mindless barbarity, the writer's cowpokes never needed any such excuse to start trouble. They do it because, to them, starting brutal fights is fun.

Seeing his string running out because of the arrowhead in his chest, Riot decides to pay back the Comanches and the dirty scoundrels who supplied them with repeating rifles. Later, he meets up with Tad, who insists on joining him south of the border for this wacky mission. At first, the men have a gratuitous fight scene, which ends in a draw and much manly laughter and camaraderie afterwards. Ultimately, the two men destroy the "Comanchero" gun dealers as well as the gun buyers, and then return home, where Riot marries Roslyn.

At the end of the book, the accursed arrowhead comes out of Riot's chest with no problem. An Army doctor comments that it is Riot's thirst for life that has defeated the original pessimistic prognosis of having a short time to live.

Unfortunately, characters like this irritated the writer of the Clair Huffaker section in the *BFI Companion to the Western*. Claiming that the author's work "is marred by a tendency towards adolescent machismo" and "lazy plotting," the BFI writer also called *The Comancheros* and *The War Wagon* "rip-roaring" and "adventurous." It does give the reader some pause considering the semantics the BFI writer gets into. Just what is the difference between "rip-roaring adventure" and "adolescent machismo?" Indeed, what seems to annoy the BFI writer is the fact that Huffaker's characters go about their "macho" activities with high spirits instead of tight-lipped grimness. There is far more violence and brutality in the works of L'Amour and Albert than Huffaker. Despite this, however, the author does seem to be saying that feelings of camaraderie can only come after two men beat each other up.

Fox's film owes more to *The Comancheros* than *Guns of Rio Conchos*. Indeed, it will be the first time Huffaker will radically change his novels for film. Previous versions of his work would have certain changes once they made it to celluloid, but *Rio Conchos* basically kept the gunrunning plot and removed everything else.

As directed by Gordon Douglas, Huffaker's traditional manly adventure comes to the fore, though there are still scenes of excessive brutality that are not to be taken lightly. For instance, a group of Apaches are out in the desert seemingly minding their own business when they are all shot dead by some assassin with a Winchester.

This sharpshooting adventurer is Lassiter (the same name as the hero in Huffaker's *Guns of Thunder Mountain*), ex-major for the Confederate Army. Richard Boone was a larger-than-life actor, and a dedicated admirer of Lee Strasberg and the Method. Here the star is physically larger than life, appearing more bearish than previously in his *Have Gun, Will Travel* days. Despite his girth, however, the actor comes through in this film with a powerful performance. As a man who lost his wife and children in an Apache massacre, Boone's Lassiter is an embittered juggernaut of a man. Throughout the film, the actor not only shows us a man who is tough and smart, but a man in deep pain as well. Taking prairie law into his own hands, the ex-officer has obsessively trailed and shot dead any Apache within sight of a settler's burned cabin.

Sitting amidst the ruins of one such cabin and guzzling some hooch, Lassiter is soon accosted by a platoon of cavalry. The soldiers are led by Cpt. Haven (Stuart Whitman), who is assisted by his black noncom, Sgt. Franklyn (the film debut of ex–NFL great Jim Brown, who will return to Huffaker Country in a few years). The blue bellies had been tracking the burly assassin and want to question him about the killings, as well as the identity of the man funneling guns to Apaches south of the border.

Nursing his own hatred, at first Lassiter refuses to cooperate. He is thrown into the guardhouse with Juan Luis Rodriguez, a Latino murderer who specializes in knife-throwing. (Don't *all* south of the border outlaws specialize in knife-throwing?) Anthony Franciosa is without a doubt the most Italian, sombrero-wearing, Mexican knife-throwing badman you've ever seen. Buried under a black wig soaked in grease, the actor tries to bury an atrocious accent under a veneer of wily enthusiasm. He is a murderer, but a likable one; and, of course, being Latino, he must also be a ladies' man. Later in the film, he takes a room and goes upstairs with two senoritas who look like they haven't been south of L.A., much less the border.

Abruptly changing his mind, Lassiter offers the colonel a chance to find the man responsible for the gunrunning. Haven volunteers to go with him, bringing along Sgt. Franklyn. From his end, Lassiter wants to bring Juan along. Incredibly, Col. Wagner (Warner Anderson) agrees to releasing a condemned murderer onto an unsuspecting public, merely because a brawling, drunken, embittered ex–Confederate officer says so!

Taking with them a wagonload of explosives, the Fab Four head south of the border. On the way, they capture a pretty Apache girl ("B" queen Wende Wagner). She doesn't speak a word of English, but her spiteful delivery of Indian dialogue, with Wagner baring her teeth a lot, leaves no doubt that she hates this quartet of non–Apaches. Using Juan to translate, the four adventurers are able to track the marauding band farther south until Lassiter and Franklyn enter a border cantina.

At first, Lassiter's attitude toward the sergeant had been one of dislike born of Southern racism. Now, seeing the bartender snub the black sergeant, Lassiter grabs the bartender's head and slams it on the bar. Taking a page out of the barroom brawl in his novel, and adding a touch of racial brotherhood, Huffaker gives us a hell of a scene, with the ex–Reb, the black sergeant and the white captain fighting side by side and turning the place into a shambles. Knowing that the brawl will summon the Rangers, the three men escape before the lawmen can catch them, riding their horses across the shallow part of the Rio Grande. Now with the border guards gone, Juan and the Apache girl drive the wagon across safely.

After a skirmish with some Mexican bandits, which our guys win handily, the group come upon a home attacked by Apaches. At first, the Apache girl sneers at the four men, seemingly proud of the attack. But when she goes inside and sees the results, including a blood-smeared baby, even she is horrified.

This is the easily most powerful moment of the film, and a testament to Boone's versatility as an actor. His expressions are subtle, but the actor uses his body to express an almost insane grief, reminding Lassiter all too well of his own deep loss. When Lassiter finds a survivor still alive in a bed (it is implied the victim is a woman who suffered rape and torture), Douglas shoots the scene from the victim's point of view, the camera looking at a saddened Boone looking at us over a bloody bedpost. We then see him pull his gun and the camera cuts away as we hear the gunshot. Then Lassiter finds the blood-stained baby. Crying as his huge bulk leans over the window sill, the actor has never been more impressive. Finally, in a burst of rage, Lassiter grabs a rifle and fires at the warriors hiding in the field outside the cabin.

That night, Lassiter is tied up so he won't attack the Apache girl. The woman cradles the surviving baby protectively, but when the infant finally dies, she bursts into tears, obviously sorry for what her people have done. After Haven takes the dead baby from her arms, he and the Apache girl look at each other meaningfully, and it is obvious the two are starting to understand each other without the use of words.

There had been doubt that Lassiter would go along with Haven's mission all the way. Now, after the massacre, the ex–Reb gives the captain information on where to find the man heading the gunrunners, ex–Confederate officer Col. Theron "Gray Fox" Pardee.

Meanwhile, Juan arrives at the cantina and wants to know where to find Pardee. When Lassiter shows up, he is forced to kill the duplicitous Juan, who had planned to sell Haven's explosives to the Comancheros.

After Lassiter is brought to Col. Pardee's stronghold, Douglas' camera pulls back and we see men, most of them in Confederate uniform, practicing war maneuvers; in essence, we are viewing a terrorist camp. Gun-toting Apaches and renegade Mexicans also wander the camp, suspiciously eyeing the newcomer.

In 1964, when the film was made, black children were being murdered and fire hoses and police dogs were the order of the day down South. Huffaker and co-screenwriter Joseph Landon are to be credited with turning his novel, essentially a swipe of *The Comancheros*, into a not-so-veiled attack on Southern racism. Col. Pardee is a would-be Hitler figure, dreaming of a day when a slave-holding South rises again.

When Lassiter is brought in to meet the great man himself, we not only see that Pardee is a rather overweight man dressed in Confederate gray, but that he is also played by Edmond O'Brien. Once again proving himself a less-than-capable player in the western genre, O'Brien effectively conveys the character's pomp and arrogance, while at the same time giving us a Southern accent that comes and goes depending on what scene he's doing. (Honestly, it must also be said that, although Richard Boone's performance in the film is wonderful, he too loses and then gains his accent at the oddest times.)

It seems that Lassiter had served under the colonel, and now the would-be despot is overjoyed at having his best man join him. Shortly afterwards, Haven, Franklyn and the Apache girl are escorted into the terrorist camp and they all meet in front of the colonel's plantation-style mansion, complete with columns. Here, the villain's residence itself recalls the glory days of imperial Rome as well as the slave-holding South, all to emphasize the colonel's mad ambitions to become a nineteenth-century Caesar.

After the arrival of the wagon, the Apache girl is ordered to join her people on the grounds as Haven and Franklin feign allegiance. (The black sergeant emphasizes that he's not agreeing with the colonel's philosophy, but just wants the money.) Unfortunately, also making an appearance is Apache chieftain, Bloodshirt (Rudolfo Acosta making his third appearance in a Clair Huffaker picture). This prompts a fight, with Douglas' camera showing Pardee cynically chewing his cigar as we hear sounds of fisticuffs and destruction.

The next scene shows all three men tied behind three horses ridden by sadistic Apaches. Later that night, feeling sorry for the three captives, the Apache girl sneaks over to them and cuts them loose.

Lassiter and Franklyn, firing rifles all the way, ride the explosive-laden wagon down a long hill, heading it towards the Apache camp with the stolen guns. Seeing Bloodshirt in the camp, Lassiter leaps at the murderer of his wife and family and is in the process of choking the warrior to death when the wagon explodes, killing all of them.

The powerful explosion shakes loose the mansion's chandelier, which crashes to the ground and quickly sets the building on fire. Seeing his terrorist camp on fire and his mad scheme ruined, Col. Pardee purposely walks back into his burning mansion, where it's presumed his idea of a slave-holding America dies with him.

At the end of the cataclysm, Haven and the Apache girl again look at each other meaningfully, then start to make their way out of the camp, the only survivors.

Rio Conchos was Huffaker's most audacious work, a slam-bang, rousing adventure which took a stand against hatred of all kinds. In the meanwhile, the novelist was also busy writing for TV. He had provided scripts for the western shows *The Lawman*, *The Virginian* and *Rawhide*, as well as *Twelve O'Clock High*. While working on *Flaming Star*, the author doctored the screenplay for the Fox western comedy *The Second Time Around* starring Debbie Reynolds. Using the pseudonym of Cecil Dan Hansen (Huffaker probably feared marring his reputation as a writer of macho westerns by associating himself with a Debbie Reynolds romantic comedy), the author handled the assignment competently enough; we can safely guess that it was Huffaker who was responsible for the gratuitous but lively fight scenes in the film.

After completing the screenplay for *Tarzan and the Valley of Gold*, it was back to Universal for the author. In 1967, Huffaker's next project was a film version of his novel *Badman*, which was originally a short story for *Ranch Romances* called "Holdup at Stony Flat." With little trouble, *The War Wagon* is as light and funny as *Rio Conchos* was grim and violent.

The film stars John Wayne and Kirk Douglas, the biggest stars ever to enact a Huffaker screenplay. Besides the humorous tone both stars lent to the project, it is the director who put his stamp on it. Burt Kennedy had made a career out of writing and directing western comedies. His *Support Your Local Sheriff* and *Support Your Local Gunfighter* are still funny today. Kennedy had also written Budd Boetticher's best films with Randolph Scott (except the classic *Decision at Sundown*).

Under Kennedy's guidance, as well as the hands-on assistance of the Duke, Huffaker's western caper story becomes a *comedy*-western caper story. In the novel, gunfighter Jack Tawlin returns to the village of Pawnee Forks, summoned by his younger brother Jess for a particular job.

At Jess' house, Jack meets up with Christine, Jess' wife. More impressed by the older, more level-headed Jack than her lazy, good-for-nothing husband, Christine is also alienated from those in town because of her saloon dancer background.

Reluctant to get into fights and weary of gunslinging, Jack decides to join his impetuous little brother in a scheme to rob a stagecoach carrying gold, which always crosses the huge bridge at Stony Flats. There is one problem though: The coach is actually a steel fortress on wheels being pulled by a team of horses. With the coach fortified with steel plates and a gatling gun mounted on a revolving turret, the vehicle is something out of science fiction rather than a prairie story.

Throughout the book, though he gushes admiration for his older brother, Jess prods him into killing a gunfighter and then getting him into a saloon fistfight with some cavalrymen. Apparently Jess harbors his own bitterness towards his older sibling.

The brothers get together with a crew of misfits to knock off the "war wagon" by having the Apaches attack the coach and diverting the vehicle over the bridge at the exact moment they blow it up. Predictably, the plotters are defeated in their attempts.

The film rejects ironies and bitterness, and instead makes things as light and fluffy as a Duncan Hines cake. Jack Tawlin is now Taw Jackson (the Duke), newly released from prison. Having been framed and sent up the river by the evil Frank Pierce (Wayne pal Bruce Cabot), the big man finds that Pierce has stolen his gold and routinely transports the yellow goodies from Taw's mine to the town bank in a, you guessed it, war wagon.

A fancy dressed, black-clad gunfighter named Lomax is not in the novel, but his appearance is welcome in the film. Kirk Douglas' take on the role is a memorable send-up. Flamboyant in dress and swagger, bedecked in rings, and never failing to twirl his gun in a showy manner, the actor almost steals the film. Having shot and wounded Taw five years before, Lomax joins him in his scheme to rob the war wagon and destroy Pierce.

Other partners are Billy Hyatt (Robert Walker, Jr.), Wes Fletcher (Keenan Wynn), his abused wife Lola (Joanna Barnes) and Walking Bear (an unusually cast Howard Keel) standing in for Iron Eyes Cody, but in a much bigger comic vein.

Huffaker's screenplay provided a light touch which met with the Duke's approval. It also has, of course, an all-out fun-filled saloon brawl in which Lomax saves Taw's life. In a romantic subplot, Billy and Lola find themselves attracted to each other, to the jealousy of Wes (a particularly nasty performance by Wynn). Several times, Wes pulls a knife on the young man and is about to cut him into chicken liver until Taw and Lomax stop him.

The basic heist plot is the same: Get the Indians to attack the coach and blow up the bridge, sending the coach to the bottom. Since Billy is an explosives expert, he brings along a bottle of nitroglycerine.

As ever, the war wagon makes its trip, but as the Indians attack, Pierce's men see it as suicide to remain near the wagon, resulting in the usual falling-out among crooks. Unfortunately, the gold that was in the wagon was dust. Since Taw is in charge of the stuff and can't touch it until things die down, he tells Lomax that in order to get his cut he'll have to keep him alive till then. Irritably, the leather-clad gunman goes for his horse and tries a running mount, ultimately falling clumsily to the ground. Douglas' fall over his horse is the laugh-filled topper to this comedy, and effectively caps an enjoyable film.

The atmosphere on location in Durango, Mexico, however, wasn't always so enjoyable. Since it was a Batjac production, the Duke became the director in everything but name only. As Burt Kennedy said, "Duke was tough on directors." Too much of a nice guy to interfere, Kennedy held his piece while Douglas was insisting he control Wayne. Though Douglas and the Duke had worked together without any major blowups, Douglas' reminiscences of the Duke reveal a friendly rivalry between the two manly actors. At least Douglas was never about to clock the Duke, as Howard Keel was ready to do when Wayne became too demonstrative in his directing.

After previewing at the Majestic Theater in Dallas on May 27, 1967, *The War Wagon* became another in a long line of hits for the Duke, grossing over $6 million domestically. This was at a time when adult admissions were 75 cents and children were admitted for 50 cents.

Apparently liking the novelist-screenwriter, Wayne had Huffaker script his next film at Universal, *Hellfighters*. A two-fisted (and two-hour) adventure about those brave men who battle oil fires, the Duke's role was reportedly based on real-life hero firefighter Red Adair.

The Duke got to know Adair quite well off-screen and his obvious admiration for the tough firefighter comes out in his performance. When Wayne learned from Adair that he and his men were shot at by Communist guerrillas in the jungle hot spots of Africa, Asia and Latin America, Wayne told Huffaker to write the skirmish into the screenplay. As the years went by, Adair would continue to admire the Duke and speak fondly of him until the hero firefighter's own passing on August 8, 2004.

Meanwhile, over at Twentieth Century–Fox, the studio was preparing to film another south-of-the-border western called *100 Rifles*. Based

7. Clair Huffaker and Hellraising in the West

on the novel *The Californio* by actor-author Robert McLeod, the film has strong elements of Huffaker's previous south-of-the-border western for the studio, *Rio Conchos*. In fact, the film essentially has the same gunrunning plot, though Huffaker reverses the theme. In *Rio Conchos*, the heroes must make sure that repeating rifles do not fall into the hands of the Indians. In *100 Rifles*, it is imperative that the Indians get the guns to stop their own extinction by their oppressors. In *Rio Conchos*, the white-hating Apaches are in league with racist Confederates to take over the west. In *100 Rifles*, Mexicans are planning to exterminate the Yaqui Indians, and even have a German military adviser to help them, at a time just before World War I.

Before you can say "*Wild Bunch* clone," you must also look at the traditional Huffaker elements: two (or more) mismatched adventurers on a mission against overwhelming odds, a kind of buddy movie with repeating rifles. Huffaker has never been especially known for having weak female characters in his works, and *100 Rifles* is as good an example as any of "empowerment" in the old west.

The Revolution has been Lightened up: Jim Brown and the incomparably gorgeous Raquel Welch in Huffaker's *100 Rifles*. These two are *not* what Zapata and Diaz had in mind during the Mexican Revolution. (Larry Edmunds Bookshop, Inc., Hollywood, California.)

To understand the film, however, one should also examine Robert McLeod's "coming of age" novel. *The Californio* tells the story of Steve McCall, a teenage wrangler adopted by a Mexican family on the California border. Since the red-headed youth grew up on a ranch owned by a Mexican, he is an expert wrangler, and has a keen eye for good horseflesh. Sent to Mexico to purchase horses, the youth is accompanied by a seasoned ranch hand, Yaqui Joe, a man who is going south of the border not to purchase horses, but to help his people.

Unfortunately, the young American suddenly finds himself in the midst of the killing fields of the Mexican Revolution. The Rurales are under the command of Col. Emilio Kosterlitzky, a German military man helping the Mexican aristocracy keep a tenuous hold on the country. However, the real villain of the book is the ruthless Sgt. Verdugo.

In a foreshadowing of Nazi persecution, Verdugo takes over Yaqui villages and lines up the villagers, personally shooting dead every third person, be it a man, woman or child, who doesn't tell him what he wants to know. During the first half of the novel, Steve has no interest in the Revolution or Yaqui Joe's passion for helping his oppressed people. But after an innocent Yaqui boy is shot in the stomach by Verdugo when the boy refuses to disclose Steve's whereabouts, Steve joins the *revolutionistas.*

The book is violent and brutally real in its depiction of the grinding poverty of the Yaquis, with Steve forced to eat food usually covered with flies. Forget the toilet facilities! Foul language is also the order of the day in merry old revolutionary Mexico, with both oppressors and oppressed referring to each other frequently as "sons of whores," "dirty sluts" and other colorful phrases.

There is also a realistic look at the usual fistic battles that cowboy heroes get into with the bad guys. L'Amour and Short were never like this. When Steve points out to Yaqui Joe that he didn't fight fair with a bullying rancher, the Indian replies, "What fight fair? You gonna fight, you better win. Kick in face, kick in balls, use ketchup bottle, use knife…"

Huffaker and director–co-screenwriter Tom Gries seems to have used this philosophy, if not the story, for their film. Yet this is still a work by Clair Huffaker. Therefore, the graphic violence depicted in the novel wouldn't get any worse on screen than an arrow going into someone's chest.

The film begins as some Rurales are about to hang the father of *revolutionista* Sarita (played by Argentinian Raquel Welch). With Welch in the film, one doesn't grouse over her lack of dramatic ability; personally, I wouldn't complain if the beautiful Ms. Welch had played Yaqui Joe.

After the soldiers pull the horse out from under the old man, Sarita jumps up and literally stands on her father's shoes, pulling him harder so the old man won't strangle. Welcome to the world of old Mexico, where a new leader is elected every other week! Into this quaint setting, we see the master villain Gen. Verdugo (promoted from sergeant in the novel), well-played by former MGM heartthrob Fernando Lamas. Years before his career would be considered something of a joke, the Latino actor gives us an interesting portrait of a would-be dictator and racial oppressor. In a politically correct world of 20 years later, one might be shocked to hear racist sentiments from a black hero and a Mexican protagonist concerning people of another ethnicity (the Yaquis), but the filmmakers of the late 1960s and 1970s had a freedom many could only wistfully dream of years later.

Gen. Verdugo is riding around in his Hitler-like touring car, lording it over the town. Along for the ride, but on horseback, is the film's Kosterlitz clone, Lt. Von Klemme (Eric Braeden, here billed as Hans Gudegast). Since the film is set in 1912 (*a la The Wild Bunch*), Von Klemme is a prewar military advisor to Verdugo. In reality, the Germans were all but promising Mexico the return of all lands captured by the United States in exchange for Mexican support in the coming world war. In the film, Von Klemme is much more benign than the arrogant Kosterlitz, and far smarter than Gen. Verdugo, though still a wily adversary. After his men capture a group of Yaqui rebels, Verdugo pulls a brand new .45 automatic from his coat and blows away all three of them with one shot.

However, up in the second floor hotel room is a swarthy young man with the appearance of a Yaqui, but with a really bad Southern accent. This poor example of cross-culturalism is Yaqui Joe Herrera (Burt Reynolds). Reynolds has natural comic timing, but his Southern accent is awful. When Herrera calls for the Yaquis to escape, the Good Ol' Muchacho is taken prisoner. Reynolds himself would refer to this role as "third halfbreed from the left," and called the film "a gritty Southwestern."

The halfbreed's incarceration is interrupted, however, by the arrival of Lyedecker, a black lawman (Jim Brown, in his second go-round in a Huffaker screenplay). For this, the film should be praised for an attempt at historical accuracy, though it's more likely they were really thinking box office due to the popularity of the ex–NFL star. The film is the first to show us a black lawman, a more common sight in the old west than most people would think from watching Hollywood films.

Lyedecker wants to place Yaqui Joe under arrest and return him to New Mexico for robbing a bank. Gen. Verdugo isn't crazy about having his executions interrupted by a black star-toter with an agenda of his own. Joe privately admits to Lyedecker that the money went for rifles, 100 rifles in fact, to be used as weapons for his people.

When Joe politely announces that he's leaping through the window of the railroad car to make his escape, Lyedecker good-naturedly gives his permission, and the Big Escape is on. The film's situations, though desperate, are imbued with humor and the usual macho adventure prized by Huffaker. Even when Lyedecker and Yaqui Joe have a fistfight near the edge of a cliff, Huffaker's tone is clearly light; these two antagonists aren't really fighting to the death, like in a Marvin H. Albert novel or screenplay. After Lyedecker pulls Joe back from over the edge of the cliff, Joe even thanks the lawman before slugging him!

When Lyedecker and Joe escape, they seize a horse and head for the hills where they meet the beautiful Sarita. Lyedecker stubbornly refuses to free Joe, insisting he return with him to face justice. The jaded black lawman also expresses a less-than-tolerant view towards helping Indians. Tracked by the Rurales, they are once again captured.

As a firing squad is preparing to shoot the men, Sarita and her Yaqui rebels climb over the high wall and kill the firing squad using some of Joe's 100 rifles. Now Big Escape Two is on! Proving that they still had it in them to run across a football field, both football players–turned–actors race across the fortress' Long Yard, causing mayhem all the while.

After this rousing sequence, we have a respite, meaning both men have a brief (and somewhat amiable) fight at the edge of a cliff. After Jim Brown reportedly said to Reynolds that his two great fears were "heights and horses," his male co-star came up with an idea. Reynolds claimed to have suggested to director Tom Gries ("My first really good writer-director," Reynolds wrote) to put the fight scene near the edge of a cliff. This entailed running cables through the two action stars as they dangled at the edge, as well as having a safety platform beneath them. (This safety platform was also used for Fox's *Butch Cassidy and the Sundance Kid* in the scene where Paul Newman and Robert Redford leap madly off a cliff into the river.)

The fight scene is performed without the sustained tension or viciousness which typify fights in Marvin Albert's westerns; instead, Huffaker (or possibly Reynolds and Brown) imbue the bit with rowdy, macho humor.

Unfortunately, before you can say "harsh reprisal," the soldiers burn down the village that sheltered our Terrific Trio. In the process, the soldiers also kill several adults and kidnap the children, including a little Yaqui boy that Lyedecker had befriended.

When the three arrive at the burned village and Lyedecker realizes that his young friend is captured too, there is a change in the black lawman. Previously refusing to fight for "damn Indians," he now becomes a

Believer. In the novel, it is Steve McKay's friendship for the doomed Yaqui boy that galvanizes him to fight the Rurales.

McLeod's novel is brutally realistic. Everyone in the revolution is a victim: men, women and especially children. Since *100 Rifles* is a major American film, it will not show the wanton murders of children. This unfortunately allows Huffaker and Gries to give us a kinder, gentler version of oppression, full of blazing gunfire, over-the-top acrobatics and phony heroics.

After attacking one of Verdugo's fortress strongholds, the children are rescued, the guards are murdered and the rebels loot the mansion, dressing up in the aristocracy's fancy clothes and helping themselves to every drop of booze. Also during this celebration, Lyedecker and Sarita do the nasty in their late host's bed, though during this entire scene, Jim Brown never once drops his pants.

In the novel, the attack on an aristocrat's mansion is far more violent. When the occupants of the house, including the landowner's and the servants' families, run outside, the rebels shoot everyone down. McLeod also shows us that after the adults fall, their children are mowed down by bullets as well.

The rebels soon form a new plan, grabbing a train filled with weapons. But how does one stop a troop train of murdering Rurales soldiers armed with rifles and a gatling gun mounted on the roof? This is a job for Fox's number one sex symbol! Showering under a water tower just as the train rolls by, Sarita has no trouble stopping the transport — or any other vehicle, we imagine. With her wet blouse and short pants clinging to her supple body, we now see the real reason for the film's popularity. The hell with McLeod's original story, the fight against oppression was never like this!

After the train is taken over, and with Lyedecker and Joe as engineers, the train heads non-stop into Verdugo's fortress.

Now, the Final Battle. Needless to say, the bad guys are defeated, but at a great loss — Sarita is killed. Verdugo's death, however, is much worse. Before you can say, "You look marvelous," a crowd of Yaquis closes in on him and his screams are drowned out in the crush.

The last we see of Von Klemme, he is sitting atop his horse far away from the killing zone. Shaking his head in disappointment, he turns and rides off, presumably using the experience with the Yaqui for some time down the line when he deals with the *untermench* back in Germany.

Joe is convinced to stay on and lead his people as Lyedecker rides back to the States, we presume a changed man.

100 Rifles delivered the goods for male fans of the genre: action, violence, a cause to fight for and, most of all, Raquel Welch. The film has strong elements of *The Wild Bunch*, which is also set just before World War I. There is a despotic *generalisimo*, he has a German advisor, there is a deal for guns, a train shootout, our badmen heroes eventually killing off the oppressors, etc. *The Wild Bunch* is a classic; *100 Rifles* is not. Indeed, one wonders how the film would look had Huffaker and Gries followed the original novel instead of the Peckinpah film. In Huffaker's next project after *Flap*, we again have mismatched adventurers out in the wild west.

Flap would be filmed by Warner Brothers in 1970 with a screenplay by Huffaker. The novel was a modern western about the misadventures of Native American upstart Flapping Eagle and his gang of misfits. The book is cynical, satirical and very witty. Though Anthony Quinn does a good job in the role, the film flopped. The novel was critically acclaimed, but audiences did not want to see a witty satire on Native American rights (or the lack of them).

In 1971, Huffaker was involved in an Italian-Yugoslavian-American co-production called *La Spina Dorsale del Diavolo*, known in this country as *The Deserter* (Somehow, this sounds better than the title's literal translation, *The Devil's Backbone*.)

Cpt. Viktor Kaleb, one of the many Serbian officers in the U.S. cavalry (played by Yugo star Bekim Fehmiu), blames the Army for the death of his wife. When Major Brown (Richard Crenna) tries to stop Kaleb from leaving, the Serb pulls his gun and wounds the major in the leg. Therefore, throughout the film, Crenna will have an unbecoming limp, reminding us of Walter Brennan on *The Real McCoys*. After this example of felonious assault, Cpt. Kaleb deserts (hence the title, apparently).

The ex-captain disappears into the southwestern desert. When the Apaches set up a stronghold south of the border, the high command (including the usually cigar-chewing, hammy John Huston) decides to send an expedition of crack troopers to stop them. Before anyone can say "*Rio Conchos* rip-off," we also must remember that this adventure is directed by Burt Kennedy, a man more attuned to the parody of *Support Your Local Sheriff* than a grim drama about running guns to the Indians. Indeed, Kennedy's light touch is missing; further evidence of this is the co-directing credit (on foreign screens anyway) given to Yugoslavian helmsman Niksa Fulgosi.

It is Clair Huffaker's fourth film about gunrunning south of the border, and by this time it looked like the author was approaching the end of his string in Hollywood. Westerns, especially the foreign ones that would give so much employment to faded American talent (like Huffaker, unfortunately), were coming to an end. The genre was declining; at first the descent was gradual, then by the 1990 all but finished.

In the meantime, the author would have one last shot in the world of film; and, as ever, the European western would provide that last shot. In 1973, the usual continental co-production deal would produce *Il Mezzosangue Valdez*. Huffaker was supposed to be the sole screenwriter on the project, based on Lee Hoffman's Spur Award–winning novel *The Valdez Horses*. The book is a coming-of-age story told from the youth's point of view, about a lonely horse breeder and his friendship with an eager young boy.

The star was Charles Bronson. In the pivotal role of Chino Valdez, the half-breed rancher, the star acquits himself well. With Bronson cast in the role of father figure in this story, one almost expected the action star to blow away the kid with a .45 if the horses weren't fed just the right amount of oats.

The novel is a well-written account of a young man growing up on the prairie and finding himself a principled yet tempestuous role model. Chino Valdez is a demonic-appearing individual with a scar running down his forehead. In the film, the scar is transferred to his arm; Bronson apparently looked demonic enough without it. Though wary of each other, Chino and Jamie (Vincent Van Patten) develop a working relationship. When the boy arrives at the horsebreaker's spread, he plans to work at the much larger Nash ranch, but never underestimate the beguiling charmer that is Charles Bronson. In no time at all, he is helping Chino bring horses into town to be sold.

When willowy blonde beauty Louise (Jill Ireland) arrives on the stage, a surly cowpoke makes a remark and Chino slugs him. The cowpoke later returns with several of his friends just as Chino is taking a drink. In the book, Chino is a wild man on the sauce; here, Bronson will hardly bend his elbow except to rein in his horse. (When offered a chance to star in a film directed by Peckinpah, Bronson reportedly said, "I don't work with drunks.")

Though Chino's penchant for wild boozing is watered down in the film (sorry about that), he is still played by Charles Bronson. Therefore, there will be the mandatory Bronson action scenes. With little trouble, Chino beats up the four rowdies who interrupt his quiet drink in the saloon.

When one of his ponies is caught on barbed wire, Chino angrily goes to the home of Louise and her obnoxious brother Maral. It seems that Maral now owns the land Chino resides on, a piece of real estate that was formerly free range. As played by Marcel Bozzuffi, Maral is a *little* too Neapolitan for the prairie, though the actor does convey an arrogant human being very well. In fact, in the land war to come, one wonders why Chino doesn't simply have Maral deported.

When Louise goes to Chino and wants the horse-breaker to teach her riding, before you can say "roll in the hay," the two off-screen lovebirds are sparking on-screen as well. The two plan to marry, but her eternally broomstick-up-his-butt brother is against the idea. Again, he sends his bad boys after Chino, and this time they hang him up and whip the daylights out of him. However, they are not just whipping any old half-breed horse-breaker with a demonic appearance, they are also whipping Charles Bronson!

Working in high *Death Wish* mode, Chino lies in ambush and uses his rifle to pick off several of his assailants. Then, in a defeatist move so unlike Bronson (or Huffaker for that matter), Chino chases off his livestock and burns his ranch. Afterwards, he and Jamie part company, never to see each other again.

The ending may have been loyal to the book, but to rabid Bronson fans (like me), this was treason! Hoping for a climax of non-stop violent retribution, we were instead treated to abandonment and hopeless despair. What's the good of being Charles Bronson without a scene where he blows away Maral with a Winchester?

The film was directed by John Sturges, the man who helmed *The Magnificent Seven*. With his career also in a slump due to the western draught, it seems that the American helmsman might not have been the only director who worked on the film. A fellow named Duilio Coletti added scenes, which might account for the film's choppiness.

Then there is another insult to a Hollywood talent. Though Huffaker is credited with the screenplay, apparently the script was "doctored" by three more writers, Massimo De Rita, Arduino Maiuri and Rafael J. Salvia. It was not an ideal final exit for a man who provided the source material and subsequent screenplays for so many enjoyable westerns.

For the creator of some of western fiction's most rambunctious hell-raisers, the times were indeed a-changing.

Huffaker died in Los Angeles on April 3, 1990. The three American icons who starred in his most popular films, John Wayne, Audie Murphy and Elvis Presley, all died in the 1970s—coincidentally, the same decade that would bring Huffaker's last work to the screen.

With the decline of the western, Huffaker's tales of wild cowpokes would be replaced by the films of Clint Eastwood. Unlike Riot Holiday and Jim Flood, the persona of Clint Eastwood would never start a saloon fight unless there were a calculating reason behind it. Cooler and slyer than Huffaker's creations, Eastwood's nameless gunmen realized that to go off half-cocked in a dangerous west was a fool thing to do, and that to survive, a cowboy had to know his limitations.

The world of Clair Huffaker was one where a man had a right to be as wild as the land he was in. Certainly, the world that we live in was privileged to have had this author–screenwriter–sailor–boxer–editor–western giant among us.

8

Saddle Up: Other Unsung Heroes of the Written Page

My deep apologies to those skilled authors who did not make these pages due to time and space constraints, but to whom as a western fan I will forever hold up as examples of talent and in some cases, genius: Thomas W. Blackburn, Les Savage, Jr., Clifton Adams, Donald Hamilton, Lewis B. Patten, T.T. Flynn, Robert MacLeod, Will Henry and one that will always stand tall in my eyes, Alan LeMay. Many of their works were made into films; some were good, some were abysmal. Hamilton also found fame in other genres besides the western, as well as writing books of non-fiction.

These men and those already written about in the previous chapters would be replaced by Loren D. Estleman, Elmer Kelton (who has written western novels since the 1950s), Brian Garfield, Ed Gorman and Bill Pronzini. Kelton set all his westerns in his native Texas. His stories had heart and the dilemmas his characters faced could not be solved so easily. Kelton was a master storyteller who forced the reader to consider the same problems his characters do, since they are constantly forced to make difficult choices. (Good examples of this are *Horsehead Crossing* and *The Hanging Judge*.)

The genre also now boasted several women. With this new blood, the previously sunny, uplifting genre now gave us stories filled with sadness and cynicism. This is not necessarily a bad thing. The western, long denied a much-needed realism thanks to narrow-minded publishers, now expanded its story ideas, allowing it to survive into the twenty-first century.

So where will the western go now? At this time, few westerns are on the nation's movie screens, and if a western is to go before cameras, they're usually cable-TV cameras.

Yet in times of misery, or when technology speeds the world up just a little too fast, I believe there will always be a market for westerns. They depict a time when folks didn't get ticketed for talking on a cellphone during traffic and your VCR or DVD player didn't go on the fritz; when a relaxing pastime was going to the saloon for a friendly drink, not watching an abysmal TV program pretending to depict "reality"; when war was mostly confined to one cattle range, not an entire planet threatened by terrorism and nuclear proliferation; and especially a time when reading a book gave more people a kick than playing Nintendo.

So for all the condescention the western has suffered through, I believe that this prejudice will not last. The snobbery of western-haters will die as surely as the sun sets and the seasons change.

Or as Audie Murphy said at the end of my favorite film, *No Name on the Bullet*:

"Don't worry about it, physician. Everything comes to a finish...."

Bibliography

Blottner, Gene. *Universal Sound Westerns, 1929–1946.* Jefferson, N.C.: McFarland, 2003.
_____. *Universal-International Westerns, 1947–1963.* Jefferson, N.C.: McFarland, 2000.
Brown, Peter, and Pat Broeske. *Down at the End of the Lonely Street: The Life and Death of Elvis Presley.* New York: Dutton; Penguin Putnam, 1997.
Buford, Kate. *Burt Lancaster: An American Life.* New York: Alfred A. Knopf, 2000.
Buscombe, Edward. editor. *BFI Companion to the Western.* New York: Macmillan, 1998.
_____. *Stagecoach (BFI Film Classics).* New York: Macmillan, 1992.
Davis, Ronald L. *Duke: The Life and Image of John Wayne.* Norman: University of Oklahoma Press, 1998.
_____. *William S. Hart: Projecting the American West.* Norman: University of Oklahoma Press, 2003.
Dmytryk, Edward. *It's a Hell of a Life, But Not a Bad Living.* New York: Times Books, 1978.
Easton, Robert. *Max Brand: The Big Westerner.* Norman: University of Oklahoma Press, 1970.
Estleman, Loren D. *Mister St. John.* New York: Doubleday, 1983.
Fox, Norman A. *Night Passage.* New York, Dodd, Mead & Co.,1956.
_____. *The Rawhide Years.* New York, Dell, 1953.
_____. *Roughshod.* New York, Dodd, Mead & Co., 1950.
_____. *Tall Man Riding.* New York, Dodd, Mead & Co., 1951.
Garfield, Brian. *Western Films: A Complete Guide.* New York: De Capo Press, 1982.
Graham, Don. *No Name on the Bullet: A Biography of Audie Murphy.* New York: Penguin, 1987.
Grey, Zane. *U.P. Trail.* New York: Grosset & Dunlap 1918.
Gruber, Frank. *The Big Land (Buffalo Grass).* New York, Rinehart, 1956.
_____. *Bitter Sage.* New York, New American Library, 1954.

_____. *Broken Lance*. New York, Rinehart, 1949.
_____. *Bugles West*. New York, Rinehart, 1954.
_____. *The Bushwackers*. New York, New American Library, 1959.
_____. *Fort Starvation*. New York, Rinehart, 1953.
_____. *Town Tamer*. New York, New American Library, 1957.
_____. *Peace Marshal*. New York, Bantam, 1941.
_____. *The Pulp Jungle*. Los Angeles: Shelbourne, 1967.
Harris, Warren G. *Sophia Loren*. New York: Simon & Schuster, 1998.
Haycox, Ernest. *Bugles in the Afternoon*. New York: Curtis Publishing Co., 1943.
_____. *The Border Trumpet*. New York: Windsor, 1939.
_____. *Canyon Passage*. New York: Grosset & Dunlap, 1945.
_____. *Free Grass*. New York: Doubleday, 1929.
_____. *Guns Up!* New York: Doubleday, 1928.
_____. *Man in the Saddle*. Boston: Little Brown & Co., 1938.
_____. *Return of a Fighter*. New York: New American Library, 1929.
_____. *A Rider in the High Mesa*. New York: Doubleday, 1929.
_____. *Sundown Jim*. New York: Triangle Books, 1938.
_____. *Trail Town*. New York: New American Library, 1941.
_____. *Trouble Shooter*. New York: New American Library, 1937.
Horwitz, James. *They Went Thataway*. New York: E.F. Dutton, 1976.
Huffaker, Clair. *Badge for a Gunfighter*. Greenwich, Conn., Fawcett Publications, 1957.
_____. *Flaming Lance*. Greenwich, Conn., Fawcett Publications, 1958.
_____. *Guns of Rio Conchos*. Greenwich, Conn., Fawcett Publications, 1958.
_____. *Guns of Thunder Mountain*. Greenwich, Conn., Fawcett Publications, 1958.
_____. *Nobody Loves a Drunken Indian (Flap)*. New York, David McKay, 1967.
_____. *Posse from Hell*. Greenwich, Conn., Fawcett Publications, 1958.
_____. *Seven Ways from Sundown*. Greenwich, Conn., Fawcett Publications, 1960.
_____. *War Wagon (Badman)*. Greenwich, Conn., Fawcett Publications, 1957.
Internet Movie Database. 1990–2004, Internet Movie Database, Inc.
Lambert, Gavin. *Natalie Wood: A Life*. New York: Alfred A. Knopf, 2004.
L'Amour, Louis. *The Burning Hills*. New York: Bantam, 1956.
_____. *Catlow*. New York, Bantam, 1963.
_____. *The First Fast Draw*. New York, Bantam, 1959.
_____. *Guns of the Timberlands*. New York, Bantam, 1955.
_____. *Heller with a Gun*. New York, CBS Publications, 1955.
_____. *Kid Rodelo*. New York, Bantam, 1966.
_____. *Kilkenny*. New York, Bantam, 1954.
_____. *Last Stand at Papago Wells*. New York, CBS Publications, 1957.
_____. *A Man Called Noon*. New York, Bantam, 1970.
_____. *The Man from Skiberdeen*. New York, Bantam, 1973.
_____. *North to the Rails*. New York, Bantam, 1971.
_____. *The Quick and the Dead*. New York, Bantam, 1973.
_____. *The Rider of Lost Creek*. New York, Bantam, 1976.
_____. *Shadow Riders*. New York, Bantam, 1982.

_____. *Shalako*. New York, Bantam, 1962.
_____. *Taggart*. New York, Bantam, 1959.
_____. *The Tall Stranger*. New York, CBS Publications, 1957.
_____. *To Tame a Land*. New York, CBS Publications, 1955.
_____. *Utah Blaine*. New York, CBS Publications, 1954.
McDonald, Archie P., editor. *Shooting Stars: Heroes and Heroines of the Western Film*. Bloomington and Indianapolis: Indiana University Press, 1987.
MacLeod, Robert. *The Californio*. New York: CBS Publications, 1966.
Miller, Mark A. "Barbara Steele: Diva of Dark Dreams." *Filmfax*, Issue 51, July-August 1995.
Mulholland, Jim. *The Abbott & Costello Book*. New York: Popular Library, 1977.
Nott, Robert. *Last of the Cowboy Heroes*. Jefferson, N.C.: McFarland, 2000.
Reynolds, Burt. *Burt Reynolds: My Life*. New York: Hyperion, 1994.
Roberts, Randy, and James S. Olson. *John Wayne: American*. New York: Simon & Schuster, 1995.
Robertson, James C. *The Casablance Man: The Cinema of Michael Curtiz*. London and New York: Routledge, 1993.
Savage, Jr., Les. *Hangtown*. New York, Random House, 1956.
_____. *Return to Warbow*. New York, Dell, 1955.
Server, Lee. *Robert Mitchum: "Baby, I Just Don't Care."* New York: St. Martin's Press, 2001.
Short, Luke (Frederick D. Glidden). *Ambush*. New York, Houghton Mifflin, 1950.
_____. *Bold Rider*. New York, Dell, 1938.
_____. *Bounty Guns*. New York, Dell, 1939.
_____. *Brand of Empire*. New York, Dell, 1937.
_____. *Coroner Creek*. New York, Macmillan, 1946.
_____. *The Deserters*. New York, Bantam, 1969.
_____. *Donovan's Guns*. New York, Bantam, 1968.
_____. *Gunman's Chance*. New York, Doubleday, 1941.
_____. *Hardcase*. New York, Dell, 1942.
_____. *High Vermilion*. New York, Houghton Mifflin, 1947.
_____. *King Colt*. New York, Dell, 1937.
_____. *The Man from Two Rivers*. New York, Bantam, 1971.
_____. *Paper Sheriff*. New York, Bantam, 1966.
_____. *Ride the Man Down*. New York, Bantam, 1947.
_____. *Silver Rock*. New York, Houghton Mifflin, 1953.
_____. *Station West*. New York, Houghton Mifflin, 1947.
_____. *Trouble Country*. New York, Bantam, 1976.
_____. *Vengeance Valley*. New York, Houghton Mifflin, 1950.
Siegel, Don and Carol Siegel. *Don Siegel: A Siegel Film*. London and Boston: Faber & Faber, 1993.
Strait, Raymond. *James Garner*. New York: St. Martin's Press, 1985.
Tanner, Stephen L. *Ernest Haycox*. New York: Twayne Publishers, 1996.
Tuska, Jon. *The Filming of the West*. Garden City, New York: Doubleday, 1976.
Wayne, Jane Ellen. *The Life of Robert Taylor*. New York: Warner, 1973.

Wellman, Paul I. *The Comancheros*. Garden City, N.Y.: Doubleday, 1952.
Yule, Andrew. *Sean Connery: From 007 to Hollywood Icon*. New York: Donald I. Fine, 1992.
Zolotow, Maurice. *John Wayne: Shooting Star*. New York: Simon & Schuster, 1979.

Index

Abbott & Costello Go to Mars 84
Abbott & Costello in the Foreign Legion 84
Abilene Town 19–21
Acosta, Rudolfo 155, 165, 175
Adams, Clifton 188
AFI (American Film Institute) 110
Agar, John 11
Airport 150
Akins, Clause 112
The Alamo 171
Albright, Lola 107
Albuquerque 36
Alden, Robert 147
Allen, Rex 56
Ambler, Eric 63
Ambush (film) 46–47
Ambush (novel) 46
Ames, Leon 46
Among the Living 109
…And God Created Woman 123
Anderson, Bibi 144, 147
Anderson, Herbert 98
Anderson, Warner 173
Andrews, Dana 22, 23, 80, 31
Angel and the Badman 103
Ann-Margret 30
Apache Rising 137, 143
Apache Territory 114, 115
Apache Trail 18, 29
Apache Uprising 51
Apache War Smoke 29
Archainbaud, George 60

Arizona Raiders 79
Arlen, Richard 50, 51–52, 80
Arrowhead 75–75
Attack of the Fifty Foot Woman 87
Autry, Gene 4, 56, 60, 73, 95
Avalon, Frankie 116
Ayer, Anne 18

Backlash 74
Bacon, Lloyd 60
Badge for a Gunfighter 153, 154–155
Badman 176
Baer, Max, Sr. 114
Baker, Diane 147
Balin, Ina 158
Bandelero 149
Banner, John 123
Barcroft, Roy 54
Bardot, Brigitte 123–124, 125, 127
The Barefoot Contessa 70
Bargerey, John 89, 91
Barnes, Joanna 177
Barret, Robert 89
Barry, Don "Red" 126
Bass, Sam 62
Beau Geste 17
Beauchamp, D.D. 84–85, 93
Behind the Rising Sun 122, 126
Bel Geddes, Barbara 43, 44
Bellamy, Ralph 109
Bend of the River 93, 97, 137
Bennett, Bruce 67

Bergen, Polly 51, 70
Bergman, Ingmar 147
Bernstein, Walter 117, 118
Best, Willie 61
Bettger, Lyle 72, 73, 81, 116
BFI Companion to Western Film 172
Biberman, Herbert 19, 20, 21, 22
The Big Country (film) 42
The Big Country (novel) 108
The Big Land 76–78
Billy the Kid 1
Bishop, Julie 63
Bissell, Whit 68
Bitter Sage 75
Blackburn, Thomas W. 188
Blackman, Honor 125–126
Blood Alley 105
Blood on the Moon 43, 44
The Body Snatcher 44
Boetticher, Budd 20, 37, 38–39, 56, 85, 88, 105, 142
Bold Rider 34
Bond, Ward 17, 23, 66, 67, 69
Boone, Richard 173, 174
Border Trumpet 14
Botany Bay 116
Bounty Guns 33, 34
Bounty Killer (film) 148
Bounty Killer (novel) 137, 138, 141, 147
Boy Who Cried Werewolf 87
Boyd, Stephen 127, 130
Boyd, William 6, 59–60
Bozzuffi, Marcel 185
Braeden, Eric 181
Brand, Max 5, 6
Brand of Empire 32
Brando, Marlon 157
Brennan, Walter 106, 184
Bridges, Lloyd 22, 23
Britton, Barbara 37, 53
Brodie, Steve 41
Broken Arrow 69
Broken Lance (film) 122
Broken Lance (novel) 122
Bronson, Charles 185, 186
Brooks, Richard 55, 110
Brown, Harry Joe 26, 38
Brown, Jim 173, 180, 181
Brute Force 68
Buchanan, Edgar 37, 39, 51, 67, 170
Buckskin Frontier 60

Bugles in the Afternoon (film) 27–28
Bugles in the Afternoon (novel) 12–13, 14, 26, 28, 68
Bugles West 62, 69
Buffalo Grass 61, 76
Bullet for a Badman 139–140
The Burning Hills 109, 110–113
Burr, Raymond 42
The Bushwackers 62
Butch Cassidy & the Sundance Kid 182
Buttons, Red 30

Cabot, Bruce 81, 169, 177
Cabot, Susan 85, 86, 87
Cagney, James 26, 81
Cagney Jeanne 81
Caine, Michael 121
The Caine Mutiny 122
Calhoun, Rory 80, 106, 113, 114, 115
The Californio 179, 180
Campbell, William 74
Cameron, Rod 24, 53, 54, 61, 65, 78, 84, 109, 123, 148
Cantor, Eddie 109
Canyon Passage (film) 18, 22, 23, 24
Canyon Passage (novel) 17, 22
Capra, Frank 103
Carlson, Richard 106, 120
Carey, Harry, Jr. 11
Carey, Macdonald 67
Carey, Phil 142
Cariboo Trail 64–65, 78
Carmichael, Hoagy 18, 24
The Carpetbaggers 122
Carradine, John 12, 68
Carroll, John 56
Carson, Sunset 63–64
Carter, Helena 28
Caruso, Anthony 78
Cass County Boys 2
Cassevettes, John 55
Cassidy, Butch 62, 82
Cast a Long Shadow 86
Castle, Mary 87
Castle, Peggie 89, 91, 117
Cat on a Hot Tin Roof 42
Catlow (film) 129
Catlow (novel) 129–130
Caulfield, Joan 80
Chandler, Lane 17, 90
Chaney, Lon, Jr. 17, 24, 38, 80, 81

Chapman, Marguerite 39
Charge of the Light Brigade 171
Chase, Borden 14, 69, 74, 75, 95
Chessman, Caryl 74
Ching, William 88
Churchill, Barton 12
Circus World 103
Citizen Kane 44
Cleveland, George 37
Clooney, Nick 10
Cobb, Lee J. 60
Cochise 65
Cody, Buffalo Bill 51, 73
A Coffin for Dimitrios 63
Coffin Gap 4
Coleman, Herbert 164
Colman, Ronald 23
Collier's (magazine) 10
Collins, Ray 48
Collinson, Peter 130
Colorado Territory 114
Comanche Blanco 82
The Comancheros 168, 172
The Command 106
Connery, Sean 55, 123, 124, 129
Connors, Mike 30
Cooper, Ben 79, 80
Cooper, Gary 13, 14, 16, 28
Cord, Alex 30
Corey, Wendall 67
Coroner Creek (film) 24, 33, 42, 52, 56
Coroner Creek (novel) 34, 38, 40
Cotten, Joseph 82
Cow Country 51, 71
Cowling, Bruce 46
Crabbe, Larry "Buster" 36, 79–80
Craig, Carolyn 115
Craig, Catherine 37
Crain, Jeanne 116
Crawford, Broderick 120
Crawford, John 146
Crenna, Richard 129, 130, 184
Crisp, Donald 32, 36
Crosby, Bing 30
Crossfire 122
Crowther, Bosley 78, 119, 147
Cukor, George 116–117, 118, 119
Cummings, Robert 24, 30
Curtis, Tony 84, 94
Curtiz, Michael 55, 157, 171

Custer, George Armstrong 28, 29, 62, 69, 70

Dahl, Arlene 46
Dakota Lil 65
Dano, Royal 165
Dantine, Helmut 63
Darnell, Linda 80
Davis, Bette 110, 123
Davis, Jim 54
Dead Freight for Piute 36
Dean, James 109
Death of a Champion 59
DeCarlo, Yvonne 51
Decision at Sundown 40, 56, 176
Decker, Albert 60, 61
The Defiant Ones 94
Defore, Don 35, 37
Dehner, John 75, 89, 115
DeKova, Frank 115
Del Rio, Dolores 155, 156
DeMille, Cecil B. 14–15, 17, 69
Denver & Rio Grande 72
The Deserter 168, 184
The Deserters 57
Destry 139
Destry Rides Again 14, 87
DeToth, Andre 25, 27, 35, 38
DeVito, Bernard 14
DeWilde, Brandon 96
Dick, Douglas 155
Dierkes, John 52–53
Dietrich, Marlene 13–14
Dinosaurus 165
Disney, Walt 69
Dix, Richard 60, 61
Dmytryk, Edward 116, 121–123, 125, 126, 127, 129
The Doolins of Oklahoma 38
Doucette, John 41, 111
Dodge, Granville 14
The Don Is Dead 152
A Don Siegel Film 158
Donlevy, Brian 17, 23, 53
Donovan's Gun 57
Douglas, Gordon 30, 67, 172
Douglas, Kirk 56, 84, 176, 178
Drake, Charles 85, 87–88, 106
Dressed to Kill 64
Drew, Ellen 67
Dru, Joanne 49

Duel at Diablo 143–147
Duel at Silver Creek 90
Duff, Howard 108, 109
Duryea, Dan 90, 97, 120, 148

Eastwood, Clint 79, 82–83, 120, 166, 186
Eden, Barbara 155, 158
Education of a Wandering Man 119
Egan, Richard 75
Eilers, Sally 39
Elam, Jack 170
Elliot, Wild Bill 33, 56, 64
Enright, Ray 24, 25, 36, 39
Estleman, Loren D. 11–12, 32, 188

Farrell, Glenda 30
Faulkner, William 63
Fehmiu, Bekim 184
Fellows, Robert 102, 106
Felton, Earl 93–94
Fenton, Frank 50, 51
Field, Sally 108
Fighting Man of the Plains 64–65
Firestone, Eddie 136
Fitzgerald, Barry 52
Fix, Paul 70, 73
Flaming Feather 71
Flaming Lance 154, 160
Flaming Star 154, 155, 158–160
Flap 184
Fleischer, Richard 75
Fleming, Rhonda 73
Flippen, J.C. 96
The Fly 136
Flynn, Errol 24–25, 63
Flynn, T.T. 188
"Follow the River" (song) 96
Foran, Dick 107
Ford, Bob 68
Ford, Harrison 55
Ford, John 10, 11–12, 14, 30, 96
Ford, Wallace 40, 70
Forrest, Sally 49
Forrest, Steve 117, 155, 157
Fort Starvation 59, 74
Forty Guns to Apache Pass 161
Foster, Dianne 95, 99
Foster, Preston 35, 36
Four Guns to the Border 107
Fowley, Douglas 40, 62

Franciosa, Anthony 173
Franz, Arthur 123
Franz, Eduard 113
Free Grass 31
French, Valerie 126
The French Key 64

Gamet, Kenneth 37, 39
Garden of Eden 23
Garfield, Brian 68, 91, 102–103, 188
Gargan, William 93
Garner, James 143, 144, 145, 147
Gehrig, Lou 18
Gentle Giant 97
Gentleman's Agreement 122
"The Gift of Cochise" (story) 24, 103–104
The Girl He Left Behind 110
Goldwyn, Samuel 24
Gordon, Leo 105, 115
Gorman, Edward 188
Graham, Fred 79
Granger, Farley 130, 131
Grant, Cary 118
Grant, James Edward 103, 168, 169
Grant, Kirby 24
The Grapes of Wrath 158
Gray, Coleen 81
The Great Missouri Raid 66–68
The Great Sioux Uprising 143
The Great Train Robbery 2
The Greatest Show on Earth 15
Grey, Zane 5, 10, 14, 57, 101, 102
Greer, Jane 41
Greenstreet, Sydney 63
Gunfight at the O.K. Corral 119
Gunman's Chance 34, 43
Gunman's Walk 109, 113
Gunpoint 164
Guns of Rio Conchos 153–154, 171–172
Guns of the Timberlands 115, 116
Guns of Thunder Mountain 153, 173
Guns Up 31
Gunsmoke 84

Hagen, Jean 46
Haggerty, Don 72
Hale, Alan, Jr. 139–140
Hamilton, Donald 108, 188
Hamlet 23
The Hanging Judge 188

Index 199

The Hangman (film) 55
"The Hangman" (story) 55
Hangtown 35
Hard Money 33
Hardin, John Wesley 65
Harris, Berkeley 139
Hart, William S. 12
Harte, Bret 10
The Harvey Girls 24
Hathaway, Henry 37
Hawkins, Jack 125
Hawks, Howard 14
Hayden, Russell 37
Hayden, Sterling 71, 72
Hayes, Gabby 37, 65
Hayward, Susan 23, 110
Healey, Myron 29, 115
Heckart, Eileen 117
Heflin, Van 30, 103
Heisler, Stuart 109–110, 111–112
Heller with a Gun 117, 118, 132
Hellfighters 178
Hell's Outpost 54
Henry, Will 33, 188
Hepburn, Katharine 118
Heston, Charlton 48, 73
Hickok, "Wild Bill" 73
The High and the Mighty 105
High Vermillion 32, 35, 50
Hills of Utah 2
Hodiak, John 47
Hoffman, Joseph 90
Hoffman, Lee 185
Holdup at Stony Flats 176
Hole-in-the-Wall Gang 52
Holliman, Earl 112
Holt, Nat 50
Holt, Tim 82
"Home on the Range" (song) 5
Homeier, Skip 112, 139
Hondo 103, 104, 105, 106, 117
Hope, Bob 66
Horsehead Crossing 188
Horton, Robert 29
Horvath, Charles 165
House of Wax 35
House on Haunted Hill 115
How the West Was Won 119
Hoyington-Huene, George 117
HUAC (House Un-American Activities Committee) 46

Hull, Henry 66
Hunter, Tab 109, 110, 111, 112, 113
Hurricane 109
Hurricane Smith 72
Hurry, Charlie, Hurry 34, 46
Hurst, Paul 18

In Old Sacramento 64
Ireland, Jill 185
Ireland, John 49, 172
The Iron Mistress 78
Ives, Burl 42

Jaeckel, Richard 81, 155
Jagger, Dean 70, 73
James, Frank 62, 66–67
James, Jesse 1, 39, 62
James Garner (biography) 143
Jesse James 14
Jesse James' Women 85
Johnny Cool 74
Johnny Eager 103
Johnny Reno 81
Johnson, Chubby 85
Johnson, Nunnally 157, 158, 159
Johnson County War 85
Jones, Buck 82
Jones, L.Q. 155
Jory, Victor 60, 61, 65, 71, 72, 108
Jurado, Katy 156
Juran, Nathan 87

Kane, Joseph 53, 54, 64
The Kansan 59, 60–62
Kansas Raiders 39
Karlson, Phil 65, 66, 80, 109
Kay, Gordon 142
Kazan, Elia 122
Keel, Howard 177, 178
Kelley, DeForest 75, 81, 136
Kelly, Jack 86
Kelly, Paul 85
Kelton, Elmer 188
Kennedy, Arthur 93
Kennedy, Burt 176, 178, 184
Kennedy, Douglas 25, 54, 65
Ketchum, Blackjack 109
Keyes, Evelyn 17
Kid from Spain 109
Kid Millions 109
Kid Rodelo (film) 120

Kid Rodelo (novel) 120, 132
Kiel, Richard 35
Kilkenny 108
Kimbrough, Jim 18
King Colt 33, 34
King Creole 157
Knox, Alexander 25, 126
Kolker, Henry 77
Kristofferson, Kris 31

Ladd, Alan 77–78, 116, 123
Lake, Veronica 35, 36
Lamas, Fernando 181
Lampert, Zohra 165, 168
Lancaster, Burt 47–48, 94, 158
Landon, Joseph 175
Lane, Allen "Rocky" 56, 165
Langtry, Lillian 118
The Last Fast Draw 132
The Last Hunt 55
Last of the Pony Riders 73
Last Stand at Papago Wells 114, 120
Lauter, Harry 165
Laven, Arnold 148, 150
The Law and Jake Wade (film) 55, 136–137
The Law and Jake Wade (novel) 134–136, 143
Lawson, John Howard 63
Lawson, Linda 147
Lee, Ruta 141, 147
The Left-Handed Gun 109
LeMay, Alan 133, 158–160, 188
Leonard, Elmore 32
Leslie, Joan 25, 26–27, 54
Lewis, Jerry 18
Lewis, Joseph E. 20
Lewton, Val 44
"Little Joe" (song) 87
London, Jack 102
Lord, Jack 55
Loren, Sophia 117, 118, 119
Lorre, Peter 63
Louise, Tina 55
Love Me Tender 116, 157
Lundigan, William 18, 29
Lyles, A.C. 80, 81, 139

Macauley, Richard 69
MacLane, Barton 28, 81, 107
MacLeod, Robert 179, 180, 183

Macready, George 26, 39
The Magnificent Seven 119, 186
Mahoney, Maggie 108
Malone, Dorothy 75, 88, 91
Man Behind the Gun 89, 139
A Man Called Noon (film) 130–131
A Man Called Noon (novel) 103
The Man from Laramie 30, 93
The Man from Skiberdeen 132
Man from the Alamo 85
Man from Two Rivers 57
The Man in Black 148, 154
Man in the Saddle (film) 26–27
Man in the Saddle (novel) 25–27
Man of the West 137
Mann, Anthony 75, 93, 96, 97, 98, 137, 142
Marauders' Moon 32
Marlowe, Hugh 28
Martin, Dean 149, 150
Martin & Lewis 66
Marvin, Lee 169
Mask of Dimitrious 63
Matthews, Carole 107
Mayer, Louis B. 47
Mayo, Virginia 77–78, 80, 114
McCall, Mary, Jr. 53
McCord, Ted 110
McCrea, Joel 16, 17, 35, 36, 107, 114
McGann, William 60
McGavin, Darren 141, 142–143
McIntyre, John 106, 149, 155, 161
McNeile, H.C. 64
Meek, Donald 12
Menjou, Adolphe 69
Menken, Adeh Isaacs 118
Meredith, Judi 147
Meyer, Emile 107
Middleton, Robert 136
Milland, Ray 37, 39, 74
Miller, Colleen 93, 106–107
Miller, Winston 76
Millican, James 28, 29, 52
Mills, Mort 141
Mister 880 47–48
Mitchell, Cameron 75
Mitchell, Thomas 12
Mitchum, Robert 38, 43, 44
Monster and the Girl 109
Montana 24–25
Montana Mike 24

Montgomery, George 65, 80
Moore, Mary Tyler 150–151
Moore, Terry 81
Morse, Gov. Wayne 24
The Movies That Changed Us 10
Mulford, Clarence 5, 6
Murder My Sweet 41
Murphy, Audie 39, 42, 79, 87–88, 94–95, 98, 138–140, 142–143, 158, 160, 164–165, 167–168, 189
The Music Man 43
My Son John 48

Nader, George 106
Naish, J. Carrol 35, 54
The Naked Spur 97
The Narrow Margin 93
Naschy, Paul 130
Nathan, Paul 48
Nazarro, Ray 115
Nedell, Bernard 37
Nelson, Ralph 143
The Nevadan 88
Newman, Paul 182
Newmar, Julie 24
Nichols, Dudley 11, 14, 117, 118
Nielsen, James 95
Night Passage (film) 94–99
Night Passage (novel) 94, 95, 98, 99
No Name on the Bullet 88, 189
No Way Out 146
Nolan, Lloyd 18, 29
None Shall Escape 25
North by Northwest 93
Northern Pursuit 63

O'Brian, Hugh 49
O'Brien, Edmond 69–71, 72, 76, 77–78
O'Brien, Joan 169
O'Brien, Margaret 117
O'Brien, Pat 81
"Old Buttermilk Sky" (song) 24
Olivier, Lawrence 18
"On the Atkinson, Topeka and Santa Fe" (song) 24
100 Rifles 178–184
Oregon Trail 63
O.S.S. (Office of Strategic Services) 34
"Outcasts of Poker Flats" (story) 10
Overholser, Wayne D. 86
Owens, Beverly 139

Owens, Patricia 136

Page, Geraldine 104
Paper Sheriff 49–50, 57
Parker, Colonel Tom 158
Party Girl 137
Patten, Lewis B. 92, 188
Payne, John 36
Peace Marshal 20, 59, 62, 75
Peck, Gregory 56, 123
Peckinpah, Sam 71, 83
Peppard, George 149, 150–151
Persoff, Nehemiah 170
Pickens, Slim 150
Pillow Talk 137
Pine, William 36
Pitts, ZaSu 73
Platt, Edward C. 139
Play Dirty 121
Poitier, Sidney 143, 145–146, 147
Ponti, Carlo 116–117
Pony Express 73–74, 76
Posse from Hell (film) 164–167
Posse from Hell (novel) 153, 154, 164, 167
Powell, Dick 41, 43
Powers, Stephanie 30
Presley, Elvis 55, 115–116, 154–157
Preston, Robert 17–18, 43, 44
Pretty Woman 11
Price, Vincent 35
Production Code 23, 125
Pronzini, Bill 188
The Pulp Jungle 59, 62
Pursued 38, 43

Quantrill, Kate 27
Quantrill, William Clarke 67, 79–80, 82
The Quick and the Dead 119, 131
Quinn, Anthony 17, 117, 118, 184

Rackin, Martin 115
Rage at Dawn 74
"Ragtime Cowboy Joe" (song) 2
Rails into Laramie 90
Raines, Ella 53
Raintree Country 122
Ramrod 34–35
Ramsey, Ward 165
Ranch Romances 74, 176

Rand, Ayn 63
Randolph, Donald 89, 93
Rawhide (1937) 18
Rawhide (1950) 23
The Rawhide Years (film) 93–94
The Rawhide Years (novel) 92–93
Reagan, Ronald 57, 109, 110
Rebel Without a Cause 110
Red River 14, 106
Redford, Robert 182
Reed, Barbara 39
Reed, Donna 18
Reed, Walter 165
The Reformed Gun 137
Remarkable Andrew 109
Renegade Posse 137, 138, 142
Return of a Fighter 19, 31
Return to Warbow (film) 142
Return to Warbow (novel) 142
Revere, Anne 66, 67
Reynolds, Burt 181, 182
Reynolds, Debbie 176
Richards, Paul 89, 91
Ride Clear of Diablo 97
Ride the Man Down (film) 53–54
Ride the Man Down (novel) 34
Ride to Hangman's Tree 164
A Rider in the High Mesa 31
The Rider of Lost Creek 132
Rio Conchos 172–176
Ritter, Tex 2, 24
Rober, Richard 26, 27
Roberts, Julia 11
Robertson, Dale 65, 78
Rogell, Albert 24
Rogers, Roy 2, 33, 56
Roland, Gilbert
Rooney, Mickey 35
Rosenberg, Aaron 74
Rough Night in Jericho 149, 150, 164
Roughshod 84, 112
Rush, Barbara 71–72
Russell, Jane 80
Russell, John 26, 27, 80
Ryan, Robert 44
Rynning, Capt. Tom 80

The Sacketts 132
Saddle the Wind 55
San Antone 54
Sands of Iwo Jima 103, 105, 106

Saturday Evening Post 10, 48
Saturday Review 14
Savage, Les, Jr. 4, 7, 91–92
Sawyer, Joseph 18
Saxon, John 165
Schaeffer, Jack 132
Schary, Dore 44
Schiaffino, Rosanna 130
Scott, Randolph 20–22, 25, 26, 27, 29, 36–38, 39–40, 56, 60–61, 65, 84, 88–89, 105
Scott, Zachery 63, 107
The Searchers 105
Sears, Fred F. 114–115
The Second Time Around 176
"See What the Boys in the Back Room Will Have" (song) 87
Selander, Lesley 71, 82, 88, 89, 90, 142
Serling, Rod 55
The Set-Up 44
Seven Men from Now 105
Seven Ways from Sundown (film) 160–164
Seven Ways from Sundown (novel) 154
Shadow Riders 131
Shalako (film) 123–128, 129
Shalako (novel) 121
Shane (film) 78, 115
Shane (novel) 132
Shatner, William 82
Shelby, General Jo 62, 76
Shepard, Patty 130
Sherman, George 171
Sherman, Harry "Pop" 34–35, 59
Showdown 139
Shumate, Harold 20, 22, 60, 61, 62
Siegel, Don 155, 157–158
Sierra 27
Silva, Henry 74, 136
Silver City 50–53
Silver Rock 54
Silverheels, Jay 106
Simmons, Jean 149
Simpson, Mickey 90
Sinatra, Frank 74, 151
Singin' in the Rain 46
Siodmak, Robert 48
Sirk, Douglas 88
Sitting Bull 62
Smash-Up: The Story of a Woman 110
Smith, Alexis 25

Smith, (Marshal) Tom 20
Smoky Valley 108
The Sniper 122
Soldier Blue 82
Son of Belle Starr 85
Spelling, Aaron 115
The Spoilers 52
Springsteen, R.G. 120, 139, 141, 142
"Stage to Lordsburg" (story) 10
Stagecoach (1939) 11–12, 19, 31, 115, 117
Stagecoach (1966) 30–31
Stagecoach (1986) 31
The Stalking Moon 82
Stampede 54
Stanwyck, Barbara 16, 28
The Star 110
Starrett, Charles 114
Station West (film) 41–43
Station West (novel) 41
Steele, Barbara 158
Sterling, Jan 73
Stevens, Charlie 34, 47
Stevenson, Venetia 161
Stewart, Elaine 97
Stewart, James 75, 84, 94, 95, 98, 99
Storm, Gale 66
Storm Warning 110
Straight from the Shoulder 109
Strait, Raymond 143
Stranger on Horseback 107
Strangers on a Train 48
Strode, Woody 124
The Strong Shall Live 128
Sturges, John 74, 186
Sturges, Preston 16
Sullivan, Barry 161, 163, 164
Sundown Jim (film) 18, 19
Sundown Jim (novel) 18
Support Your Local Sheriff 176, 184
Sweet Smell of Success 94
Swenson, Karl 155

Taggert (film) 107, 120
Taggert (novel) 119
"Take Me to Town" (song) 87
Tall Man Riding (film) 88–91
Tall Man Riding (novel) 88, 89, 92
The Tall Stranger 114
Tarzan and the Valley of Gold 176
Taylor, Don 46
Taylor, Elizabeth 122

Taylor, Forrest 39
Taylor, Robert 46, 55, 135, 136, 139
Teal, Ray 111, 113, 165
Tension at Table Rock 75
Terror by Night 64
The Texas Rangers 65–66, 79, 80
That Jane from Maine 134, 137, 203
Thaxter, Phyliss 44
Them 67
Thomas, William 36
Thorpe, Richard 47
Tilghman, Bill 2
The Time of Their Lives 98
Tinling, Jim 18
To Hell and Back 86, 87
To Tame the Land 102, 132
Tobey, Kenneth 161
Tobias, George 139
Tomorrow the World 112
Totter, Audrey 27
Tourneur, Jacques 23, 44
Town Tamer (film) 80–81
Town Tamer (novel) 59, 80, 81
Tracy, Spencer 103, 122
Travers, Bill 145
Treasure of Ruby Hills 107
Trevor, Claire 11, 12, 14
Trouble Country 33
Troubleshooter 14, 15, 16, 19
True Grit 121
Trumbo, Dalton 63, 109
Tucker, Forrest 28, 40, 71, 72, 73
Tumbleweed 87
Twenty Million Miles to Earth 87
Two Women 118
Tyler, Letty 37

Uncertain Glory 63
The Unforgiven (film) 94, 158
The Unforgiven (novel) 158–160
Union Pacific 14–17
U.P. Trail 14
Utah Blaine (film) 113–114
Utah Blaine (novel) 113–114

The Valdez Horses 185
Van Cleef, Lee 120, 164, 166
Van Eyck, Peter 93, 125
Van Patten, Vincent 185
Van Sickle, Dale 82
Vengeance Valley (film) 47–49

Vengeance Valley (novel) 32, 47, 48, 49
The Virginian 2, 5

Wagner, Wende 173
Wake of the Red Witch 105
Walker, Robert, Jr. 177
Walker, Robert, Sr. 48
Wallace, Irving 110, 112, 113
Wallis, Hal 48
Walsh, Raoul 114
War Wagon 176–178
Warner, Jack L. 26, 78, 116
Warpath 29, 52, 68–70
Warren, Charles Marquis 73, 75–76
Wayne, Aissa 169
Wayne, John 11, 13, 14, 15, 30, 48, 103, 104–106, 154, 168, 169, 171, 176, 177
Weaver, Dennis 144, 147
Webb, Robert 116
Weisbart, David 158
Welch, Raquel 180, 183, 184
Wellman, Paul I. 168
Wescott, Helen 51
West Side Story 110
Western Films: A Complete Guide 68, 91, 103
What's So Bad About Feeling Good? 151
Whelan, Arleen 35
Where Angels Go, Trouble Follows 97
White, Jesse 87
Whitman, Stuart 168, 171
Whorf, Richard 110

Widmark, Richard 55, 74, 135, 136–137
The Wild Bunch 71, 121, 150, 179, 181
Wilde, Oscar 81
Wilke, Robert 96
Williams, Bill 65
Williams, Guinn "Big Boy" 26, 37, 41
Willingham, Mary and William 79–80, 141
Wills, Chill 54
Wills, Henry 165
Windsor, Marie 65
Wings 51
Wise, Robert 44
Wister, Owen 2
Witney, William 80
Woman of the Town 60, 61
Woman They Almost Lynched 27
Wood, Natalie 109, 110, 111–112
Wood, Sam 46, 47
Wooley, Sheb 29
World in My Corner 161
Written on the Wind 88
Wyatt, Jane 60, 61
Wynn, Keenan 177

Yates, Herbert 26
"You Can't Go Far Without a Railroad" (song) 96–97, 98
Young, Tony 120
The Young Lions 122
Younger, Cole 67
The Younger Brothers 67

www.ingramcontent.com/pod-product-compliance
Ingram Content Group UK Ltd.
Pitfield, Milton Keynes, MK11 3LW, UK
UKHW042004140426
5217IPUK00015B/976